WEALTH AND WELFARE

WEALTH AND WELFARE

By JEREMIAH GOTTHELF

HOWARD FERTIG
NEW YORK · 1976

First published in English in 1867
Howard Fertig, Inc. Edition 1976
All rights reserved.

Library of Congress Cataloging in Publication Data
Bitzius, Albert, 1797-1854.
   Wealth and welfare.
   Translation of Geld und Geist.
   Reprint of the 1867 ed. published by A. Strahan,
London.
   I. Title.
PZ3.B549We6 [PT1819.B6]   833'.7   75-4947

Printed in the United States of America

WEALTH AND WELFARE

By JEREMIAH GOTTHELF

ALEXANDER STRAHAN, PUBLISHER
56 LUDGATE HILL, LONDON
1867
Facsimile of the title page of the original edition.

CONTENTS.

PART I.

	PAGE
I. A Happy Home and a Happy Custom,	1
II. The Happy Custom interrupted,	30
III. A Love at First Sight,	63
IV. How One Quarrel breeds Another,	77
V. Old Things seen in a New Light,	95
VI. A Moral Victory,	124
VII. The Blessing of Peace,	144

PART II.

I. An Eventful Night,	167
II. A Churl's Hospitality,	191
III. Maternal Diplomacy,	216
IV. The Lovers Meet,	247
V. Family Councils,	272
VI. A Ray of Light,	295

PART III.

	PAGE
I. A Young Girl's Ordeal,	331
II. Pros and Cons.	367
III. An Honest Wooer,	399
IV. Silent Sorrow,	435
V. The Holy Season,	456
VI. Death the Reconciler,	473

PART I.

I.

A HAPPY HOME AND A HAPPY CUSTOM.

TRUE happiness is a tender plant; noxious insects ever hover round it, an impure breath kills. Man is appointed its gardener, and has for his wages blessedness. But how few there are that understand their business; how many themselves introduce into the close cup of the flower that flower's deadliest foe; how many look on unconcerned, or even amused, while hurtful insects settle, gnaw, and fret, and the blossom fades! Happy he who looks up in time, and with ready hand saves the blossom and kills the foe; he preserves his heart's peace and saves his soul alive, —these hanging together like body and spirit, this world and the next.

In the Canton of Berne are many fine properties, many substantial farmhouses, where dwell many a worthy pair well reputed for their God-fearing ways and good household management, as also for an amount of wealth, garnered up in barns and granaries, chests and troughs, which this frivolous new-fangled generation, turning everything into money because it wants so much money, has no conception of. Over and above these stores, however, in such a house as we are speaking of there is always a round sum kept for the casual wants of the good folk themselves, or their neighbours, the like of which you might look for in vain, from one year's end to the other, in the mansions of many of the gentry. Very often this sum has no fixed place. Like a familiar spirit, by no means a bad one, it flits about the house, now here, now there, sometimes in the cellar, sometimes in the barn, sometimes in the parlour, sometimes in the great carved chest, and sometimes in each and all these at once, and half-a-dozen more. For should a piece of land bordering on the farm chance to come into the market, it gets bought, and has to be paid for in ready money, neither father nor grandfather having ever been known to be in debt, but paying for whatever they bought on the spot, and, of course, with their own money. Again, should there happen to be among family connexions or friends, or even fellow-parishioners, a respectable man, hard pushed or anxious to make a purchase, this money migrates hither and thither, not as an investment, but a temporary convenience for an indefinite period, without either bond or interest—merely upon the faith of a heavenly reckoning by and bye, the other world being still believed in as it ought.

In church and market both, you may see the farmer dressed in decent homespun, while his wife is at the housework the first in the morning and the last at night, nothing appearing on the table but what she has herself cooked, nor any wash getting poured into the pig-troughs without having been well stirred to its depths by her own bare arm.

If any one should wish to see for himself one of these specimens of honourable industry and independence, let him go to Liebiwyl (I don't mean Liebiwyl in the Köniz district—I don't know that there is one there), and he will find a handsome farmhouse facing the south. The glitter of its windows in the sunshine is seen from far, and every year it is washed with the fire-engine; consequently it looks quite new, though in point of fact it is more than forty years old, and affords a convincing proof of the benefits of washing for all and everything, houses included.

A wide, beautifully carved balcony, shaded by the projecting roof, runs along the upper storey, and a terrace-walk round the house, paved near the stables with small round stones put close together, and near the rooms with broad massive flags. Fine pear and other fruit-trees stand about the house; everything is luxuriant and green. A hill protects it from the dreaded north-east wind; but from the front windows there is a view of the mountains that in their changeless majesty defy the vicissitudes of time, and of human life.

In the evening a visitor to this comfortable home would be sure to see, sitting on the bench beside the door, smoking a short pipe, a man whom to look at he would never guess to be far on in his sixties; and from time to time, on the door-step, a tall figure with pleasant face and neat attire, to whom the man constantly seems to have some observation to make or some question to put. This is his wife. Farther back, by the fountain, stands a well-grown handsome youth watering a pair of fine brown horses, while his elder brother carries straw into the stable; and close by a merry girl-face pops up every now and then from among the flowers and bushes to know whether her mother wants her to come and help in the house, or to complain about the caterpillars on the cabbages, the cats in the lettuce-beds, or the blight on the roses, and ask her father what is to be done in the matter. Meanwhile servants and labourers stream in leisurely from the fields, one hen after the other jumps up on its perch to roost, while the pigeons keep strutting and cooing to their ladies as assiduously as ever.

Such a picture as this might have been seen by any one passing the farmhouse of Liebiwyl for the last five or six years; and if the stranger had put a question to a neighbour, or to some old woman leaving the door with something under her apron, as to the character of its inhabitants, the answer would have been much to the following purpose :—

They are uncommon good, and awfully rich folk.

When the farmer and his wife had married, some thirty years before, they were pronounced the handsomest pair that had stood side by side in the parish church for a long while back. More than a hundred conveyances had accompanied them, and a good number of friends on horseback besides,—riding being more usual then than now, and even women taking to it sometimes, particularly at weddings. The marriage festivities had lasted three days, and there was no stint in the matter of eating and drinking; indeed, the abundance was such as to be talked of all over the country. On the other hand, wedding presents had poured in till they hardly knew what to do with them. Two whole days were spent in receiving and storing them, and extra hands had to be got in for the purpose; but there was no farmhouse in the whole district that stood in such wide repute.

Such an establishment as this, on the largest scale, perfectly free from debt, and having a considerable sum of ready money besides, is not to be met with everywhere. And the owners did not hold it only for themselves. They knew that the rich were God's stewards, and would have to give account of the talents committed to their charge. When any one asked them to stand sponsors they never said nay; and they were not of opinion that, since the rise in the price of wood, the poor no longer required it to burn. Their servants were far better cared for than is usually the case; it was not supposed that things could be done in a day, or that it was a waste of good milk to give it to them. In short, they were thoroughly worthy people, and dwelt in peace and concord such as is seldom to be met with. All the year through there was nothing but love and kindness between them, nor had they ever been heard to give each other a cross word. If ever under the sun there were people to be found who had all they wanted, and nothing more to wish for, surely they were these. A happier family you would nowhere find. So ran common report, and to all appearances it was perfectly correct; and yet even here, as elsewhere, it was true that each had to bear his own burden, that each found his burden heavy, and that most of life's burdens have this peculiarity, that the longer and more uninterruptedly they are borne as burdens, the heavier they grow, and that their weight may at length come to be so insupportable as to swallow up every other feeling, every blessing, and every enjoyment. The family had indeed fared very well together, but for all that there is a something to be got over everywhere,— only as yet this something had been a mere passing matter, had not grown into a chronic mood, and never came before a third party.

Strange enough that the one thing that most frequently sets men by the ears should so often come between married people and make a division,—I mean money and this world's gear. It is only when an instrument is in perfect tune that it responds agreeably to the most skilful hand ; if out of tune it can yield nothing but discord, be the player ever so practised or the touch ever so light. Else one might suppose that the very community of interest between a husband and wife, to whom the property equally belongs, and who equally suffer from any mismanagement, would preclude all possibility of discord here. But this is the very thing I want to insist upon : peace, or the absence of peace, do not depend upon external circumstances. They have their seat in the heart. Possibly my readers may be inclined to demur to this as a general principle, to say : 'True, if all the wealth be on the husband's side, or he be the only breadwinner, and the wife bring nothing into the common store ; or if everything comes from the wife and the husband live upon her means, it must indeed be hard to keep things straight, for the one will be tempted to suppose himself put upon, and the other will chafe under the sense of perpetual obligation ; or should the husband be a stay-at-home and the wife be fond of company ; or when he wishes to turn his money to the best account, and she knows nothing of economy and squanders it all on her back; or if he be good-natured, and she possessed with the demon of covetousness ; or he anxious to keep up the respectability of his house, and she a screw who counts the coffee-beans and grudges every one their food,—why, there must be disputes, and there is no help for it.'

No doubt of it. But disputes are not all. There is something even worse than disputes : a chronic antagonism of character, not so much owing to positive faults as to constitutional peculiarities on both sides, and consistent with mutual affection and agreement in the main.

Our worthy pair, for instance, were both respectably descended ; neither could look down upon the other. The husband had inherited a property with few encumbrances, and the wife had brought him a good dower. Both were managers, and spent little on superfluities ; both were anxious to make the best of their means; went seldom from home ; both were good-hearted, obliging, and benevolent. According to the custom of the country they had a common purse; the wife went to the money-box as freely as the husband, and neither thought of writing down an account of incomings and outgoings. The said money-box had but one key, and when either asked for it the other never inquired why it was wanted.

Christian, the husband, was of an easy-going nature. When actually at work, few surpassed him in activity and skill, but it cost him a good deal of effort to set about his work. He was given to putting off, from one day to the other, and what did not suit his inclination to-day was like enough to suit him no better on the morrow. However fine the weather, nothing could induce him to set about one of the more important summer operations in the middle of a week. When all around him were in a fidget, he would calmly observe that if the weather continued as it was he would set about it on the following Monday, but in the middle of a week he would not: his father before him never did so, and he was a man the like of whom it would be well if one could meet now-a-days. If the following Monday did not turn out fine, he would patiently wait another week, observing that he had never seen good hay made in the wet, and that when it had rained enough it would be sure to take up. Hence he was generally the last in the district to get his work done, and for many things was invariably too late. But he argued that if one did not kill one's people with over-work, one need not be blamed for that ; and that though cattle were not human beings, still one must be reasonable with them, else what was the use of having reason ? Many there were who grudged a day's rest to man and beast, but he could not see that they got much by it: their profits all went to the doctor or the butcher. All the animals on his farm were dear to him, and when he had to part with one it was a wrench to his heart. Consequently he seldom did so, nor could he be tempted by the highest price to let a creature go to which he had once become attached.

Again, if he could drive any one, or do any one a service by the loan of a horse, he never refused ; was, generally speaking, remarkably ready to oblige, but he was not fond of giving money. It cost him a pang indeed to part with it for any purpose. People did not know how hard a thing this was, he would say, till they had money of their own, and then, once it was gone it was no easy matter to get it back again.

Now Annie his wife was of a very different temperament. She had been an energetic, impetuous girl, who went through whatever she had to do with spirit, and got over her work in half the time that others took to do less. In her youth she had gained vast credit for this, and even in her old age she found a pleasure in being first and foremost in everything. It was in her, she said, and no one knew how much time was to be saved in the course of a year by setting about things promptly, one might almost do with half the number of hands. She did not wish to be covetous—God preserve her from anything of the kind; but when people had children they should remember that the property had to be divided among them, and if the parents could not manage well with the whole of it, how were the children to get on with half or a quarter? Added to which, she concerned herself much about the number of poor that were to be helped, and for whom one had never too much. For Annie was singularly kind-hearted, and could never deny any one; she would almost give the clothes off her back, eatables in any quantity, nay, even money slipped readily through her fingers if she happened to have it at hand. All day long, poor people, especially women with bags, were to be seen coming and going about the house. Ill-natured people, indeed, declared that she was thus liberal partly to get a good name, and partly for the pleasure of hearing what went on in other houses, and that the poor woman who gave the worst reports of the neighbours' wives was sure to get the most. But this was only the language of envy, and showed that the speakers knew nothing themselves of the simple kind-heartedness that prompted Annie's gift.

In one thing, and that the main, Christian and

Annie were entirely of one mind. Both desired to manage their property so as to give a good account of it before God; both wished to do right, and yet to leave their children comfortably off. Only, each had his own peculiar way of setting about this: Christian was anxious to keep together what he already had, Annie to make more, and in every way to turn their capital to the best interest, so that they might be the better able to help the needy in their distress.

Such were their conflicting peculiarities; but these interfered less with their mutual comfort than might have been supposed. It did indeed often appear to Christian that his wife was too kind, gave too easy credence to every gossiping old wife, and that what got wasted in this manner would make a pretty round sum at the year's end. But as he was not in the habit of telling every passing thought, he had plenty of time for counterbalancing reflections. He would remember that every human being has some fault or other, and he preferred his wife being too good-natured to having her too hard, and, on the other hand, she was a good manager, she spent nothing on mere display, and, when there was work to be got through, worked for two, and did not want a maid to dance attendance upon her. Therefore he was bound to put up with something, and he might easily have had one who would have spent far more and accomplished far less than his Annie.

On the other hand, Annie would often tingle to her finger-ends when a butcher offered a larger price than she ever looked for—the cow giving but little milk, and being no beauty either; and yet Christian could not make up his mind to part with her, refused the tempting sum, kept her in the stable, where she took up a place that might have been better filled, and kept saying to every one that she was the best cow in all the villages about, and that you might look far and near before you saw such a handsome beast. And often, too, she would be ready to jump out of her skin when the sun was bright in the sky, and the corn ripe in the fields; and yet, because it did not happen to be a Monday, Christian would sit quietly before the house, or set about twisting the straw-ropes, that were ready long ago in other houses; and when at last *the* Monday came, and with it all the troop of labourers that Christian considered necessary, and for whom Annie had to cook, and there chanced to be a cloud in a corner of the sky, and because of that cloud Christian with all his labourers would stand about the door from breakfast to dinner, doubting and discussing whether it were advisable to begin or not, and bring them all in to dinner, without a single ear having been reaped,—why, at such times, Annie would grow sick with vexation, and feel as if a stone were weighing on her heart. But then she, in her turn, would consider that every human being has his faults and burdens, and that if Christian were not thus dilatory, she would have no drawback at all, and might well fear some far worse trial. And so she would not complain; other women had more to bear; and what would it profit her if her Christian were prompt and alert, and the first in all undertakings, if at the same time he were violent and irritable to her and others, and cared for nothing but money and bargain-making? She would not change him for hundreds of others; for if he were not the first in the cornfield, neither was he the first in the public-house; and if often the last in the hay, he was never the last to come from market or merry-making; and, taking one thing with the other thus, she had nothing to find fault with, and it would be a sin to complain, since after all she did not know any one that she would change her Christian for.

Now, when a man or woman argues in this strain, it not only shows that they have the right kind of spirit, but that they are in the way to be contented with their lot, whatever it may be; that they can feel genuine thankfulness towards God, extract the sting from misfortune, and the bitterness from the faults of their fellow-men. But where, the field of vision is narrowed, so that people no more see the good, but the bad only; when they become more and more sensitive to defects, and less and less so to redeeming qualities,—then indeed misery is at hand, and an abyss yawns, from whence arises the ghastly spectre, Discord. Like the Austrian soldier caught in the thicket, the unfortunate mortal is tied and bound by his own thoughts, as by the hair of his head, to what oppresses and hurts him; nor can he get rid of it; he groans, moans, chafes, struggles, whimpers, but all in vain; he is fast in fetters, against which no file prevails. His fellowmen cannot help him, and God will not, for he who has chosen such a bed of thorns has forsaken God.

Christian and Annie then were, we see, happy, and on the way, moreover, to greater happiness, because they were in the habit of weighing themselves and their circumstances in the scales of that gratitude which the creature owes to God.

True, it did sometimes happen that one or the other got a rebuke now and then, but so covertly delivered that less sensitive hearts would never have found it out; that, for instance, Christian, when Annie offered to bring him in a scrap of meat into the little back-room, would reply, 'Well, I should not be sorry, if you have any left.' This Annie felt as an affront, because she was conscious that, out of charity, she had given away many a little bit which Christian might else have had, and perhaps had missed. Or again, when Christian kept demurring and delaying, and setting to nothing, with so many people to receive a day's wage without doing a day's work, Annie, every limb twitching with impatience, would at last burst out, that if they did not know what to do, she could set them to water the cabbages, which Christian resented, being well aware that they had enough to do, if only he could decide about it, and that it must be a nuisance to his wife to have to cook for so many who did nothing, and yet required board and wages none the less.

Such thrusts as these did not indeed often occur, but they would escape now and then. However, they were not exasperated by rejoinders, as is too often the case among cultivated people. The one who had received the tacit rebuke held his peace, because he felt it deeply, and was pained by it. But, however sharply it might penetrate, it did not smart long, or fester, there being two reasons why such hits as these never caused bad blood between the pair.

Annie's mother lived with them. She was a remarkably intelligent woman, and warmly attached to her son-in-law. She had lived before with another son-in-law, who had treated her disrespectfully and unkindly. There she had to give up everything and require nothing, to bear much and silently. Here she had it all her own way. Christian would ask and take her advice, just as though she were his own mother; and if she had a fancy for anything, or there happened to be something particularly good to eat or drink in the house, he never rested till mother had some of it. And if anything was the matter with her, he would go himself to the doctor, and beg and entreat him to exert himself and do his best, let it cost what he would, for that if they lost their mother, he did not know what would become of them. Thus the old woman plainly saw that she was not in his way, but that he wished her life and comfort so long as it pleased God to spare them, which is not always the case. Accordingly, if she saw that a chance word had struck deep; that Annie was angry,—perhaps actually cried, and bemoaned herself as not having deserved such injustice, and preferring to die to putting up any longer with it, the good mother did not pour oil into the fire, but rather replied, 'Dear child, you do not even know what real sorrow is, and that is the reason why you take a little word so ill; but Annie, Annie, beware. I am always frightened when I see young wives make so much of trifles, lest the Almighty send them some real misfortune, that they may know for what tears were given, and when complaints are lawful. If you had had my fate, you would thank God for such trifling vexations as these, and see in them a sign of His mercy. Only think of what I had to go through.' And then she would relate to Annie some anecdote out of her own life, illustrative of her husband or her son-in-law, and of her own toleration, but for which, things would have been even worse than they were. True, this mode of reasoning did not at first answer very well with Annie, who would reply, 'Yes, but I am not you; and what difference does it make to me that you were still worse off? that does not make my case any the better.' So Annie would indeed say, but for all that her mother's eloquence had its effect; it calmed down her vexation and revived her love. When she had quite come round, she would playfully reproach her, and declare any one would suppose that Christian was her child, for she preferred him to her, and, let him say or do what he would, he was always right. Positively, if Christian were to snap her nose off, she believed her mother would approve him for it.

But the good woman could take Annie's part as well. When she had aimed some sharp shaft at Christian's heart, and her mother plainly saw that the arrow stuck in the wound, she would creep about after him till she found him in a quiet corner, and beg of him not to take it ill. He knew well that Annie was of an anxious temper, and she had never been able to cure her of this on account of all she had had herself to undergo. But as for meaning anything unkind, that indeed she was far from doing, and if only he were satisfied, the mother knew well that her daughter was so. Christian was not one who grew suspicious and unreasonable in proportion to another's humility. He would assure his mother-in-law that he was not angry, but only regretted that Annie should feel herself obliged to think for him. All things could not be done at once, and to rush at them in a violent hurry, without any previous consideration, was what he could not bring himself to, nor had he ever seen any good come of it. However, he knew everybody had ways of their own, and that Annie meant well, and therefore, though he could not help feeling these things, he did not resent them: people must be patient with one another; each had his own faults; and what did they come into the world for but to learn and practise forbearance?

Thus it was that the mother-in-law, like a guardian angel, smoothed over the little rifts that she observed; and if there were others that she did not observe, or could not close before the going down of the sun, another good spirit took the matter in hand, and they got closed and smoothed.

This last was an ancient and beautiful family custom, which has exercised unbounded influence for centuries past; blotting out and doing away with all germs of discord, and preserving peace in the hearts of those on whom God's blessing rests, and who shall see their children's children. Whoever came last to bed, husband or wife as it happened, said the Lord's Prayer aloud; and heavy indeed was the sleep if the other did not wake up and follow it with sincere devotion. When they came to the petition, 'Forgive us our trespasses, as we forgive them that trespass against us,' and man and wife were conscious of discord, or at least dissension, it seemed as though God's voice were speaking with them, and the words trembled on their lips. And then when they went on, 'And lead us not into temptation, but deliver us from evil,' every grudge that they had nursed against each other vanished away in a feeling of deep contrition before God; and heart opened to heart, and faults were acknowledged, forgiveness asked, and affection expressed, —both owning that they were only happy in peace and concord; though sometimes the evil spirit would come, one knew not how, and make everything seem dark and clouded before the eyes of the mind, and fill the heart with anger and discontent. But when this prayer was said, it was as though a stronger than he entered the soul and scourged the evil one thence, so that he had to take flight whether or no, and then the man seemed to awake from a bad dream, and, instead of dark and gloomy night, he looked all at once into a sweet sunny garden, such as that which met our first parents' gaze when from the desert into which they were expelled they looked back upon their Eden ; and oh! how eagerly he rushed into this garden, fearful lest he too, like those hapless first parents, might be shut out from it, and never know rest any more. And this sunny garden was peace and love between man and wife; and were the whole world offered in exchange, he would not give up this paradise. And thus the freshness of their early happiness would revive, and in cheerful humility each would confess his own failings, and beg to be forgiven, and promise to contend valiantly with the foe when he came again, as he surely would. Then they would fall asleep in sweet peace, and when a new dawn coloured the sky, they woke up with refreshed and strengthened spirit. Nay, it was as though the early days of their married life returned; they longed for each other's presence; their eyes were constantly meeting, and Christian unconsciously followed Annie about the house, and Annie went as constantly to the door to see whether Christian was in sight.

Thus years passed away, and at length the good mother died. This was a heavy blow to all in the house. A good spirit died with her, and they missed her grievously and long. Christian would often declare that he did not believe such another mother-in-law was to be found throughout the world, and no day passed without his quoting her: 'Mother used always to say...'

The other blessed domestic influence, however, did not die, but abode with them, uniting their hearts ever more and more, and helping them to bear whatever trials life brought them; for in all lives there come heavy blows; just as there are storms in every summer, and the brighter the summer the louder the thunder of the occasional storm.

God had blessed them with children, in whom they had their delight. But the hand of the Lord came upon them, and, one after the other, took away the fairest and dearest of these, till at last they began to fear that they should be left alone in the world. They found it very hard to be resigned, and it was long long before they could sincerely say, 'The Lord gave and the Lord hath taken away; blessed be the name of the Lord.' They often tried to do so, but conscience kept them silent, for they knew their hearts held another language, and that God read the heart. But they sustained each other, and at night, when praying together, one began, 'Our Father,' and the voice failed, and tears came, the other wept too, and for a long while neither could get through the prayer. Yet still they would not give in till one or other could, even though at each petition fresh tears came; and behind each, as it were, the lost little ones appeared all alike, whether the will, the bread, or the kingdom reminding of them, and the mention of trespasses waking a fear lest in any way their parents should have sinned against them. When at length they had so mastered all emotion as to reach the end, and could join in saying, 'Thine is the kingdom, the power, and the glory,' then peace would descend, then the waves of anguish would be laid. They would picture their children, with their grandmother, in that glory of the Father; they would look forward to the time when they too should be waked up by that Father's might, to be all together once more, for ever and ever. Then they found themselves able to talk together of the lost ones, how good and dear they were, what they had said, and how each parent felt when first the dread of their death broke upon them. From the dead they passed on to the living, to their hopes and joys regarding these; how they resembled those who were gone, and each day grew more and more like; and how it seemed as though their children loved them better than they used, and did all in their power to fill the empty places. Gradually these living ones assumed the place of the dead, —were like the flowers that covered their graves and hid them from their parents' sight; for three children, as we have already said, were left to Christian and Annie—two boys and a girl.

The youngest was his mother's favourite; the girl her father's darling; the eldest dear to all. In the main, they took after their parents, and grew up good and promising. They were not required to vex their brains with overmuch learning, but they were well grounded in their Bible, which both father and mother considered the chief point, having hitherto got on very well themselves without much skill in writing and ciphering,—for we must admit that in these two points neither was an adept. When Christian had to write his name, he took as long a run as if he were about to leap a six-feet ditch; and when Annie and the butterman differed in their reckoning, he had but to take out his bit of chalk to convince her at once; she knew very well why.

But it was different as to work. Here Annie could show her family the way, and in her opinion they could never begin too early; something or other children must have to do, and it had better be useful than mischievous. Christian, however, opined that it was not well to set them tasks so soon; it only did harm, and made them dislike work; whereas, when reason came, they would take to it of their own accord. At all events, so it had been with him, and no one could say he was not able and willing to work. This difference of opinion occasionally gave an opportunity for mutual forbearance and forgiveness; for when Annie lectured, Christian would break in, 'Well, I would not force them; if they liked it, they could soon do it.' Or when he looked complacently upon their idling, Annie would suggest that he as well as they might be better employed. But all these rubs got smoothed over by the good spirit that nightly extracted all bitterness from the hearts of both.

Something however of this told upon the children, for children are like a white wall,—however clean the hands laid on it, by and bye they leave their traces there. Christy, the eldest, who attached himself specially to no one, was a quiet soul, who said little but felt deeply, and lived more in his own thoughts and feelings than in the outer world, consequently he often seemed idle and apathetic. Lizzie was a pretty girl, but she would talk of work a whole day through before setting to it; when once, however, she fairly did so, she could distance most girls; but this occurred but seldom. The poor were not partial to her; they thought her proud and extravagant; and yet, if there was anything to be carried to or done for an old woman, Lizzie was always ready. Young men, too, pronounced her haughty, because she was not so familiar with them as other girls; and vain, because everything became her; and she always looked as if she had just stepped out of a bandbox. Andrew, the youngest, was a handsome youth, quick, active, efficient, like his mother ; like her too, he was rather anxious and impatient; and before his father finished one stable, he would have fed and cleaned half the stock seven times over. All three were rather silent, but when they did speak, they could say a good deal in a few words. Christy, the eldest, was the only one who ever waxed really talkative; but a glass of good wine would sometimes open his heart, and then he showed that he had more in him than people supposed.

The more marked the individual characters in a household, the more agitated and chequered its life, whether it appears so outwardly or no. However fond they may be of each other, each member of the family has something that tends to repel ; each has a sensitive point that often gets a rub ; each his own separate domain in which he tolerates no intrusion ; each his peculiar pretensions, which he puts forth as it were unconsciously and accidentally, but the neglect of them, even if unexpressed by look or word, wounds deeply. Such claims, such pretensions as these, are considered all the more valid, because they are never directly urged.

Now, each of these young people had a strongly marked individuality, and therefore his or her special claims on parents and brothers ; and the neglect of these drove a splinter into the heart, which, although silently borne, after the manner of the family, yet was painfully felt none the less.

For instance, Christy was of a sickly constitution, liable to feverish attacks, which sometimes left symptoms behind that resembled those of consumption. He consequently required to be humoured as to work, food, attention, medical advice, etc. His family did their best, but as his looks did not always reveal his sensations, and as he expected whatever he suffered to be found out without his expressing it, it necessarily followed that he sometimes believed himself neglected, uncared for, and in the way.

Lizzie, too, had her own pretensions. She was a bright joyous creature; and who could say whether in the bottom of her heart a wish might not lurk to be no longer pretty Lizzie, but a farmer's wife like her mother? Accordingly, she liked to attend all dances and merry-makings; not, of course, in Cinderella fashion, but better dressed than any one else. But her brothers were not always inclined to escort her, and she could not go alone; nor was her father always ready to give money for every project of the kind; and her mother was usually on his side, and would say, she had been no dowdy herself, nor ever used to be looked down upon; but such requirements as Lizzie's she had neither had nor heard of. She should like to have seen what her mother would have said to them! This grieved Lizzie, and she often fancied she was looked upon as in the world only to be of use to her brothers, and that no one cared for her interests. She was just good enough to work, but if she wanted something more, there was no sympathy for her.

Andrew, too, who was naturally well aware that he must one day inherit the farm, would have wished to see work pushed on more vigorously, more money laid out on improvements, and he often thought no one remembered him ; nay, that every one spent as much as they could, and did as little, just to prevent his being over well off. Not that he was covetous, but he was anxious ; and this persistent anxiety, which he never chose to express, appeared in the eyes of many to be pride, while others again pronounced him covetous, because he was so much at home, and so careful in looking about things, while the others went about and spent money freely.

Neither father nor mother was aware of these secret feelings in their children's hearts ; but the mother had from early childhood acquainted them with the peacemaking domestic spirit before mentioned. She had taught them the Lord's Prayer so well, that they never said it by rote,—that it was to them first a sea into which every cause of vexation fell and got swallowed up, and then a ladder to lead them to heaven. More particularly, as regarded the brothers, who slept together, and generally prayed together, the result was that the morning sun very seldom rose on the shadow that darkened either heart the evening before. Lizzie had not the same advantages; for as she was alone in her room, she lacked this special opportunity of reconciliation; but her brothers' good-nature came to her aid, made them regret any cause of offence that they had given her, and be all the more good-natured to make up for it; and then her father's tenderness for his darling would often induce him, if he saw her vexed by any refusal of his, to go and buy something more expensive than she had originally wanted, so she had but little to complain of.

Thus, then, the family lived on in prosperity and general esteem, till an event, apparently of no great consequence, threatened entirely to destroy their happiness.

II.

THE HAPPY CUSTOM INTERRUPTED.

CHRISTIAN found himself called upon, not merely, as heretofore, to pay his quota to the parish fund, but to take an active part in its management, to become a trustee, to assume official duties as one of the local authorities. This is in itself a burden, and involves no small personal responsibility, and in many places, it is strange to contrast the amount of this personal responsibility of unpaid parish officials with the entire absence of it in the case of richly-salaried members of the Government. Where, from a mistaken principle of personal liberty, the rule is invariably to decide in favour of individuals against the corporation, and, out of spurious humanity, to prefer the rascal to the honest man, this responsibility becomes a positive danger, a sword suspended by a hair over the head of the parish guardian.

Christian, from his ignorance of all legal matters, and inability to write, found his position a very difficult and expensive one. He had not only to pay out of his own pocket for all assistance, but to depend entirely upon others, and to follow his adviser as a blind man does his dog. This particular danger, however, he was less aware of than Annie; for women have generally greater prescience than men. All this public business that took Christian away from his own and the work of the farm was particularly distasteful to her; however, she did not harp upon it, or, as wives too often do, make a necessity still more intolerable. But further, she had a strong suspicion of the man of whose assistance Christian availed himself, and often warned against him. He seemed to her, she declared, false, far too plausible and flattering, and always needy; just the one to do for sixpence what another would not do for a thousand pounds. However, Christian could not do without him; good advice was scarce, and in many parishes not to be had even for money, and Annie herself could point out no one who could give better; so, in order that he might not be tempted to wrong them, out of want, she expended as much as possible upon him; whenever he came, had him into the back parlour, where there was always some dainty for him that he could not get at home. But there are people who not only are dissatisfied, give them what you will, but infer that they have you entirely in their power, and can fleece you unobserved and unpunished. When they have got to this pitch, they generally play a double game: their poor victims pay them; and they are bribed by others to cheat and befool them, reckoning that they can get twice as much from two sources as from one. And there are more who live upon this plan than is generally supposed.

Christian was a trustee; he had other people's means in his hands, whether in money or deeds I do not know, perhaps both—for title-deeds are not invariably where, according to strict law, they should be; and when a Government and a parish official, or a clerk, for instance, are one and the same, whole fortunes may melt away. But how make the Government official responsible? The innocent parish authorities, or the still more innocent members of that parish, have to pay the costs, and to discover by their own experience that little thieves may indeed be hanged, but that great ones go free.

Now nothing could be further from Christian's intention than to wrong any one, but he was bamboozled as follows:—There were people who wanted money, and Christian's adviser being in their interests, persuaded the good man to invest with them what was in his hands, and to give up the titledeeds. He told Christian that the parish approved, that he had laid the matter before the guardians, and they had authorized the transfer, therefore that he need be under no anxiety, whatever happened, it could in no way affect him. When once this was done he would be free from all responsibility and anxiety, and he, the adviser, would take care to have all the proceedings entered in such a way as to insure him perfectly and for all time. Christian liked this prospect, and had not the remotest suspicion; but Annie was not so easily satisfied; there were five thousand Bernese pounds[1] at stake, and that was not a sum to trifle with; it would be better, she thought, to go to some regular lawyer about it,— in money matters one could never be too careful.

But Christian, for his part, was never given to say more than was absolutely essential, more especially about business, for he did not like to betray how little he knew of it, being at heart ashamed of his ignorance, though content to leave his children in the same plight. And further, he did not know whom to trust if he was not to trust his adviser. If he were a rogue, why, then, there was not an honest man left in the world; and if so, what was the use of running hither and thither when one had plenty to do without that? He was, indeed, consti-

---

[1] The Bernese pound, which is always the one alluded to in this story, is an imaginary coin, in value about half a florin, or tenpence of our money.

tutionally distrustful, but on this very account slow to seek new advisers, being firmly persuaded that if his old friend was not to be trusted, there was an end of probity on earth. But he was willing to hope he was safe in his hands. If Annie would only be quiet things would go straight, and all must be well, for no one said a word to the contrary.

This went on for several years, but gradually there crept out of the parish council-chamber, no one knew how, a rumour of Christian's having grievously tampered with the public funds, and being answerable for many thousand pounds. Annie, who seldom went from home, but for all that was in the habit of hearing not only what was done and said, but a great deal more, soon heard that there were heavy claims against Christian, and that, were not his private means so good, he would be bankrupt. This was a terrible shock to her, though she felt sure there was great exaggeration. However, she insisted on Christian's going at once to his *factotum*, and seriously inquiring how things stood; but the latter only laughed at him for heeding such foolish gossip, and assured him it would be well if everything in the world was as safe as his affairs. He would answer for that. He was indeed a poor man, but he had a conscience, and perhaps a better one than many rich men; therefore

Christian need have no anxiety. What had been done had been properly done, and he would willingly undertake to make up every farthing lost on that account. With this comfortable assurance the farmer went home, comforted his wife, and there was another interval of peace. But again the affair got talked of, and more seriously than before, and again terror woke in the hearts of both, and now Annie would not rest without Christian's consulting a real lawyer. It was long, however, before the lawyer could be got to give any opinion at all. He had not seen the documents, he said; but at length he inquired whether Christian had had a written authorization of his proceedings from the parish.

'Not I,' was his reply. 'I was told that none was necessary; that it was all written down in the parish registers, where it could be found when wanted, and that it was not worth while having a duplicate.'

'Well,' said the lawyer, 'if the matter is inscribed in the parish books, no proceedings can be taken against you, at all events.'

Accordingly, Christian was again at ease, for he never doubted that it was thus duly inscribed; but Annie was not so confident, and insisted upon his going to ascertain the fact at once. So off the farmer went, grumbling the while, and brought home for answer that the clerk had said he had not time to look just then; he had more to do than women wotted of, but Christian might rely on all that was correct being written down in the book; he knew his business. Once more the matter went to sleep, and Christian kept saying that people might say what they liked against him, but when a man had the parish books at his back, no one could touch him,—no, not the very devil himself.

But ere long one of those who delight in carrying unpleasant tidings, but do not wish to have their names mentioned, crept quietly to Annie, and confided to her that there really was no record of the transaction in the parish books; that it had been a regular conspiracy to defraud Christian, and that the clerk was trying to hush things up, and avert the catastrophe as long as possible. But sooner or later Christian would have to pay. So much was certain, and it were best to do so as soon as possible; perhaps, if he were prompt, something might still be got out of the fire. All this was a sore thunder-clap for poor Annie, and all the worse because she could not conceive what was to be done,—except, indeed, that Christian should go at once before the council and expose the villany; and, above all, to the parish clerk, and tell him that he was a rogue and a lying fellow, and that he would have nothing more to do with any of them; they might shift for themselves. But the

THE HAPPY CUSTOM INTERRUPTED. 37

new adviser said this would be of little avail; Christian might, however, demand an extract from the parish books, and if this were not given at once, he might have it claimed by a lawyer, and then they would know what was or was not to be found there.

And so it was, and after much circumlocution, Christian at length arrived at the certainty that the parish books contained not one single word of the whole transaction; the matter had, indeed, been discussed before the board, but no resolution had been come to; it had been thought best to leave it to Christian's own responsibility. Accordingly, it was decided that he must pay up the five thousand pounds; nor could he recover from any quarter, his treacherous advisers abounding in the most plausible excuses, and laying all the blame upon others.

I hardly know whether to say that this loss fell upon the farmer's family like a thunderbolt, shattering their happiness at once, or to liken it to a venomous worm, gradually destroying their peace. Neither simile is quite accurate; the blow was indeed heavy and sudden, but after it the worm was still living, and at its poisonous work.

Five thousand pounds are nothing for a merchant; he snaps his fingers at a loss like that; it in no way cripples him, even if it sweep off much of his ready money; he is accustomed to reverses,

—to-day up, to-morrow down. But it is otherwise with the farmer. With him prosperity is a slow, but steady affair; small losses are made up by small gains, a bad year by a good; and in this way, if he be economical, industrious, and escape heavy calamities, by little and little he gets on. If great trials come, if all his cattle die, or his house and furniture be burnt down, he is thrown back for years; but still he generally submits with admirable resignation. What, indeed, is the use of fretting? 'tis the Lord's hand that has done it; and men do not mock at such losses as these, nor do children and grandchildren bring them up against him.

But if he loses money in any exceptional manner, through his own folly or the rascality of others, then he is in great danger of forfeiting his peace and eating his heart out, as we country folk say. He cannot soon replace what is gone; perhaps his whole remaining life will not suffice to replace it, and then, what will his children and children's children say of him?

Christian and Annie had indeed laid something by, but they found difficulty enough in doing so. He was not clever in management, required too much time and too many hands in all farming operations; and Annie was a kind-hearted creature, and money melted in her hands she hardly knew

THE HAPPY CUSTOM INTERRUPTED.

how. It was natural that this five thousand pounds, when they had to replace it, should seem to them an immense sum indeed, the fruit of their whole life's labour.

Then, again, the children were grown up; this loss could not be kept from them. What would they say? How would they bear it? In the country, children share their parents' toil and see its results; they know their possessions and their debts, and form their own projects accordingly. In this case all three were marriageable. Might not this affair injure their matrimonial prospects,—the report of it even more than the fact itself? Everything gets exaggerated, and where one misfortune of the kind has occurred, others seem probable. People are afraid to run the risk. And, indeed, if their children were to marry, where were they to find a dower for them? If they were called upon to give them anything just now, they must strip themselves entirely, must even borrow, and either come to poverty and contempt in their old age, or bid the young ones leave them empty-handed. A time of want hovered night and day before Annie's imagination.

Indeed, this could not fail to embitter the spirits of husband and wife alike, for with the money they had lost a large portion of their life. We all feel that life is a great gift,—it is one with which we have to win much, very much; with temporal life,

life eternal. But many there are who look upon this temporal life as merely meant to gain temporal wealth in,—who, indeed, speak of eternal life as the highest good, but appear to understand thereby only worldly gear, at most a wife and a fortune, and hence they estimate their life by the amount of money they have scraped together, as a mole might its strength by the mounds it has thrown up. Therefore, if all gains be at once swept away, they fall into brooding despondency; cannot help brooding continually over what is gone, and how it went; for they really and truly have lost not only their money but their life,—their life having consisted in money-making. Now, Christian and Annie were thoroughly worthy people, better you will hardly find in town or country; but they were too much given to estimate a man's worth by his wealth, and the success of his life by what he had made. If he had inherited so much, he ought, they thought, to have acquired so much, and to leave so and so much behind him. . . .

They knew no better. If they had not learnt much arithmetic at school, they had been accustomed to calculations of this kind from their youth up; and if Christian never said it, still he had over and over again thought, as he took his place in a public-house, 'Here sits a hundred thousand Bernese pounds.' Do not despise him for this; there are other than he who do not know that if a man were to win the whole world and injure his own soul, he would not only have wasted his life, but incurred a heavy sin.

They went about, this poor husband and wife, for days and days, as though they had been knocked on the head, and kept continually thinking over one only subject, 'Five thousand pounds, five thousand pounds.' The children were less overwhelmed than the parents; they had a long life before them, which offered them hopes in abundance as compensation for this loss. Lizzie appeared to feel it most; perhaps she feared that it might seriously affect her dower, or frighten away some one she had in her eye. But at all events there was nothing here of what too often occurs elsewhere; the children never reproached their parents,—nay, they did what they could to cheer and encourage them. But where parents direct their children's thoughts exclusively to money, and keep other considerations out of their sight, it must needs be that their teaching recoils against themselves; if mischance befall them, they have to bear the anger and reproaches of their children, and, when they grow old and useless, the impatience of these children at their prolonged life.

Here, however, love had long prevailed, and the old custom of the children 'honouring their father and mother, that their days might be long in the land that the Lord their God had given them.'

But as it is with him whose house and all inside it is burnt down, so was it now with Christian and Annie. At first the calamity filled their soul, inducing a sort of torpor; then projects of reparation flashed through this torpor like flames through smoke. They took to devising means of replacing their loss, and to turn over in their minds where the blame lay.

Christian had no house to rebuild, but he began to ponder persistently the best means of regaining the lost five thousand, and by and bye, whenever he saw a poor woman creep up to the door, the idea occurred : 'She is carrying off money's worth with her; and what is the use of my pinching and sparing with the right hand, and giving away whatever is portable with the left?' Our good Christian was like many, who believe that the right way to economize is to restrict others.

Annie again began to recall how often she had warned Christian against parting with the money; how she had advised him to seek for better counsel; and how consistent she had been in her dislike and suspicion of the treacherous friend. Also, she took to calculating whether it would not be possible to get through the work with fewer hands; and when she went through the stables and saw two or three cows as fat as they could be, but nearly dry, she could not help reflecting how much money they would bring in if parted with. All this, however, went on inwardly; was soon over, like a mere lightning flash. No angry words were spoken; each was affectionate to the other; and they went to their nightly sleep in peace and concord, if with heavy sighs.

But at last came a day when it seemed as though some evil influence were at work devising and contriving how events could come about in the most unlucky way imaginable. There are such days when cross-purposes succeed each other like a flock of wild-geese, till at length long pent-up vexations overflow, and the storm breaks out.

When the stable was visited in the morning, a horse was found to have slipped his head out of the halter and hurt himself a good deal, so that he could not be used that day; in the cow-house, too, there was something wrong, and when they came for linseed for the animal, it was found that mother had given the last of it to a poor woman for whom poultices were ordered. The servants were wasting their time to and fro in the stables, so that nothing was done in the fields; and, while others had got in their second hay-crop in excellent order, Christian's was left exposed to the rain. In the evening came a butcher from Berne to visit the sick cow, and he could hardly be got out of their stable, he was so anxious to make a purchase or two, and went on offering the most unheard-of prices. It was a time, he said, when fat cows were hardly to be had, and butchers were at their wit's ends; for whether there were cattle or not, townspeople would have their meat, and the butcher might find it where he liked; as far as they were concerned, cut it out of a cabbage-stalk if he chose, so only they got it.

However, Christian went on smoking his pipe unconcernedly, and replied: 'You have had your answer: once for all, I am not going to part with them. If a Berne butcher can give that price for them, I can afford to keep them at that price.' All the arguments that could be used, all the butcher's assurances that other cows would be far more profitable to the farmer, went for nothing. Annie heard the discussion with an impatient heart, kept going in and out of the stable, and at length could not refrain from telling the butcher that he was a sensible man and knew what he was about, and that if it were she, she would gladly deal with him.

This was a thrust that went home, but Christian took no notice, only said to the butcher: 'You have heard what I mean to do, and if I were you I would not stay here any longer. If you've any other job in hand to-day you have no time to lose.'

Soon after this came to the house a poor old woman, who had a sick son. She had maintained him pretty well, she said, hitherto ; but just now the distress was great ; her son was beginning to recover, and the doctor had ordered him wine, but how was she to get it ? In such cases as these, Annie was the general resource, and it was seldom that any came to her in vain. The poor mother wiped her eyes before she began her story, and then had much to tell of her son ; how good to her he had always been, and how he had fallen sick, and they were in real want ; they had had nothing warm to eat that day, and now she was told to buy wine, and had not a penny in the house, and did not know where to turn for one. If Annie would for God's sake lend her some pence, or, if it were possible, a half-crown, why, then she should indeed be relieved, and she would spin in return for it as much as ever Annie saw fit. For if her son were to be taken from her, she did not know what would become of her; he was one of a thousand, he was.

Annie was in extreme perplexity. As to wine, there was not a drop in the house, as was often the case, and a few pence were all she had in her pocket. She did not often leave herself in such a plight as this ; but she had just stood godmother; and since the harvest she had had no butter to sell ; eggs too had been scarce ; in short, she had made nothing, and Christian happened to have the key of the money-box in his pocket. Yet she could not let the woman go away thus. Her son might die; and if so, she should never have another quiet hour in her life, nor could she depart in peace; but for all this, it went horribly against her to ask Christian for the key. Meanwhile, she set down the poor woman to something warm, and went to look for Andrew, who had plenty of money, but he had gone off with the butcher, and taken the key of his chest in his pocket; her other son was in the stable, but all belonging to him in Andrew's chest. Lizzie had lost the key of the little coffer in which she kept her money. Everything seemed bewitched. At last Annie took her courage in both hands; she went out and said, 'The key of the money-box, please, at once!'

Christian turned very red, was a long time fumbling for it, and finally gave it, with the words, 'Well, I had meant to try and keep something for the morrow.'

Now, such a speech as this Annie had never yet heard; it roused her thoroughly. She gave Christian a look that he had not met before; but she could not say a word. She rushed frantically with her key into the house, and when she gave the half-crown to the old woman, her hands trembled so that the grateful recipient stopped short in her fervent expressions to ask, 'But, dear heart alive, what ails you? are you vexed to part with it?'

'O no, no,' replied Annie, 'it is nothing of any consequence; I always am this way when I have been a long time without being bled; it will soon pass off.' And Annie strove to compose herself; for no strange ear had ever heard a complaint, no strange eye had ever seen a tear in hers, except on grounds that all admitted natural. Whatever might happen between her and her husband, Annie would not have it trumpeted about the streets. But on this occasion her self-control cost her a mighty effort, and she tried to dismiss the poor woman sooner than was her wont, she found her presence so intolerable a restraint. There seemed, however, no end to the good creature's thanks, and this not only out of gratitude, but astonishment at Annie's sudden change of manner, and a hope of discovering its cause if she lingered on. When at length she was obliged to go, she went up to Christian and tried to get him into talk, but he did not even answer her. No doubt, thought she, they have had words; and in her conjectures on this head, she almost forgot the half-crown that was to buy wine for her son's good.

As the old woman went off by the front door Annie darted out through the back, pretended to have something to do in the pig-styes, and when once she was out of the way of men and maids, she crept to a bean-field, which often serves as a beautiful green curtain to hide what is not meant for the eyes of all.

There she gave free course to her tears, and thought that if her heart's blood could flow as fast, there would soon be an end to her sorrows. She could not keep herself up; she was obliged to sit down among the beans; the ground seemed to reel under her, and eyes and mind grew as dark as though a pall had bound them round.

So then this was henceforth to be her fate : she alone was to suffer for Christian's misfortune; she was to turn away the poor, to make the innocent pay for what they had had nothing to do with. This she considered a great sin, to squeeze out of the needy what one had lost through one's own weakness and the roguery of others. How often indeed they had talked this over, and agreed that if a rich man had a loss, it was always the poor that had to make it good; for that people would rather stint them than deny themselves their superfluities; and now, were they to act in the very same way? And what would be the result?—a mere nothing, not worth counting. Christian could afford to refuse large sums of money for useless beasts, and to go on in all his old ways; and yet, because of a trumpery half-crown, she had to be spoken to in a tone which pierced her very soul. She saw plainly enough that there was no longer any love felt for her; that she was the scape-goat who was to endure all that others brought about. Had she not warned, had she not counselled? But she was not attended to, was not believed; and yet she was to be the one to suffer. If there had been a single spark of affection in Christian's heart for her, he could not have behaved so. And besides, was it his property only that had suffered? had she not brought in enough to entitle her to give an alms if she chose? Yes, indeed! If she had ever been an expensive wife, or an exacting, or an idle one, there might have been some excuse for him; but all round the country there was not one who had brought in more, and worked more; and she begged to know if nothing was to be done to please her, and helping the poor was all her pleasure; and was not that better, pray, than dressing up and gadding about? And the more she wept, the fuller poor Annie's heart seemed to grow, till she really thought it would burst outright! Dark angry clouds gathered athwart her soul; she thought in quick succession of separating, going away, packing up, claiming her own fortune, speaking her mind out freely, leaving her husband for good and all. Every such project died away as soon as it rose: some for her children's sake, some on account of what the world would say. But just as fire licks up water, and dries wet places, so does anger consume sorrow, and stop the flow of tears; and when she observed that she was being looked for, her mood became much akin to the weather we often see succeed a storm,—it rains and thunders indeed no longer, but neither does the sun shine, —the sky looks threatening and gloomy, and no one knows what will come next. Annie left her hiding-place, and suddenly made her appearance, as a clever woman can, in the midst of her household, without any one knowing exactly where she had been, or when she came back.

The children indeed were aware that there was something wrong, but no one inquired what it was, and all went to bed as early as they could.

Christian smoked his pipe as usual before the house. When once he had sat down, he was generally unwilling to get up, and glad as he might have been to find himself in bed, the effort of going there was so unpleasant, that he would, if left to himself, sit till midnight, without making up his mind to rise. On this occasion he did sit out long all alone, perhaps not only from habit, but from that uncomfortable feeling familiar to us all when we know that another is offended with us, and wish to make it up, but are not sure whether that other is inclined for peace or war, and cannot bring ourselves openly and good-humouredly to beg to be taken back into favour.

At last, however, he went to bed. He was the

last. He said his 'Our Father,' but he had to say it alone. Annie did not join in with him. When he had done, he waited a while. Annie continued speechless; he did not know whether she was asleep or awake, and he could not speak the first word. The question, 'Are you asleep?' stuck in his throat. Ten times at least he thought of putting it, but it was not to be got out, so he laid himself down in silence. It was the first time they had ever omitted to exchange the pious wish, 'God give thee a good night!'

Now, Annie had not been asleep, but she was resolved not to break the ice. Christian it was who had grievously offended against her, Christian it was to whom the first word belonged; and for this first word she waited, not that she knew herself whether she would make peace with him or not, but at all events she would tell him that her heart was almost broken, and that if this was to be the way things went, she would not put up with it any longer.

When Christian prayed, 'Forgive us our trespasses, as we forgive them that have trespassed against us,' she wondered whether he remembered his trespass of that day against her. The prayer over, she expected him to speak; but when he laid himself down to sleep without a benediction or a good-night, she said to herself, 'So then he meant it; so then all is over! If he cannot any longer see and confess his faults, I am an unhappy creature indeed; but I won't let myself be quite trampled upon for all that.' Strange how Annie kept thinking, not of the forgiveness of sins, but merely of their confession, and how well this confession became Christian; and now that he omitted it, she saw in this a new offence, and one that she could not possibly overlook; and when, in addition, no good wish was spoken, it seemed as though between her and her husband a broad deep chasm yawned, never more to be overpassed.

Often, indeed, she felt as though she must speak, as though it were too terrible that they two should lie down thus in strife and wrath, and let the sun rise upon them so, but such impulses were constantly checked by the angry pride that suggested that she had to show once for all that she was not to be thus trampled down and victimized for the faults of others, or treated as if she had been some mere scullion, or had come to her husband empty-handed.

All night long no sleep visited her eyes, but no repentance either her heart. She rose before dawn to escape having to say to Christian, 'God give thee a good morning,' or to thank him for his wish of one; and this was the first day that they ever begun without a loving blessing. Sadly and silently the hours wore on, and when evening came, Christian was the first to go to bed. He yearned for his wife's voice again, which all the day long he had not heard. This silence had pained him, for he loved her, and he had been reflecting that although indeed she was far too kind to the poor, and wasted a good deal in that way, attracting all the rascals and idlers as sugar does flies, yet that in other respects she was economical, and always industrious; that he might have had one who was far harder to live with, and that every human being had some fault, only some more and some less. He had planned telling her that sulking did no good; that they had lived in peace and concord nearly thirty years; and that it was not worth while beginning a new plan now. Annie came, said her prayers, but said them silently to herself. If Christian would not even wish her good-night, she did not see why she should say his prayers for him. Meanwhile, he was longing to hear the familiar words, and meant to join in, but when no sound was heard, and Annie turned round to sleep without so much as a good-night to him, he hardly knew what he was about. He never reflected that he had gone to bed in silence the evening before; his mind dwelt only on Annie's omissions. 'Very well, then,' he mentally resolved, 'she will have it so; she shall see that I too can change. I am not going to let myself be dictated to by a woman in this way; I did not come into the world for that.

What is a husband for but to decide how things are to be? If she chooses to sulk, let her as long as she likes for me; I shall never ask her what is amiss.'

Thus it was that Christian's wrath kindled, and, as is always the case with slow natures, it was enduring. Annie had expected that he would inquire why she did not pray aloud as usual, and determined upon that to have a thorough explanation. But now when Christian neither inquired nor spoke a word, she said to herself, 'Well, then, if you will have it so, so be it; but I never thought you had been such a hard-hearted man, nor could I have believed you cared so little for me;' and she very nearly burst into a violent fit of crying, so full was her heart. But anger prevailed and drove away emotion.

Thus both lay down that night in bitter mood, rose the next morning speechless, and a melancholy time began for the whole family.

When once a grudge firmly establishes itself in the heart, that heart becomes selfish. Its range of vision, and still more of sensation, narrows. As the spider can only catch the flies that venture within the sphere of its net, so anger is only sensible of things connected with its cause, all in the world besides is a mere nothing; the aggrieved neither sees nor hears, or, if forced upon his attention, he rejects it. When once harmony is destroyed within the soul, and an exclusive feeling gets the upper hand, the man becomes limited; and just as Archimedes, absorbed in his calculations, was heedless of the capture of his native city, so a thoroughly angry man hardly cares for his own interest, and a thoroughly discontented man is indifferent to the enjoyments of all around him.

Let any one passion, in short, become dominant, it will resemble the uncontrolled fiery element which devours all within its reach, and only dies down when nothing is left it to devour. Let married people have a chronic grievance against each other, and it will colour the whole household; everything will go to swell it; all other feelings gradually weaken; the thoughts, perpetually exercised on this subject, become dull and blunt to all beside,—nay, one might almost say that the vision grew impaired, things most essential being unseen, things dearest uncared for. This condition comes on little by little, one scarce knows how,—for if the devil goes about, as we are told, like a roaring lion, he still oftener glides round in breathless silence; and hell is very like an oven which is not heated to the utmost all at once, but feels at first only pleasantly warm.

So was it now with our poor pair. They bore about their grievances locked up in their own hearts. At first they were careful to conceal them from servants and neighbours, and outwardly things went on much as before, only Christian intentionally refused to sell his cows, intentionally employed as many hands as he could, and set about work in the most dilatory way; and Annie, who saw all this, became on her side all the more openhanded, and told many a poor woman in Christian's hearing to come soon again. Thus one defied the other, each dwelling upon the five thousand pounds, equally feeling that it ought to be made up, only differing as to the method; and the more unsuccessful they naturally were in thus making it up, the more their inward disaffection increased. It was their children who first suffered from it. Their parents took less and less interest in their affairs,—hardly indeed heeded them; the children might come or go, neither father nor mother asked where or whence. Now, undutiful children like such indifference, but to loving hearts it is indescribably painful.

Formerly, when Lizzie came back from any gaiety, her mother delighted to hear how it had gone off, who had been there, etc., and knew how to elicit, by judicious questioning, much that the young girl was glad to tell. Young men got discussed, so as to show plainly who would be welcome as a son-in-law, who not; and such conversations gave Lizzie an opportunity of opening her heart about her rivals, and saying to her mother, 'Really, mother dear, I must

THE HAPPY CUSTOM INTERRUPTED. 57

positively have a new bodice. There were girls there from houses where they have hard work to pay the rent, but not one of them had such a shabby bodice as I; and as for silver chains, I have only those I had at my first communion, and they are so slight and old-fashioned, no well-dressed girl would wear them.'

Thus appealed to, her mother could hardly object to new purchases being made, and, if once she gave her consent, father seldom said nay to his Lizzie. But now all this was changed.

She always encountered sour looks if she wanted to go out; and when she came home and tried to entertain her mother with the account of her gaieties, either met with silence, or was told that Annie did not care for such things, and that in her day girls stayed at home and took some of the trouble off their parents, instead of flaunting to every merry-making, like the birds to a millet-field. Or, if anything were said of dress, of a hat or a new petticoat, her mother sighed and gave no answer, or lamented that, when once things had gone wrong, every one came with his wants and conspired to bring about utter ruin; she should have expected Lizzie to be more reasonable. Then, if the girl shed tears because she could no longer get at her mother's heart, and her father chanced to ask her what the matter was, and she replied that she could no longer please any one, that every amusement was grudged her, that this made her so miserable she should just take the first comer if it were only to get away, all the comfort she had from him was, 'Very well, then, take him, and then come and ask me for a good round dower; it's all one. It will be better to be ruined outright, we shall at least know then how we stand.'

Now, this made Lizzie very miserable. She was a good girl, and truly fond of her parents, but she did think it hard that she was to be the only sufferer, and merely to live and work for others. If the farmer's son is anxious to become a farmer, why should not his daughter aspire to be a farmer's wife? And now Lizzie's prospects of attaining this desirable condition were to be all quashed because her father had lost five thousand pounds, and found it difficult to give her a dower!

This was a hardship indeed.

The eldest son of the house was, as we have said, of a sensitive nature, and had often before fancied that he was not sufficiently considered; but now this was oftener his opinion than ever, and not always without cause.

Formerly his mother's eye would detect the changes in his face, and take measures accordingly. 'Christy, my boy, I have made up a draught for you to-day, you must not go to work;' or she would call him into her bedroom, where she had put by some dainty for him, that he might not try his stomach by the harder fare of the labourers. And if he did not soon mend, she would propose sending to the doctor, or even having him over, 'for then he can see for himself what ails thee; messages are not always carried right.'

Now all these attentions were over; his mother hardly ever asked him how he was, or if he revealed his case by loss of appetite or by sighs, she was capable of saying: 'You must not notice your symptoms so much, you will soon be better; the more we coddle ourselves the worse we are.'

Or, if he were really ill, obliged to take to his bed, alarmed about himself, and anxious to see the doctor, his father would perhaps say that there was no having a doctor for him all the year through; for his part, he was sick of doctors, and had now no money to throw away upon them, but the poorer he got the more his family wanted, and so on.

Now, such speeches pierced young Christian to the heart. He thought that, short as his life would probably be, they should not grudge it him, but now he saw it was too long for them, and they could not wait till his time came. He often wished that he could die that very day, that their consciences might reproach them. They would be sorry then, when they had to take him to the churchyard, and reflected how little they had attended to him, and that he might have been alive at that hour if they had not grudged him money for a doctor. Then the idea of marrying would occur to him, that at least he might have some one to look after him, and he would creep around, visit places he had better have shunned, spend money in public-houses, and so forth, till he fell sick again, cared no longer for girls, touched no more wine, and nursed the idea of a speedy departure.

But it was the youngest son, Andrew, who suffered most of all. His mother had been accustomed to say to him, 'Andrew, the sooner you can bring me a daughter-in-law the better pleased I shall be, but mind these three things: choose one who washes more than her face, one who is stirring and not afraid of the pig-trough, and one who has her wits about her, and can give a ready answer. I shall be glad of a little rest, and if you bring me a girl such as I describe, she will not have to complain of me.'

It is true that Andrew used to reply, 'Mother, I am in no hurry at all.' But for all that he was fond of talking over the girls with his mother, and hearing what she thought of this one or that, and what she knew of their parents, and even their grandparents; for Andrew laid great stress upon a good name, and would only marry into a respectable family. He was determined no one should reproach his wife with her origin, and while he valued well-gotten wealth, he would not have married the rich daughter of dishonest parents, if she had had a cheese-vat full of gold pieces, and the prettiest of faces into the bargain.

Now a young fellow like Andrew cannot tell a family's antecedents and belongings. All he sees is the girl's own conduct, and even this he often sees through a glass darkly, and persuades himself that out of a light-minded girl will proceed a well-behaved wife; but alas, what a mistake! It is therefore fortunate for a young man to have a mother with whom he can talk rationally about young girls, and who does not believe that the kingdom of heaven lies in a full purse, or that it does not matter whether her son marries a fool or not—she herself being wise enough for two.

Andrew had already lived a good many years in the world, and had thought of more than one girl in a vague undecided way : 'Shall it be this or that? this is the prettiest, that is the merriest, and a third is a very devil to work,' but never yet had he met any that made him feel, 'This is the one I will have, and no other, and if I cannot get her I will take no one else, and perhaps I shall hang myself into the bargain.'

On one fine Sunday it occurred to him that he might as well go and take a bath once in a way.

Accordingly he set off, stuck a beautiful rose in his hat, put on his best necktie, said that he was not to be expected to supper, and that the horses must be fed without him; there was no telling beforehand what might keep one. As soon as dinner was over he set off alone, for his brother was in one of his doleful moods, and to take a servant with him—as is often done, to eat and drink with his master's son, and to fight for him as well—was a thing that did not suit his taste.

III.

A LOVE AT FIRST SIGHT.

IT was a hot day, the dust lay half a foot deep on the roads, and when Andrew came out of the bath he felt like a new man altogether, as if he had wings, and could fly over hill and dale. Two merry fiddlers challenged to the dance, and the nailed shoes clattered heavily on the unsteady floor above. Very quietly he went upstairs into the dancing-room, where he saw about half-a-dozen couples stamping about, and a dozen girls standing against the wall, who would willingly have shown off their own paces and stamped with the rest. Andrew, however, did not belong to the soft-hearted race who take pity on all forlorn damsels, and think that they are only created to satisfy any wish that a girl may form. Besides, with us, in our country districts, a dance is no light matter, for a partner cannot be got rid of at the last stroke of the bow, and left to fare for herself thenceforth. If a youth offers his hand for a dance, a whole bevy of hopes are raised in a girl's heart. First of all a bottle of wine, which her partner is to order, then a dinner, some dainty roast or other, then a pleasant walk or drive home, and finally a merry wedding. All this is conjured up in the mind when a young girl gives her hand for a dance, and this hand of hers is like the key of a cupboard full of splendid things, that are all your own if only you know how to turn the key. If, therefore, her partner lets her go again after a dance or two, or a few empty compliments, all these bright hopes die down, and her heart is full of grey ashes, as ours too would be if, having seen the rosy dawn colour the sky, that dawn were followed by no sun, but by the return of night.

Therefore it was that Andrew was slow to commit himself, for none of the girls there suited his taste. He therefore asked for a pint for himself only, and sat down at the table, undisturbed by the angry glances that, like so many flies or wasps, would gladly have destroyed his comfort if they could. But he went on drinking his wine in the most cold-blooded manner, and thought to himself that if nothing more attractive came in, he would just finish it and be off.

Speak of the evil one, as they say, and he is there; and so it often is in happy hours,—the angel we long for suddenly appears in our path.

When Andrew looked up next, he saw a young girl standing at the door, of a quite different type from any of the others. She was not richly dressed, nor exactly beautiful, according to our country standard, but he could see at a glance that she was one of the right sort, and belonged to respectable people; and the exquisite cleanliness and modesty that pervaded her attire and demeanour gave her, as it were, an appearance of proud refinement, which prevented any of the young men there from going up to her. Andrew, however, felt himself a person of some consequence, and was not ready to suppose any one too good for him; and so, although the girl was a stranger, he was no way daunted, but rose up at once and asked her whether she would take a turn with him, to which she replied that she would with pleasure.

They danced several times together in the large bare room, looking like a king and queen among common people, and the longer they danced the more they enjoyed it; they kept such good time and were so well matched in every way, that both thought they had never had so satisfactory a partner before. After a while Andrew proposed to treat the young girl to a bottle of wine if she would allow him, to which she first replied that there was no occasion for it, for she was not thirsty, but afterwards gracefully consented.

It was plain to see that she was pleased with

Andrew, and as she was a stranger in the place, and saw that he did not know her, she was all the more free and unrestrained, and did not ensconce herself in a tiresome taciturnity. When they sat down to their wine, and the waiting-maid asked if she should bring something to eat as well, Andrew said by all means, if she had something really good. But to that the girl objected, saying that she had been pleased to drink a glass of wine, but had no time to eat; her father would soon be coming to fetch her, and they had a long way to go before getting home.

Andrew, however, comported himself like one who knew what was due to his own dignity: to the waiting-maid he said that she had received his orders, and to his partner that she must not be punctilious, a few shillings more or less made no difference to him; and if her father did come, there would be plenty to eat what was cooked. If, however, she were willing, he proposed to take a few more rounds while the refreshment was preparing; he had never met with any girl with whom he so much enjoyed a waltz. The young lady did not say nay, and they danced again, danced on lightly and joyously, till it got rumoured in the kitchen that there was a pair upstairs the like of whom had never been seen there before, and one scullery-maid after another thrust in her black face through the door to snatch a look at them.

Even after dinner was announced they could not resist a few more turns, though the maid kept beckoning to them, fearing lest it should grow cold. But Andrew felt as though he could not bear to unwind his arm from his partner's waist, as if once he let her go she would vanish away, and he should see her no more. At last, however, they moved towards the table, though the young girl maintained that it was really too much, and that she was determined to pay her share. She had not come there to gormandize; but her father having some business on hand, and she nothing to do, she thought she would just look on at the dancers to divert herself. As to the fiddlers, she would say nothing; but she was resolved to pay her share of the bill; if he was so free of his money, that was no reason why others should not be equally so. Andrew meanwhile was wondering who his partner was, and she who he might be, and both kept beating about the ·bush, but each wanted to know the other's name before giving up their own incognito. However, neither succeeded. Andrew was much struck with one difference between this girl and others; having asked what business her father had on hand, and been told that it was a purchase of wood, his next question was whether their home was too small, and this afforded the young girl a fine opportunity of relating how many acres of land they had, how many sheaves they made up, and how many bundles of hay she gave the cows every year; but not a word of the kind did she say; merely that their house was not a convenient one, and the stable very bad. She made no boast of anything; however much he drew her on he could not even learn how many pigs they kept. Accordingly the young girl heard nothing either. Andrew was generally rather fond of boasting of their fine horses, how many they kept, and what they might get for each of them; but on this occasion he could not for the life of him have said a word about them, though his companion gave him many an opportunity of doing so. He felt as though such boasting would degrade him in her eyes, and that those who boast most have least to boast of. While they were thus parrying each other's questions with equal caution, the waiting-maid came up to say that the young girl's father was below, and desired that she would come to him at once. 'Tell him I will be down instantly,' said she, but for all that she did not rise, drank Andrew's health, went on talking, and seemed to have forgotten her father's message.

Then up came the waiting-maid again, and informed her that her father would drive off alone, if she kept him waiting any longer; he could not keep the horse standing under the trees for half a day.

'Let him go,' said Andrew, 'I will take you home, if you have no objection.'

At this she blushed and said, 'No, that I cannot do, but thank you all the same, and God be with you,' and held out her hand. Andrew took it, and seemed as though he had something to say, for which she waited, but before he could find the right words, the maid rushed in again, and called out, 'Make haste, make haste! the old man is in a downright passion.'

'Good-bye, good-bye,' said the young girl, and tore herself away.

'Wait one moment,' cried Andrew, but she was already down the steps, first asking the maid, as she flew past her, who that young man was.

'I don't know,' was the reply ; ' he was never here before.' Then the young girl got silently into the car, silently bore her father's reproaches, silently, drove home with him, and felt the while as though they were driving into a desert, where there was no more joy, no more sunshine, nothing but heartache, and a long weary time before one came to die.

As for Andrew, he remained standing stock still as if stupefied; and when he went to the window to snatch a look at her father and his conveyance, and find out whether they were familiar to him or not, all he saw was the cloud of dust they had raised. At this a pang shot through his heart, and he went on gazing into the dust, hoping the wind might blow it away, and give him another sight of her; and long after dust and vehicle alike had disappeared, he kept looking that way, his heart growing every moment heavier.

'I would give a thousand pounds,' thought he, 'to know who she was;' and while so thinking, he was aware of the waiting-maid behind him.

'Make out my bill,' he said abruptly, as if fearing that she might read his thoughts in his back.

'Three francs and a half,' was the reply; and while she was taking up the money, he thought he might venture to ask who those people were.

'That was the Dorngrüt farmer; he lives in one of the villages down yonder; I don't know in what parish exactly, but he must be awfully rich. You have overpaid me. I said three and a half, and you have given me four francs.'

'Keep it for yourself, then,' said Andrew; 'I don't want it.'

'You are a strange youth,' said she; 'most give too little, and you give too much. But do you know what would please me better even than the half franc?'

'No, indeed,' returned he.

'Well, then, a waltz with you; you are such an uncommon good dancer.'

'Oh, by all means; just one turn or two.'

'Now, then, fiddlers, play your best, play fast; faster, for if the landlady finds out that I am dancing, she will fly at me tooth and nail; she is in extra bad temper to-day.' And the music having struck up, off they set; the young girl leaping like a kid in her enjoyment; but for all that, she did not omit, when a pause came, to put the question : 'Where do you come from?'

At first it struck Andrew that since his first partner did not know this fact neither need his second, but on second thoughts he told her; for how could he tell that he might not be inquired after?

'So that's who you are,' said the waiting-maid; 'I have heard a good deal of Liebiwyl, but have never yet been there. The Dorngrüt farmer's daughter asked where you came from, but there is no telling what one does not know. Shall I bring you another bottle of wine? You won't be setting off so early as this—the evenings are long now.'

'No, I shall drink nothing more,' said the young man.

'Then you must take one other turn with me.' And after that she would have another and another; and no one can tell when she would have stopped had not the landlady appeared at the door to look for the poor girl, who had forgotten all about her, but, at the first sound of her shrill voice, fled like a leaf before the wind.

'So you are still there, you wonderful dancer,' the

landlady went on, turning her attack upon the unfortunate Andrew; 'I should think you had had dancing enough by this time; but, however, if you must go on, you had better ask me than one of my maids. I should like to try whether you waltz as well as they all say. Strike up, fiddlers;' and, without further ado, Andrew had to lead out the fat landlady. He began to think he was bewitched, and to wish himself far away, lest after the landlady should come the cook, and after the cook the bath-woman, and after the bath-woman the poultry-girl, and after the poultry-girl the nursery-maid, and after the nursery-maid the host's daughters, and so he be kept waltzing round and round till morning; and what would people say then? However, deliverance came in the shape of the landlord, who appeared at the door, calling out that he had been wondering what kept every one upstairs to-day, and that if this went on he would send the fiddlers away. He thought that a woman of his wife's years might have shown more sense, and, after having had three husbands and fourteen children, she would have had done with dancing. But he had often heard that death was the only cure for folly. However, she would be so good as to cut it short, for there were people downstairs who wanted something to eat upon the spot. 'Let them wait,' said the landlady, 'we had to wait till they came. As for you, you are a brute; and I'm not going to be ordered about by you, but shall dance with whom I like, and as long as I like. Come, young man, we will have another round,' and so saying she turned to put her hand on Andrew's shoulder, but no Andrew was there; her hand met only empty air, and she stood paralysed with amazement.

There was a thundering burst of laughter through the room, and the landlord cried out, 'Well done, he has run away from you!'

'Where can the young fellow be?' said the hostess, looking round the room in vain; 'the old gentleman must have gone off with him.'

This provoked another peal, and her husband bade her look about for her lost partner, observing that if it were as she supposed, he wondered she had not been carried off at the same time, as had chanced to her betters before now.

While the pair were exchanging these amenities, Andrew, who had got out upon the balcony, and so into the road, had already left the house far behind. Sometimes he seemed to fly, sometimes he felt as though he could hardly crawl; now he was again dancing with the young girl, now he was feeling that he had seen her for the last time.

He formed plan on plan for finding her out. He

would serenade her by night, or he would go to her father, under pretence of buying hay or straw, or selling a horse or cow; for a farmer's son has many ways of gaining admittance to other farms if he be really set upon it. But none of these schemes pleased him entirely; he went on forming others which pleased him no better, and found himself at home before he knew it.

The others had all done their supper, but his mother had kept his for him. In other days she would have sat down beside him and asked where he had been; and one word would have brought on another till both knew all they wished. Now, however, she merely put his supper down before him; did not even ask whether it was hot, did not tell him that he had come back in good time, did not, in short, speak a word, but kept coming and going as though he were not there; so he could not put any question to her, which disappointed him much. For many days he kept hovering about her, but whenever he adverted to the Sunday, some ungracious word or other closed his lips. At length he thought he had found a favourable opportunity; he was alone with her in the granary, reaching her down grain for the pigs :—

'Mother, do you know the Dorngrüt farmer?'

'What makes you think of him?'

'Why, I saw him last Sunday.'

'How did you know that he was the Dorngrüt farmer?'

'Oh, I happened to ask.'

'What made you think of asking?'

'Nothing particular, only I had danced once or twice with his daughter.'

'Ah! just so,' returned his mother; 'while one is toiling and hoarding and fretting at home for your sake, you gad about and flirt with every silly girl you meet.'

'I do not think, mother, that you have much to complain of in me; I do all I can.'

'Yes,' said she, 'and you frequent dancing-houses and the like. I think you might leave that alone, remembering how we stand here. But so it is with one's children; when most we need them, they are all looking out for themselves, and give not a thought to their parents.' Andrew could make no further reply; he was too much aggrieved. Surely he thought his mother must know how he loved her, and how little he deserved such reproaches; never had his father had to lay down a single farthing of damages for any wild conduct of his; if he were paid for the work he did, he should get high wages; and it was hard indeed if a farmer's son might not take a bath and dance a little once in the year or so.

Such were his thoughts, but they did not make him undutiful; on the contrary, his feeling was that it behoved him to show his mother (and some one else too) that he was better than she had thought him, and in case any one chanced to inquire about him, to have deserved a good character as a worthy fellow, and one who got through what he took in hand as well as any under the sky. And if sometimes bitter moods arose, and tempted him to be wild and reckless, he fancied he saw the young stranger lift her finger and say, 'God keep me from such a one.' Then he restrained himself, and behaved as he thought a girl who wanted a good husband would have him do. But for all his planning he never got to Dorngrüt to see her again. No one encouraged him; and indeed he had not the heart to think of introducing a young wife into their household as things now stood there.

IV

HOW ONE QUARREL BREEDS ANOTHER.

AS the future possessor of the farm, as well as in order to please his mother and gain a good reputation in the country round, it had occurred to Andrew that he might venture to take a more active share in the management,—might occasionally make some suggestions to his father, or propose to take the trouble of certain operations entirely off his hands. At first his father had been pleased and proud of such a son, and had often said to himself, what a first-rate farmer he would be. Indeed, if the elder man's experience had seconded the zeal of the younger, the lost five thousand pounds might soon have been replaced. But now mistrust and jealousy began to work in the father's heart. He imagined that Andrew had been set on by his mother to manage the farm in her way,—hastily, eagerly, on a new-fangled plan, such as his father and grandfather had never known. He would not allow his son to be put over his head, was resolved people should not have it to say how clever a fellow he was, and that things went on better since he had taken them in hand. No, he was but a bad son after all who did not plough in his father's furrow. He, for his part, should have been ashamed to seek to rule while his father lived, and when he lost him, he went on in his footsteps, and things had gone well enough. But the world was waxing worse; now-a-days children despised their parents, and every urchin believed himself wiser than his grandfather. For all that, so long as he lived he was not going to give up the helm, and they should see who was master. From this time forth poor Andrew had a bad time of it; it was enough that he should advocate any measure to insure its failure; his father ran counter to him in everything, and if he himself chanced to blunder through inexperience or precipitation, he never heard the last of it, while what he did well, remained unnoticed.

Andrew lost heart when he found himself so misunderstood, and was accordingly reproached for his listlessness, and told that he was great indeed in talk, but when things had to be done but a poor hand after all. This, however, he could have stood, for he knew well that parents' failings are to be patiently borne, if only these reproaches had been made in private. But the ways of the house had entirely changed in this particular, and this it was that so distressed him; he could almost have wept over it. Formerly, all were so guarded in their speech, that no angry word was ever heard, or at all events never heard by strangers, and for this the house was famed far and wide; for when an angry word is never spoken peace must needs prevail, and where peace is, detraction cannot assail.

But now it was quite otherwise. Christian and his wife did exchange many and many a cross word, and reproached each other without a scruple. Christian was always inveighing against his wife's wastefulness, and telling how such and such a neighbour was of a different stamp, and how much egg and butter money she had made over in the course of one year to her husband. But then, to be sure, there were not always two beggars at that door, waiting for three others to come out before they went in. With such a thrifty wife, farming must be a pleasure, and saving easy; but now, do what he would, there never was any money laid by; it all got scattered to the winds. Annie, on her side, was sure to pay her husband off; observing that, at all events, she had not fooled away five thousand pounds; nay, that she could help many and many a poor soul, without spending even the interest of such a sum, and that there was surely some difference between the poor and the rascally; nor did she find in Scripture any blessing promised to those who fattened up the latter. As to milk-money, it was not she who bought and sold cows, and she had only to deal with what was brought in to her. Of course, if work were set about in proper time, there would be better fodder. She knew men who could make half as much again out of their farm.

When they had exchanged observations of this kind, it would sometimes happen that Christian lost all self-control, and protested before servants and labourers that he was sick of his life, and that if his wife did not leave off casting that five thousand pounds in his teeth, he should have to take himself off. Meanwhile Annie would be weeping in the kitchen before the maids, and saying it was well her mother was not alive; she never could have endured it; and if she saw how her daughter was treated, it was enough to make her turn in her grave. She had not deserved such conduct; what she gave away was her own, and no one had a right to interfere with it. But she only wished she was dead and out of the way, and then Christian might take one of those who managed so well with milk and egg money. Perhaps then she might be valued once more, and Christian might often remember his Annie, who now could do nothing to please him, let her strive her best.

HOW ONE QUARREL BREEDS ANOTHER.

The words that fall upon the ears of servants meet with no barren soil, but rather one in which they can spring up a thousand-fold, and when sprung up they are not stationary, like wheat or any other crop of the kind, but they wander from house to house, and sow themselves in other ears that stand open day and night. There is another remarkable peculiarity too about these servants' ears. In some respects it would be the grossest injustice to say that they are ears that hear not, for they sometimes hear a hundred yards off, through closed doors and solid walls, and yet there are things to which they remain hopelessly impervious, and you may tell them these a hundred times a day, and find no trace of them on the morrow. Curious, indeed, but common, these anomalies.

But it was not only servants who heard and repeated in this case. Lizzie would occasionally impart her troubles to a young friend; would tell how there was really no living at home; and how she should be glad to marry the first who came, merely to make her escape. But this was never to be breathed to any one, at which caution the friend would be indignant, and vow that wild horses could never draw the secret from the recesses of her breast. Yet she had no sooner got home than she would say, 'Mother, there's sad work going on up yonder; Lizzie herself has been complaining to me. I would not belong to that family for any money. No indeed! and if either of the young men took a fancy to me, they could not get me, I can tell them.' But nevertheless we suspect it would not have been safe to make the offer.

Neither again could Christian the younger, or Christy, as he was called, when he had had a few glasses of wine, refrain from giving a few expressive hints; and when he was out of spirits, and believed himself neglected, he was the more communicative. Nay, the very beggars who received good things at Annie's hands, snapped up odd words here and there, and almost forgot to thank her in their haste to go and spread them further.

On desert islands plants will sometimes be found belonging to some far-distant zone, and men racked their brains to know how they could have got there, till the learned, taking pity upon their ignorance, informed them, in scientific terms, that the pollen of flowers flew about in the air, and adhered to the legs and wings of migratory birds, which were often driven by mighty winds out of their course, across the trackless ocean, and glad to rest on the first land they saw. As they lighted there, this flower-dust, falling off them, would germinate, and spread till the desert island grew rich with vegetable life. Now words are like these wandering seeds; they are spirits of the air; they fly on the winds, adhere to men's ears, and are often dropped here and there, to spring up and bear fruit long after those who disseminated them have forgotten them. They who witness their subsequent growth marvel, and cannot fathom the mystery, not knowing how rumours may spread far beyond the sphere where they had their origin, nor how long and circumstantial a history may grow up from a chance word that falls upon a beggar's ear.

Accordingly our luckless family were talked of on all sides; for the less cause for censure they had hitherto afforded, the greater pleasure there was in censuring them now, and their neighbours indemnified themselves for past silence by present discussion, much as many who fast to-day will do by an inordinate meal to-morrow. More or less all around felt a certain pleasure in this. 'You see,' they said, ' what comes of these people who want to be better than others, and how fond of money they were at bottom, for all their liberality. We never got so much praise or good repute as they for hospitality and open-handedness, but yet we should be ashamed of making such a fuss about a five thousand pounds.'

The women, more especially, could not conceal their satisfaction. They were sorry for Christian, they said; any sensible wife might have got on with him, and many would be glad to have half as good a husband. When one came to speak with him one saw that he was by no means wanting in intelligence;

indeed, few could give you a better account of a thing than he. But as for Annie, the grave and sedate, they must say she was rightly served. She had thought herself wiser than the rest of the world, had despised other women and shunned their society; had held her head above them all; and as for beggars, she had made them so exorbitant in their demands, that there was no possibility of satisfying them. They were capable of throwing the bread you gave them in your face and bidding you give it to the dog; saying they knew a house where there was bread of the best for the poor. Yes, she had thought herself spotless, and that the angels would never rest till they had her with them in heaven, and now every one might see that she was no better than the rest. For their part, they had always maintained there was little merit in behaving well when people had it all their own way, but now that trouble had come, look how she went on. Perhaps she might be glad enough to consort with them now, but it was their turn to give her the cold shoulder; formerly she had thought herself too good for them, now she should see that they did not hold her good enough.

Thus the women ran on; their husbands, however, cut the matter shorter, and Annie found more favour in their eyes than Christian.

People must be blind, they observed, not to see who it was who first drove the cart into the hedge, and now was unable to extricate it. Nothing was more ruinous in a large farm like that, than always to be behindhand with the work, as was Christian's way. In the house, where Annie ruled, everything had its right time and place; nor had any one ever heard of the servants being kept waiting for dinner. And whatever Annie had under her care, she tried to dispose of for the best, whereas there was no getting anything out of Christian's hands, and he was a perfect fool at a bargain, any schoolboy might cheat him. They, for their part, could get on very well with Annie, she was such a well-mannered woman, but with such a husband no wonder that she should sometimes let fall a sharp word. However, it would be a good thing for many were there no worse women in the world than she. To which the wives retorted, that they only wished their husbands had her to deal with, and they would soon change their note; but men were an unreasonable race, who approved of everything except what their own wives did.

All this gossip pained no one so much as it did Andrew. He could have borne the rest quietly, but he was always thinking of the Dorngrüt farmer's daughter inquiring about him, and finding out where he came from. And now what would she hear of his home? Was not its former good name gone? Would she not be told that it was an unhappy household; that strife and dissension dwelt there, and that, though they were once wealthy, they would not long continue so? Things could not go on thus much longer. A girl had better look twice before she let herself be entrapped in that quarter, but indeed no one who was not positively in despair would. Andrew knew well that the good report it had taken a whole century to win might be lost in a few years, and who had so much cause to lament this as he, to whom the property was eventually to descend?

He felt more and more that if ten thousand, ay, twenty thousand pounds had been lost, and peace and love retained, he should have been happy, and would never have said a word. He fancied too, that a mere monetary loss would not have dismayed the young girl; but, if he judged her rightly, she would never enter a house divided against itself. Day by day his hope of showing himself at Dorngrüt grew fainter.

That Sunday seemed like a beautiful dream, which often brought the water into his eyes. For a long while he kept his grief to himself, hoping that some better hour might come, in which his mother would question him as of old, and then he would lovingly tell her everything, everything in his heart; perhaps she would see how much harm this way of going on did to her children. But, alas! his mother was occupied only with her own sorrows, heeded not those of others, and the good hour did not come.

At last Andrew could no longer bear his distresses alone. He complained of them to his brother, who had always looked upon him as a favourite, but on finding that he was a fellow-sufferer, extended some of the compassion he had felt for himself to Andrew's case, and both came to the conclusion that things were getting worse and worse, and that, by hook or by crook, they must seek to remedy them. They determined to interrupt their parents the next time they quarrelled, and to tell them that it did no manner of good, but only embroiled things further. If they remonstrated gently, surely it would be well taken, more particularly if they pointed out to the one who began the strife how wrong he was, and prayed him to be gentle, for God's and his children's sake. This was the best plan they could devise, and when, moreover, Christy showed himself full of interest in Andrew's love-affair, and said everything must be done to bring it about; that he would prowl round Dorngrüt some early day, and if he heard a good report, try to get admission into the house, and see and hear how the girl was minded; Andrew's spirits began to rise, and he thought, after all, their parents would not go on long so badly when they saw how they grieved their children by it; they would surely put some restraint upon themselves; they had at least a warm heart for their children.

To their sister Lizzie, however, they said not a word of all this. They looked upon her as half a child and half a stranger, who had no right to take a part in family discussions. Farmers' sons are pretty much like cats, who are reputed fonder of places than people; while their sisters are like doves, who daily fly, far and wide, and readily follow other doves to strange dovecots. The sons are conservatives, the daughters radicals; the first think everything is theirs by right, the others gladly take refuge away from home, and, sheltered under foreign protection, feel safer and stronger in urging their claims against the fraternal aristocrats, and snatching as much as possible out of their claws.

Both brothers were really very fond of Lizzie; but, as she sometimes displayed a little vanity, they enjoyed teasing and putting her down; while she, who was well aware that she had a better head than girls in general, took this ill, and paid off the brothers for their lofty demeanour by many little satirical speeches,—nay, sometimes she told tales of them to her parents; in short, she acted towards them in true radical fashion, which they little heeded, only becoming the more stately and reserved towards her.

But however well meant Christy and Andrew's

HOW ONE QUARREL BREEDS ANOTHER. 89

endeavours to restore peace, they were by no means successful. Their parents misunderstood them; they fared like some bungling practitioner, who attempts to probe a wound or lance a sore that is not ready for such treatment.

As soon as they attempted to check the wrangling of their father and mother, they were reminded of their filial duty, and asked since when it had become the custom for children to interfere when their parents were conversing with each other. The poor parents never reflected, that if you take away the corner-stone, the whole house falls, and that if they sinned against that fundamental law, never to dispute in their children's presence, they could not expect from them the old reverence,—nay, that where parents do wrong, filial love prompts a rebuke, just as parental love does when children err. It belongs to the wisest to give counsel and reproof; if then the children are the wisest, shall they not reprove?

This was not, however, the parents' view. They did not discern that they themselves were no longer what they once were, but morally sick, and their children the vital energy by which they were to be restored to health. And whenever silence was imposed upon them, the latter attempted to justify themselves, and would say: 'But, father, I do think it is not worth while to be so cross about it, as mother is right; if things were managed as she says, they would go on better;' or, 'Father is not so far wrong either; one cannot always get things to go one's own way, one must be guided a little by circumstances.' Now such expressions cut both ways. What was meant as a palliative, was felt by one party to be a justification, by the other an accusation. It was merely casting oil into the flames. Whoever felt self-aggrieved by the remark, looked upon it as a sign that the speaker was a partisan of the other, grew the more angry and unreasonable, and the contest the more complicated and inveterate. Andrew, whose activity was repelled by his father, and who not only considered his mother's charity good for the credit of the house, but had the same tendency himself, often took her part, which offended his father, who loudly protested that his son could not wait his death to snatch at the helm; that he made a mere tool of his mother, and aggravated every difficulty; and that if he were away things would go on better. He could see what they were at: they wanted him to give up the farm to Andrew, but that he would not do while he could move a finger. Lizzie, who was Andrew's very opposite in character, and not particularly devoted to his interests, sided with her father, and whenever her brother opened his mouth, would take a part in the discussion, even though hardly knowing what it was about. If her mother told her to be silent, her father got all the more indignant with his son, and once, when Andrew found himself alone with Lizzie, he threatened that if she opened her mouth again on these subjects, he would take her by the shoulders and put her out of the room. He would teach her not to mix herself up with everything, and she ought to be ashamed, to her very heart's core, of ever saying a word against her mother.

'Do it, pray,' Lizzie would answer, 'do it if you dare, and think you are the only one entitled to speak. But the house is not yet yours, and so long as I must be in the cage I have every bit as much right to speak as you. And I wonder that you are not ashamed to behave to father as you do; you might be sorry for all he has to suffer from mother's ill-temper.'

'Mother's ill-temper!' cried Andrew; 'I should like to know which is the most ill-tempered, father or mother?' And so they went on, and often indeed would have come from words to blows if the elder brother had not interfered.

So then, what had been meant for peace became a fresh incentive to war, just as at a fire, the hose intended to save one house in a street, often spread the flames to the next, because themselves set on fire by the heat. Instead of the quarrel between the parents getting made up, the children took to quarrelling amongst themselves, and one quarrel begat another. Thus the family life grew sadder and sadder, and this made Annie so miserable that she often prayed to die, and her husband, for his part, was just as wretched.

One morning—it was the Sunday before Whitsuntide, Christian took it into his head that he should like cakes for breakfast. There had been some baked on the Saturday, and the whole household had partaken of them, but they were baked in such liberal measure that some were always left; and very often no one would eat them the second day. On this occasion, however, Christian took a fancy for some; whether it was a mere freak, or because he had just seen two beggar-men go away, I cannot exactly tell, but so it was. Christian asked for some with his coffee, and Annie told him there were none left, but she would bring him some rolls.

'Why, that is strange,' replied he; 'yesterday there were ever so many over, and none this morning! Go you, Lizzie, and look; you will be sure to find some.'

'You have heard me say that there are none,' said Annie, 'and after that you surely need not send Lizzie to make sure.'

'But what has become of the cakes?' inquired he.

'They are all gone, and that is enough,' said his wife.

'So we've come to that,' broke out Christian;

'beggars snatch the very cakes from under one's nose. Bread is no longer good enough for them, and we shall soon want bread ourselves, for they will eat us out of house and home. That is the end of it, when women care more for beggars than for husband and children.'

'I don't know,' replied Annie, 'what makes you want cakes this morning; it is only in order to get up a quarrel; over and over again there have been some left, and you never thought of them, so that they would have wasted had I not given them away. You have often said you did not like cold cakes.'

'That has nothing to do with it,' cried Christian, 'but you want to bring me to beggary or to my grave, you —'

'Father, father,' entreated Andrew, 'just think, it is Sunday, and what will the servants say if they hear us quarrelling again?'

'But why should mother have given away the cakes?' said Lizzie; 'she might have thought that father would like some.'

'And pray, what have you to do with it?' cried Andrew; 'mother has known what she was about long before you were in the world.'

'I have as much right to speak as you have,' retorted Lizzie, 'and am not going to be put down by such a one as you are.'

'What sort of a one am I then?' inquired Andrew.

'An ill-tempered, conceited, tyrannical fellow,' was the reply.

'Wait a moment, you mischief-making chatterbox,' cried Andrew, darting at her, but she ensconced herself, with shrill complaints, behind her father, who took her part angrily.

At that the poor mother, who had gone out when Andrew alluded to Sunday, opened the door which led into the kitchen, and said, 'O Andrew, remember Sunday; are you not ashamed of being heard by all the church-goers? You lecture others, and cannot control yourself.'

This silenced Andrew at once. 'Don't be angry with me, father,' he said, 'I did not mean to dispute with you; and if it is your pleasure that this girl should say whatever she likes, so be it,' and out he went.

That morning the household was all at sixes and sevens. As soon as the quarrel began, the servants went off after their own devices, and when Andrew summoned them, one emerged from this corner, the other from that, as though disturbed in mischief, and no one went back to clear the table, which remained as it was till nearly mid-day.

V.

OLD THINGS SEEN IN A NEW LIGHT.

ANNIE could not get her son's words out of her head. It was the Sunday after Ascension; what, indeed, would people say, if, on such a day, not one member of the family were to be seen in church? They would be sure to invent some malicious reason for such an absence. Some one or other must go. But Annie found nobody whom she could send. If the family were to be represented at all, it must be by herself; and if she meant to go to church, she must dress herself accordingly. Alone and unaided she set about this, glad that she required no assistance, for her mother had always taught her self-reliance, and declared that hands were given us to help ourselves, and that we must give account of the use we have made of them, as well as of every other talent.

Annie made no particular haste that morning; she

did not want to join the crowd; her mood was not a communicative one, and her heart was too full of its own sorrow to have room for the interests of others.

She had about a mile and a half to walk to church, and came across no one on the road; for on such a day all men were anxious to arrive early in order to secure seats. She felt strange and dreamy, very solitary and very sad, like one doomed to wander on and on indefinitely, with no object, no home, no one waiting for her. The bells still sounded, but ere long they ceased; she heard nothing but her own footsteps; not even a dog barked in the valley; the grave could hardly be more silent than this. If she were really alone in the world, if she were to find no one in the village, no one in the church, no one anywhere, —if all had passed away through that invisible door of which the Lord only has the key! Then the last solemn peal sounded from the church tower, and Annie folded her hands and felt a ray of comfort, and yet she trembled too, for she seemed to hear blend with its tones a voice like that of a judge who summoned her before him.

The church was quite full, and there seemed to be no place left for Annie, who stood in a corner by the door. 'If it were to be so with me when I die,' thought she; 'if I came to the gate of heaven and found no room to enter in, were obliged to turn away because I came too late!' And again her heart sank, and her eyes filled with tears. Meanwhile a labourer's wife, to whom she had often shown kindness, kept beckoning to her, but Annie did not notice it till some one in the nearest seat pulled her sleeve, and then she saw how anxious the poor woman's face was, and that she had got a good place beside her for her benefactress. Annie walked up humbly, and took the offered seat as a great favour. 'Who can tell,' she thought, 'if I do come late and heavy laden with my sins into the kingdom of heaven, whether some poor woman may not beckon to me, and share her place with me for the sake of the little good I did her on earth?—that would be a rich reward indeed.' And as she sat down beside her poor neighbour, she almost felt as though she were near her good angel, and had won a safe place, from which no one could expel her, and which would be hers throughout eternity.

When the singing was over, the pastor began his prayer, and the congregation stood up. It grieved Annie to rise from the seat, where she had felt a few moments of heavenly rest. She imagined what it would be to have reached heaven, and then to be cast out, perhaps into that dark abode where there was wailing and gnashing of teeth. Before her rose her vanished days, contrasting with her present: those were bright with peace and joy, these wrapped in gloom and sorrow. She could partly tell the difference between heaven and hell. Yes, she too saw no end to her misery. When this short hour of quietness was over, she must return to quarrels and strife; no one, no poor woman would be there, to invite her to a place of shelter. The old wretchedness awaited her,— not that of a mismanaged harvest, which ends with the bad year, but that of a misguided soul, which endures too often, like that soul itself, eternally. Oh! if she need never go home again; if she could but lay her weary heart down in some still corner, where it might rest till some lowly place in heaven were ready for her!

These thoughts were interrupted by the minister's voice giving out his text, which was as follows: 'But I say unto you, I will drink no more of this fruit of the vine, until I drink it new with you in the kingdom of God.'

It seemed to her as though the pastor had been reading her heart, and had chosen those very words as a promise that her wish should soon be fulfilled, and she freed from all her troubles and taken into rest. Yes, she would be glad to die. And yet an indescribable sadness gradually came over her. At first she thought, 'My death would be a blessing to myself, and good for all; for if I were once gone, perhaps they would remember what I had been to them, and when anything went wrong, look back to how it was in my time, and say to themselves, "It was a sad thing for us to lose our mother."' But soon a dismal fear intruded: 'Would any one indeed mourn if I were to die? would tears be shed as they carried me to the grave, and heard the earth rattle upon my coffin? Would Christian hide his face in real or pretended anguish? And Andrew, what would he say? would he really feel it an affliction? Ah, if I could have died three years ago! I know what they would have felt then. Christian would have gone about as if the heart had been taken out of his body, and he had nothing to do but to follow it. But now, now, perhaps, there would be none to stand around my bed; and when they came in and found me dead, it would seem as though a weight had fallen from their hearts, and a stone of stumbling been taken away. O God, if my mother only knew how I stood and how I should end; never could she have believed it! And I used to think that when my time came, people would say, "We have never seen a death cause such sorrow; all were weeping for her, so that you could hear them ever so far off; she must surely have been a good woman."'

Burning tears welled up from Annie's heart and coursed freely down her cheeks. To die, to be taken away as a stone of stumbling, as a weight upon the heart, as an obstruction to happiness, that was fearful indeed, and she had so ardently desired the very reverse. Quite overwhelmed by her sadness, she could scarcely refrain from weeping aloud, and grief destroyed all power of thinking, till these words of the pastor's rang through the night of her spirit :

'Jesus had partaken of His last meal with His disciples ; He, being conscious that it was the last, attached an enduring blessing to it, bequeathed to us this Supper as an imperishable inheritance. But when we partake of our last meal with our families, none of us know that it is our last. Well were it for us, therefore, to look upon every meal that we share as such. Nor would there be anything improbable in such a supposition, for how many a father of a family who sits at table at mid-day, is laid on his bed a corpse by night; how many a mother has death struck down while the meat she had cooked remains unfinished ; how many a youth has been brought home dead on the morrow, who revelled at supper at his father's board the evening before ! Yes, it were indeed well to consider each meal our last; it would favourably influence our demeanour. Gladly would we leave behind us, as a memorial, a wise saying or a loving word, so that, long years after, some one might still say, "I cannot forget his conversation the last time he sat at table with us, when there was no idea of his dying so soon. I have often wondered whether he himself had any foreboding; but at all events it has been my consolation to know in how good a frame he was taken away." But if during this last meal there had been evil communication, if the Giver of all good had been outraged while His gifts were enjoyed, think how those left would feel when looking back to it, and how the departing feels in that last moment, when all the past flashes upon him at once, while recalling his words during his last supper, and reflecting what a memory they leave behind, what an evidence they afford of the state of his soul!

'Or, if the gifts of God are being received in strife and enmity, with a grudge in the heart, malicious thoughts in the mind, perhaps angry words on the tongue, and God call a member of the family away, with no opportunity of making peace, retracting, and asking forgiveness; when he dies unreconciled, think you not that a double-edged sword pierces his soul? And how must it be with those he has left? Must they not, for the rest of their days, recall with anguish that one of their number was taken away out of their midst at enmity with them?

'Therefore, let every meal in every house be taken as if the last; eaten as was the passover by the Israelites in the house of bondage—in haste, and with loins girt for departure into the wilderness; for so should the Christian be ever ready for his journey into that dread valley of death that lies between us and our promised land.

'But, since the business of every day, the stir and excitement of common things, hinder the soul from gazing up into the region of a higher life, let none omit at least to regard that holy feast which commemorates our Lord's last earthly meal, as his farewell meal also. Not only let it be considered a farewell to sin, but a farewell to whatever belongs to us here below, a signal of departure from among our friends and kindred. Let us ask ourselves, Have we done our best for them? Have we injured none among them? What name, what memory shall we leave behind? Do we part in peace? Will their tears and regrets follow us? Will their hearts remain true to us? These are questions that we shall do well to put to our souls. Think thus, all of you, when you drink of the fruit of the vine this evening in your homes; think, as the sun goes down, that your last hour is about to strike, and put these questions to your conscience: How stands it between me and mine; what retrospect shall I bequeath to them; how will our hearts part, if to-night the parting comes? I know well enough that this will flash a fierce light into many a heart, and reveal a dark stain on many a conscience, for discord is too common between us, anger and discontent too plainly read on our faces.

Therefore hasten to make peace, to make amends, to redeem the past. There are three months between Whitsunday's sacrament and the next, and who can be sure of living through them? Young and old, strong and weak, are alike struck down by the Lord's arm. Do you not feel your mortality in every limb, does not the beating of your hearts justify my words? Delay not, then, to amend yourselves, and to restore all breaches. Why is it you hesitate to come to so holy a resolve? "I am not in fault," says one; "I was sinned against in the first place." "Yes," says another; "and I am not sure whether, if I make advances, they will be responded to." A third pleads that, "if things were set right to-day, they would be all wrong again to-morrow." A thousand such pleas creep out of the recesses of men's souls; these are the old mouldering cerements, used a hundred times before, in which they are wont to bury all good resolves. Did Jesus urge such excuses in the garden of Gethsemane? Did He make any conditions when He cried, "Father, forgive them, for they know not what they do?" any reservations when He offered himself on the Cross? No! nor did He make any either when He commanded us to forgive seventy times seven in the course of one day, and to take the beam out of our own eye! Therefore be reconciled with men, that you may be reconciled with God; forgive your debtors, in order to have your debts forgiven; be not extreme to mark your brother's fault, if you do not wish to be dealt with by the Lord according to your own sins. Delay not, oh delay not; He comes like a thief in the night. Remember, too, your brother has something against you, believes himself as much injured and offended as you do. There is but one way of settling these accounts, and that is by forgiving and forgetting.

'Therefore, whoever thou art, who wilt approach the altar and art angry with thy brother, first leave the altar and be reconciled with him, and then return. Heaven is the abode of eternal peace, nor may they enter there who leave strife behind them, or bear anger in their hearts.

'Therefore, purge yourselves from all such sins, that when the Lord comes you may joyfully depart, leave a blessed memory on earth, and find everlasting peace in heaven.'

Such was the minister's address, and his words sounded to Annie almost like those of God; they met her case, and answered to her thoughts, as exactly as though an all-seeing eye had been reading her soul. One after the other they came, striking upon her conscience till she was almost overpowered; and, when the sermon was at an end, she seemed to be left standing on the edge of a fearful abyss, and to hear a voice cry, high above her head,

'Woman, woman, thy time is nearly over; save thy soul alive!'

She did not dare present herself at the sacrament. She left the church with many others, though she longed too to approach the table of the Lord. But it was only her body she felt that was properly arrayed; her soul shrank back, lacking the wedding garment. Like one who has been saved from imminent peril, but scarcely yet knows how or where he is, she wended her way home. How long she was going she knew not. But they were expecting her. Andrew was standing at the door looking out, and the voice in which he called out, 'Mother, are you here at last, and what has been keeping you so long?' showed that he had been uneasy.

The dinner was quite ready. Lizzie had cooked it, and was now fussing in the kitchen to hide the embarrassment of a bad conscience, which she would fain have got rid of, but knew not how. However, when her mother asked whether she had got the cooking done, Lizzie replied very good-humouredly, and with many more words than were needed. Their father was still absent. 'He had gone into the wood,' they said.

There indeed poor Christian had been sitting long, and with a heavy heart, although the sky above him was so bright, and the earth laughed with joy. 'It can never go on thus,' he was saying to himself, 'there is no comfort in our meals; the children interfere with everything; the servants no longer respect me, one goes here, the other there, and at last they will be too many for me, and I shall see what I inherited from my father go to the dogs. No; this can go on no longer. But, what to do? To stand one's ground, and show once for all who is master, were the best plan, if there were no children, but if one thwarts them too much they will run away and bring more disgrace upon us. To drive away those accursed beggar-women with a whip, and, when one crept into the house, to push her out, neck and crop, might indeed put an end to the hateful system. And yet, what should I get by it, but to be vilified all over the country? If a woman will squander, no one is cunning enough to hinder her. To separate would be the best plan, and to let each take their own money and manage it in their own way. But how to do about the dower? If I had that to make good just now, it would pinch me sadly. And then I have really no particular fault to find with Annie. If she were less absurd about beggars, did not think herself bound to support every scamp in the country round, and left off reproaching me about that five thousand pounds, I should have nothing to complain of. On the contrary, I am almost as fond of her as ever. For in all other matters she is good and careful, and there is not a sign in the calendar but she can tell you all about it. As to the faults that beset most women, I really don't think she has one of them. But I am not going to hear any more about that five thousand; I was not made guardian to please myself, and if any one ever grieved over a loss, I have done so, and the more, because I see that if we go this way to work, we shall never replace it, but throw good money after bad. And yet it is not so much the five thousand pounds either. If we were only as comfortable as we used to be, and Annie was her old self again, I should not care about it. To be sure, I might make over the farm to the lad, and live in the back-room, but I am ashamed of giving it up with less than I got with it; people would laugh at me; and besides, I should be sorry for the fellow. If we can't get on with the whole, how would he after paying his brother's and sister's portions? And, moreover, I do not know how Annie could stand it. There are many instances of mothers deprived of the housekeeping, and having nothing more to do, getting wrong in the head; and it would be particularly trying to one who has always been accustomed to manage a large concern, and is fond of giving. No; I do not believe that she could endure having everything taken away from her, and for this I would never be responsible; she has been a good wife after all. Then, too, if once people get wrong in the head, there are many instances of their being treated no better than cattle; not that this could ever happen to Annie if I lived to see after her, but no one knows who may go first. I knew a woman who got melancholy because she was deprived of household management, and had nothing to do or give, and who, after her husband's death, was treated like a lunatic, shut up, and never seen. Not that Andrew would behave so, I am sure; but no one knows what kind of a wife he may get, and there is no telling what a wife may make of a man. There are plenty of instances of a worthy youth becoming a very devil of greed and folly after his marriage; if he be unfortunate and get a bad wife, such a one is capable of wearing out seven husbands, and the devil himself may take lessons from her in tormenting. But what I am to do I know not, only things cannot go on so any longer.'

Up to this moment Christian had been thinking, but now he fell into a mere vague sense of perplexity and dejection, from which he was roused by a sound of bells wafted by a light breeze over the wood. It announced the close of the morning service, and admonished the departing congregation to return in the afternoon, that the seed which had been sown might be dug down deeper into that strange ground of the heart, where the good seed has such a tendency to scatter or die down. 'I ought to go home,' mused he, 'if I mean to be in good time for dinner, but I don't know how it is, I never like going; when I get near the house, I always feel as if some one were standing at the door waving me off, or as if something wretched and wicked were about to happen there. Formerly, it was not so; formerly I was like a boat upon a current that every moment flowed stronger; the nearer I got to my own door the quicker I walked, and often indeed ran. Ah! that was a happy time.' And once more Christian fell into a reverie, till at length his wish forced its way in words, and he cried aloud, 'O that it would but return!' But how to bring it back he knew not; no scheme satisfied him, ponder as he would. Mournfully he rose and set out homewards, his gloom being sometimes of an angry and bitter, and sometimes of a gentle melancholy cast, according to the nature of the cloud that shadowed his soul. But none of these shades of feeling were visible on his countenance, which was pretty much like a deal-table, of the same colour, look at it what way you will, whether in sunshine or rain. Such a countenance as this has its inconveniences as well as its conveniences, but statesmen and rogues would often give a good deal to possess it.

With this aspect, then, he returned and took his place at the head of the table, and it was piteous to see how rapidly and silently every one ate, almost as if each felt himself in a hornets' nest; the fact was, they all thought Christian's countenance portended thunder and lightning upon the least provocation; for all saw that behind that gloomy mask some inward struggle was going on, but no one saw that he was even more ready to weep than to storm. Indeed, people sometimes do storm just to prevent their tears. However, everybody's object seemed to be to get away as soon as possible. Annie herself merely took a few mouthfuls, and returned to the kitchen, which pained Christian exceedingly; for he was not aware that she did so, not from any ill-will to him, but merely because her own heart was so full. She felt as though it must burst, whereas he set all down to ill-temper and sulkiness, and determined that the mischief chiefly lay in this, that Annie never could forget a grievance, but kept brooding over it all the week, so that when he himself had dismissed it, and wanted to be on good terms, she had it all ready to cast at him again,—worse this than cooking the dinner on Sunday and having it warmed up every day throughout the week,—so that there was no enduring it, and he was weary of his life. As soon as he could, he too rose from table and stood a long time out before the door, not knowing what to do with himself. He would rather have remained at home, but he was afraid of a quarrel, did not like to find himself alone with Annie, not being in a disputatious mood, and yet he was reluctant to leave the house. But at length his indecision ended in his setting off, though he walked a good way before it occurred to him where to spend his afternoon. Annie had been watching him out of the kitchen window, and had wondered whether he would go or stay. If he stayed they two would be alone that afternoon, and then she would make a clean breast of it to him, would humble herself and beg his pardon, and beg him to go on differently in future, not only for her sake and the servants', but more especially for the children's. But she could not make up her mind to ask him to stay at home; what would he think?· Yet when he went, not even once turning round, and when she saw him no longer, the tears burst forth like a mountain-torrent after a thunder-storm, and she hurried in.

On fine Sundays, especially where there are no little children, a farm-house is often very solitary in the afternoon. You may go round it more than once without coming across a living thing, except perhaps a pig, that gives notice of his existence if you go near his trough, or a horse that neighs over the empty manger. Perhaps on a third or fourth round you may discover some Jack or Peter sleeping on his back under the shade of a fruit-tree, but often you must knock at the door—knock repeatedly, loudly but patiently, and at length, at about the seventh or eighth knock, an irritable voice may be heard to call from the back-door: 'Is any one knocking?' This is the voice of the farmer's wife, who had taken refuge in the back-room from the hosts of flies, with the intention of reading some book of devotion, but had been irresistibly attracted to the broad bed in the corner, and there enjoyed a delicious nap in the unwonted stillness, till the unwelcome knock disturbed her.

And so, on this especial Sunday afternoon all had flown with the exception of Annie, who was left in charge of the house. At first, she too, having closed the door on the last maid, went into the back room and laid her head on the bed, not from sleepiness, but because it was heavy with sorrow. She felt inwardly convinced that she must soon die, and she resolved not to die at enmity; but how should she set about making peace? Christian became daily more repellent and estranged, and would not bear the least word from her. And so she mused and wept in very hopelessness, till a knock at the door disturbed her. She delayed answering it, for a farmer's wife does not willingly make her appearance at the house door with red eyes, and she would have been glad if the visitor had passed on. But as he persisted, her good heart did not allow her to pretend, as is often done, that there was no one at home. She feared it might be somebody sick and in distress, and would not burden her conscience with the neglect of such an appeal, but, wiping her eyes and smoothing her hair and straightening her cap, went to open the door, and found the policeman there asking for a signature.

In point of fact, this was but a pretext for conversation on his part, behind which again lurked the hope of a good dram, for this is often what a policeman coaxes out of an old woman to whom he brings the latest news of the district; and indeed, generally speaking, Annie was not averse to a chat with him, and he got something or other that he liked before going away. But on this occasion she was in no mood for a chat, merely opened the upper half of the door, and told him Christian was not at home, and that he must come again. The usual questions as to when he would be back, and where he was gone, were cut short, and when the policeman turned to the weather, observing that it was fine, and that he hoped it would last, she said it was best to take the weather as they got it, and narrowed the opening in the door, so that he discovered he was an unwelcome guest, and mournfully moved away, in hopes of a chat and a dram at the next house, where he was scarcely seated before he began to tell how he had found things at Liebiwyl: the farmer's wife had red eyes and knew nothing about her husband's movements, and he would only ask whether the right kind of a wife ever remained in ignorance on that head.

Meanwhile Annie closed the door, smoothed the bed in the back room, went out by the back way and made the round of the house, looked into the stables in which she had not been for long, and paid a visit to her pigs, who greeted her with friendly grunts and snorts, for which she rewarded them by flinging an armful of fresh grass into their trough. From thence she passed into the orchard, went from tree to tree, admiring the promise with which they were decked, estimating the value of the different sorts of fruit; and as a field-marshal arranges his troops for battle, so did she mentally divide and apportion the respective crops according to their kind, —these for keeping, those for selling, these for preserving and drying, those for cider and brandy; and so she came to the flax, which sprang up thick and straight, and on towards the hemp, which proudly looked down upon it. Thus she passed from one thing to the other, and all were flourishing and beautiful; and as from a grass hill behind the house she surveyed them all, her heart wellnigh leaped with joy, for she had never seen things in better order, and a finer farm there nowhere was. But then came back the old sorrow, just as in wet seasons a shower succeeds to each gleam of sunshine: 'All this is ours, and how happy we might be with it, and yet we are worse off than the poorest labourers; not because of want; we have enough for ourselves, and even for our children, but because we we are not right within, because bad weather there has spoiled everything.'

Annie sat herself down and looked across the rich country, and saw it full of promise and beauty up from the valley's depth to the mountain tops; saw how the sky circled and blended with all on which her eyes rested, and how from this harmony came light and rain, and the wondrous power of the mysterious life-fostering dew. Yes, the glory of the prospect lay in this union of earth and heaven, and this peace between them; heaven showering down its influence on earth, earth praising heaven by its fruitfulness and beauty. And she thought how heaven should in like manner encompass human life; how each day, which is a little life in itself, should begin in heaven, and how, when the hours of toil are over, and evening has come, and sleep weighs on the weary eyelids, we should seek to have our place of rest on the confines of both worlds, where angels go up and down, and keep watch over the sleeping pilgrim who has fallen asleep in the Lord, that when the sun returns he may awake in the Lord, strengthened by heavenly rest for earthly activity. 'And used it not to be so with us?' thought she; 'when night came and rest summoned us, did we not lift up our souls and seek peace and repose in and with God, and lay aside the woes of earth, and cast all angry thoughts into the sea of forgetfulness? Then it was well with us; each morning we took God's blessing with us into the business of the day, and each evening we cast away whatever of earth's impurities we had contracted. But now we cast none of them away; now we go to sleep in misery and discontent, strife and anger, and evil spirits come in the night, and by wild dreams foster that anger and strife. And in the morning no bright sunshine beams into our souls, no blessing of God is carried into the day, only the old wretchedness which has grown since the evening, which daily grows and grows till it encompasses our whole life, so that our eyes can discern no heaven, just as in bad weather clouds gather thick around the mountain tops and hide the sky.' Thus it was that Annie for the first time really appreciated the amount of her sin in first leaving off their common prayer, and saw how from that moment grudges and grievances had rooted themselves in their souls, and what had been wont to pass away had become permanent.

True, indeed, she had gone on praying for herself, but her prayers had found no echo in Christian's soul, had smoothed no unpleasantnesses, still less had they soared to God; they had left her own soul dark as before, and gradually become mere words, which rolled off her lips as stones roll in the river's bed. The light from above had ceased to light her spirit, earth had grown drearier and darker day by day.

Thus she dwelt upon her own sin, and no longer attributed the origin of their unhappiness to the loss of the five thousand pounds, which fell more upon her husband than herself, but to the severing of that spiritual bond which had so long kept them in love and concord; and she it was who was guilty of that severance. This discovery, which flashed through her like lightning, shook her spirit to its depths. She had failed to see and understand this, which was yet so palpably true! And she had narrowly missed taking this guilt with her into the other world, going there laden with the sighs of her children, whose enjoyment she had spoiled, if not their natures. Now she understood how easy it was to discover the mote in another's eye, while failing to see the beam in one's own. Alas for her had God judged her as she had so often judged her husband!

An infinite humility came over her; she felt how deeply she had erred; no punishment seemed great enough, nor did she deprecate punishment,—rather desired it, felt that it would do her good, would convince her that God's eyes, of which she had so long been unmindful, still rested on her; that His hand was over her still. But she equally felt that it behoved her to make amends for her faults; it grew plain to her that it is only they who from their heart confess their sins who shall have them forgiven, and not merely confess them once in a way in hopes of immediate forgiveness, but confess them in love that nothing can embitter,—that persists in its confession even if forgiveness be withheld, and unkind treatment persisted in. She knew now that everything depended upon her, and that she must lay her hand to the work at once, for might not the Lord come as a thief in the night and reckon with His servant? She knew that she—she first and foremost of all—must knit again the ravelled tie; that this great and holy achievement was appointed to her.

One often reads of heroes whose efforts, and martyrs whose endurance, were superhuman; and as one reads, the feeble and timid tremble, while bolder spirits wish the days would return when energy could win such triumphs, and execrate our monotonous unexciting times, when the only foe left to combat is *ennui*. But there is this peculiarity about us men: we estimate greatness and force only by weight, number, length, and breadth; we have no other scale for spiritual things but what the journalist employs in his narration of battles, in which the importance of the events is calculated according to the number of dead left on the field, and the amount of powder expended.

But for all that, there are heroes and martyrs still left, and scope offered for martyrdom and heroism every day. Wherever there is a divine energy implanted in men, it will infallibly exert itself; there is no stream on earth but finds its channel. True greatness knows how to be great in little things, while barren pride is ever waiting for some opportunity to become great, and waiting in vain; and indeed, if such opportunity came, it would only reveal its inherent littleness, just as a vain man, who is always striving for a title of some kind, either spiritual or secular, never cuts so poor a figure as when he has got it. Genuine heroism, the true martyr's spirit, is to be found in life now, as heretofore, by those who can recognise it not only when publicly chronicled and applauded, but in every one of our daily relationships, and who can believe that it flourishes elsewhere than on battle-fields, stakes, and scaffolds.

The humility springing out of that love that beareth all things, endureth all things, is not easily provoked; that, divinely implanted, endures to the end; endures, be it for life or be it for death, in full persuasion that the Lord's will rules over that of men, and that His will must be bowed to for our own purification, and for the good of others, in great and small things alike ; this humility, we say, is the spirit from which all heroism and all martyrdom now-a-days proceed.

This humility it was that now came over Annie, and made her rejoice to endure whatever God saw good to appoint for her, and resolve never to give in till things were restored to the state in which her mother left them. This done, she could again venture to return to thoughts of her mother, and found out how these had of late been gradually fading away from her mind. But now she could lift her eyes to her again, and a peace and good hope long unknown rose within her heart. 'They come from my mother,' thought Annie ; 'she is rejoicing over me, and would encourage me to the right course, as in her life she ever did by her good advice and blessed example.' When Annie had thus struggled and triumphed, sitting up there on the grassy hill, she raised her eyes again, and all things seemed fairer than ever ; the sky no longer to encompass earth, but to touch it, to be blent with it,—heaven and earth one. Till now she had never known how, when the kingdom of heaven is within us, our footsteps consecrate each spot a heaven on which they tread.

Strengthened as with fresh life she went down to the house, and met a friendly welcome even from the pigeons and the hens, who followed her to the kitchen-door and waited till she brought them food, and sat watching with pleasure how cheerily and peacefully they shared it. Then out came the dog, wriggling through the pigeons and the poultry, and laying his head on Annie's knee, not the least annoyed at the cat—who had already taken up her position there—giving him a tap or two, for she had drawn in her claws, and was only playing with her old companion. This good understanding of theirs delighted their mistress, who stroked them alternately, but it brought tears into her eyes too. If cat and dog could be brought by the force of habit to live thus amicably, how could man and wife, whom God had created for each other, mutually worry and harass and become more and more antagonistic the longer they lived together?

Thus she sat, till, as evening drove the birds to the woods, and the poultry to their perches, one inmate of the house returned after another, each after his own fashion; those who had still some work to get through, hurriedly enough, those who had only to eat and sleep, slowly and deliberately. The maids came along at a quick pace, but stopped now and then at the hedges to pick a leaf or flower, and took that opportunity of turning to look whether any one were following them, in which case they would possibly adjust their shoe-tie, or their bodice, to give them time to ascertain whether the person following had something more to say to them. Andrew came in dejectedly from the wood; Christy more cheerfully from the direction of the village; and Lizzie slipped in at the back-door, no one knew whence.

But still Christian was wanting, and Annie looked out anxiously after him. At last he came along, slowly, irresolutely, like a ship driven back from the harbour by contrary winds. Annie's heart beat hard as she saw him come with sour visage and reluctant step, for she could not know what was in his heart. She lost all courage, and had to run into the house, instead of speaking a few words of friendly welcome, as she had fully meant to do, and this grieved her husband, who noticed how suddenly she turned away.

'Can she not even say good-evening to me good-humouredly?' thought he; 'not even leave off sulking on Sunday?' and he was ready to turn away again; and came in with a sourer face than ever, not noticing Lizzie, who sidled up to him as if there was a secret understanding between them, and she had something confidential to say. But when her father appeared as if he was not aware of her, she pushed away the dog, who wanted to fondle her, and went off into the garden to her flowers. Meanwhile Annie had made the coffee, fried the potatoes; everything was ready on the table, the coffee-pot stood on the edge of the stove, and the servants came slowly in to supper.

Annie made a strong effort, strengthened herself in her faith and humility, behaved more cheerfully than her wont, and had a pleasant word for every one. What she had long left off doing, she now did again; she handed every one their coffee, and to Christian first; then she came round with the milk, and as she knew that Christian was fond of the skin that gathers at the top of the jug, she took a spoon and put the most of it into his cup; and when he said 'Nay, stop, I have got enough.' she replied, 'Do you take it, there is plenty for the others.' This surprised Christian; he thought things were coming round, and became chatty, and told many a droll story that had been long unheard; so that those around were amazed, and concluded he had been to the public-house, and had a few glasses more than usual. But he had not tasted wine the whole day long; only when Annie poured the best of the milk into his cup it pleased him; he felt as if once more at home, and that had a more cheering influence than many measures of wine.

'After all,' thought Annie, 'Christian cannot be so very angry with me;' and her confidence increased, and when everything was washed and put by, she went out and joined the others by the kitchen-door, took a friendly part in all that went on; one kindly word brought on another, no one knew how, and the moon was high in the sky before the household separated.

VI.

A MORAL VICTORY.

ANNIE was the last to go into the house. She shut the doors, looked round as usual to see whether the fire was safely out and everything in its right place. Twice she did this, for her heart was again beating violently, and her little room seemed a sanctuary she hardly dared to enter. In silence she undressed, in silence sought her own little corner, and, once there, sat long endeavouring to pray as she used to do, but it seemed to grow more and more impossible; the words would not come; when she moved her lips, no sound was heard; it was as though some unseen power were arrayed against her, resolved to detain her in the fetters of recent habit. She felt herself dragged down to her pillow, and all within her cried out: 'Not to-night! oh, not to-night! compose thyself, gain strength, wait till morning, you will do better then, morning is the right time!' But then she seemed to hear the minister's voice, telling how the mother of the family might die before the meat she had cooked were eaten ; how heaven was the abode of eternal peace, and how he who would find a place there, must neither leave quarrels behind him, nor take angry feelings with him. Again she strove for utterance, and the great drops gathered on her brow, till she raised her spirit to God with groanings that cannot be uttered : 'Father, hast Thou forsaken me?' and at once it seemed that the dark influence that stood before her soul vanished away; that the chains that bound her were broken. The words came freely to her lips, and slowly and tremblingly, but fervently and distinctly, she began to pray, 'Our Father which art in heaven,' etc.

At the first sound of her voice Christian started as though he had heard the tocsin ring ; then he sat up and also began to strive for utterance, and to join in the prayer ; and when Annie came to the petition, 'Forgive us our trespasses, as we forgive them that trespass against us,' and fairly broke down at the words, trembling all over, and her voice a mere sob, he wept with her, and weeping finished the prayer. And now it was as though that prayer were a sun,—dispersing the dark clouds that had been lying round them before, and preventing them from seeing each other's faces ; but now the sun prevailed, scattered the clouds, which God's own hand, it seemed, lifted more and more, till they were quite lost in the blue, and all was light and clear; no shadow remained, and their hearts lay open to each other.

Annie was the first to break this holy silence, by accusing herself and begging for pardon; but Christian interrupted her. She had nothing to ask pardon for, he said; it was all his fault; if he had heeded her, it would never have happened.

Each wondered to find the other's heart so tender and loving, and perfectly unlike what they had supposed it to be; at one little word sufficing to bring about a reconciliation, and yet at neither having ever thought this might be the case, but assuming that an explanation would prove useless. It was only Annie's humility, in taking the whole blame upon herself, which broke through the disguise.

This is the very reason why God leaves the future dark to our gaze, and draws a curtain before the human heart, that we may learn, in true courage and submissive trust, to do what is right, without inquiring what our success will be, or measuring the effort with the reward. Often, indeed, what scared the unbelieving as unheard-of boldness, is so easy and rapid to faith that the Christian hardly traces his own agency in it, but attributes all to the grace of God.

So was it now with Christian and Annie. For a

long time they could hardly trust their ears ; they could not realize their recovered happiness, trembling at every word, fearing to chafe some sore place in the heart, and to see the demon of strife raise its hideous head once more.

They chose their words as tenderly as a loving mother closes the wound of a darling child, and this revealed to each the strength of the other's love. And when at length they were quite sure they were under no illusion, that neither had the least undercurrent of angry feeling, but forgave from the ground of the heart, humbly acknowledging his own weakness, and longing and thirsting for the old peace, the old happiness ; that neither looked for too much from the other, but would strive, with heart and soul, to do his own part ; then a joy suffused their spirits such as they had never known before ; it might almost be likened to what is felt by one who dreams himself in the place of endless woe, and wakes up to see God face to face in heaven. It was the joy of the angels over the lost and found ; the joy of the father clasping his returning prodigal in his arms. As all that they had felt and suffered since their hearts had been mutually closed came welling forth, each wondered at the other's tenderness, and Annie wept and said—

'Oh! if I had but known, all would have been right long ago ; but why did I lose faith and confidence so completely? I see now that, when once we lose faith and confidence in God, we become godless, and when we lose it in man, we become loveless; and he who is godless and loveless, walks in deep night, and has hell within him.'

But Annie's regrets were interrupted by Christian's, for this, he said, had been his very case. In short, they could not sufficiently marvel how they had completely misunderstood each other, each attributing hate to a heart aching with love, and confounding sorrow with anger. It was as though one had been speaking Spanish, the other Hungarian, while both believing they used the same language, and consequently misinterpreting every word and sign. They were never, as we said, weary of inquiring into the utter mistakes they had made, and at each explanation their mutual confidence increased, and their amazement at their own blindness.

First Annie would declare that the whole fault lay with her; that it was as though she had not only turned the key upon their hearts, but taken it away, so that it was impossible to open them. Had she not left off their prayer in common, all this wretched time would never have been; they would have continued one in God; for what earthly cares divide during the day, must be joined anew by heavenly grace each evening; so her dear mother had always taught.

Then Christian would console her by assurances that he too had not been what he ought; he was quite conscious of that; and if she had closed their hearts, she it was who had opened them again, and more than made up for her errors. And if this had not happened, he would never have known how much more precious peace is than five thousand pounds, and how gold is not everything,—nay, is nothing; for where peace is wanting, the richest man is far worse off than the poorest, who has peace. He had often been provoked at observing how much happier his servants and labourers seemed than himself, and how much more they enjoyed their meals; now he had learned, by his own experience, what Jesus meant by saying, 'What shall it profit a man to gain the whole world and lose his own soul? or what shall a man give in exchange for his soul?' He never could have realized this so thoroughly if he had not himself experienced it. The words 'Money, money,' 'Rich, rich,' used for ever to be ringing in his ears, and when he heard of a stranger, his first question was, 'Is he well off?' Now, however, 'Peace, peace,' 'Pious, pious,' would sound in his ears; and when he wanted to know the worth of a man, he should put his question in a different form.

But the crowning touch to their happiness was the thought of their children. They knew how this gloom had recoiled upon them; for if one limb of the body suffers with the rest, so still more must one member of a household when spiritual sickness befalls another, particularly when that ailing member has much to do with the conduct of affairs. They were well aware how their children's innocence and youthful mirth had decreased of late, as though the misunderstanding between their parents were a blight to their souls. They saw too, how this misunderstanding had contracted their hearts, so that they had had no room for their children, only for their own covetousness and discord. They had not only failed to take due interest in their children's affairs, but had actually occasionally felt as if those who ought to be their greatest joy were in their way, were almost a burden.

But now that their hearts had again grown large, their children's happiness was once more theirs, and they thrilled with joy, thinking how they would rejoice to see all quarrels at an end, and the old parental tone restored.

They went on speaking of their children's prospects with loving and earnest interest, till at last Christian turned to the inquiry—

'But tell me, Annie, how it was you ever managed to get your heart opened once more, and to pray aloud as of old? I had often and often planned a formal explanation with thee; but, in the first place, I knew ten to one I should have only got angry over it, and thou also, for I had got it into my head that all the faults were on thy side, and, besides, I could not bring myself to it in spite of my wishes; a hatchet could not have opened my lips, I do believe.'

Upon this Annie began to tell her experiences: how an inner voice had seemed to warn her she must soon die; how she first felt as though she were the last and only human being left on earth, and must hasten to overtake the rest; and next had a vision of being borne to the grave, leaving none to weep for her, and finding no room in heaven any more than she would have found in the church, but that at length a poor woman made way for her. And then how the pastor had said it were well to look on each meal we partake of as our last, more especially the Lord's Supper; and that we must learn to make peace and to keep peace, for there were no quarrels admitted into heaven; and how each should beware of believing that he was wholly in the right, and the other party in the wrong, but rather contrariwise. Also that (though how she felt at his words she never could describe) one resolve became firmly rooted within her,—the restoration of peace; for she would not lose her place in heaven, and her death she believed was near. But for all that, it had been long before she found out how to set about it. It was late in the afternoon when she first saw clearly that she must begin at the very point whence discord had sprung, and that, in fact, she it was who, by her discontinuance of prayer, had been guilty of it all. Now then, she knew what her part was to be, but never had she thought Christian's heart was all the while so inclined towards peace. She had expected to have to pray alone, long, long before it melted, and hence discouragement had wellnigh kept her back, only, having begun, she never would have left off.

'But,' she went on, 'when you at once sat up in bed and joined in prayer with me, methought you had been long buried out of my sight under the earth, and I seeking and groping for thee in vain, and all at once there thou wert, well and hearty, borne back to my side by angels, once more mine, never to be lost again till my death. Now I know that when you carry me to the grave you will weep indeed, and when the earth falls upon my coffin you will bury your face in your hands, and think, "After all, Annie was good, and if I could I would not marry again. I and the others have had a heavy loss."'

To which Christian replied, 'No more of that; I will not hear a word of dying; but this I will say, at whatever time you had died, I should have forgot everything whatever; everything but how good and dear you had been to me, and how you had managed for us all, and been cleverer than any of us. But don't talk to me of dying; we are just going to begin a new life of real concord, and whatever pleases thee shall be my pleasure too.'

'Listen to me, Christian. You were always a kind one, and now kinder than ever, but there is still one thing that I want. You will never persuade me that I am not near my end; I feel so strangely happy, I know it must portend death. But we won't dispute about that, but leave it to God, who will order all well. Only one thing you must promise me. Next Sunday, which is Whitsunday, we will receive the sacrament together, as a token of full and thorough forgiving and forgetting, just as though it were the last time we were to partake of it, and the parting was to follow thereupon; like the Israelites eating the passover, all ready for their journey, and prepared body and soul to follow the Lord's call whenever it should come. And when we have all met around the Lord's table, I shall feel, I think, quite secure of peace in time and eternity; I shall know that, having celebrated so solemn a festival of reconciliation, nothing more can ever come between our souls. As it is, I still feel anxious as though the enemy who had divided us so long were lurking near, but, this done, all will be well, and I shall be able to say, with a thoroughly happy heart, " Lord, let thy handmaid depart in peace." '

'Hear me, dear Annie,' said Christian. 'Not another word about dying; I neither will nor can bear it, for I don't see why you should just go and die now that we are about to live in peace. I should not,—I must say it,—think it right of God to take you away now. But with all my heart I consent to receive the sacrament with you next Sunday, and the children will gladly do the same, and rejoice to find our game at cross-purposes over. And it's very well, too, that people who have been talking us over, I am well aware, should see us at the Lord's table; they may then talk on as they will, but they must feel that things are not so bad since we can venture there. It is curious, I don't indeed understand much about religion, and have not been much in the habit of going to church, it was not often convenient, and a man like me has so much to think of, he can't always keep spiritual matters in his head; but I confess I never went to church or sacrament without resolving soon to go again, I always felt so comfortable after it. It was, so to speak, with my soul as with my body, after a bath, taken once in a way: my spirits were better, I seemed to see more clearly, and could take things more quietly. I have many a time thought that, just as we used formerly to put away any little trifle between us by praying together, so on Sunday one should put away all that has hung over one during the week, and that if we made a point of purifying our souls, as we do of putting on a clean shirt on the Sunday, there would be much less misery and mischief in the world. But if a man of my stamp does sometimes get an idea into his head, he is likely to be slow in working it out, be it ever so good. But things must be altered; and on Sunday I'll go with you gladly, and then God and man may see whether we love each other or not.'

The rapture of recovered affection kept sleep far from our worthy pair; day began to dawn, the sun rose, its joyous beams came as heavenly messengers, reminding mortals of the glory of God, and of their duty to work while it is day.

Happy indeed was the uprising of husband and wife. New life blossomed within their hearts, or rather, it was the old life that had emerged from the evil that hid and choked it, and which was valued a hundred times more than before, because it had been lost and was found. They did not noise their happiness abroad; they gave it no special name; the household went on as usual, but a quiet blessedness shone in their faces, and it was downright touching to see how these elderly people kept hovering about each other like a couple of young lovers the day after the wedding. Christian was constantly coming in to light his pipe in the kitchen, and he was scarcely out of it before Annie was after him to tell or ask something or other.

Their children observed the change, but took no notice. But when Andrew was feeding the horses at noon, his father joined him in the stable, talked over the stock with him, asked whether, in his opinion, it were well to make any changes; perhaps it would be better to sell off and buy new blood; if Andrew thought so, he might go to Berne the first Tuesday in the month,—that was the best place for purchases; and he ought gradually to accustom himself to such dealings; they must be undertaken sooner or later, and the sooner he learned them the cheaper would the lessons be. Andrew hardly knew whether he was standing on his head or his heels, but he good-humouredly followed his father through the stables, and whatever he suggested was approved.

Meanwhile, it was very much the same with Lizzie and her mother, who were planting cauliflowers. The mother began to discuss Lizzie's wardrobe, went over its items one by one, spoke of having a set of shifts made for her as soon as the stitcher was to be had, and pronounced her Sunday jacket worn-out, and a new one essential. Lizzie might do as she liked; either go that very evening to the shop, and see whether the right thing was to be got there, or wait till there was a fair somewhere near, where there would be a better choice.

This speech of her mother's quite bewildered Lizzie; she hardly knew whether she was dreaming or not, and her conscience began to stir, and to ask whether this was the proper reward for her yesterday's rebellion. At first she could not trust to the change, thought it was not in earnest, or a mere trap to lead her on, and so she only returned vague answers, and waited to see what would come next. But when nothing came but one kind word after another, no reproaches, no retractations, then Lizzie marvelled, and she thought, 'Oh, if it were always so! but things will soon alter.' However, they did not alter; nothing was to be heard but pleasant, kindly words; the whole household seemed pervaded by a new impulse, and its machinery revolved rapidly and cheerily. It was as on a warm March day when the sunbeams pour down on the earth's dormant life, colouring all the vegetable world, and filling humanity with hope and thanksgiving.

Now peace and love between parents is neither more nor less than the sun of the household. If this be clouded that household is plunged into winter, girdled with frost, smitten by wind, snow, rain, and its members grow gloomy, apathetic, and inert; but if it shines forth storms are stilled, rain ceases, a glad activity sets in; and as larks sing best in a blue sky, so cheerful songs are heard around the house, and each one bestirs himself as though his wings were beginning to grow. Lizzie kept dancing after her jacket and worrying the tailor; Andrew had long talks with his father, and hovered in silent delight around his mother; and with a cheerful heart, but yet his head on his hand, as though it were aching terribly, Christy the younger sat behind a tea-pot which his mother had already filled twice for him unbidden, his father having of his own accord offered to send for the doctor. Thus the week passed away without a single drawback, for day by day peace seemed more steadfast and pervading, and before Saturday Annie had no more anxiety; she knew that it was to be permanent, no mere morning cloud ready to vanish away.

Saturday came, and with it its evening rest, which here, as in many other houses, was rigidly observed. It is a custom that on Saturday, after six o'clock, after the ringing of the last church-peal, all work shall cease; people would rather finish whatever remains to be done on the Sunday morning than then. Whether this is a remnant of the Jewish Sabbath, or merely a setting apart a portion of time for silent preparation for the coming sacred day, they hardly know; some look upon it one way, some another. At all events, it is peculiarly welcome to young people, especially to servants ; who seldom enough employ it in meditation and self-communings, but devote it to personal affairs, for which they have but little time during the week,— pay visits to the tailor, the shoemaker, the village shops, hoping to combine pleasure with business. The young fellows get together, and the girls keep flitting hither and thither like moths around a candle, or children who run away from you in play, calling out meanwhile, ' Catch us, catch us if you can !'

Supper was over, the live stock all fed and cared for, the maids had fluttered, the men-servants slouched off. On the bench before the house sat Andrew and his father. Christy was standing by in an idle mood, Lizzie making nosegays, when out came the mother and inquired—

' Have you told them ?'

' No,' replied Christian ; ' you can do so best.'

' So indeed I can,' said she. ' It is my wish that we should all go together to the sacrament to-morrow. You are well aware that there has long been something uncomfortable between us. We both meant well, your father and I, but we did not rightly understand each other. It was not on our own account so much as on yours, for who do the parents care for but the children ? But I was the most in fault in the matter, and grievously indeed I erred. I have found this out now, and told it to your father, and he has forgiven me.'

'But mother,' said Christian, 'I have been as much mistaken as you. I too have overlooked what constituted happiness, and when we might have enjoyed it have banished it by over-anxiety, and in this I was worse than you. If I had been a little wiser, the loss of the five thousand pounds might soon have been got over.'

'O daddy, we won't contend about it now any more. I know in my heart's core how wrong I have been, and that my anxious ways have vexed not only you, but the children, and that I made them unhappy all the time I was fretting about their welfare. But now I know that wealth and welfare are two very different things, and I hope they too have learnt this for the whole of their lives. God has taught us this lesson, so there is nothing to regret; but one thing I wish, and that is, that you should all heartily forgive me, so that when I have to go away from you, you may all be at peace with me, and bear me no grudge either before men or before God.

'But, mother,' broke in Andrew, 'what are you thinking of? We never did bear you any grudge, or father either. We have all along regretted that you fretted so much about the money, and we knew well it was on our account; that used to grieve us uncommonly, but we could not alter it. All the week we have observed that something had happened; have thought that it was like a cloud passing away from the sun; everything has seemed different, and we have felt as if on wings. Yes, gladly indeed will we go with you to-morrow to the sacrament, not with any idea of forgiveness, but to thank God for bringing things round, and still less with any idea of your death. Mother, you shall find out henceforth how much we love you. But it is well that every one should once more see that we have no quarrel with each other, and dare to present ourselves together before God and man.'

'Yes,' said Lizzie, 'I have behaved ill to you, mother, and sorry I am for it; but if we are to go to the communion to-morrow I must rush at once into the village to the tailor's; he has again been promising and not performing; and if I do not get my new jacket I cannot go with you, for it is impossible that I should appear in the old.'

'Thou art always the same, Lizzie,' said her father, 'with nothing but nonsense in thy head, otherwise thou wouldst not give thy jacket a thought, but dwell on what a thing it is when brothers and sisters go together to the Lord's table in mutual peace and reconciliation, that they may be reconciled to God also. Remember that if you are always set upon vanities you will be unhappy, and make all about you unhappy. I know now the meaning of the words. " where your treasure is there will your heart be also;" if the treasure be lost, the heart must needs sorrow; therefore it behoves us to seek out for ourselves a treasure that we run no risk of losing, for whose sake we shall not get to hate God and man. No, my Lizzie, this evening thou wilt not go after thy jacket, but let jackets rest; and indeed, wert thou to read a chapter it would do thee no harm. Thou must not look at what I do; I have more to do and think of than thou hast, and besides, I don't need to be always reading when I want to dwell on what is good. I know many a verse thou dost not know; people are too conceited now-a-days to learn anything thoroughly, and there are many new-fangled teachers who are half-ashamed of the Bible, and turn the Catechism into ridicule. I have often thought what must come of this in the end, and that we need not be surprised at our children thinking only of jackets when we speak of the sacrament.'

'O daddy, don't be angry with me; I just said that, and meant no harm, but I'll willingly stay at home, and it is not true that my head runs upon nothing but jackets. When God reads my heart to-morrow, He will see that I can think about my father and mother, and how to behave so that they may truly love me. Dear little mammy, you believe this, don't you?' said Lizzie, resting her elbow on her mother's shoulder, and stroking her cheeks as little children are so fond of doing.

'Ay, ay,' said the mother, 'she is a good one at bottom, though at times one hardly knows what to make of her, and is half inclined to think she has nothing but pranks in her little head; but when I come to die, it will be seen that Lizzie is behind none in housekeeping, and has more in her than mere fun and vanity.'

Thus the family sat together in serious and loving discourse till late evening. Many subjects were touched upon, but the main topic was Annie's firm belief that she was soon to die, and that on the morrow she was to receive her last sacrament with them all. Whatever the others could say to dissuade her, she held fast to this opinion, gently and cheerfully, speaking much about presentiments and analogous cases in her family, her children the while growing more and more depressed, till at last their father proposed that they all should go in and read a chapter; they were quite sure *that* was true, and there was comfort to be got out of it, whereas no one knew how much or how little there might be in the rest, and it only made one melancholy to dwell upon it. His hope was that the dear Lord would long permit them to live together in peace; He had seen their disunion, their love must now be well-pleasing in His sight. Accordingly, they proceeded to edify themselves with God's Word, and, in a serious mood, almost as if on the eve of a first communion, each betook himself to rest.

VII.

THE BLESSING OF PEACE.

SOLEMN and still should Sunday ever break, the presence of the Lord thrill the trees of the garden, the sigh of repentance stir the spirit, the prayer of the heart tremble on the lips. So was it in the Liebiwyl farmhouse on this Whitsunday. In each breast there was still the sorrowful remembrance of their unworthy, unholy dispute one short week before, hence all the more serious their present mood, the more fervent their usual prayer, the more kind and gentle their bearing. Their feelings found no special expression in words or actions, but revealed themselves rather in the tone of the voice, in the promptitude with which each despatched his work, the sympathy with which every remark was received, the liking to be together even in silence. Even Lizzie was deeply moved, never gave her new jacket a thought while putting on her old, was early dressed, looked out a beautiful sprig of rosemary for her mother, and offered one to each brother, but on this occasion they did not wish for any. All waited before the door for their mother, who had still to give instructions to the maids, and to see to things in general. She sent out word indeed that she was not to be waited for, but not one of the party would have left the house without mother, and not one got impatient, or called out to know whether she was coming; and when she appeared, making many apologies, Christian said—

'We would gladly have waited for you longer; it was for our sakes you were detained; each of us has only got himself to think of; you have to care for us all.'

It is a beautiful sight to see parents wending with their grown-up children to the church where they had them baptized in infancy, and able not only to say, 'Lord, here we are; of those Thou hast given us, we have lost none;' but able also to thank Him, in that the parents have been sanctified by the children, and look on them not merely as props to their body in old age, but helps to their souls. When a whole family goes in this way to the Lord's Supper as to their last earthly meal, in believing confidence that the Lord will not hereafter divide what here He finds united, that, although indeed death may interpose like a shadow, and hide one or the other for a while, yet that soon that shadow will vanish in the light of eternal life,—this, we say, is a beautiful sight. In such a family there abides an energy of trust, faith, and love, which the world cannot give, which the world does not even know.

Soon they were no longer alone. They fell in with others; friendly greetings were interchanged; this one slackened his pace, that one quickened it, because they did not like to walk apart on the way to church, but in good-fellowship with their neighbours. But why should we only somewhat accommodate our steps to those of others on the way to church, and not on the way of every-day life as well? Only a little effort, only a degree less selfishness, only a short practice were required, and we might all walk on together in harmonious measure, a company of holy ones throughout life, instead of eternally diverging, because the one insists on shortening his step, just as the other takes to lengthening his.

The church-goers gazed in amazement at the party of five, but the feeling was not expressed in words; each, however, had his own explanation, which he purposed to propound at dinner-time; and indeed there was hardly a house where the circumstance was not discussed that day. Annie's emotion in church the week before had not passed unnoticed ; but, though there were theories in abundance, nobody hit upon the true solution, which could only have been divined by one who possessed the spirit from whence it had emanated. And this spirit is rare; hence so many misinterpretations, hence such nonsense gets talked when people hear of an unselfish act; they have not the key to it in their own breast, and only believe in the motives by which they themselves are actuated.

The nearer they got to the church, the thicker the crowd; for on Whitsunday, when the sun is already warm, many an old granny, who has hitherto been hindered by cold, and muddy ways, can manage to get to church and refresh her soul with the Lord's Supper; she knows not what next winter may have in store for her, and would seek God while she may.

Early as Christian and his party were, they had difficulty in finding seats. Those who can should always be in time; late-comers are seldom in the proper frame, any more than the pastor who breaks off worldly business to betake himself to his holy work. Our spirits are wondrous things: they must be earnest and solemn before they can be earnestly and solemnly impressed; just as the winds must cease to blow, before the waves can go down and the sea be calm.

Now, when we are seated quietly in the silent,

spacious church, perhaps some sweet strain is played on the organ, or some beautiful text occurs to our mind, whilst the bells are summoning those without. And just as in a dark cellar, the eye gradually dilates, and takes in many an object unseen at first ; so too our soul dilates, and becomes susceptible to many influences against which it had been closed before ; and when the minister comes—a sower to scatter holy seed—that seed falls on hearts opened wide, instead of meeting only with outward ears, and those, ears that hear not.

The minister opened the sacred volume, and gave out his text: 'What lack I yet ?' At first the words appeared to Christian and his family to promise little applicability to their own case—they repeated them, and pondered them, but knew not what to make of them.

Then the preacher began, referring to his last sermon, and reminding how he had admonished them to partake of this holy communion, as a last, a farewell communion, in love and charity with all men. But we were not, he said, concerned only with what was behind, but with what still lay before us ; we had not merely to take leave and depart, but to gird ourselves for the onward journey ; and hence the question applied to all : Am I prepared ; or, if not, what lack I yet ? Have I all that helps on to the kingdom of heaven ; if not, what is it that I am short of? This was a matter in which men easily deceived themselves, and it was always a deception to suppose that we had reached the goal. Many there were who confidently expected to go to heaven, and were perfectly satisfied with themselves, cited themselves as an example, complacently looked down upon others, and knew how to dress out even their faults as virtues, hoping God would count them such,—much as a man will sometimes try to deceive others by giving out a common stone as a costly jewel.

For instance, when one contemplated death afar off, and in a general way, one might suppose it easy to die ; but if the time suddenly came, it would seem a very different matter : the easy would grow hard, and the unsuspected force itself on the sight. His hearers should remember the rich young man, who came so confidently to Jesus, believing it an easy matter to win eternal life, because he had hitherto kept the commandments. He too had inquired, 'What lack I yet?' 'Go, sell that thou hast, and give to the poor,' was the reply. For this the young man was not prepared, and he went away sorrowful, lacking the Christian spirit of obedience unto death ; lacking the love that prizes God above all, and our neighbour as our self ; being ready for all that he was inclined to, not for what the Lord required,—loyal till his loyalty was put to the proof,

—deficient in the Spirit that leads into all truth, suffices for every emergency, and gives a child of God power to act up to every claim, as to the apostle Paul it gave that of speaking to the point before every judge.

Now, there are thousands who resemble the rich young man in their ignorance of what they lack. They live quietly on in the grooves in which father and mother lived, give no offence, and find none, but unconsciously they are living only for temporal things; these are their good things, and for them they are accustomed to plan and care supremely; these master and govern them, and they know it not. If then anything unusual occur in their history, if God require a sacrifice, stretch out His hand for their money, shake their habits, send them losses, make their tastes clash with those of others, embitter their life in any way, then, then they discover how they stand, on what their heart is really set,—discover that circumstance is their master, not they master over circumstance; for God's Spirit it is that they lack. In their anxiety about money they forget God; they have neither trust in Him nor submission to His will; they go away offended, become embittered against their fellow-men, cannot rise above the power of habit, and so peace and concord are shattered, because built only on outward circumstance, on a wonted way of life, and not on the living Spirit that is ever ready for any sacrifice, ready to pluck out the eye and cut off the hand lest offences come. He, the pastor, would have them all remember how often their peace had been thus disturbed, how often their own mood witnessed against them that God was not their chief object; that they were too weak for the smallest sacrifice, succumbed beneath the slightest claim, and grew dejected and discouraged. Yes, he would have his hearers reflect how many men, and many families, outwardly and inwardly failed in this manner, because they never found out what it was they lacked. This was Whitsunday, a day that by its every recurrence attested that God would give His Spirit to them that asked it; and he wished them to recognise that this Spirit is the highest gift that God can bestow on men, and that on our winning it, hinges our eternal life.

This is the Spirit which in Christ overcame the world, and overcomes it still in each one who is His. More precious is it than silver or gold. Time cannot affect it, death cannot destroy; it secures happiness in every relation, peace in every household, enjoyment in every heart; it gives a foretaste of salvation, it is the key to the kingdom of heaven.

This spirit it was which the rich young man lacked, which so many of us lack, and without which it is easier for a camel to go through the eye of a needle than for a rich man to enter heaven, because he sets his heart on his possessions, and forgets that there is something far above gold, which alone insures welfare, stands fast in life and death, in health and sickness, in each change and chance of the world; and hence, when money brings him trouble, or can yield him no more comforts, such a one is like a man who, having fallen into the water, and being unable to swim, does but hasten his fate by his agonized struggles. He has not presence of mind to see the hand that is stretched out to save him; he does not seize hold of it; he pushes it away; he sinks.

Thus the pastor; and then he passed on from the general to the particular, and applied the subject to the varied phases of daily life.

Christian and his family felt as though he were reading their hearts aloud, pointing out the error that had led them to the very verge of the abyss, as well as the only means of help by which, indeed, they had already been holpen.

Wonderfully touched and comforted were they to recognise, in the various emotions of their souls, the influence of that spirit they had so long lacked; to feel, that it was the day of Pentecost in their hearts, that they had received a gift above all others, for the want of which the whole world cannot compensate; to see that the Lord had led them into darkness only that their souls might yearn for the morning, and their eyes turn to the east till the sun should rise. Absorbed in pious emotion and amazement, they listened to the laying bare of their hearts from the pulpit, in presence of the whole congregation. Nor did it offend them that the minister should thus reveal and expound their secrets to all around; it seemed fit that he should do so, as though their experience were common property, not to be hid under a bushel, but placed on a candlestick for the good of others. Often they felt as though they could hardly refrain from confirming and illustrating what the minister said. If he had even named them, it would have waked no anger, for they thought every child in the church must know to whom he alluded, and they only wondered that all eyes were not fixed upon them, that those seated at a distance did not rise to look their way, that everybody pretended not to be aware who the preacher had in his eye.

At the conclusion of his discourse they felt themselves strengthened in their good resolves; and when he invited all to come to the Lord's Supper who heartily wished to be His disciples, the call sounded to them, not, as of yore, a mere general invitation, but a special summons to themselves, which they were bound to obey. And when they drew near to the table, they went, not as having a right to go which they did not choose to forfeit, but rather as if drawn thither by a special attraction, an unseen power,—like the thirsting to the water-brooks, or the lost child to the father he once more descries. Everything was absorbed in a blessed sense of communion with the Father and the Son, through the Spirit that dwelt in them; and as a token of this communion they received the outward sign of the Supper, and felt an inexpressibly strong conviction that neither the world, nor death, nor Satan could ever separate them from their God any more.

Seriously, solemnly, but with joyful hearts, they went away from the Lord's house edified.

The stream of people soon surrounded them, and it seemed strange that they should be mingled with it now as they had been before, and yet no one should make any allusion to their having been the subject of the sermon. Nay, they were amazed to hear one observe that the minister preached nearly every other Sunday against covetousness; it was plain to see he had not much to call his own. The speaker confessed that he, for his part, was weary of hearing the same thing over and over again. Another said that he had observed plainly enough that the pastor was pointing at him, and he might have let that alone; on a Whitsunday it was not very fitting, he thought, and people ought to be left in peace. Not long ago he, the pastor, had called upon him for a subscription, he forgot to what, and he had not given him anything, had told him that one had one's money for one's-self, not for others, and that it behoved one to make sure, first of all, that one had enough. And now, to go and make a whole sermon upon him; that he did not think fair in a minister! But he would pay him off, and not enter the church again for six weeks at least. A third had some other objection, a fourth ditto; while it seemed as if each had heard a different discourse, only for the most part they agreed in disliking it. He could preach better, they said, if he chose; a week before, he had given them a sermon enough to rouse the dead; but he did not often care to exert himself, and it was not very creditable to have the power to do well, and not the will.

There were a few, however, who took no part in these comments, but went their way in grave silence; in them the minister's discourse had gone home; their hearts were too full for disputation, nor did they care to admit how right he had been. We are wont to cover up our inmost feelings more carefully even than our bodies; and the covering is often so thick that no eye can pierce through it, not even our own. And this we do from a dread of being misunderstood, and having our most intimate feelings ridiculed by those who cannot share them; for just as children will treat the costliest jewels as common stones, so common minds will mock at what is above them in proportion to its height.

Accordingly, it never occurred to Christian, Annie, or their children, to give their neighbours their version of the discourse, nor to tell them how it was borne out by their own experience. Indeed, they were almost glad that others' ears had been holden, and that what they believed so clear to all remained obscure; and they only briefly said that, for their part, they had liked the sermon; that they were of opinion every one might find something in it to suit his case, and that if all did as the pastor bade them, it were no bad thing for any.

But when the quiet afternoon was come, and the servants were gone their ways, and a sweet Sunday stillness reigned around, they all gathered in the shady orchard, and, seated on the cool grass, beneath a widespreading apple-tree, began to speak of what had been going on within them. To all alike the sermon had been a mirror in which they had more or less clearly beheld their own inward condition, and all admitted how right the pastor had been in declaring the Spirit of the Lord to be the one thing needful; how their unhappiness had arisen from making money, and not this Spirit, the centre and aim of their life; and how it was this Spirit alone which had stilled the storm in their hearts and family relations.

THE BLESSING OF PEACE.

It was marvellous to them all how the preacher had spoken what they had felt, as though he read their hearts, and clothed their thoughts in words, making them clearer to them than they themselves could have done. They knew that he was very slightly acquainted with them, and no third person could have given him this information; for they themselves had hardly possessed it till now; and as to the occurrences of the last week, they were not guessed at by any. So they could only explain it by a Divine dispensation; God still, in these our days, speaking by the mouth of His servants, still inclining the mind and touching the heart; for who indeed is it who guides the preacher to his text, and makes that text live within him, till it expands into a sermon, which comes as a special message to one man and not to another? Shall He, without whom no hair falls from our head and no sparrow from our roof, have no power over our spirits? Shall He who reveals Himself through night with its solemn speech, day with its cheerful language, and every flower that blooms in the field, not also be made known by preaching, and in whatever way He will? So at least our good people reasoned, and found great comfort in believing that God had looked upon them and directed the minister's thoughts.

And not only had the text become a living thing

in the minister's mind, but his sermon lived in their spirits ; that is, it intermingled with their life, and this life found expression in many various ways through the wonderful play of thought, even in apparently secular talk, in which a stranger might have discerned mere good-nature, no trace of a holy spirit or lofty aspirations. But the Spirit of the Lord pervades field and fruit, weed and flower, and if it be really in us, it reveals itself in all relations of life, and in every word we utter. They are very inexperienced who would confine it to any set phraseology.

'I am getting old,' said the father ; 'I feel that I can no longer overtake the whole affairs of the farm, and perhaps, indeed, much might go on better than it does; but I don't well know how to alter now. I would not hinder the young people in any way, so perhaps it were well that I should give up, and let the children manage. If they understand each other, I don't see why it should not answer.'

'I quite agree with you,' said the mother; 'they would manage very well. You and I will move to the back-room, or perhaps we can build over the stove ; that would not cost much ; and if they ever wanted help or counsel, why, there we should be, and the young ones would often be glad of us. Only, the proper thing would be, that Andrew should marry, else I don't see how they could get on. Lizzie won't be here always, and if Christy were to marry, and his wife took up housekeeping, when Andrew came into possession of the farm it would be a blow to Christy's wife, and not turn out well.'

Andrew interrupted his mother, and declared he would not hear of such a thing,—would never turn them out. He should only be too happy to do all he could to help his father, as in duty bound, but the latter must still be at the helm. As to marrying, he would not hear of it; he did not think he should ever marry, and certainly not merely to drive away his mother from the kitchen; he loved her too well for that. She had managed capitally for thirty years, and it was doubtful whether they should ever find her equal.

'Why,' interposed Christy, 'one or other of us will have to marry, I suppose. As to Lizzie, there is no question that she will. Now I, for my part, don't intend to marry. Such an invalid is not fit to be the head of a family, and I might easily fall in with some one who would bring me to the grave before the first six months were out. No, no, I shall remain with thee; we have always been brotherly, and shall continue so. Thou must marry, and hast thyself admitted that thou hast some one in thy eye, which I should have made known long ago, only it went out of my head in our misery. However, it has not gone out of thine; for since then thou hast never gone to a dance, or stirred a step from home at night.'

Andrew reddened, and would have denied this, but his mother broke in—

'Tell me now, what was that about the Dorngrüt farmer's daughter? You once questioned me about her, and there was something particular in thy manner; I snubbed thee at the time, and have often regretted it, but I did not know how to begin upon it, so said nothing. Is she still in thy mind?'

'Oh, not particularly,' said Andrew.

'Come now, speak out openly. If it is so, something may be done. Many a one has kept a thing of this kind all to himself, and crushed it down, and regretted it afterwards,' urged his mother.

'Well, then,' said Andrew, 'I will just tell the truth. That girl did take my fancy, as no other ever has done. I don't believe there is another fit to hold a candle to her, and at once thought to myself: "She, or none." And so I still feel, but I see very well that nothing can ever come of it.'

'Why so?' inquired Christian. 'Have you asked her?'

'No,' returned Andrew; 'but I know it for all that.'

'How can you know it when you have never asked? things often turn out differently from our expectations. Is the girl engaged to any one else?' suggested the father.

'Not that I know of,' replied Andrew; 'and I did not mean that, for I fancied that I was not altogether disagreeable to her, though, to be sure, one may easily be mistaken. But there is something else.'

'Well, tell us what it is,' said his father. 'Is there anything wrong about her people?'

'Why, that's matter of opinion,' answered Andrew. 'Her father is very rich, and awfully covetous; and as I have heard, he thinks no one rich enough for his children, or else insists upon conditions that there is no standing. He has already settled two of his daughters on such terms that his sons-in-law are to be the only ones to inherit, and their brothers and sisters to go their way empty-handed. This I would never consent to; I won't see my brothers and sisters wronged, and feel that my children, and children's children, will have to suffer for it; and when people come together upon such an understanding as this, one sees pretty plain what spirit they are of, and we know what comes of a spirit like that. I don't want any more than my share; Christy's and Lizzie's belong to them as much as mine to me, when it comes to a division, which God grant may not be the case for many a long day.'

'Dear brother,' said Lizzie, 'if this be all, don't disturb yourself about me. Christy was only in fun, and there is nothing serious going on as far as I am concerned, and if I can promote your happiness thereby, I will gladly remain single. It would have been lucky for many a one to have kept unmarried. I know how well off I am with father and mother, but it's always uncertain how a husband may turn out.'

'You know,' said Christy, 'how we stand together, and if the girl really suits you, make what arrangements you can, and depend upon our doing our utmost to help you; and if father likes to give up the farm to you for a fair sum, I for one have no objection to it.'

'I won't hear of that,' replied Andrew. 'Father and mother shall hold their own. I will never consent to let them tie their hands on account of a child. I am not going to set father and mother aside for the sake of any girl, and now that we are so happy together, we won't bring in any cause of disturbance.'

'You would please me exceedingly by marrying,' said his mother. 'When I come to die, and die I shall before long, it will be a great comfort to me to have seen thy wife.'

'Mother, don't speak of dying; you must not die; and don't talk to me of a wife either.'

'But I will talk,' said Christy. 'Things are not always to go on in the same way, and there is no harm in making an experiment. The chief thing is to know whether the girl likes you or not; if so, everything else will come right. Have you heard anything of her since that evening?'

'No,' said Andrew; 'I did not see any use in inquiring, when the best thing seemed to be that I should forget the whole affair as soon as possible.'

'There you were wrong,' returned Christy; 'and I will find out all that is wanted for you. I have set my heart on your getting a good wife, and since mother is longing so much for a daughter-in-law, she must have one before next Easter, or my name is not Christy. Father, give me a little money in my pockets, and I will go on some errand or other —cows, horses, sheep, never mind what—to the Dorngrüt farmer, and perhaps I shall have an opportunity of speaking to the girl herself, and finding out how the land lies, and what the best way of setting about the matter is.'

'Do as you like,' said Andrew, 'and thank you for your offer; but I won't have you commit yourself. You are all only too kind to me, but I shall not forget it, you may be sure of that.'

'A week ago I never could have hoped for this state of things,' said his mother; 'and if any one had told me of it, I should have disbelieved him. But with God all things are possible, and since He permits misfortune to break in upon us like a thief in the night, why should He not cause joy too to burst forth suddenly like the sun from its chamber, when He sees our hearts are ripe for it?'

'Hark! what is that?' cried Andrew, springing up from the ground. The slow strokes of a bell came one by one through the air. The whole party rose. 'The alarm-bell—where is the fire?' they cried. There was no smoke to be seen, but then they could only sweep a small portion of the horizon from where they were. They hurried to the house, and in a few minutes Andrew, with his fire-hook on his shoulders, with the bucket hanging to it, was seen hurrying as hard as he could to the church-tower, where the bell tolled more and more eagerly for help, and the happy family picture had vanished away, swallowed up in the troubles and turmoil of the world.

But though the form had vanished, the spirit remained,—the living spirit, which ever generates new forms, fair offspring witnessing to its existence and energy.

PART II.

I.

AN EVENTFUL NIGHT.

WHO is there who has not often remarked the difference in the sound of bells, and experienced what opposite emotions they excite in the human heart?

Sublime and solemn, as though from heaven, they peal, when summoning mortals to the house of God, there to humble themselves before the Almighty, to raise themselves to the All-merciful; mournful the toll of the funeral-bell, blent as it ever seems with the rattling of earth on the coffin-lid, and the darkness of the grave; gentle and sweet the vesper-bell, a kindly greeting at the close of day, a welcome invitation to repose, a call to lay ourselves down beneath a Father's care, and to leave all our concerns in His wise hand. But when the fire-bell rings, terror thrills every soul, women turn pale, children weep, men listen with eager ear and throbbing heart. It sounds from the steeples round like the wail of wives, the sobs of orphans, the crackling of flames, and the longer it rings the more intense its appeal, the more fraught with anguish and alarm. Men gather together in their distress, all eyes are strained to catch the dismal smoke that shows the place where the fire is raging, and the help of the brave needed.

Around the engine-house, which, as usual, stood in the middle of the village, with the public-house near, and the church a little to one side—around the engine-house, Andrew, the Liebiwyl farmer's son, found half the village assembled, some gazing at the rolling smoke at a distance, which rose ever thicker and blacker to the sky, others handling hose, joining pipes collecting buckets, calling out for horses, which no one, however, would supply; asking for a bit of candle in their lanterns, as evening was drawing on, few admitting that they had any candles of their own, but signifying that the shopkeeper would give some for money. As soon as Andrew came, he inquired where the fire was, which no one could tell him for certain, only it was a great fire, and every moment a new house seemed to catch.

'Where was the torch-bearer, the engine-driver?' he cried, for nowhere was this functionary to be seen; upon which he was told that he had not been in church morning or afternoon, and must be gone off on business of his own, either after a wife or a cow, probably the latter, the Berne butcher having bought two from him in the course of the last week.

'Which of you will take my hook? Give me the torch,' cried Andrew abruptly; 'if you cannot get horses here, go as quick as you can for mine, but make haste to follow, otherwise it will be a disgrace to the whole parish. These are the things that show what sort of people there is in a parish, whether good for anything or not.'

His sharp words made an impression on many, all the more that they were spoken by a young fellow who had never come forward before in any way, and hit hard at certain grey heads who aspired to parish dignities.

'If such a mere lad as this was to thrust his finger into the pie, he would have nothing to do with it,' observed the village bailiff; but prudently waited to make the remark till Andrew's rapid steps had already carried him out of hearing. 'Such a young blockhead does not know that horses should always be fed before they are taken to a fire, should have a peck of oats at least, if not two, for who can say when they may get anything to eat next? And by the time they have done their oats they are very often not wanted, everything being burnt down.'

Meanwhile the firemen were off with measured

step, and with them went many others who could not stay quietly at home when there was help to be rendered.

The farther they got the mightier rose the pillar of smoke before them, and floated away into a great black cloud, a second firmament of darkness; hence the more than ever doleful wailing of the bells, and the denser the crowd hurrying to the fire. They had no need now, as often is the case, to stand still before every house to inquire where the scene of the calamity was, and carefully look for some scarcely visible grey thread winding up from earth to heaven. No! there was the burning hamlet before them, the dread scene of a fierce strife between the devouring element and the energy of human beings, the winds rushing to aid the flames, but man, too, hurrying to the help of man.

Andrew and his band forced their way valiantly into the very heart of the strife, sought out the most perilous position, sought, too, for the chief fireman, but found him not. Everywhere confusion prevailed; too many gave orders here, no one there at all; indeed, things went on best where every one did what his instinct prompted. Andrew, like a wise general, had desired his party to keep together as much as possible, but in this, fate, that ever delights in dividing, was too strong for him. The firemen rushed with hooks and ladders to the burning houses, and tried to snatch from the flames their prey, at the risk of falling victims themselves; while those who had buckets placed themselves near the engine, to relieve the weary in keeping the hose properly supplied,—Andrew, meanwhile, as torch-bearer, flying along the lines, ordering and encouraging, pressing the idle into the service, pushing the irresolute into their proper places, and experiencing to the full the immense difficulty of keeping up a systematic and efficient play of water at an extensive conflagration. But light as a bird, and bold as a lion, the danger roused all his energies; he felt as though strong enough to bend a world to his will; on his way to the scene of action could have sung and shouted if only it had been decorous, and, in the absence of such outlets to his excitement, had run so fast that those behind him had kept continually calling out that no one could keep up with such a pace.

Such was the condition of triumphant energy in which he arrived at the spot; but who does not know the rapid transition from one stage of excitement to another—how impetuosity becomes impatience, and impatience irritability? The first thing he had done was to form a line of water communication; and the louder the fire roared the more energetic his efforts,—being possessed by the very same spirit which intoxicates the young hero on the battle-field, and drives away the possibility of fear. True, this spirit borders on the ludicrous when displayed in trivial matters, such, for instance, as keeping a line of buckets together, but even the vague consciousness of its character does not extinguish it in him once it is kindled, it glows on the same till at last it perverts itself into violence. Andrew began by hurried, but courteous requests—'Would people be so kind as to lend a hand? Might he beg?' and so on. But when gap after gap appeared in the line he had taken such pains to form, he left off all unnecessary phrases, and by his abrupt commands offended and drove off many whose services he required. At length he began to swear and storm, contrary to his habit, and to push people not over gently into order. Seeing two young girls talking under a tree, he rudely disturbed them, and sought to press one of them into the service.

'Can't you gossip at home, you —?'

'For goodness sake don't be such a clown,' said the young girl, turning round towards him, and Andrew saw the face of the Dorngrüt farmer's daughter, and she his, and both gazed as though they were petrified, could not speak a word, and for a moment stood motionless amongst the busy crowd. Suddenly cries of 'Room, room! make way, make way!' were heard on all sides, and the well-known Soleure fire-engine came crashing through the trees towards a pond, and behind it a stream of men with hose, scattering everything on their way, so that when Andrew looked round next he neither saw his line of bucket-bearers nor the young girl. We are bound to admit he cared little for the first, but he looked everywhere for the last, went in and out among the trees, took to running up and down, looking at every girl, but no longer after the water supply, till the engine-driver sharply asked him what on earth he was about, and bid him keep the people together for another half-hour at least, by which time they would have got the fire under.

Andrew went to his post; but how gladly he would have run away, like those whose defections he had been so hard upon a moment ago! Zeal and energy were over, and though he still kept moving about rapidly, it was not so much to look after the gaps as to look into the face of every girl he saw; as to how often he stumbled over buckets thrown aside he took little heed, though each time the incident was greeted with peals of laughter. It was true he made his rounds, but in point of fact he was hunting, not after idlers, but the farmer's daughter, and often he ran up against a tree, bringing his torch into peril of its life. But nowhere could he see her, turn where he would, and the more prolonged his disappointment the greater his vexation, not only with his duties, but with her who ought surely, he considered, to have stayed somewhere near where he might have been sure to come across her again,—not remembering that at night, in a strange place, where everything was seen by the uncertain light of flames, and obscured with smoke, it was not very easy to know where exactly one was. All at once his line of water-bearers was rent asunder, and before he could count ten he found himself alone, and in silence, except that he could hear the engine-driver swearing and cursing he knew not why, when suddenly it occurred to him that the pastor had come to return thanks. This thanksgiving service every one attends; the moment the rumour runs that it is about to begin, work and order are over, and the crowd converge from all sides to the point where the pastor is standing on a stool, or the charred fragments of a burnt-down house, or an inverted tub or pig-trough, as the case may be. As soon as this idea flashed into Andrew's mind a weight fell from his spirits, activity returned to his limbs, he flew away with the rest; for where could he have a better chance of meeting his lady-love again than in this general assembly? The fire had been subdued; it was only right to thank Him who is the giver of all strength, and without whose blessing none of our efforts succeed. This time the pastor stood on a balcony. 'Torchbearers to the front!' was the cry; and Andrew had to place himself close to the balcony, from which the minister began to return thanks to God and man. But not a word fell on Andrew's ear, he was all eyes looking for the girl of his heart. By a dexterous manœuvre he contrived to mount on some beams, could look over the heads of the crowd, and turn his torch in all directions, but in none was she to be found. Hundreds of faces he saw, but nowhere the right one; or if sometimes he fancied he had discovered her, the face soon changed before his disappointed eyes, now into that of a monkey, now into a sheep's face, which are far commoner we all know than the face of a lovely girl.

The thanksgiving was at an end; the crowd dispersed; the firemen blew their horns, called out the name of their home, and the different parties gathered round their torch-bearer as round a standard. Andrew had forgotten this part of the business, and had he not been reminded of it by a chance companion, would have wandered off alone, and gone on with his search, but dignities ever bring their burden. The party had been nearly got together, and were on the move homeward, when Andrew bethought him he should like to take back a testimonial of his presence at the fire. Some assured him it was not necessary; their buckets, left behind, which would be brought back by the burnt-out villagers, would be the best evidence of their having been there. But Andrew was bent upon a testimonial, asserting that firemen were often suspected of having been absent when wanted. The majority were strongly inclined to waive this formality, being terribly hungry and thirsty, and anxious to find themselves in some distant public-house, where they would have a story to tell. Andrew instantly came in to their departure, and promised to follow them, and this pleased all parties; his band went off, with the exception of one who preferred to remain with him, and he himself had another chance of continuing his search. Very slowly indeed he proceeded to the schoolhouse, often pausing, forcing his way through whatever group he saw, and proceeding in such dilatory fashion that his comrade remonstrated : 'Thou wilt come to mischief, it's not fit, after a fire, to be poking one's nose everywhere in this way.'

But for all his lingering and prying he found the young girl nowhere; not in the schoolhouse, where at last he procured his testimonial, not in the public-house, where, in spite of all the protestations of his comrade, he would go in for a measure of wine; he had to leave the village whether he would or no, without hitting upon a single trace of the young stranger.

It was a beautiful night, the stars were sparkling in the sky, the burnt village glowed through a transparent veil of smoke like a place of torment, and its inhabitants, flitting around their devastated homes, looked to Andrew's eyes like shadows of the lost, or spirits of evil reviving the fire.

Outside the village several roads diverged; but the greater number ran through a fine oak wood where the majestic trees stood wide apart, and the brushwood grew scantily. This night all these ways were unusually fraught with loud life. Crowds of those who had come to help were hastening home, laughing and joking, singing and shouting; the engines rattled noisily over the ground, the awakened birds chirped anxiously to each other, and the flickering torches threw a strange weird light around. The general excitement grew ever wilder and louder, for the Berne peasantry, difficult to arouse, when once roused are difficult to quiet down, and nothing sets their blood in greater commotion than the stir at a conflagration. The abrupt shock of the fire-bell's first sounds at once quickens its flow, the rapid transit to the scene of action increases its speed, the work and danger there makes it mount higher and higher, and when to all this is added a measure or two of wine upon an empty stomach, the blood positively boils, and on the least provocation bursts out into fury.

Hence the uproar, the screams, the frantic mirth, and the loud disputes that now filled the wide forest. Every engine which drove through the throng was the occasion of a fray; young men fought till they bled for the tittering girls whose tender hearts had impelled them in numbers to render assistance at the fire, or to seek other tender hearts there; old village feuds set the fire-hooks going, and many a one dug into human flesh as though it were burning wood. And when this kind of thing once began, it spread like a contagious disease, or like a fire, quenched here, only to break out there, till there is nothing more left for it to fasten on.

Andrew walked with his comrade quietly and proudly along; when too much pressed upon, he warded off the crowd with a strong arm indeed, but gently, and kept steadily on his way, till he got far into the wood, where, in advance of him, he heard angry words, blows, and women's cries, but it was in a dark part of the wood, and his torch the only one just there to shine through the avenues of oak branches. All at once he heard, as he thought, the same feminine voice which had admonished him not to behave like a clown, and upon that rushed into the fray. Vain was it for his friend to entreat him to turn aside, or put out his torch, for that if he interfered with it in his hand he would come in for hard blows. Andrew would go out of his way, he declared, for no one, nor put his torch out either, the use of it being to give light in dark places. The louder the dispute, the more he quickened his step. His comrade behind him, who, seeing Andrew was not to be dissuaded, mentally resolved that, since ill luck would have it so, it was much the same to him; it would not be a matter of life and death, he supposed, and for the sake of a few blows, more or less, he would not desert a friend.

As the Trojans and Greeks waged war for Helena, so here, too, a group of young fellows were disputing for a maiden, not in words, but blows, according to the custom of their fathers. When Andrew threw his torch's light upon the scene, he saw many a bloody face, but, as he had presaged, saw his own young girl in the midst; accordingly he forced his way into the ring like a proud ship-of-the-line through the breakers, his good comrade behind him, in full expectation of a shower of blows. But all at once there was a rush above his head, and Andrew fell as if struck by lightning. In every quarrel in which many are engaged, there are sure to be some who like to keep a whole skin, and yet to take a prominent part, and these lurk at a little distance, and wait an opportunity for a good safe blow from behind. One of this kind it was who had struck down Andrew with his fire-hook, the blow, however, had been intended for the torch, whose revealing light came so inopportunely.

'Wait, thou accursed murderer, and I will pay thee off,' cried Andrew's comrade.

The word *murderer* created a panic among the disputants; no one wanted to be mixed up with so grave a charge, and before the speaker could turn round, he found himself left alone with the wounded man, who lay there stunned and bleeding, while his comrade observed: 'This is just what I told thee would happen,' and urged him to rise.

But move, pull, raise him, do what he would, nothing succeeded in arousing Andrew, and his friend remained standing there in utmost perplexity. At length a man came along through the wood, and, having heard the story at full length, proceeded to say: 'Do you know that, to the right there, about a rifle-shot off, there is a little cottage, I will show it you; there you can get a cart and drive off with him; when once you overtake the rest, you'll do finely.'

However, the comrade was reluctant to follow this advice, and leave Andrew alone.

'You blockhead,' went on the stranger, 'he is not likely to run away, and no one will want to steal him; and, if you stand by him all night, he may chance to bleed to death.'

'Perhaps people will come by and help him,' suggested the friend.

'I doubt it,' returned the other; 'it seems to me

as though we were the last, but I don't want to persuade you. Do as you like, I won't detain you. Good-night.'

'Stop, stop,' cried the comrade, trying to prop up Andrew against an oak; 'and now, then, come with me as fast as ever you can, I am not sure of the way.'

'Gently, gently,' said the other, 'or else find the way out for yourself;' and slowly following the quick steps of the former, both disappeared in the wood.

A long time elapsed, and then there was a rustling through the trees, and two men came driving up in a cart.

'Look,' said one, 'that's the place, where those three oaks stand together; he is lying against the middle one.'

They stopped at that middle oak, but no one lay there; no one was to be seen lying far or near. The woods were silent and empty, all life was suspended, the frightened birds had sunk again to rest.

There stood the poor comrade aghast; nowhere was his friend to be seen, nowhere a trace of him. Those were the three oaks, sure enough, there was no such other group near; and there was blood about them, and traces of a man having lain under the one in the middle. A vague fear seized hold of him, he looked all about with the torch into every mousehole, and up every tree; now cursed his own folly (he might have known it would be so); now the man who by his advice had led him astray. Suddenly a dark thought crossed him: could the villain, he thought, have sent me out of the way that he might do as he liked with poor Andrew! And this thought went on, getting darker and darker, and his terror greater and greater, till at length he was driven to impart it to his companion, and to ask whether he had any knowledge of the man who brought him to his cottage.'

'Don't be uneasy,' replied the latter; 'one sees no sign of trampling or of anything wrong by the oak, and if the man had had evil intentions, he would only have pointed out my cottage from a distance and not come up to it himself, which he must have known would connect him with the circumstance. But your friend must have come to himself after you left him. What of that, you are sure to find him in the next public-house.'

Which of us is not ready to believe what is pleasant and probable besides; for there it was that Andrew had appointed his party to wait for him. Accordingly, his friend settled with the owner of the cart, and hurried to the place of meeting, where a great crowd was gathered, but no Andrew was there, nor any of his band. They had all left, he was told, but whether they had been joined by a wounded man or not, no one could say for certain. Some thought they had, others thought not; others again begged that they might not be teased by such foolish questions, they had not time to answer them, and a pretty thing indeed it was to expect them to give account of every bloody face they had seen,— there were sure to be plenty after a fire like that. So the poor comrade had to go on his way, comforting himself as well as he could, but still his heart was ill at ease.

'If I had only stayed by him. Who was it put that cursed cart into my head? Can it have been the devil who lured me away? I thought at the time he did not look like other men.'

And so he went on cogitating till he was at home again; and once there, he hardly dared to inquire for Andrew, but had a good mind to send a child to the engine-house with the torch, quietly creep back into his own quarters, and pretend that he knew nothing of the matter, and had not even been at the fire. But, however, he could not quite make up his mind to this,—as indeed, thank God, men seldom do carry out a hundredth part of what occurs to them,—and soon he found out that no one had seen Andrew, and that all looked to him for information about him.

Accordingly, he began to narrate, and his narration was all the more marvellous that he tried to conceal the fault with which his conscience reproached him, yet which, after all, was no fault, but a mere error of judgment very excusable after such a conflagration, and with such an empty stomach. He gave increasingly startling and confused accounts of how his leaving Andrew came about. The more questions put to him, the more his story grew; and of this story, which went on increasing in length and mystery, every one gave his own version, which versions resembled each other about as much as black and white, or an elephant and a snake. According to some, Andrew had been killed and buried in the wood; others whispered that the devil had had a hand in carrying him off; and others, again, hinted that his comrade, who had for a long time past been penniless, and knew that Andrew's purse was generally well lined, had the true clue to the mystery.

Meanwhile, at home they were anxiously looking out for their son. Christian kept impatiently pacing the terrace before the house; Annie was standing outside in the road, and both kept calling out to know whether the other saw him coming. Hours of miserable suspense passed thus, and Christian had just resolved to go to the village and inquire, when a woman passed by, and said:

'Good people, you are waiting in vain, he will never return to you.'

'O God! what do you say? what has happened?' cried poor Annie; and Christian shot down from the terrace like a hawk whose nest is attacked.

'I dare not tell you more,' said the woman, 'you might be frightened; such news always comes too soon. Good-day.'

Annie had grown pale as death, and could hardly gasp out, 'Oh, what is it? what is it?'

'If I had known that I should frighten you so much,' replied the woman, 'I would not have said a word, but I can't say any more. It's dreadful what things happen now-a-days.'

At this Christian lost all patience, and cried: 'Will you speak out or not? We are not to be made fools of in this way.'

'Don't be so hot,' replied the woman; 'if you won't be frightened, and get angry with me, to be sure I will tell you what I heard in the village. They say that Andrew is lost; some will have it that the devil has spirited him away, and others that he is dead and buried in the wood between here and the village where the fire was. Goodday.'

This time no one heard her salutation, for Annie had laid her head down on the garden wall, and was sobbing convulsively, while Christian tried to comfort her: 'Don't take on thus, I am sure it's not true. Come in, that people may not hear, and I will start off to the village, where I shall have better news, but, any way, it is strange that he should not be there.'

He tried to lead Annie in, but she fell fainting to the ground, and he had much to do before he could bring her round, as also to send for Lizzie and Christy, who were in the fields busy with the potatoes, and it was only when they had heard the sorrowful story he could get off.

For years and years no one had seen Christian move at such a pace. As soon as the villagers discerned him from afar, the news spread: 'He is coming! he is coming!' and every one got out of his way. The women dived into their kitchens, the men shot round the corner into the stable, only a staring lad or two remained in the street, curious to see how the staid farmer could run. But, when he had passed, the women poked their heads out over the kitchen door, and said: 'Ay, ay, he does not cry, but Annie, his wife, will cry finely. Well, well, so it is—to-day red, to-morrow dead! One might have known that something of the kind would happen; where there is nothing but quarrelling, the Lord is sure to send some token of His anger against such goings-on.'

This amiable comment, however, Christian did not hear; but finding there was no one about to give him any information, made straight for the public-house, where, from the landlady's more rational account, he gathered that all hope was not lost, that the mystery lay in Andrew's disappearance, but no one knew anything further; that Hans Sami had been with him last, and must be able to solve it, if he would, but that his story was so strange and inconsistent no one knew what to make of it.

'Very well,' said Christian. 'We'll get the truth out of him one way or other,' and steered at once to the house where Hans lived. But there he had no small trouble before he could get in, and went round and round knocking and calling in vain, till at length he spied the farmer's wife in the dairy, and darted in to her, nor rested till Master Hans was brought forward, and then he cross-questioned him sharply. On the whole, Hans told his story pretty truthfully, except that he painted the individual who induced him to leave Andrew in very dark colours indeed, and left it to be inferred that there was something unnatural about him. But that Andrew was dead he declared he did not believe, though what had become of him he could not conceive.

'Well then, we must go and look,' said Christian; 'and you will come with me and show the spot where you left him.'

'I am very tired,' pleaded Hans, 'and have not closed my eyes the whole night.'

'Very well, then, we will take a horse and vehicle, and see that you are ready to set out with me in an hour's time.'

Hans was glad enough to consent to this, so soon as he saw that Christian was not angry with him, and declared that no one was more interested in finding out the truth than he, not only for Andrew's sake, but that it might be known he had not left him in the lurch.

Christian felt very strange as he went back; his legs shook under him, and more than once a cloud gathered before his eyes, so that he had to stop and lean up against the hedge. He was full of hope that things would not turn out so bad after all, and tears of gratitude and relief flowed freely; but now that the excitement of extreme terror was over, body and soul were alike weak, and he could hardly drag one leg after the other; so that he was longer getting home than he intended, and at the first sight of his slow gait, Annie, who with all his household was waiting out in the road, exclaimed:

'O heavens, how you look! He is dead, then, is he? O Andrew, my Andrew, shall I never see thee more?' and again the tide of anguish overflowed.

'Don't go on so,' said Christian; 'nothing of the kind; anyhow Andrew is not dead. He must have come to himself when he was alone, and gone off to wherever he is now. But we must look for him. Christy, give the brown horse a feed, and get the vehicle ready; I will just change my coat.'

And then up he went to the house, sat down on the bench, and desired to have some water brought him, he felt so strange. Of course, he was at once assailed by fresh lamentations and entreaties to say what was the matter with him; sooner or later it would have to be heard, and the longer it was kept back the worse it would be.

In reply he bid them all compose themselves. 'It was nothing serious; but something had taken away the power of his limbs, as it were; it must have been running so hard, and it would soon pass off. Annie should put him out a clean shirt, and he would go off at once.'

'O no, father, you shall not go,' replied Annie; 'Christy can drive, you are ill, and the brown horse is so wild, no one knows how terrified I should be if you went.'

'Hans Sami is to go with me,' returned Christian.

'What of that?' replied his wife; 'he cannot cure thee, and when people are taken as thou art, lying down is the best thing. No one knows whether you might not, which God forbid, have a stroke, or something really bad, if you were to go knocking about. No, indeed, thou must keep quiet, and if not soon better, Lizzie shall go for the doctor. Perhaps bleeding might do thee good.'

Say what he would, Christian had to give in, and let Christy drive off; and anxiety for the one present somewhat diverted Annie from her anguish about the absent. The right sort of woman ever devotes herself to what is nearest, and does not forget to help those within her reach because unhappy about others far away.

Christian was made to go to bed whether or no, and to drink a basin of warm broth; and Annie sat beside him and kept off the flies, while Lizzie stood outside watching for tidings, if not for Andrew himself. Before long her mother joined her, having stolen away from her sleeping husband, and a little later Christian came out, for anxiety did not let him sleep long; but gaze as they would, far as the eye could reach, there was no one to be seen. Poor Annie burst out:

'Yes, so it is; but who can believe it till it comes to pass? Yesterday everything was so beautiful, we were all together so happy and joyous, and how is it with us now? Now we are desolate, our boy is gone, and we must weep our hearts out, just when we might have been so happy. O that men would remember to love each other while they are together; no one can tell how soon they may have to part!'

II.

A CHURL'S HOSPITALITY.

IN the heart of a woody district, and immediately surrounded by rich meadow land, stood a large grey building, the back of which had all the freshness of a recent addition ; near it stood a wood-pile, a barn, and a dwelling-house with small windows, and a roof pressed down over them, looking for all the world like a hat drawn down over a thief's eyes to hide their expression. All sorts of things lay around ; preparations for building, and implements of various kinds ; the pigs enjoyed the fullest freedom, ducks and hens the same ; and in an open shed stood a short pinched-looking man, with sharp nose and cunning eyes, making straw ropes for the coming harvest. Near this shed was the housedoor, which led through a dark smoky passage into the kitchen, and out of this door came, with rapid step, a young girl, who bore no traces of smoke, being neatly, carefully, and gracefully attired, and said:

'Father, we shall have to send for the doctor after all; he does not waken,—what do you think?'

'What I thought at first,' muttered the man; 'that you should have left him alone. What was he to you, and what good have we done by putting ourselves about for him?'

'But, father,' pleaded the girl, 'he might have died.'

'And if he had? He will have to die one day or other, and perhaps it would have been better for him now than later.'

'But, father, what sort of conscience should we have had if we had left him lying there, and then heard that he was dead?'

'Ill weeds are not so soon killed, and you don't know whether his comrades may not have been to look after him, and a pretty story there will be when they do not find him, and the mischief knows what will come of it.'

'However that may be, father, here he is now,' answered the girl, 'and scolding won't better things. But will you come in and tell us what you think of him? We have made wine poultices, and now my mother says she will try cold water; and if that does not answer, she does not know what to turn to next.'

Twisting up his rope, and laying it with the

others, her father replied: 'So it is, we are not half ready with our own things, and yet go and plague ourselves with other people. But I would have you know, once for all, that we have got to mind our own business, and leave other folks' alone. What can we do for one who does not know how to take care of himself?' And, growling the whole of the way, he followed the girl, over the high doorstep, through the long passage, encumbered by implements of all kinds, into a bedroom, the door of which she opened, when he muttered: 'You need not have brought him into the house, and given him the best bed, I think; those one picks up in the wood one puts into the stable, and he would have got well sooner in straw than in a feather-bed.'

'Father,' returned the girl, 'he belongs to a house where they are not accustomed to lie in straw.'

'Why did he not stay at home, then? he might have lain where best he liked for me.'

'Hush, hush!' whispered a tall thin woman in the room, holding back the blue bed-curtain as she spoke: 'hush, he is moving.'

Lightly the daughter stepped up behind her, while the farmer stood at the foot of the bed, and gazed at a pale young man lying there, with head bound up and closed eyes, but with a quivering and twitching of the hands which showed that consciousness was returning, and that he wished to move, but could not.

'He don't want doctors,' said the farmer; 'he'll soon wake up of himself. It was not worth while to come darting out like a shot and make such a to-do about the first idle fellow you came across.'

Upon that the wounded man slowly opened his eyes, looked languidly round, and slowly closed them again. Then suddenly, as though a sense of strangeness had come over him, he started up in bed, looked about him with wonder, and asked: 'For God's sake, where am I, and what is the matter with me?'

'Why, where should you be but here?' said the woman.

'But how did I get here?' inquired Andrew.

'Look here, girl,' said the mother, 'you tell him;' and she made room, and Andrew saw before him Mary Anne, the Dorngrüt farmer's daughter, with her eyes modestly cast down.

Andrew felt such a faintness come over him that he was obliged to lie down; but he did not close his eyes any more.

'You tell him all about it, child,' repeated the mother. 'Meanwhile I can be doing something in the house.'

A CHURL'S HOSPITALITY.

'Well,' observed the farmer, 'it's a good thing, at all events, that you have come to yourself; there's no need for the doctor, and you'll soon be better. When I have finished my load of ropes, I will come back and see if you can get up.'

And so both father and mother went off, and neither had the least guess at what was stirring in the two young hearts. Mary Anne had never been able to forget her tall slender partner, and at many a market and place where men congregate she had turned her dark eyes round in vain; and often, in the midnight, when the wind shook her window, she had started up, thinking, 'Perhaps it's he!' then sadly buried her head in her pillow, and pondered and wondered whether he knew at all who she was, whether she should ever find out who he was, and above all, whether they should ever meet again. She should never forget him, that was certain; and if they were only to meet in the next world, she should recognise him at a glance. And the gloomier the prospect before her, the deeper was his handsome image engraved on her heart; but still she dared not let her parents know the secret she nursed there. If she had admitted that she loved a youth of whom she knew nothing, not even whence he came, nor what his name, they would have said: 'You are a fool, a good-for-nothing. Did one ever hear of a girl taking a fancy to a man to whom she could not even fix a name, nor knew whether he had or had not a penny, nor what sort of folk he came of?'

Therefore she silently hoarded his image in her inmost thoughts, out of sight of all, and no day passed without her thinking, 'Does he still remember me? would he know me again if we met?'

And then with that image she contrasted another, that of an old man of seventy, with thin hair, red eyes, and a snuffy nose. And if any one had been beside her at such times, they might have heard the words: 'I never will or can do it, and if they insist upon it, I shall die.'

Dorngrüt was hardly three miles from the village where the fire was, and stood back from the road. When cloud upon cloud of black smoke rose up to heaven announcing the conflagration of fresh houses, and the bells clamoured more and more wildly for help—according to the beautiful custom of the country, no one who had arms and legs at their disposal could sit inactive at home. Farmers' daughters ran off with their maids, farmers' sons with their servants, and many a worthy grandsire limped away, a bucket in each hand,—buckets being too often forgotten by the thoughtlessness of youth, though so essential at a fire. Accordingly, every one from Dorngrüt, with the exception of the master and mistress, had run off to the flaming village; and Mary Anne had worked valiantly there, but had got separated from her party, and was looking for them, when all at once her secretly-cherished image stood before her; she chided it, and like a ghost it vanished away. She got pressed again into the service elsewhere, could not go and seek this image, had to pass bucket after bucket through her hands, while the ground positively burned under her feet. Twice she tried to make her escape, but was driven back to her post. And when at last the thanksgiving set her free, she could only reach the outmost ring of listeners, had to look out for her party and their engine,—for girls are not fond of passing through the wood alone, and prefer having male companions; in short, she was one of the last to leave the scene of the fire, with a large party, and the escort of the engine.

Very slowly, each relating his heroic deeds, and how without him either the minister would have been burnt, or a woman, or a house, and how, if their particular engine had not been there, no living thing, to say nothing of dwellings, would have been left standing, the party were proceeding through the wood, when suddenly a girl, who had turned a little off the road, shrieked out—

'O Lord, O Lord! a dead man, a dead man!'

The procession halted, girls screamed, young men ran to the spot, lanterns were called for, and timidly

Mary Anne crept behind the rest to where a tall slight youth was lying beneath an oak, his pale face on the green grass, blood streaming down his cheeks, blood staining the ground about.

Mary Anne now made her way nearer, where the lanterns gave a bright light. There he lay whom she had secretly borne in her heart of hearts, found, lost, there he lay—dead! She neither screamed nor fainted, but felt as though an iron hand were pressing her very life out, when some one exclaimed—

'No, he is not dead! he is quite warm, and I think I feel his heart beating.'

'Very well, then,' said the engine-driver, 'let us get off before he comes round, otherwise who knows whether we may not be drawn into the scrape?'

The circle dispersed, the young men were about to mount again, and the engine-driver had just given orders to march, when Mary Anne came forward and said that would never do, that they could never leave him lying there, as they should have to answer for it before God and man.

'Come, come,' said a young fellow, 'we have nothing to do with that; he got here without us, and he may get away without us. No one knows who he is.'

'No, we cannot do so,' insisted she; 'and he is

a respectable farmer's son somewhere up country; I have met him before. If we take ourselves off and he dies, our whole district will be disgraced, not a farthing shall we ever get for any purpose, and if any of our houses take fire, no one will come to help us. Surely you don't want to have it said that our woods are the haunts of murderers?'

Now Mary Anne stood high in the estimation of her neighbours. It was not the first time that she had carried a point, and her words made an impression, for they began to consult how to move the sufferer. Mary Anne gave orders to one of her servants to run home the shortest way he could, and to fetch a cart with straw, and meanwhile the young man could be lifted and carefully held by two on the bench of the engine; and upon being asked where on earth he was to be taken, since he could not even say who he was, she replied that they need not concern themselves about that, he was not the first that she had harboured, and would not be the last. Her two brothers, who were present, raised objections, but were not listened to; and thus it was that Andrew had been brought to Dorngrüt. The farmer had growled not a little over it; but his wife declared she had never yet sent a sick beggar away, and it would indeed be scandalous if a farmer's son were left to die in the wood, for that a farmer's son he was, ay, and one of the most re-

spectable, might be easily known from his shirt,—
she did not know when she had seen one so fine
and white.

So it was that things had come about; and that
Andrew was in Mary Anne's own room, for she had
given orders that he should be carried in there, and
felt that she would not, for all the treasures in the
world, have had him anywhere else, and now her
parents were gone, there he was holding out his
hand, and saying—

'You are no longer angry with me, are you? but
indeed I did not know that it was you.'

'How should one be angry in such a confusion?'
returned Mary Anne; 'a person ready to take
offence must not go to fires.'

'It was very unlucky that the water-cart should
come just then, as if dropped from the skies,' said
Andrew, 'else I should have told you how sorry I
was; afterwards, look for you as I would, I could
not find you. But how in the world did I come
here?'

Upon this Mary Anne related the course of
events, suppressing, however, the prominent part
she had taken in their direction, and then she
asked Andrew to tell her how he came to be all
alone under the oak-tree.

His narrative was more straightforward. He said
that he kept thinking that he might possibly meet

her again, and assure her that he had not recognised her, otherwise he would assuredly not have been so rude and boorish, that it was not his wont to be so, but that things had vexed him, for, arrange the people as he would, the next moment they all got wrong again. He had fancied he heard her voice, and hurried on to make sure, when all at once he felt as though struck down to the centre of the earth, and that it got darker and darker the deeper he fell. After that he knew nothing more, till he fancied he heard the sound of voices, and with great difficulty opened his eyes; but she was standing behind her mother, and he did not rightly see her, till all of a sudden it occurred to him that the girl behind the elder woman might be the one he was looking for, and that thought opened his eyes again, and brought him to himself.

'But how did you know me?' asked Mary Anne.

'How should I not?' returned Andrew. 'I should have known you amongst a thousand; but did you know me?'

'I fancied that it was you,' replied she, 'but I could not be quite sure of it till I saw you recovered. But do you know where you are?' she inquired.

'I must be at Dorngrüt,' said Andrew.

'What makes you think so?'

'Are not you the daughter of the Dorngrüt farmer?'

'Who told you that?'

'The barmaid who waited upon us.'

'So then you knew where I was to be found, and never took the trouble of inquiring how I got home? That was not very polite conduct; and yet you pretend to have remembered me.'

'Do not take that ill, pray; a hundred times and more I thought of coming, but you said nothing about it to me, and I had not time to ask you.'

'Perhaps,' said Mary Anne, 'you were really unable to come, your master would not give you leave.'

Andrew stared, but seeing a roguish smile playing around her lips, he replied: 'You are only joking; you must surely know who I am.'

'How should I know it?' returned she. 'I asked no one, and your name is no more written on your brow than any one else's.'

'Did you never, then, wonder who I was?' inquired Andrew.

'Why, about as much as you wished to see me again,' answered she. 'And whom was I to ask? my father, or our Dobbin? But, joking apart, who are you?'

Upon that the young man told her, and he had no occasion to say more; for who and what the Liebiwyl farmer was, was as well known at Dorngrüt as is the pedigree of one noble family by another. He made no boast of the land, nor the live-stock, nor the wealth they had; he merely praised his brother and sister, his father, his mother,—told how kind they all were to him, how united and loving. The previous evening came full into his mind, the tears stood in his eyes, his heart overflowed in words; and more devoutly than before any minister, with glowing heart and moistened eyes, Mary Anne sat and listened, when in came her mother with the coffee and an omelette, and said she had just made them, and wished to know whether he could take anything.

We have many stories current about the way of exorcising spirits, and getting rid of supernatural appearances, and are told how devout Capuchins have often to be called in for the purpose; but no one takes the trouble to tell us how the heart is to be expelled from the tongue, the soul from the eyes, both driven into a dark hiding-place, a door shut upon them, and that door firmly bolted; and yet there are many who exercise this marvellous influence without ever suspecting it, many mothers, many fathers, who nevertheless chafe and scold at this very closing and locking of the heart that they have effected. But it is curious how often it happens that we know not what we do, and curious too how like hearts are to marmots, which only venture out of their holes, in solitude and freedom, when no wind is stirring, but the sun shines full and warm.

Both became dumb at once, and their hearts crept out of sight. Then Andrew said she must take no more trouble on his account, he wanted nothing, and would set off at once; and Mary Anne asked—

'Do you know who he is? he is the Liebiwyl farmer's son. How often we have heard of them from beggars and others!'

'Indeed! is he?' replied her mother. 'But there is no hurry about leaving; take a cup of coffee first, and eat something. There, girl, you give it him, I have got the pigs to look after, only I was afraid of its boiling over.'

But it was not so much to look after the pigs that she went off, as to tell the farmer who Andrew was, for he kept grumbling about this way of bringing in people without knowing anything of them, and getting talked of, and having a bad name. When, however, he heard who Andrew reported himself, he said—

'If this be true, he comes from a good place; but many a one pretends to be some one he is not, and the sooner he goes off the better pleased shall I be. If old Jacob hears of this, no one knows what he will say. We must be careful, wife; you know how suspicious he is.'

Meanwhile, Mary Anne was waiting upon her

guest; and what made this office still more delectable, was that she had to feed him where he lay, and to hold the cup while he drank; and no one knows how endearing a process this is.

Andrew had indeed protested against eating and drinking, but being ministered to thus was so pleasant and appetizing, that he ate and drank he hardly knew how. To be sure, it was rather difficult to swallow so, but for all that he thought he had never tasted anything so delicious as this food, and that he should like the meal to go on for ever. In short, it was a sweet intimate helping and being helped, such as can happen but seldom, and was therefore all the more prized.

Then back came the mother, and brought in her husband to have a cup of coffee, and all the pleasant intimacy was over and gone. The farmer was monosyllabic; did not even inquire how many cows they kept at Liebiwyl, whether they made cheese, nor how much milk they got in; while Andrew, in the meantime, began to yearn after home and his mother, and to suffer from the suffering which he well knew his absence must occasion his family, as no one knew where he was, and in such cases lies are sure to be spread. Mary Anne tried to comfort him by saying that no great anxiety would be felt about a young fellow of his sort; they often stayed out all night, and no one knew where they were, and he was, she dared say, no better than others. To which he replied that he had never been an hour away without his mother knowing where he was, nor had he ever before been absent from breakfast.

'Well, you are an exact one,' broke in the mother. 'I hardly ever heard of such; it would be a happy thing for us if our boys were like you.'

And she would have proceeded further—mothers delighting in blaming their sons nearly as much as in praising and hearing them praised (blame being, indeed, very often only a bridge to praise),—-but her husband interrupted her, and said—

'If he only knew that the young man could bear it, he would drive him to some place whence he might get home that day.'

'What are you thinking of?' burst in Mary Anne. 'Why, he has only just come to himself, and his head is still as hot as fire,—you may come and feel it if you like.'

And so saying, she laid her hand on Andrew's brow, who knew no longer whether it was hot or cold; but never had he felt any application that he found half so pleasant. He fancied, with that hand on his brow, he could cross the sea to America, and never care to look round.

Mary Anne went on to say that it would be more to the purpose to send some one over with a message; her father must surely see that. She would go and look for a person to set out at once; there were plenty who would be thankful to run, no one knew how far, for sixpence.

'If he chooses to go,' growled her father, who was not inclined to find out how hot Andrew's forehead was, 'why should you oppose him? He must know better than you do what he can bear, and what they will say at home.'

Upon that Mary Anne held her peace, grew red all over, and went out. Andrew understood the farmer's drift, and saw plainly that he was not welcome, but burdensome, and this his pride would not endure. Therefore he said he had already enough to thank them for, and would give no further trouble; he should at all events be able to reach the next village, and there he should be sure to procure a horse for love or money.

The old man said that he would not press him to remain against his inclination; and that if he wanted any one to bear witness in what state he had been found, he should be ready,—for that of course he knew who had knocked him down, and meant to prosecute them.

Andrew answered that he was not quite certain about it; and even if he were, he should not prosecute; a blow more or less was of little consequence, and the money he might get as compensation would not give him half so much satisfaction as the prosecution would bring him in of annoyance, and, moreover, he was in no need of it.

'Every one has his own way of thinking,' said the farmer; 'but where I have a claim, I have a claim, and, for my part, I would never give it up, if it cost me my head, not to say my last farthing.'

Andrew did not reply to this, nor enter into what they thought at home upon these subjects, but began, though still weak and tottering, to prepare for departure, when in came Mary Anne in haste, to say that two men had just driven up and were inquiring for him; but that surely he would not go, now that he had an opportunity of sending a message home.

'Why, he can ride now,' said the farmer; 'and since he insists, 'tis no fault of ours even if he be not fit for it.'

Meanwhile the mother had brought in Christy, who manifested a most hearty delight at seeing Andrew again.

'And just at Dorngrüt, of all places,—that's the most curious part of it,' said he.

'Why should that be curious?' inquired the farmer; 'is not Dorngrüt like any other place?'

'Why, you see—,' returned Christy, embarrassed, and stopped short at a wink from his brother.

Mary Anne opened her eyes wide; she guessed

something was coming which she would gladly have heard; but Andrew, who observed a displeased expression on the farmer's face, and did not want to have his game spoiled by a precipitate move, which often answers very well with young girls, but seldom with their fathers, replied—

'We sold some trees last year. We rent a small wood that stands in the middle of our property, and kept off too much sun, and we were told a good deal of that timber had come to this house.'

Christy looked amazed at hearing this, but was wise enough to hold his peace; and the farmer wondered how they had sold it, calculated what the dealer must have got for his commission, and finally settled that he had been a fool to deal with him, —that when one had horses to draw it, it was better to buy timber standing.

'So it seems to me,' said Andrew; 'and if you need any more, you can come to us direct, without any to-do, and you shall have what you require, and not at an unreasonable price either, for the wood wants further thinning, and we should have no objection to carry a load or two for you, without charging anything; it is only your due.'

It will be seen that Andrew was not devoid of cunning; but neither was the farmer, who did not fall into the trap laid for him, but observed that just at present he had all he wanted, and that there was plenty of time to look about him for the future.

During this conversation, the good woman of the house had brought in spirits and bread and cheese, and insisted on Christy and his companion partaking, and completing their story. Accordingly Hans added the proceedings of the evening before, and how Andrew had persisted in poking his nose into every group they passed, why, he could not think, it was not his way in general; and Christy told how, when they heard of a man having been carried into Dorngrüt, and the account of him tallied with Andrew, he thought he must have given a shout that would make a hole in the sky.

To all this Andrew only lent half an ear; he would fain have spoken a private word or two to Mary Anne, but this was impossible. Her brothers had come in, the room was full of ears and eyes, all on the watch as he saw, and therefore he felt uncomfortable, and proposed setting out.

All were about to leave the house, when Mary Anne said he positively must have fresh bandages put on, which would soon be done; they might all go and prepare, she should not be long; by the time they were ready the bandages would be on. But not a soul stirred, not even Christy, who thought it was no use to wait out of doors; and that if once brought out, the brown horse would never stand still. Therefore the bandages had to be set about in the presence of every one, but they took a good deal of time.

At length all was ready. Andrew lingered on, thanking, inquiring how much he was indebted to them, and begging that they would come to Liebiwyl and receive some return; not indeed that he could ever repay what they had done for him,—but for them he should not have lived till morning. All this was wearisome to the farmer, who hurried out to cut it short, it being no part of his code of manners that his guest should precede him. No sooner was he gone than Andrew felt in his pocket, said he believed he had left his handkerchief in the bedroom, and returned to fetch it, though the mother begged he would not trouble himself, her daughter would bring it, and Mary Anne at once turned back for that purpose, but this did not induce Andrew to stand still.

'Don't give yourself the trouble to look,' he said, 'you don't know where it is.'

And both disappeared, while the brown horse pranced and capered and reared up straight, so as to engage the full attention of the farmer and his wife, till finally Andrew came out, handkerchief in hand, and Mary Anne behind him, but only as far as the threshold, and then vanished before he was in the car, though we do not conceal that this was only hat she might look after him longer from a side-window.

Andrew ought not to have gone away so soon; but he saw how unwelcome he was, and no money could have induced him to remain. He did not know if that was the farmer's way in general, or whether he had some special objection to him individually, though why he could not conceive. However, he could not endure the movement of the car; his head pained him fearfully, so he determined to remain in one of the nearest public-houses (and they stand so thick that there is no need to go far to reach one), and bade Christy drive on at the brown horse's best speed, that his father and mother might be put out of pain.

The joy Christy occasioned when he came within speaking distance may easily be conceived, especially as, at the first sight of him returning alone, deadly terror had filled every heart anew.

When Annie heard where Andrew had been found, and how he had fared, she clasped her hands above her head, and said she must be dear to the Lord God, for He had arranged everything just as she would have had it; true, she was grieved for the poor people whose houses had, as it were, to be burned down for her sake, but she must contribute all the more liberally to make up for it. That, however, the Dorngrüt farmer should not have kept Andrew longer, but actually have seemed glad to be rid of him, she really could not get over. They surely needed not to have been ashamed of him; and granting that he had given trouble, there were those who would be only too glad to make it good. She wanted Christy to tell her whether or no Andrew had contrived to get anything arranged or not. But Christy knew nothing. He had only heard that the farmer's daughter had insisted positively on Andrew being lifted up and taken to her home, and that had amazed every one, for her people were known not to be over-ready to receive guests; but she was so bent upon it there was no turning her. Further he knew nothing, but he owned he too had been made indignant to see how ready they were to get rid of his brother, more particularly when the motion of the car gave him so much pain.

Annie was never weary of inquiring whether the Dorngrüt people had known who they were, how the girl herself behaved, what sort of a looking woman the mother was, what kind of a house and farm they had, and in what order, and whether Andrew had spoken out to the girl, or left things as they were. And the more she heard the more vexed she became, not only with the farmer, but with her boy Christy, who, like a young simpleton, had let the best opportunity escape him, without making any use of it. He was the very person to send to a place if you wanted everything to be embroiled. If she could only have had the least idea where Andrew was, no power on earth should have prevented her going over herself, and she would wager the best cow in the stable that she should not have come thus empty away, and that Andrew would still be lying in that smart room of theirs, with its sofas and its covered chairs, which Christy talked of,—not that she thought much of a place where things were so untidy without and so smart within. In short, Annie was cross and impatient, and if they would have let her, would have set off upon the spot to look after Andrew and the state of affairs. Lizzie offered to go at once, if her mother wished it. She could see to Andrew; and if there was anything to be done at Dorngrüt, it would perhaps be managed better by a young girl, to whom no one need pay any particular attention, than by a woman like her mother, for every one would find out where she came from, and read in her face a hundred yards off that she had something important on her mind.

'Ay, indeed!' said her mother; 'a likely thing that you should be chosen for the purpose; you are not discreet enough for yourself, let alone for others. No; I must go myself and see what is to be done.'

The good woman was in a perfect fever till her husband came in, and said—

'Be quiet about it; if it is to come to pass it will, without our fussing ourselves. It is too late to go to-day, but to-morrow we can drive over and see how the land lies.'

At this postponement Annie got very red; but when she looked into Christian's good-humoured eyes, the flush subsided, she held out her hand to him, and said—

'Thou art right; come in with me, child, and read me a chapter.'

III.

MATERNAL DIPLOMACY.

THAT night Annie could not get to sleep, and two contrary currents of feeling kept contending in her breast. For no one has done with conflicts here below; so long as the heart beats, one must still succeed another; therefore they only are at perfect peace who have passed through death into life eternal. Annie had as yet married none of her children, and she believed herself near her end; and where is the mother who would not fain see one at least, if not all, safely and happily settled before she closes her eyes?

Andrew was her especial darling; his happiness seemed to depend upon the decision of very strange parents, and she kept revolving how best to get round them, and obtain their consent, for she could not but believe that, were the case properly put, all would be well.

Therefore, on this occasion, it was not the sun that waked her, for she was up long before it, getting together cushions and everything she could think of to make Andrew's journey easy, and opening so many doors that everybody in the house awoke in terror lest they should have overslept themselves, as they saw the mother all ready for departure; but they soon found out who it was that had mistaken the time.

Christy betook himself to the stable, Lizzie to the kitchen, and their father sat up in his bed, still sleepy, and rubbing his eyes, when Annie came in with an armful of clothes, which she had taken out of the chest.

'See, father,' she said, 'there are your things. I would get up, if I were you, and then you need not hurry yourself, but you'll be ready when the time comes for starting.'

'Am I to go with you?' inquired he.

'Why, of course,' replied his wife, 'who else should?'

'I thought you and Lizzie were to go,' said Christian. 'What o'clock is it? I don't think it's more than half-past three.'

'What should I do with Lizzie if anything were to happen? and I am afraid of driving alone with the young horse.'

'Take the old one,' said Christian; 'he is quiet as a lamb.'

But Annie said he had been out yesterday, and one must consider animals a little when one could. But the fact is she preferred the Dragoon, as he was called, because he was so handsome that people stood still whenever he came rushing by. She desired the maid to bruise some oats and to take them to the stable, and gave orders that the harness should be made bright, and the horse carefully rubbed down and combed, so that there might not be a particle of dust in his mane, or anywhere, otherwise Andrew would be vexed. The cushions of the car, too, were to be well shaken and brushed, and when at length Annie made her appearance at breakfast, Lizzie burst out laughing, and asked whether her mother was going to a wedding, she was so splendid one dared hardly look at her. And when her father, too, came out, equally imposing, she grew serious, and asked what they really were going to do that they had made themselves look so smart, quite like a bridal pair. And indeed these two elderly people had a noble appearance in their handsome attire, in which there was nothing gaudy, but everything of the very best, and, in Annie's case, of very expensive materials.

The mother answered her questions by a rebuke.

'Will you never learn to be sensible, child, and do you suppose that you are to be the only one to dress out, and whose clothes signify? Believe me, when there's a wedding on hand, people take some notice of a father and mother, and very often they go for far more in the matter than a young gosling like you. Those folk yonder shall know that we too have a home over our heads, and are not quite nobodies. And if Andrew has told them whence he came, and two shabby scarecrows were to make their appearance, one calling himself his father, the other his mother, would they believe him? No, no; they must learn that here too we are people of some consequence, that there is no need to be ashamed of us, and that we are well able to pay, if they are not able to give a night's hospitality to a sick person for nothing!'

'Are you then actually going to Dorngrüt itself?' inquired Lizzie. 'If so, remember what I said on Sunday; I am still in the same mind.'

To which her mother replied that it would depend upon how they found Andrew, and what he wished; but that if they were to go to those people, come what may, they must be well dressed.

'Father, have you money in your purse?'

'Enough, at all events, for to-day,' said Christian, pulling out a handful of small coin, amidst which a few five-franc pieces shone out.

'What are you thinking of?' said Annie; 'would you go from home with no more than that? See, you have got the key: do take a good full pocket-book with you; you can put it in your breast if it's uncomfortable in your breeches pocket, and indeed it will show the better there, even if you don't draw it out; and let me too have a handful. One never knows what may happen, and it does not look well to have to ask one's husband for every farthing, especially in a strange place. The idea of going to such a distance with so little money about one! Formerly it was never thought of. Where I was brought up, no farmer would have dreamt of going out with the plough unless he had at least a hundred dollars in his breast-pocket, and at that time there was still gold to be had; now, one never sees it.'

At length things were fairly under weigh. Christian's pipe was lit, two servants were holding the Dragoon, who comported himself so wildly that Annie began to tremble. Lizzie received her last instructions as to how much butter she was to sell when the butter-man came round; and Christy reminded them that what had been said by him two evenings before remained in force, and that if they could make a satisfactory bargain they were not to think about him.

'Now, then, in God's name,' said Christian; and the Dragoon took a leap forward that sent one servant flying right, the other left, Lizzie giving a scream as though she had been stabbed, and a second when he grazed the gate-post so closely it seemed as though he must upset the car, and then all rushed into the road to watch how he would go on. He went on well enough; when once Christian was firmly seated, a horse had to obey him. Even the Dragoon, though foaming and chafing, found himself compelled to proceed as his master pleased, and not according to his own inclination.

'Who are these coming along at such a rate? They must be well-to-do, to judge from their appearance, more particularly from their horse,' said a stout man in a white cap, to a slender youth who was standing before the inn-door, his hands in his wide coat-pockets.

The young man, instead of replying, went straight up to the car, while the horse neighed loud, and turned his head towards him, and a handsome woman from within exclaimed—

'Why, look! there he is. I declare I never knew such a thing; for God's sake, how are you?'

'Here,' said her companion, 'take the reins, Andrew. This horse is a very devil to pull. I won't drive him again in a hurry; my arm is quite stiff with holding him in.'

'Why did you take him?' remonstrated Andrew. 'He has been long in the stable, and is always frisky; the mare would have gone much more quietly.'

'Your mother would have the Dragoon,' said Christian, getting out with some difficulty, the steps of the car not being very convenient; then lifting down his wife with a strong arm.

It was only when they were safely landed on terra firma that the questions and the wondering fairly began—on their part, as to Andrew's adventures—on his, at his parents' stately aspect. They were soon joined by the landlady, who came out full of excuses for being so untidy that she hardly dared to show herself, and pressed the pair into her best room; and before Andrew, who accompanied the Dragoon to the stable—an attention the latter acknowledged by much neighing and pawing—could rejoin them, they were all on the best terms possible,—the landlady enlarging on her treatment of Andrew's wound, and how, to be sure, he was one in a thousand: so handsome and well-mannered a youth you would hardly find up country or down, and Annie, in return, unable to conceal her anger at the Dorngrüt people having got rid of her son so cavalierly, announcing that it was their intention to go on there to thank them, and settle with them, that they might find out Andrew's parents were not destitute any more than themselves, and, thank God, wanted nothing for nothing.

The landlady applauded her resolve, and owned she should be very glad that the Dorngrüt people should be made thoroughly ashamed. They were the proudest and worst-conditioned set far and wide, yet thought that whatever they did was right. It was only the daughter, who was still at home, who was different from the rest; she did not grudge a little help to the poor, and could speak civilly to folk. The landlady only wondered where they had picked her up, or whether it was possible she could really come of their stock and yet be so unlike them; you don't usually find sweet pears on a crab-tree. Be that as it may, the girl was really a good girl; and if she could do anything to help her to a worthy husband, it would be the greatest delight to her, if only to prevent them compelling her to marry that old clown. It was not only that she was sorry for the girl, but that her parents should sacrifice her and get still richer thereby without any further trouble, that she owned did provoke her uncommonly.

Naturally, Annie eagerly inquired what these prospects of marriage were, and asked Andrew if he had heard of them; but he remained quite composed, and merely said there was nothing in it, people talked a great deal too much these long summer days.

'But, my fine fellow, there is something in it,' insisted the landlady, 'or I should not have mentioned it. And you suspect it yourself, or you would not have clenched your fist and gone on as you did when I told you of it yesterday evening.'

'But what is there, then?' cried Annie impatiently.

'Why, as to what there is,' said the landlady, 'it's one of those old stories which are always getting repeated: they want to make the girl a means of adding new possessions to the old. At Schüliwyl yonder, there is an old fellow, but a rich one, who has had three wives already, and brought them all to the grave. He indulges himself, but no one besides, and his temper is such nobody can live with him. He has heaps of poor relations, however, who would gladly be his heirs, and on that account try to do impossibilities, and for a time work like a horse for him without any wages, and for wretched fare, but at last it ends in their running away; and then he does all he can to injure their characters, and prevent them from getting another place. The devil, people say, would have carried him off long ago, only he wants a pair of such, and can't find another to match; in the meanwhile, he has put it into the old chap's head to marry. And now, what does he do?—Look out for some poor girl to whom his money might be of use? No, thank you; he must needs have the prettiest and the richest to be had in the whole country round. At first she only laughed, and could not believe he was in earnest, and used to amuse herself with him, but now things are changed, for she sees her parents have taken up the idea seriously, and insist upon a marriage; and from that time she has avoided him all she can; but that won't help her, she will not escape him; and when he once gets her, won't she pay for it? But her parents are bent upon it, the old skinflints that they are.'

'But why,' inquired Annie, 'should they be so? Would not a well-to-do young man suit them just as well?'

'My good woman, don't you see through them?' cried the landlady. 'They think there will be no children, and that if the old man lives ten or twenty years the girl's prime will be over, she will be a rich widow, and at length everything will revert to their property. That's their speculation. Now, with a young fellow they could not expect this. In short, it would have been settled long ago, let the girl have protested ever so much, but that there was a hitch about settlements. The old boor says none are wanted; if he dies, his wife can take all he has, for clearly she is more than thirty years younger than he. But the farmer insists upon settlements; he says people can never know, and that if his daughter were to die before her husband, he would get her dower, and her parents would be losers rather than gainers, which they by no means intend. So old a man, he argues, ought to reflect that he is very lucky to get a young wife, and ought to be ready to pay for it. However, the other refuses to tie himself down; and who knows whether he may not be speculating on a fifth wife, and hope, as he has got rid of three already, he may be equally lucky with the fourth?'

The longer the landlady's story, the greater Annie's indignation; she begged to know how far it was to Dorngrüt, and which was the way there. She would see for herself, she said, what such people looked like, whether they had horns on their head, or were outwardly like others.

But Andrew objected to this. He knew that his mother was little skilled in concealing her feelings, and that her anger would be sure to burst out on such an occasion as this; he could imagine all the cutting things that would get said, and if once an open feud arose, good-bye to all hope. No; he had not the hardihood to set everything on one cast, he would rather trust to prudence and discretion, and began to dissuade his mother from her intention, on the plea that they were a long way from home, and that he wanted to get there, that he had thanked them all at Dorngrüt quite sufficiently, and that they should only be disturbing them now, as he knew they were going to cut their hay.

Naturally, the father's instinct led him to take

the son's side, but Annie was more obstinate than usual; and as for the landlady, she held that it could do no harm whatever for the Dorngrüt people to see that there were others as good as themselves.

But Andrew became very earnest, went out of the room, and called his mother after him, while the landlady congratulated Christian upon having such a son, and observed that nothing was wanted now but to find him the right wife.

'Yes, if we only could,' said Christian; 'but when we thought we had, it all comes to nought.'

'Is it not the case, if I may venture to ask,' said the landlady, 'that he has had the Dorngrüt farmer's daughter in his eye? The people who were with the engine gave a strange account of the girl's manner when they found him in the wood, and would have it that it was not the first time they had met.'

'There was a something, but it will come to nothing,' replied Christian. 'Not long ago they danced together, and the girl took the lad's fancy; but now he himself will see that there is nothing to be had in that quarter but worry, and no more want to have anything to say to her than I do.'

'Oh,' said the landlady, 'I would not give up the point so easily as all that; a pretty and rich girl is worth some trouble; as for those who fly into your mouth like flies in summer, they are good for nothing. And if I can do anything to help on matters, without being found out, I will most gladly, both because I like the girl herself, and should have all the pleasure in the world in spiting her parents.'

At length Andrew and his mother returned, and the latter had relinquished her project of going on to Dorngrüt; but one could see it cost her a pang. To think of having taken so much trouble, put on one's best things, brought out so much money, and been half-frightened to death by the Dragoon, all for nothing! She was only supported by the fact of other people, at all events, seeing the display, and what they saw would not, she knew, long remain unknown at Dorngrüt.

Our good pious Annie was a thorough mother, would have relinquished her own salvation—in part, at all events—to further her son's happiness; and when she believed he had been treated contemptuously, could assume an ostentation and pride which else were contrary to her nature. Indeed, every genuine mother resembles a hen, who pecks and flaps at the least appearance of offence to one of her chicks, only, while the hen's anxious care endures but for a few weeks, the mother's never ceases till death closes her eyes,—nay, who knows whether it ceases then? When children are gathered around a dying mother's bed, and her dim eyes turn their rapid glances on each of the weeping band, who that understands their language but can read there all the care and anxiety, the joy and sorrow, that the mother's heart has long experienced about each of them, and is now taking with her into the presence of her Father, and her children's Father, her God and theirs?

In order, therefore, to keep up appearances, Annie now proceeded to do a good deal of shopping. She went out so seldom, she said, that it behoved her to take back something to those at home, and she wondered what sort of coffee they had here. The shop is a still more favourable place than the public-house for free communication between women, and every day there are transactions and treaties carried on there which are far more amusing than the political ones that appear in our newspapers. But just because they are so important, and engage body and soul, no one has time to write them down, and yet they circulate throughout the country, fly from house to house, bring about peace and war, marriages and baptisms, while the printed news has often neither life nor influence, is a mere collection of dead facts, powerless to stir a dog from the hearth.

Annie found things to her wish in the shop; no one was there, so she could look about her, chat, buy, as long as she liked. She took her time, the shopwoman took hers, and the end of it was that she made a number of purchases which she could hardly have carried over to the public-house. And all the time she behaved so pleasantly and simply, and with such an absence of boasting, that the shopwoman was dying to know who she was, yet did not venture to ask her: for this kind of behaviour will ever inspire respect, while those who give themselves airs betray their vulgarity, and every one makes free with them. The shopwoman would not hear of Annie's carrying a single article, promised to bring them all over as soon as she had peeled her potatoes, and kept her promise too, contriving at the same time to extract from the landlady not only who the strangers were, but a few hints about the Dorngrüt matters as well.

No one knew how it came about, but the excellent dinner they had ordered was drawing to an end, the landlord sitting chatting with Christian about oil-cake and bone-dust, the landlady carrying to and fro, Annie saying that it would soon be time to set out, and that Andrew had better see whether the horse had been fed, she could not bear people to be enjoying themselves while their beasts were hungry, and Andrew replying that he was sure the horse had been well cared for, but he would go all the same, since his mother wished it,— no one, we say, knew how it happened, but just as he left the house the Dorngrüt farmer's wife was coming up the street, and Andrew could not help stopping to shake hands with her, and say that he was still there, at which she seemed both shocked and amazed, and inquired how it had happened, and why he had not at once returned to them when he found that driving pained him. She was greatly annoyed, she said, that he should have put up there, —people might think they were not able to afford having him for a few days; had she known how things would turn out, no power on earth would have prevailed on her to let him go away, whatever he had said or done. It was a good thing that she had chanced to come to the village, for now he could return with her if the walk was not too long for him. If only she had known it, she would have brought the conveyance. As to all this about not knowing, did not take in Andrew, the more that the sly face of the shopwoman behind her window caught his eye, and he could not help wondering whether the speaker had come over out of curiosity to see his parents, or because she was really annoyed at his having stayed at the public-house, and wished to have an opportunity of apologizing; however, he did not probe into the case, but behaved with the utmost politeness, as young lovers always should, for to have the mother against them is a most untoward thing.

'My goodness gracious!' exclaimed the landlady,

'if there is not the Dorngrüt farmer's wife speaking to your son!'

'Impossible!' exclaimed Annie. 'Where is she?'

'It's very true; there she is,' pointed out the landlady. 'What can she be wanting to-day in the village; she does not come in three times a year, —not even to church.'

Meantime Annie had risen, straightened her kerchief, and with great delight painted in her face, presented herself to the stranger, and insisted upon her coming in, which she at first refused, but was at heart glad enough to do, that people might see there was nothing wrong, nor chide at them as a brutal inhospitable set.

She was made to sit down and join them over their wine, and all the time she went on telling how Andrew had been brought in seemingly dead, and how she had washed and dressed his wound and brought him to; and how reluctant she had been to let him go, but there was nothing to be done; had he been bound with chains, he would have broken them, she verily believed. These spontaneous excuses disarmed the good-natured Annie. She praised her visitor's skill and kindness, and then she praised Andrew, and said life would have been over for her if she had seen him brought home dead, and great tear-drops ran down her face as she spoke.

'It was exactly the same with her,' said the other, 'though she often thought people must have much quieter lives without children. When they were little, they were about your feet all day, and no end of trouble; and when they were grown up, they went their own way, and one had to work and think one's-self to death to insure their being well off. For she could never bear that a child of hers should be worse off than she herself; people could not get on with less than they had been accustomed to.'

These remarks led the way to her telling what property they possessed, and how her children had been uncommonly fortunate in the matches they had made, for both of them were now richer than she.

Annie replied every now and then by a few sensible words, but did not let herself be betrayed into any counter boasting. In everything there was a marked contrast between the two women, Annie was so bright and clear-sighted, and for an elderly woman still so handsome; she spoke slowly but significantly, all her movements easy and graceful, so that whoever saw her felt respect for her, and wherever she was, in whatever attire, or however occupied, she could not fail to command attention and deference.

The other was got up as smartly as possible, but

there was something incongruous about it all, and nothing about her looked thoroughly clean, or sat well; she made all her clothes look like work-a-day dress, while on Annie everything seemed to become Sunday attire. The hands of the Dorngrüt farmeress were not actually unwashed, but the washing evidently did not go far enough. Her nails were ill cut, and a something untidy peeped out in all directions. Her face was not plain, but pasty and greasy-looking; she spoke very fluently, but there was no pleasure in listening to her, nor could one be sure whether she was to be believed or not. Wherever she was she thought herself bound to show her consequence, and hence provoked others to underrate her; nor when she sat down now, did she seem easy or at home. The more inwardly impressed she was by Annie's appearance and manner, the more inflated she herself became, in order to keep up with her, while the more pretentious she was, the more simple Annie grew, and this simplicity embarrassing her,—the more awkward the farmeress. Strange how very little pretension answers its purpose, nay, how it defeats it.

This by-play amused the landlady not a little; she enjoyed the discomfiture of the mistress of Dorngrüt, and could have watched it for a whole day, but Christian gave the signal for departure.

Annie repeated her thanks, and particularly mentioned their daughter, who had been the means of rescuing Andrew, said she should like to see and thank her herself, and that she should be very glad if they would come over and pay a return visit to Liebiwyl.

'It's not worth while to name it,' was the reply; 'but I should like to come over very well, only one never knows what may happen, and young girls are often very foolish.'

To which Annie made no answer; but asked Christian whether it would not be proper to make a present to the young men who had lifted up Andrew that night.

Christian replied that he had already thought of it, but was glad she reminded him, and, drawing his bulky pocket-book from his breast, took out a handful of coins and gave them to the landlord, begging he would give what he thought proper, and return thanks in his name.

The landlord was quite aghast, said there was no necessity for anything of the kind, and that not one in a hundred would have thought of it; but, at all events, this was over and over again too much,— indeed the half of it would-be so.

However, he took it; and as the farmeress was curious as to how much it was, and probably thought it would be well that others should know the landlord had received such a sum, she stayed on till the car was ready, and after many leave-takings the Dragoon set off at a spanking pace homewards.

As it always happens when people drive off, those who are left behind despatch, not indeed bullets, but remarks after them, kind and genial, or unkind and false, much more according to the source from whence they proceed than the character of the parting guests; for some there are who could not refrain from maligning an angel when he turned his back, even had he brought them ever so great a blessing.

Accordingly, on this occasion, the farmeress and the landlady stood at the door, and the latter fired off a whole volley of praise and glorification: those were people indeed, so polite and friendly to others, not an atom of pride and vanity, and yet something about them so noble and superior. And how rich they must be! the youth had paid in the most liberal way for one night's lodging, and she was afraid to say how much her husband had got; there was no one hereabouts who would have thought of such a thing; their only thought would have been of proceeding against those who had done the mischief. She had asked whether Andrew knew who it was who knocked him down, and did not mean to prosecute, but he said what was over and gone was not worth recalling; that he had to thank God for bringing him through, and that to display revenge, which was hateful to Him, would be a poor way of showing gratitude. This the landlady said had delighted her; but she should like to know how many people would have seen things in the same light. If she had had a daughter, and she had got such a husband as this youth, she should be prouder of him than of a king.

Thus the landlady; and while she was talking she was joined by the shopwoman, who also blew a loud trumpet of commendation as to the way in which Annie had shown her knowledge of what was what, and yet never beat her down in a single thing. It was not her way to overcharge, but had it been, she would not for the whole world have done so in this case; she would on no account stand ill in the estimation of such a woman. People of that stamp had more influence than was supposed; and if one of them said she had been pleased with what she bought at such or such a shop, that the things there were good and sold at a fair price, it got one on more a hundred times than if once in a way one contrived to get double the value of what one sold.

'And so it was with innkeeping,' said the landlady. 'Many a one fancied he might do a smart stroke of business, and overcharge or give bad food now and then, but he would find that from that time nothing would prosper with him; and however he might lower his prices afterwards, people would still go on saying they were cheated, because they had no trust in him. To be discreet is the great thing, and young innkeepers should be careful, for one attempt to overreach might do them an injury that their whole life long could never repair.'

Never before had the mistress of Dorngrüt returned home so heavy laden with matter for thought. She could not help pondering how happy Mary Anne might be with Andrew, and what a contrast he was to the old boor from whom even she would have shrunk in her youth, though she was not half so particular as her daughter. It is true she had often sought to comfort the latter by observing that Father had been still older than her suitor, and that if Father had done for her, Jacob might do for Mary Anne; she did not see why children should fare better than their parents. However, she was conscious that such comfort was not adequate; and would cunningly add, that it was not worth while to object so violently to what would not last long, for one so short-breathed as Jacob would never live to be a hundred. He had, indeed, outlived three wives, but was not likely to outlive four, and then Mary Anne would be provided-for for life, with nothing to do but to eat and drink, and order others about; and if she wanted coffee seven times a day, there would be nothing to prevent it.

Such had been the mother's line of argument; but still at bottom she was one who had some feeling for a child's personal happiness. It often occurred to her that if Mary Anne could become a good and respectable wife, there was no particular reason why she should accept the old man merely for her brother's sake, and to increase the family property. If Jacob still continued so obstinate about the settlement, she really thought the girl had better take the one she preferred, for she plainly saw that her heart was set upon him, else she would not have talked so often about her partner, or known him again so immediately in the wood. Perhaps the one suitor might be used to egg on the other; they must see. But, at all events, she must say Mary Anne would suit his family very well; there was something so stately about her, one often did not know whether one might venture to speak to her or not, and then she was so particular, and would shrink from many a thing that no earthly creature but herself saw any harm in. Such was the train of rather confused thought that went on in the good woman's head; and when she got home she put on a diplomatic expression of face, and imparted to husband and daughter only what diplomacy counselled. To the former she said that those were people the like of whom you would not often find, and that, if the girl herself were the only one to be considered, she could never do better. If old Jacob would not come to the point, she thought it would be well to secure Andrew, but she had not let out a single word, though that cunning puss the landlady had tried hard to lead her on; however, there was no doubt that the young folk liked each other, and if they decided upon anything in that quarter, they had every opportunity, for they had been most pressingly invited over to Liebiwyl.

To her daughter, however, who kept circling round her like a cat around boiling milk, she remarked that those were strange people, to whom she did not take much, people that she hardly knew whether to call genteel or common; they seemed to have very little to boast of, but they had flung about their money as though they had a gold mine at home; she could fancy that they were Baptists, of whom there were many in Emmenthal. Yes, that was no doubt it.

'But, mother, Baptists don't dance, I have often heard,' replied Mary Anne.

'Ah, there you are; you have always got that foolish dance in your head, as though dancing were the chief thing in life. Depend upon it, you'll come to no good if you let your mind run on such trifles; it prevents you thinking about useful things, such as the price of flax this year, the best time for sowing beans, and how to contrive to get married so as to satisfy your father and mother.'

Meanwhile there was not much said in the car by the homeward-driving party—perhaps because their minds were too full to be at once relieved by words, just as sometimes the blackest clouds can neither rain nor hail, however inclined. Annie only expressed her anxiety about Andrew's head, he himself was fully engaged with the Dragoon, and Christian was very sleepy, and had to smoke hard to keep himself in any degree awake.

At home, they were waited for with most eager curiosity by those left behind; the time seemed to pass more slowly than ever before; they were always looking out too soon and wondering what kept the car so late, and what would be brought back in the way of purchases and news; and when at length it appeared, great was the commotion all around the house, out poured welcomes from every hole and corner, even the animals took their part, the sheep bleated, the horses neighed, the dog went wagging round each as they got out, and on the bench beside the door stood the more reserved cat, waiting with arched back for a fitting opportunity to offer her modest attentions. No positive questions were put, but the moment was impatiently desired when, hunger and thirst having been satisfied, and superfluous ears got out of the way, everything might be asked and told.

Although Andrew was very tired, and his head ached sadly, he too waited for the auspicious moment, for he had felt a good deal surprised at the silence of his parents.

Lizzie was dreadfully disappointed that the whole of their story should consist merely in their having seen the mistress of Dorngrüt, and even of her they would say but little, for both father and mother were cautious in their daughter's presence, which she naturally resented.

'It was a pity she had not been there,' she observed; 'things would have got on a little further than that.'

At length she learned that there was not much to be done at present, because there was something going on in another direction, and where there were many thorns, you must look awhile before you thrust your hand in, if you would not get well pricked.

Upon which Lizzie pronounced that they must be horrid people to treat a daughter so; that, for her part, she could not love her father and mother a single moment longer if they proposed such a match as that, such a perfect slaughter and sacrifice; and that she thought the right sort of girl would run away from them as fast as her legs could carry her, at all events that was what she herself would do.

At this Annie sighed, and Christian smoked vehemently.

Andrew's eyes, however, filled with tears. He could see, he said, that they had something on their spirits, and well he knew what it was. Those people did not please them; and although suitable as to position and wealth, they were not sure about their principles. He saw all that, but, alas! there was no having everything in this world; now the fault lay in the girl herself, now in her parents. He himself did not like them either, only he loved the girl so much, and more than ever since he had seen her stand with downcast eyes beside his bed, and had taken her for a spirit; he could not give her up. But she was really quite unlike the rest in everything; it was not he alone who thought so, every one agreed in it. All her ways of thinking and feeling were different, and often one could see that she was ashamed of the others. And then she would be a long way from them, in the course of the year they would not often meet, and once with right-minded people, all the good in her would be able to come out unhindered, which as yet it never had had a chance of doing.

'There is no saying,' said Christian; 'blood is blood, and breeding is breeding; but I will not oppose thee on this account, thou art old enough to judge for thyself, and thy heart is set upon her.'

'Father,' replied Andrew, believe me I too am anxious to do right. I know it concerns my whole life, nay, perhaps it concerns eternity as well, and I have often thought I had better remain single, I should know then where I stood. But this is not God's will for us, and parents too are anxious to see their children settled. But, believe me, I will not enter into this affair blindly, or think all right because my own heart is set on it. Nothing can be done in a hurry, and it will be strange indeed if with time I cannot get to the truth of things; and if I find out that she is in any way inclined to evil, depend upon my giving her up, even if it breaks my heart.'

That night poor Andrew got but little sleep; his heart was so heavy he hardly felt the pain in his head. The very atmosphere at Dorngrüt was displeasing to him; he felt disgusted with their way of thinking and acting, and could hardly help saying, 'God, I thank thee that I am not as they.' With a wife of the Dorngrüt stamp he needs must be unhappy, that he knew; nor could his father and mother ever put up with such. Where a house has had a certain character for generations, and the family a settled way of life, marriage is a far more serious thing than when two meet in the streets and set themselves down in the first cheap lodging they find. And in a respectable farmhouse the difficulties are greater than in a higher rank, for in the latter the household is managed by a regular staff of servants, whereas in the farmhouse it is the wife who rules and gives the tone to everything. Now, Mary Anne seemed qualified to suit: modest, kindly, neat, active, and not unused to give orders. She was obedient to her parents, the dog and cat were fond of her, poultry and pigeons followed her about. All these were good signs, but they were only external; as to her real inner nature, he had not had time to get at it, and he knew well that mere good sense might lead a girl to differ outwardly from the rest of her family, while all the while she was at bottom essentially the same, which fact would only appear after marriage, when, having attained their aim, people let their real character have free play.

Now Andrew's experiences had often shown him into how unlovely and almost monstrous a thing a pretty young wife could develop. If it were to be so in his case! if his parents' grey hairs were to be brought with sorrow to the grave, and he had helplessly to look on! and again his eyes filled with tears. How such a thing should ever come to pass in this particular case, he could not, it is true, conceive, but he resolved to proceed with the greatest caution.

It is, however, a very difficult thing to look

through a smooth white satin skin into the bottom of the heart, and to discover whether deep down there lies the spark of eternal life, or the beginning of corruption, whether dust and ashes or healthy energy are to be our portion. It is not science that can help us here, spectacles are useless, age will not save us from absurd mistakes; indeed, childish eyes see truer, and those see best of all who have eyes like children's, undazzled by the glare or dust of the world.

IV.

THE LOVERS MEET.

WHEN lovers wish to meet unobserved, they must either choose the deepest solitude or the densest crowd; extremes touch here, and the instinct of youth teaches what the experience of age confirms. If a girl wishes to have a good look at her suitor, or a suitor to discuss future happy prospects with the girl of his heart, a busy market-day will suit them as well as a twilight solitude; and they may probably sit in a quiet corner of a full room half the day long without any one noticing them, for when the fiddles are going each has enough to do to look after his own enjoyment, and has no time to watch others.

Now, when Andrew went to look for the handkerchief he had forgotten in his room at Dorngrüt, he had seized that opportunity to make an appointment, but he had chosen not a crowd, but solitude, chiefly because he was not well acquainted with the customs of the family with regard to markets; and to fix as a place of rendezvous with Mary Anne a market which half or all her household attended, would have been dangerous, while to lead her to one to which they were none of them in the habit of going, would have been suspicious, and probably she might not have been allowed to find her way there.

However, he knew a place, retired in situation, where there was a mineral well, celebrated for its virtues, but the inn there was not celebrated, for either the people had nothing at all for you to eat, or made you pay for it in a way that you were likely to remember. Their idea was that their position gave them a right to extra profit, and that if only a hundred guests came, they were to extract as much from them as they could have done from a thousand. But the public did not understand such calculations; and as in general it is more set upon a good inn than a mineral spring, the place was not only solitary through its situation, but through the absence of all company, and he who wanted perfect quiet might find it there Sundays and week-days both.

Now Andrew had whispered day and hour, and the name of this place, into Mary Anne's ear, and she had nodded assent, and this was why he was so confident, and so little wished for the interference of others.

Long had he sat there on the day appointed, and no Mary Anne came along the woody path, or up the steep incline from the plain. Gloomy clouds gathered in the sky, a cold wind swept along, and dark and chill grew Andrew's spirits; anxiety and disappointment strove there, and as it always happens when we have waited long, a hundred causes successively occur to one, each of which is worse than the other, and exasperates us more, till at length, when we are thoroughly out of patience, anger suddenly breaks down into anxiety, all sorts of terrors oppress us, and increase every moment the torment of suspense. Oh, waiting, waiting is a hard thing; to go on waiting in vain is horrible; it is a rack which no law can put down, a mode of torture which never becomes obsolete. But do not let us forget what waiting must be at the gate of heaven, when no porter comes, no key is turned in the lock, no welcome greets us, no loving glance looks through the key-hole, no rustling of wings promises us admittance, but the darkness grows even darker and colder, and we realize that for ever and ever *the door is shut*.

'Did she understand me? Will she come yet? Has she been, and gone? Has she lost her way? Have they prevented her coming? Has she not chosen to come?' These were the questions that Andrew went on putting to himself in his ever-increasing vexation, for all the week long he had pictured to himself how, as he approached the house from one side, he should see Mary Anne coming along by the other, and that they should meet to the very minute before the door. But now he had been there a whole hour, teased with questions as to whether he would bathe and dine; 'he had only to speak in proper time, for in such an out-of-the-way place a dinner could not be got by magic, though people often seemed to suppose they had but to think of a thing, and there it would be.' Andrew at first evaded the question, but at length he ordered dinner, so the waiting-maid brought in plates, saying she would bring the rest as soon as the boy returned with the bread, but the good-for-nothing fellow always loitered so long Andrew would probably have to wait a while, —thus opening a conversation which might either run upon the defects of her mistress and the bad management of the house, or take the turn of a flirtation with the handsome youth, as the case might be. Then the door slowly opened.

'God greet you both,' said a voice, and a young girl entered the room, blushing deeply; while the waiting-maid rose from her seat, and replied—

'God greet you well. What can I do for you?'

Andrew too had turned very red, either out of surprise, or annoyance at the waiting-maid being found sitting so near him, but he jumped up at once and exclaimed—

'Welcome, in God's name, cousin! so you are here. What good luck brings you?'

Mary Anne at once seized the cue, and replied, 'You too are a welcome sight; I was on my way to you, and now I can speak to you here, which is much pleasanter for me, as I shall get home in better time. It is not nice weather to be on the roads, but the matter was pressing.'

'Come away,' said Andrew, 'and tell me about it. I hardly knew who you were at first.'

And really this was not to be wondered at, for Mary Anne was not attired in her best, but rather disguised, wore a thin short petticoat, a serge jacket, coarse linen sleeves, and a horse-hair cap on her head; in short, she was dressed rather as a working girl than a rich farmer's daughter; but for all that she was so really lovely and refined that she showed it is not always the feathers that make the bird.

The waiting-maid said they should have their talk out to their hearts' content. If they liked, she could take them to an up-stairs room, where there were fewer flies, and they were sure to be alone. Not, indeed, that they were likely to be much disturbed here; she had never been in such a place, no one came but the miller and chimney-sweeper,—not even a beggar.

Now, the more disaffected a waiting-maid is with the landlady, as a rule the more gracious she is to guests; and why should she not? After all, hearts yearn to hearts, and if the landlady is too lofty to accept a waiting-maid's sympathies, why should she not devote them to visitors?

The room was very small, the springs of the sofa had given way beneath much sitting, the table wabbled; there was not the least pretence to elegance, and yet it seemed a quite beautiful room to Andrew and Mary Anne, and, as they sat down side by side on the sofa, they felt too happy for words, they had too much to say to know where to begin, till at length Andrew sighed out—

'I thought you would never come, and that I should have to return without anything done.'

'It is a wonder that I am here at all,' said Mary Anne; 'for a long time I did not know how to manage, and thought I should have to give it up.'

'What, did you ever think then of not coming? Could you have had the heart to disappoint me, and let me wait in vain?' cried Andrew.

'Do not be angry,' returned Mary Anne; 'but if it had not been all as quick as lightning, I should have refused at the time.'

'Do you not, then, care for me at all, and have I

deceived myself in fancying your heart was somewhat as mine, and I a little dear to you?'

At that Mary Anne looked at him sadly and tenderly, and the tears came into her eyes; then she slowly replied—

'You do not know how I am situated. It is not my way to go about the country here and there; this is the first time that I have given any one the meeting. Even if I wished it, I should not be allowed. We have always more than enough to do, and my father won't hear of any one's will but his own. And I have long felt that there was no use in my coming, that it could only make my heart still heavier than it is, and that the best thing I could do would be to put the whole thing out of my head and forget that I had ever seen you.'

'That would have been strange conduct,' returned Andrew; 'and after that I should have thought no girl was worth a penny. As to what you say of your father, surely it is not a hopeless case; we can get over that.'

'I fear it is,' sighed Mary Anne. 'But then, on the other hand, I so wanted to see you once more, and to tell you you must not be angry with me because my parents behaved rudely to you, and let you leave when you had hardly come to yourself, and were not fit to move. They were so afraid of old Jacob, whom they want me to marry, hearing anything about it, so afraid too of our getting to like each other, and disturbing their arrangements. For, as I said, whatever my father wills must get done, cost what it may, and however evil the consequences. This made me feel anxious to tell you how it was, that you might not feel angry with me, or plague yourself further about me, for there is nothing to be done. Still, I thought I should like to be with you once more; perhaps we shall never meet again in all our lives.'

'What an idea!' cried Andrew. 'Things won't turn out so bad as that; as yet we have made no serious effort, and I am not so easily to be diverted from a purpose; but first of all I must know whether you care for, and will have me. After that, I should like to see any one force you away from me to marry old Jacob or any one else. But first of all that point must be settled. What do you say?'

'I need not take long to answer that question,' replied Mary Anne. 'If I were not fond of you I should not be here; I would have gone to meet no other man in the world, nor behaved so ill and told such a falsehood for his sake. But if I had let them know at home I was coming to meet you, no power on earth would have induced them to consent, so I pretended that I was going to see a godchild of mine not far from here, to whom I took no present last New-Year's Day. Even so they objected, and said I might wait till the next New-Year came round; and if it had been fine weather for out-door work, I should not have had a chance. As it was, I went and cried to my mother, and told her it was too cruel, that, once married to that old fellow, she knew I should never get out, and yet that now, while I was still at home, a few hours even were grudged me, and I was treated more hardly than any servant-maid. That went to my mother's heart, for she would not be so unkind if it were not for my father, and she does a little know what pity means. So she persuaded my father, and told me to be off and say no more about it, but to do nothing imprudent, or Heaven knew what would happen. And now I am dreadfully anxious all the time, and only wish I were at home again.'

'Then you have no pleasure in being with me?' asked Andrew.

'Oh, do not plague me with such questions,' said the poor girl. 'You do not know what it is to be in constant terror lest some one should see and betray you, or to have to think of the reception one will get on your return. This is the last day of happiness I shall ever know, and even this cannot be happy, because it brings me nearer to what is worse than death. You do not know what it is to feel thus.'

'Well,' said Andrew, 'perhaps I do. At all

events, I have not always been the happiest of mortals ; I too have sometimes felt quite indifferent to everything but what concerned myself, felt that I must weep, let the sun shine ever so brightly. Yes, I can understand it.—So then you have no objection to me, and would consent to marry me if you might have your choice ?'

'Do not speak to me about it,' said she, 'it only makes my heart heavier ; and besides, when I look at you I must always think of old Jacob with his blear eyes, and the very thought sickens me.'

'So then personally I please you better than the old fellow ?' asked Andrew.

'What a question !' cried Mary Anne.

'But if the old man had my person he would suit you ?'

'If I had known that you would take pleasure in tormenting me I should never have come. No indeed, it is not merely old Jacob's appearance that goes so against me. Sometimes I fancy I could put up with everything, if he were not so ill-tempered and every way vicious. Oh, it is fearful to be with one who has everybody's curse, for whom no one prays, and to have one's hands tied as to any possibility of doing good. This frightens me most of all, for I know I can never bear it patiently, but shall get into a passion, and no one knows what I may come to. Your family, on the contrary, have a high character; I should learn good from them, and I know how much I need this. And I can sincerely say that I have had a deeper feeling than personal liking for you, and can't help thinking that if God were as merciful as people say, He would preserve me from falling into the hands of such a fiend as Jacob.'

'Ah,' said Andrew, 'you must preserve yourself, and not look out for miracles. Still, if you are really in earnest, you may perhaps consider that God brought us together that you might cleave to me, and I stand in the breach and do battle for you.'

'What do you mean by earnest? How can I be more earnest than I am?' inquired Mary Anne.

'I mean,' said he, 'earnest as to your own soul, and as to God. I do not suspect you of want of sincerity; but I know I have often found myself bringing God in when it was really myself I cared for, and speaking of my soul's good when it was my body's pleasure I was set upon. All I mean is that if you were really anxious about your salvation you would have laid that before your parents, and if there is a drop of good blood in them they would not have said another word. I don't pretend that we are the best people in the world, and we have had our differences, though, thank God, they have worked themselves away; but at the worst of times,

R

when there was most worry about money, if any one had said that his salvation was at stake no one would have uttered another word.'

'It is not so with us,' said Mary Anne; 'grieved am I to say it, nor would I to any but you. I might urge this plea as long as I liked, I should only be laughed at for my pains, and told I need not trouble myself about anything of the kind; all that was needed was a rich husband and settlements, and the rest was no affair of mine. Money is all they care for, and they treat me as a fisherman does the poor worm he puts on his hook for bait. I am nothing to them; they neither think of my body, soul, life in this world or the next, but merely of money, and they heed my prayers and entreaties just as little as the fisherman does the writhing of the worm at the end of his rod.'

'That's bad,' said Andrew; 'but they must have some religion surely?'

'I suppose so,' replied Mary Anne; 'they have been taught like others, but I am sorry to say I don't see much sign of it. You can't believe how often I tremble beneath our straw thatch, where cursing goes on all day long, and a prayer is seldom heard; where the talk at dinner is such one fancies it might stain the walls, and no creature goes to the Lord's Supper. If it thunders, or at night-time, I am always thinking how easily a spark might fall, and we might all be burnt to death before any one observed the fire, and then where should we go? And if sometimes I do say that we ought to remember that there is One above us, and to behave accordingly, I am told to look at home, and laughed at for being such a fool as to believe what the parson says, and to think all true that is in the Bible. You have no idea how it frightens me to be amongst such, and I have often prayed God to help me to get away, and now He will; but to get where?—to a far worse place.'

'Hush, hush,' said Andrew, 'have a care what you are saying. The Almighty is not to be dictated to; and if we act rightly, what He sends is always good; but then we have to act.'

'God knows I can't help myself,' said Mary Anne; 'but only think how one must feel in such a state of perpetual terror,—misery before one, and every day bringing it nearer, and nowhere a helping hand, and no shelter to fly to. Think if you wanted to be saved, and were thrown still living into Satan's clutches, think how you would feel, and if you would always know what you were saying.'

'If you do feel thus,' said Andrew, 'do not despair, help will come; we are no longer heathens, and I don't suppose Christians can be guilty of more cruel conduct than in the times when men sacrificed to Moloch. I have loved you from the first moment I saw you; but since I have known your people and your home, I own I have often felt uneasy. They seemed to me a rough lot, and set only upon earthly things, and these will not bring peace or make us happy, as I have found out; and I have been afraid you might be of the same way of thinking as the rest of your family. If people do not understand each other on these points, nothing can go well, and if we cannot submit ourselves to God, what chance of submitting to a fellow-creature? And to speak out plainly, I have been afraid of bringing a person into our house who did not understand prayer, or desire to be a Christian, and to labour after peace. I know that a daughter-in-law would have an easy time of it with my parents, but to see them made unhappy by her is a thing I never could stand. But now, keep up your heart, for things will come about, you will see.'

'Alas!' said Mary Anne, 'if I could only live in a house where I need not tremble by night, and had peace by day, I should think myself in heaven, even if there were no great riches there. But be sure it can never be. My father has made up his mind, and when once he has done so there is no turning him. I may struggle and fight it off for a while, but to no purpose; I shall have to give in at last.'

'Hear me,' said Andrew; 'if you will engage yourself to me, and be constant, I shall be very much surprised if anything prevents our marriage, but all depends upon yourself; if you are not steadfast, all is over. If you resolve to be so, give me your hand, and say, " Yes, in God's name."'

Mary Anne grew pale and red alternately, tears streamed down her face; she raised her hand slowly, laid it in Andrew's, then fervently said—' Yes, in God's name,' and fell sobbing on his breast.

Silently Andrew pressed the hand that lay in his grasp, and for a long time neither spoke a word; it seemed as though both were praying, as though an angel were hovering round the betrothed to bear up to heaven what was living and throbbing in the heart of each. Then Andrew took out his watch, and said—

' Keep this as a token. I know none is needed, but I shall like to feel that you have something of mine; and when you hear it beat, think that my heart beats as constantly for you.'

Mary Anne looked at the handsome heavy watch and chain, and replied—

' I should dearly like to have it, but dare not take it; I could not hide it safely, I should be always in terror of my father or mother finding it. But yet I should like to have something from you.'

' What can I give you?' asked Andrew. 'If I had thought of it, I might have brought a ring or a chain, but now I have nothing.'

'I should not dare to take either ring or chain,' said the young girl, 'but give me a piece of money, it matters not what, and I will give you one; no one can find that out, and when we look at them we shall think of each other as well as though they were the handsomest presents in the world.'

The exchange was made, and now the betrothed pair seemed for the first time fully at ease, and able to tell each other every thought of their hearts.

Mary Anne confessed all her experiences that day she drove off with her father, without even having heard who Andrew was. She had danced with many a one before, but never had she felt the same. During the whole time she had seemed to be saying —'He or none;' and when she lost sight of him, it was as though heaven were closed. For a long time she could not laugh, could do nothing but brood and brood, and her mother had often remarked that there was something suspicious about it, but how could she tell her? Go where she would she could nowhere meet him, and every Sunday, as it came round, she used to think—'What if his banns be given out to-day?' every Friday, when she heard the bells ring, she pictured to herself that they might be ringing for his wedding. But since her parents had begun to torment her about old Jacob, she had thought of Andrew more constantly than ever, and she did not believe a night had passed that she had not seen him in her dreams. 'But you,' she suddenly asked,—'you knew who I was?'

At this Andrew coloured, and said she must not be angry with him, and he would tell her exactly how it all happened.

But Mary Anne crimsoned, and she was very nearly angry, saying she would not hear of a love that went on unspoken for a whole year, while one knew very well all the time where a girl was to be found, and yet never took a single measure to get at her.

Andrew had a good deal of trouble to obtain a hearing, and entreated that she would not be so hasty; when she knew all, she would be satisfied. He then went on to relate the state of the family at that time, how when he wanted to speak to his mother she would not listen to him, and so he lost all courage, more especially as he had heard how rich they were at Dorngrüt, and that her father was bent upon rich sons-in-law, inheritors of the whole of their parents' property. Then he dwelt upon it as a remarkable coincidence that as soon as they all became reconciled and happy together, and he had opened his heart to his parents and his brother and sister, and they been all kindness and concurrence, the fire-bell should have rung, and he and Mary Anne been brought together at the burning village. He must believe all this was the result of something higher than chance, and therefore he was full of hope that all would be well, else why should things have dovetailed so singularly?

Mary Anne had some difficulty to reconcile herself to Andrew's having known where she was without finding her out, and declared had she been a young man she could never have acted so. However, now that she understood the case, she would forgive it, but indeed and indeed he must promise to love her dearly, to love her better than anything in the world, as she would love him, else she should never have the courage to stand up for herself. But now she wanted to know how things were to be managed, and what he would do next.

This was a very important point, and required a great deal of consultation. Mary Anne thought there was no time to lose, for old Jacob had been rather more conformable about settlements of late; and if he once came round, her father would be for giving out the banns at once. Therefore, whatever had to be done had better be done quickly. Finally, Andrew determined that the best and most manly course would be his coming at once to Dorngrüt and asking her father for her hand, but then Mary Anne must have courage to stand by him and declare that they were engaged, and that she would have no one else. Mary Anne, on her part, would have better liked Andrew's father to come over, for then she could have kept herself in the background at first,—girls rather preferring to shilly-shally in such matters, much as a cat does with a mouse, which does not, however, suit every man, and many a match gets broken off in consequence. But she foresaw that, according to Andrew's plan, it must come out that they had met on this day, and then she should have nothing but unkind words so long as she remained at home. 'However,' she concluded, 'if it must be so, I will make up my mind to it for love of you, although you have been a whole year without inquiring for me.' Only she foretold it would not answer, and to fail in such a decisive step would be very bad, it would not leave anything to be done afterwards. At all events, he must not get angry, he must remain civil and quiet, let them say what they would, that they might have no pretence to forbid him the house for good and all. She trembled all over already when she thought of it, but he was not to be angry with her, happen what might.

Andrew became more and more fascinated with the young girl the more he saw of her; in spite of her homely attire she was so exquisitely clean and neat, and she had such a pretty little way of speaking, without any affectation, straightforwardly and sincerely. Then her whole manner, her very way of eating, pleased him, and he wondered and wondered how she could come of such a stock. For, as Spaniards are almost all dark-complexioned, and English people fair, as in youth at least every one shows some national characteristic in his face, so human beings have a family type, a family hue, a family atmosphere as it were, and all members of the same house more or less partake of it. But she seemed to have nothing in common with her people, within or without, and at last he was obliged to inquire whether she had been long at home; and then found out that almost all her early days had been spent with a grandmother, a very dear though peculiar woman, of whom she was so fond that when she lost her she wished to die too. She had, she said, been very long before she could at all accustom herself to the ways of her home, and had always thought they were less fond of her than of the others, and that nothing she did pleased them. When her sister left, things got a little better, and her mother would indeed often listen to her, but her father never liked her till now that he could make her profitable to him. Indeed, he had been vexed at her for coming into the world, and never got thoroughly reconciled to it.

Oh, how swiftly a day may run away, and what an infinite difference there is between hours spent in a first undisturbed interview with the girl one loves, or in a long night of pain on a lonely bed.

How tedious time is then, how second after second, like a drop of blood wrung from our tortured frame, drops heavily into the ocean of former seconds, and the hours stretch out in endless perspective like a sandy desert, where there is neither shade nor rest! But how time flies, and morning becomes evening unawares, when for the first time two loving hearts lie open to each other, when eyes read love in mutual eyes, ears are filled with sweetest sounds, and lips drop words of tenderness unchecked!

Thus it was that evening now came suddenly upon Andrew and Mary Anne; and she began to say she must go, and he to plead for a few minutes longer, till at last there was no help for it, they had to part, and, as the song has it, 'parting pains.' This they experienced, and all the more because their next meeting was to be so momentous, possibly so painful. Willingly would Andrew have accompanied his love, but she positively refused him; fields, she said, had eyes, woods had ears, and when there was any mischief to be made, ill-luck would bring people across one that were supposed to be a hundred miles off. They parted therefore at the house-door, after the barmaid had wished them a good journey, and begged them to come again, saying that if they had anything to settle between them in which she could be any way useful, they had but to speak; for Andrew was well aware how a kind word and a bright coin bear fruit a hundredfold in barmaid-nature, and therefore never grudged them.

Mary Anne had a sad and anxious walk home, for when her lover has left her side a girl's heart is given to sink, even when the course of love seems likely to run smooth, still more when abysses yawn and monsters threaten.

Who is there who has not heard of the Devil's Bridge, and of the dark caverns on the other side, and how beyond lies a peaceful lovely district, where the waters flow gently, and the meadows are bright in sunshine and musical with cattle-bells? But one who stands on this side the Devil's Bridge, in a wild valley hemmed in between rocky walls that rise to the sky, with the savage Reuss thundering and foaming at his feet, and the storm raging behind him, he longing the while for the peaceful meadows on the other side, for the even pathway and the soft grass, only he meets no bridge, sees but the abyss and the leaping of the wild torrent, hears but the rushing of the storm while the setting sun sinks behind the rocky wall, and night is added to the gloom of the scene,—such a one, I say, may imagine how Mary Anne felt. She had had a glimpse afforded her of the happy land of wedlock, where the sun of peace shone, the Lord's blessing abode, where words of love made every day sacred, and life a Sabbath of the Lord; but before her feet lay the abyss, and from out the abyss a monster rose and stretched out his arms towards her, and over the abyss there was no bridge, and behind her the driving of the storm. The parental will might have been this bridge; then indeed only one step were needed, and she would stand in the land of Canaan, that goodly land and longed-for. But no, this will was not a bridge, was far rather the storm that drove her to the abyss out of which old Jacob's hateful eyes leered nearer and nearer!

Can there be anything more horrible than parents perverting themselves into evil spirits to urge their children forward in the way of destruction? And what must be the feelings of a child who clearly sees her position, sees both the dark abyss and the holy land, and goes home to parents who with one word might open out to her the glories of the latter, and will not, she knows, speak that word, but are willing to sacrifice her to the Moloch whose arms are stretched out from the abyss. Well may it be imagined how such an unhappy child must feel; and if she weeps her eyes out, who can dare to blame her, or bid her be reconciled to her doom? But that there should be such parents may seem an unheard-of and incomprehensible thing to some, and yet, alas! it is to be witnessed every day.

We still hear, now and then, of dark and ghastly deeds done in heathen lands, and as we hear and shudder, we say, 'Thank God, those times are over with us, and the car of Juggernaut no longer rolls along our roads.' And yet there is heathenism in our very midst, and human sacrifices are still rife, and the horrible, crushing, mutilating car of godlessness rolls daily over prostrate thousands.

It has often been observed that so soon as a human being sets up an idol, he offers to it all he has, and this we see daily illustrated. If a man's gold be his idol, he sacrifices to it life, honour, children. If ambition or rank be the idol, life, money, children, are all remorselessly offered up; and if the latter complain, there is a terrible outcry made over filial ingratitude,—their future was secured, but they would not understand their own good, plainly as it was placed before them. Now this is idolatry, and idolatry ever claims victims.

True, most of these parents shelter themselves under the plea that children do not know what is for their good, and that parents must exercise their judgment in their behalf. No doubt young people will often behave childishly, and when they see a doll with red cheeks and long curls in a shop-window set their hearts upon it, and cry till it is theirs. A refusal may in such a case be judicious, but to force upon them another and an uglier doll instead, is unjust and tyrannical. However, this folly of children and ruthlessness of parents is not to be prevented by any law, and will break out in all states of society. The only remedy for it is Christian wisdom, which knows how to prize every one according to his real worth.

We may therefore easily imagine with how heavy a heart poor Mary Anne proceeded on her way.

V.

FAMILY COUNCILS.

VERY different from Mary Anne's was Andrew's return to his home. He was full of hope and joy; the girl of his heart was won, and in every respect seemed as if made on purpose for him. As he went on his rapid way, his spirits rose and rose, and by the time he reached Liebiwyl he had not a doubt remaining that all would be well, else there would be no justice in heaven and earth, he vowed. It was rather late when he got back, but there was still light in the window; his father he found smoking his pipe on the bench outside the house; indoors, his mother was reading her Bible, Lizzie embroidering a collar, and Christy dozing beside the stove. Although Andrew protested that he wanted nothing to eat, the table was laid in a moment; and while he was at his supper mere commonplace remarks were exchanged as to the weather, the look of the country, promise of fruit, and so on. It was only when Lizzie had cleared everything away, and the whole family party were assembled, that the mother inquired—

'And now, what news? Did she come, and what did she say?'

Upon which Andrew began to relate how he had had to wait a weary while, and how they had pretended to be cousins; and next, all that Mary Anne said to him, and how she was dearer to him than ever, and he was terribly sorry for her, and how they had talked all day without a single creature coming in who could betray them.'

'So then you have had no disappointment,' said his mother. 'I was sadly afraid they would never let her come, or send some one after her.'

'Yes, but think, mother, what it must be for her to go home and to be obliged to conceal all that her heart is full of, more carefully than a rogue conceals his stolen goods. And yet there is nothing in it that she needs to be ashamed of, but rather just what father and mother should be the first to hear; and she dare not tell it, because they think their girl's heart like their granary, into which nothing is to enter without their previous arrangement, while love is a thing that comes in no one knows how, cannot be guarded against, even if one would. I could not help thinking how differently I should fare when I got home. I should be waited for, I knew, and I pictured to myself finding you all exactly as I did: my father on the bench, mother behind her Bible,—and I could hardly wait till I got home to tell you everything I had seen and heard; I felt as if I was being drawn hither with ropes. Oh, you don't know what a delight such a coming home is, and how happily one goes to bed after one has been able to unload one's whole heart.'

'Yes, children, that's how it ought to be,' said Christian; 'and now let us all be careful to keep it so. We must behave like people whose house very nearly caught fire through their heedlessness, but fortunately they were able to put it out, and cannot guard too carefully against a spark for the rest of their lives.'

'Yes,' said Lizzie, 'so it is, that's a very good idea. But I can hardly wait to see the girl, and keep wondering what she can be like, so to have bewitched Andrew. I am not one of the ugliest going, but let me do what I will, I have never carried anybody so completely off their legs as she has him. Those to whom I give a rebuff don't go and hang themselves, and those who ask what portion my father meant to give me, and to whom I say, 'I flatter myself a good prolific ewe, and a set of new shift-sleeves,' go off with themselves and look after me no longer, let me smile ever so sweetly, and open my eyes to their utmost. Neither have I been tempted to hang myself for any of them, nor would I have taken the pains to run a mile after them; I should have grudged shoe-leather. So I can't help wondering what this love is, whether people only fancy they feel it, or whether God has really made some hearts quite different from others, so that they take fire and set on fire in this odd way. I must say such a flaming love as this is a very pretty thing, and would please me too, and that is why I want to know whether one can do anything to insure it, or whether one must be specially created for the purpose.

'You are a foolish Lizzie,' said her mother; 'you mean no harm, but these are not subjects to joke about. Idle jesting leads to no good, and you know nothing of love as yet; it is a mystery that no one can fathom, nor is any one secure against it. I don't believe in love-potions, though there is a man in Soleure who pretends to make awfully good strong ones, and sells them awfully dear too, though he says they do not pay him. But there are certain times when you feel as though some one suddenly threw a stone at you and knocked you down at once—I could tell you a case in point, —and so it must have been too when Andrew met his sweetheart.'

'Mother, what could you tell? Mother, what was it?' said Lizzie; and the rest looked inquiringly.

'Well, child,' said Annie, 'since no one knows how much longer I may have to live, and you may take warning from it, I think I will tell you. When your father was courting me, I only made fun of him at first. I was a merry girl just like Lizzie, and fancied I would have any one rather than him,—would not have him at any price. But once, at a Langnau market, I saw something, and I felt as though some one had thrown a stone at my heart, and from that hour I was a changed creature, and I said to myself, "He or none;" and though I was ashamed of it, and tried to hide and work off the feeling, it was all in vain, and before it had gone on very long we were called in church.'

'Mother, what was it you saw?'

'Well, I will tell you openly,' she replied. 'Such things should not remain concealed; who knows whether they may not be useful to others, and if there is anything I can say I must not put it off. It was market-day in Langnau, and I had been dancing with a rough sort of young man, the farmer Truber's son, and we had gone on in a very wild boisterous way. All at once I fancied some one called me; I looked round, but there was no one speaking. I danced on, the call was repeated, and some one seemed to come outside the window and beckon to me three times. I did not know who it was, only the eyes looked as familiar to me as my own. I forgot young Truber and the dance, and rushed away outside. However, I saw no one, not a creature like the one who had beckoned to me; but behind, in an angle of the house, I saw our daddy there, whose back was turned to me, but I could perceive that he had his handkerchief in his hand. At first I fancied his nose must be bleeding, but no, he was wiping his eyes, and had been weeping. At that moment I felt as though a stone fell on my heart, and from that hour I could not bear any one else, and, as I said, before I could guard against it, my heart had cried out, "He is the only one for thee," and what I went through before he came after me again, and things got settled, no one knows. Day and night I used to see him wiping his eyes, and till we were married not a night passed but the thought awoke me. Therefore, Lizzie, no jesting; you do not know what may happen to you. And think how dreadful to have laughed some one away, and then just as he was leaving to feel the stone fall on the heart, but too late, he will not return, and goes after some one else.'

'I don't know,' said Lizzie, 'if my heart were

weighed down by a stone of a hundredweight, that I should care to run after anybody. Many a one has asked me to give him a meeting, but I never did, at least I never went to any place expressly for his sake.'

Andrew got red, but his mother rapidly interposed—

'You remind me of one who in the middle of summer laughs at those who in winter-time sit by the stove, and wear woollen stockings. It is nowhere written that what suits not one can suit no other. How many appointments are made to meet in a respectable public-house,—and why not, there is nothing improper in it? It is the custom of the country, and a modest girl may safely practise it. And, child, what do you think you would do if we wanted to mate you with an old sinner, if we ridiculed and tormented you, if your father and mother were resolved to sell you, and your brothers were like devils hunting a poor soul, and a fine young fellow loved you and you him, and there was not a corner in the house where you could speak a word in comfort, and yet your heart was full, and you must either accept an appointment or take up with an ugly old boor,—eh, my girl, what would you do then? It's all very well for you to crow now, but think of what I have said, and put yourself a little in Mary Anne's place, and then what would you do, girl, what do you think?'

'Alas, mother, I think nothing, and I should do what you wished me.'

'You are a foolish puss,' said her mother. 'But now, children, go to bed, and thank God that He has enabled us to talk together in love and peace once more, and pray that it may ever be so.'

'Don't be angry with me,' said Lizzie to Andrew; 'but the fact is, I am jealous of the girl whom you love better than you do me, and shall continue so till I find some one that I love better than you. But I should like to see her. I wonder whether she really is such a paragon that there is no one to compare with her; that would be a melancholy thing for the rest of us.'

'Thank God, dear Lizzie, for this,' said her mother, 'that He has given different eyes to each of us, else it would be sad indeed. Now, to me my husband is the best of all men; I nowhere see finer children than my own; and one of these days you will be meeting with somebody in whose eyes you too will seem the prettiest and dearest lass on God's earth.'

Andrew did not wait long before he put his project into execution; but still he had to share the common experience whenever an interval, however short, lies between resolving and carrying out a resolve. The coming to a decision consumes our strength; when the decision is, as it were, born, the bearing energies are exhausted, and a period of lassitude supervenes. One seems to have fallen from a mountain height into a deep valley, and action rises before one like another mountain; there is no leaping from the one peak to the other, we have to gird up our loins for a new effort, a fresh start, which is always trying to human indolence. Critical actions do not indeed very often occur, any more than women bring forth every day; our life is mostly made up of a daily succession of daily habits. But to go a-wooing, especially under unfavourable circumstances, is a very critical action indeed, and even when one has resolved upon it all is not done, and every day that passes between the purpose and its accomplishment increases our inclination to shuffle the latter off to some one else's shoulders.

Andrew regretted a hundred times not having assented to Mary Anne's proposal that he should send his father over, and felt how self-will involves a retributive scourge of a merciless description. Indeed, it is the general custom amongst us that the lover's father should play the wooer to the parents of the bride, should go over and say—

'My lad likes your daughter, I suppose you have nothing much against it, and that it will suit you?'

Or sometimes, in more elaborate fashion, as, for example, that father, who knocked one evening late at the window, begged the old people to look out, and then began—

'It is God's will that my boy and your girl should come together; I have had to make up my mind to it, and so will you, but I should like to ask what dower you mean to give her,—about a thousand pounds, I fancy?'

'I approve the match,' returned the other party, 'but I can't think of giving more than a hundred pounds.'

'You don't mean it?' said the other.

'Indeed I do, not one halfpenny more, and even that is too much.'

'Then,' replied the former, 'it is not God's will that the two should come together; the Lord's purposes are unfathomable, and His ways past finding out. Good-night; no offence, I hope?'

'Quite the reverse,' said the other, and quietly closed the window.

And the reason of this custom of sending the father to woo, lies, first of all, in the wholesome primitive belief that parents should take thought for their children's welfare in every relation of life, and comes down from the good old times when children did not suppose themselves emancipated as soon as weaned, or look down superciliously on their parents as soon as able to blow their own noses. There is an infinite difference between unjust constraint and pious foresight; between parents who only want to pair money-bags, prop up fortunes, and unite title-deeds, and those who deprecate their sons taking wives of the daughters of Moab or Canaan, and desire to see them wedded to virtuous women of their own land. Then, again, there is another reason why, if the father approves the match, he is pleased to undertake the office, and why a mother will often dispute it with him. It affords such a good opportunity to speak well of their children; and blessed are that father and that mother who, on such an occasion, can sincerely testify—'Not once has our child made our hearts to ache; the blessing of God has rested upon us and our family from the beginning till now.'

Both father and mother would gladly have gone to plead Andrew's cause, but he had willed it otherwise, and now he did not like to confess his timidity, and to say plainly—'Father, you go; I dare not.' Therefore he persisted in his first resolve, and went. But, to be sure, what a composing and rehearsing went on in his head till he got to Dorngrüt! Who is there who has not observed this process in a young minister big with his first sermon, or a schoolmaster about to give his first lesson, or a representative concocting his first speech which is to electrify the assembly?

But Andrew conned and rehearsed harder than they all, how he should deliver himself when he got to Dorngrüt; and the nearer he drew to it the more he laboured; but however correctly he got up his speech, when he went over it next he was sure to find the opening sentence had eluded him, or that there was some dreadful entanglement somewhere, till at length he resolved this could not be the proper plan, something else must be thought of, it would never do to be like a boy who could not get his lesson by heart. 'I shall know what to say,' he thought to himself, 'when I see how the wind blows;' and with that he turned aside, and soon found himself seated behind a pint of wine in the public-house to which his parents had come for him.

The landlady had not much comfort to give him. 'True, the girl,' she said, 'was well worth an effort for her own sake, but as to fortune he might easily do better elsewhere, for she would not get much, she was sure, unless the father could be legally compelled to provide for her. But the rumour ran that the banns were to be published next Sunday between her and Jacob, and the poor child's resistance would be all in vain, for what the old father wanted done, must be done, come what would. Still, to try could do no great harm. They could not eat him, but, if she might advise, he would take a present with him. That always answered, and insured some civility of behaviour, even if his suit were rejected. And again, she would advise him not to be soon cowed, otherwise he had better not go there at all; he might depend upon it a high tone would answer best, particularly with the old man. If people were very amiable, he was sure to set them down as mere fools, with whom he might take what liberties he liked.'

Andrew profited by this counsel, bought a sugar-loaf, carried it off, as well as some coffee, and marched on calmly and composedly—as one who has commended his soul to God does into the thick of the battle—to the Dorngrüt farmhouse.

Very soon it stood before him, half old, half new, half grey, half white, nor could he say which part of it pleased him best. Not a creature was visible, no dog barked, no cock crowed; all was still. Such a silent house as this has a mysterious and eerie character about it, one fancies there must be something portentous within, and knows not whence it will break out; and the longer one knocks the more uncomfortable one grows, and the more vague terror there is in one's expectations.

So it was with Andrew; he knocked the first time and waited, knocked again and waited, waited longer, knocked a third time with quick beating heart and strained ear, still the silence of the house continued; but how he did start, to be sure, when suddenly a voice behind him called out—

'What may you want?'

He looked round, but saw no one, and stood petrified with horror, when the same voice repeated—

'What may you want to-day?'

And this time, looking in the direction whence the voice came, he saw a long nose peer out of the bean-stalks in the garden below, and finally the whole face and form of the farmer's wife, who very slowly disentangled herself from the beans around her, and advanced towards him, apparently revolving how she ought to proceed.

Andrew greeted her as politely as he could, but she did not invite him in, merely asked him to take a seat on the bench beside the door. There he gave over his bag into her hands, said that he had been passing by and had thought he would bring a small token of his gratitude for the trouble and expense they had had on his account. The farmer's wife said—

'O dear no, I had never thought of such a thing, it's not at all necessary; pray take it back.'

But Andrew insisted upon it, and soon got her to accept it, though saying all the time—

'Well, if you make a point of it, but there was really no occasion.'

She went in; soon after a cheerful crackling was heard in the kitchen, and when she returned she had quite a friendly expression in her eyes, sweetened as it were by the sugar.

'Andrew must wait awhile,' she declared; 'he should not go away without taking something warm. But really, to go to such an expense, it was quite out of the way.'

Andrew declared himself in no hurry. The farmer's wife sat down beside him and shelled her beans, and as bean after bean fell from her lap into the basket, so word succeeded word, till gradually Andrew got upon the subject of marrying, and said he wanted a wife, if he could find one that suited him; and this he could say, he should not turn out to be a bad fellow towards a wife, or charge his conscience with any unkindness, for though it was easy enough to load a conscience, it was hard to get it unloaded again.

'Indeed!' said she; 'then a wife would have no hard time of it with you?'

'That would she not,' said Andrew; 'and though I won't say that she might not be richer elsewhere, yet, after all, a person can't eat more than enough, or be more than comfortable, and plenty and comfort she would find with us; and as to kind treatment, I trust she could not do better.'

'Ah,' said the farmeress with a sigh, 'it would be

a good thing if it were so everywhere, but riches and happiness are two different things. Many a poor person is as happy, or happier, than many a rich one.'

'Indeed, yes,' said Andrew, 'and I have often felt a deep pity for some women who have plenty of money, but a brute of a husband, and have longed to knock the old fellow over. If I could get such a one as your daughter, I think I should let her have everything she fancied, and would run barefoot over thorns as far as Basle to save her trouble. If it could be brought about, that is what I should like, and so I trust would my parents, who, though they have not seen her, have heard nothing but good of her.'

'I don't suppose you are in earnest,' said the farmer's wife, 'and besides it's too late. Mary Anne has got a lover, and everything is settled, else you would have suited me, and I believe the girl would have had no hard time of it with you.'

'I rejoice,' returned the young man, 'that you do believe this, and, therefore, I hope that you will speak a good word for me. Things can be altered, and I have reason to hope that the girl herself wishes they should.'

'Ay, I know that she is sadly against old Jacob, but it will do her no good, except that he'll use her worse for it afterwards,' said the mother. 'That's what they do, the wretches that they are. If you accept them willingly, they reproach you with having run after them, and if you refuse them at first, and then take them, they make you pay for it, so that one is ready to die in the beginning, but afterward one gets over it. I have gone through it all, and know how it is.'

'For this very reason,' urged Andrew, 'be a true mother to the girl, put some spoke in the old fellow's wheel, you will never repent it as long as you live; I will do all in my power, not only for her, but you.'

'Hear me, my dear,' replied she; 'it's of no use. My husband has a grip like a bailiff's, and what he once holds in it can never be got out again. And he is set on this marriage with old Jacob on account of our boys. That's the only use he seems to make of his girls, to get them well married, and to contrive that their brothers shall inherit after them, and so the property increase, instead of diminishing, and the boys being made poorer by their sisters. And true it is old Jacob is rich, and, if everything happens as expected, our boys may one day profit by it not a little.'

'But,' asked Andrew, 'are the boys alone, then, your children, and should not you care for one as much as the other?'

'How should I know?' was the reply. 'This is

the custom, and one follows the custom. I don't say that I am not sorry for the girl, but what can be done? she must fare like the rest of us, that's what we are in the world for. Otherwise, I should not have at all objected to you. When our old man dies, I could have come to you. He can't go on much longer; he often coughs at night till he turns one's stomach, and for hours together has to sit up in bed. I have not had an over good time with him; if ever I wanted to spend a penny myself, and that not on useless things, which was never my way,—he would wrangle with me half a day, and if the Lord chose to take him I should not regret him, only that then I should be still more badly off. The lads behave now as ill to me as they can, and if once they came into the property, I should fare worse than any dog in the parish. They would take everything, and never give me my portion, and if I laid a complaint against them they would only treat me still more hardly in consequence. One has often seen what becomes of an old woman when people would rather have her under ground than above. And so it has struck me that I might have lived with you when our old man is gone, and had my allowance there; you would have seen to it that I got it all right, and have let me spend as much of it as I wanted—not all, of course, there would be sure to be some left which you might take. I was wonderfully struck with the way in which your mother could buy and order, and felt that, if I could but do the same for one month, I should be content; but never in my life have I been allowed to order, nor ever shall now, God help me! But often and often my heart has been like to break when I thought how many thousand pounds my husband had with me, and took them all as coolly as though they had been as many pence, and how I never had any share in them, but have lived the life of a dog for forty years, for I was still quite young when I had to take him, sadly against my will, for I wanted to remain single a while, and enjoy myself a little. Mary Anne will be better off, for, please God, her old man cannot live forty years, twenty at most must be the end of it, and then she will be finely off; but still, twenty years is a long time, and a cross old fellow is, a horrid thing.'

Meanwhile something warm had been getting ready, midday was drawing on, one began to hear distant voices and barking from the fields. The farmer's wife made Andrew enter, saying he would be a little more out of the way in-doors, and there was no occasion that the servants should see him. Accordingly, he was marshalled into the familiar room where he had lain unconscious and recovered; into Mary Anne's room, the safest in the house, for a young girl's room is seldom intruded on by any whom she does not herself admit there. And about such a young maiden's room, whether large or small, handsomely or meanly furnished, there is ever a mystery, or at least the veil of a mystery; often this veil conceals a sanctuary, and then blessed indeed the hand that lifts it; often, too, just the reverse, and then better would it have been for the hand to wither than to have laid a fatal hold on that veil.

Andrew disregarded the soup that stood on the table, and kept looking in silent devotion around the room—that room which to him was a sacred spot,—when the door opened, and Mary Anne entered. She started at sight of him, changed colour, and, as she silently shook hands, trembled violently.

'Your mother is not ill-inclined towards me,' he said.

'Ay,' said the mother, who hurriedly came in as he spoke. 'Just look at each other, and eat as fast as you can, and then the sooner you go the better. Nothing can come of it, and if the old man heard of it, we should have an awful storm to no purpose.'

'But, mother,' said Mary Anne, 'you cannot surely wish to make me so unhappy; you must have some feeling for me.'

'Hear me, my dear,' said her mother. 'You know as well as I do what your father is, and how little I have to do with anything. And besides, it really is not worth while to make such a fuss about one husband more than another. They are all pretty much alike in the end, some a little better, and some a little worse. There is not much to choose; and if one can't have things one's own way, one does not die of it, you may depend upon that, otherwise there would have been an end of me forty years ago. One gets accustomed to everything. For forty years I have never had my way, therefore I don't expect things to go now as I would have them. I say, once again, if our old man were gone, and he can't be here very long now, I have faith in you that I should do better with you both than elsewhere. But it's no use to want the impossible; and if one can get a good cup of coffee now and then, one learns to put up with much that at first would have made one leap into the air.'

Such was the mother's strain of consolation, but it was of no sort of avail; there must be some congruity between the comfort offered and the nature to be comforted, and often enough people run on without knowing whether their consolations are oil or water poured on the fire.

Accordingly, as we have said, these arguments of

her mother's were quite thrown away upon Mary Anne. And as for Andrew, she saw no necessity for attempting to comfort him; probably she thought that one who had but to hold out his little finger, to be jumped at by so many girls, would not break his heart if he failed to get the first he fancied. All she wished was to get him away. But Andrew was otherwise inclined. He sat beside Mary Anne, and did not get on at all with his food, though the mother kept reminding him that there it was getting cold. Mary Anne, too, made no semblance of going away. Then her mother brought in word that they were all returning to the fields, and what would her father say if he did not find her there? The young girl declared that of late he had been so often cross to her that a little more or less would make no difference; and that she would go on no longer hanging between life and death, that she wondered whether her father could have a right to treat a child in such a way that he might as well kill her outright, and that this she would ascertain once for all.

'You poor fool,' said her mother, 'try it with him if you dare; you will soon see what a father can do.'

'Yes, mother, I will, for I believe it's just courage that's wanting, and that if a girl be but firmly resolved, and does not heed cross words, or even blows, a father cannot compel her to act contrary to her will. And if he uses me too badly, I shall run away, and I know where to.'

At this her poor mother was terribly dismayed, for she herself had long lost all courage, and did not wish to come in for the storm Mary Anne might raise; she, for her part, was afraid of blows, and knew of no refuge where she would be welcome.

Therefore she begged her daughter to go off to the field at once; and told Andrew she felt sure he would rather not occasion any unpleasantness, and that if he took her advice he would be off as soon as he could. He had no great loss, after all, in her daughter. All the property went to the boys, and she knew nothing of housekeeping; such a young fellow as he might do a hundred times better, and if she were he, she would not take any more trouble where there was nothing but vexation to be had. But the poor woman might just as well have spoken to the wall, neither of the lovers paid the least attention to her, and while she was expending her breath in vain they were carrying on a private conversation of their own. At length she got thoroughly angry, and said—

'I tell you, for the last time, to go, and if you won't go, look to yourselves. Whether it be the old man that comes in, or the devil himself, I have no more to do with it. Look out for yourselves.'

VI.

A RAY OF LIGHT.

THE door opened, and in the old man came.

'Lord have mercy upon us, there he is,' cried his wife, and vanished.

'Here's a pretty thing,' said the farmer, but by no means in an angry tone; 'just as the proverb has it, "When the cat's away, the mice play." Have you come across each other again behind a hedge?'

'No,' said Andrew, 'this time I have come of my own accord. My father and mother are getting old, and have long wished me to marry, but until now I have not felt inclined. Now, however, I wish to ask you whether you will give me your daughter. She will not be unhappy with us, nor will she be ill off. We have a property on which we can live, and some capital besides; we are only three, and I am the youngest.'

'Indeed, indeed! well, you don't beat about the bush, at all events; you come to the point pretty quickly, young man; just as if you dropped from the heavens and thought I had nothing to do but to jump at your offer, and say, "Yes, with many thanks for the honour you do us." But that's not my way, and things are not so easily settled as all that. What do you say, girl, shall I say "Yes" at once?'

'I should like it, father,' replied Mary Anne. 'I don't know what I could have against it.'

'Indeed!' said the farmer. 'You don't know, don't you? you have forgotten all that has gone before, I suppose. Why, this seems to me to be already a settled affair, and nothing left me but to speak whatever is laid down for me. Well, well, things are come to a pretty pass now-a-days.'

'No, father,' said Mary Anne, 'nothing of the kind. I am glad that you happened to come in; no one thought of settling anything behind your back. But this I say now, and always will say, Old Jacob I will not take; I cannot marry a brute.'

'Why don't you offer me a cup of coffee?' said the farmer; 'or is it not meant for me?' and he took a seat at the table, adding, 'It's hot weather to-day.'

Then he began to speak of this and that, inquired whether they made cheese at Liebiwyl, and other questions of the kind; in short, put Andrew through a regular examination. At last he inquired—

'Where is your mother all this while? Tell her to bring a bottle of wine; it never tastes better, to my thinking, than after coffee. I have had none to-day; I was in a hurry, something told me I was wanted at home.'

The mother was out of doors, and keeping at a safe distance. She felt exactly like a boy who has put the match to a toy-cannon, and is listening anxiously for the explosion, but meanwhile prudently keeps his face as much out of reach of it as possible.

When Mary Anne came out, the poor woman started, and felt as if summoned to execution; but when she heard the message, she joyfully inquired—

'What! has he given his consent, is the thing settled?'

'He has said nothing about it,' replied her daughter; 'he goes on as if he had never heard of anything of the kind, and talks of cheese, milk, and goats till one is almost wild with impatience. I never can understand my father.'

'Depend upon it,' said her mother, 'he has had a dispute with Jacob. The old foxes! They want to outreach each other, that's what it is. Father likes to have two strings to his bow.'

Upon which she took in the wine, and was amazed to find how peacefully and cheerfully things were going on, the old man conversing with Andrew, not indeed as with an equal, for the farmer was of opinion that earth did not hold his equal, and no old noble could be haughtier than this old boor, who took his stand not merely upon his wealth, but on his sagacity and penetration. A youth like Andrew was naturally, in his estimation, infinitely beneath him, and this he gave him to feel by many innuendos and much contradiction, after the manner of some of our notabilities. Andrew, who was modest, but not in the least subservient, skilfully parried several of his observations, and watched for an opportunity to come to the point, as a cat watches a mouse, but long all in vain. At last the farmer inquired—

'So you are to have the farm?'

'Certainly,' said Andrew; 'and if you give me your daughter, she will have no need to be anxious about ways and means.'

'There are farms in the upper country,' observed the old man, 'that I would not have as a gift; and if there be debt upon them, it must be a wretched hand-to-mouth business. I suppose your affairs are settled, and that you won't have much to part with to the others?'

'Nothing is settled as yet,' said Andrew; 'but they will not deal hardly with me. They are all kind, and wish the farm to be properly kept up. The land is not indeed quite level, but none of it is bad land, and, if it is properly looked after, you'll not find many a farm in the low lands more productive.'

'I have heard to-day,' observed the farmer, 'that a load of timber I thought I had bought is not coming, and I have two or three trees too few. Could I get them from you? The last time I saw you, you said something about selling wood.'

'Oh, we do not exactly sell wood,' replied Andrew, 'but if any one is in want of some, and we can do him a good turn, we never refuse. In our woodhouse there is very probably some timber that may suit you; come over and look for yourself.'

'So you have a store by you ready for sale?' asked the farmer.

'Not exactly that. But if we see a tree on the go in the wood, or elsewhere, or one that is damaging the others, we cut it down in winter, and saw up what will be serviceable as timber. My father thinks it a good plan to have it by us, and then, if wanted, there it is ready; there is nothing he dislikes so much as having to scour the whole country to get a thing.'

'Well, if you think you have timber by you which is good and well-seasoned, it is possible I may come over next week, if a horse is to be spared.'

'I am sure we have,' replied Andrew, 'and as much as you will want. But now, may I ask about your daughter,—will you agree to my offer?'

'Why,' said the farmer, 'there is no great hurry about that; we have plenty of time for discussion, and we are not so tired of the girl as to be anxious to get rid of her at once. We can talk of the matter another time, and if I come over next week one thing may lead to another.'

And further than this Andrew could not bring him, despite the most diplomatic expedients; nor, when he observed that the sun was getting low, and he must be off, was he given any reason to believe that he might remain the night, all that was said was that the days were long, and the moon would be up about ten. So he had perforce to leave; but before he went he earnestly entreated that the farmer would not fail to come over the following week, and bring both wife and daughter with him, they had never yet been to Liebiwyl.

The farmer's opinion, however, was that there was no occasion for womankind to see the whole world, and that if he were to drive them everywhere he went himself he should have overmuch to do; anyhow, he was too old to begin the plan. More he would not say, or let any one say; he gave neither time nor space for a single word or sign behind his back, but accompanied Andrew into the road, and kept such a sharp look-out over house and road that not a mouse could have done anything unobserved, let alone a young damsel. When he was thoroughly convinced that Andrew was really safely off, without attempting any further approximation, he went back to the house and took the women sharply to task about his coming there at all, and his reception as though already an accepted suitor. His wife pleaded perfect innocence. She showed the sugar-loaf (the coffee she kept to herself), and said he had brought that as a present, in return for her nursing of him, and that she had been obliged to ask him in and set something warm before him, according to universal custom, but had thought of nothing further. But Mary Anne had come in, and then they had gone on like two fools; she had often told her to go away, and that no good would come of it—the girl herself would tell him that,—but she could not get her to stir.

Mary Anne did not try to make out half so good a case. She openly admitted that she had told Andrew she should never say him 'No;' he had only to obtain her father's consent; but as to old Jacob, come what might, she would not have him,—rather would she let herself be roasted like coffee-berries.

'That remains to be proved,' said her father.

And not one word more; nor did he storm at her, which amazed her exceedingly; but the mystery was solved on the morrow by her mother telling her how old Jacob had angered him, and he was bent upon angering Jacob in return.

The old suitor had, it appeared, consented to settle his fortune on Mary Anne, and had been persuaded to appoint a meeting with the Dorngrüt farmer on market-day, at a given public-house, in order there to draw out the contract, so that the banns might be published at once. Now, Jacob had never made his appearance, but had sent over an idle scoundrel, a kind of rich man's hanger-on, such as is everywhere to be found, and asks nothing better but to cheat and mislead farmers. And with this fellow the master of Dorngrüt was expected to come to a final understanding, nay, the rogue had even presumed to hint that there was no such great hurry about the settlements after all, and that, if he liked, he might have the banns published in the first instance. At this her father had flown into a passion, and asked the fellow whether he supposed he had to do with a schoolboy who did not know that this was a mere trick and attempt to take him in. But he had only to tell Jacob that the whole thing was at an end, and that he was not to suppose he could make a fool of the Dorngrüt farmer. According to what the go-between said, old Jacob had a pain in his back and could not bear the drive; but her father would listen to nothing, went off in a huff, saying he had had enough of delay, and there were better matches for his daughter than an old sinner like Jacob. 'Just then,' her mother went on, 'he heard a whisper from one of our lads of Andrew's being at our place, and thought nothing could have happened more opportunely to aggravate old Jacob, and therefore it was that he did not storm,—on the contrary, was quite pleased to find him. And, who knows, things might yet turn out well, if only our daddy were soon to be taken before Jacob comes round; if not, he will be over here and giving the wheel another turn. Or, indeed, father may have changed his mind, but that I do not think; he loves money dearly, but tyrannizing still more, only, if any one tries to be cleverer than he, and to overreach him, that makes him so angry he forgets money, and will fly off in quite a new direction. He is a curious one is our daddy.'

Such was the substance of the mother's narrative, to the opening part of which Mary Anne had listened with delight; a stone seemed lifted away from her heart, and heaven opened above her head, but before it ended the stone was slowly lowered, and the sky darkened, and the old misery wrapped her round and round. Imagine the situation of one who has ventured far out at low water on a rocky promontory, and now finds himself surrounded by the rising tide, all hope of retracing his steps cut off; he has to wait, to look out over the boundless sea, to watch the waves foam and rise, to feel them playing round his feet, ever higher and higher; and he knows not how high they may come, knows not the state of the tide, is at the mercy of the winds and the moon, on both of which it depends, whether in a few hours he shall be able to walk safe and sound to the mainland, or be washed ashore as a corpse by the remorseless water. So is it with a young girl who sees a paradise before her, yet dare not stir a foot or venture in, has to wait she knows not how long, six days, six weeks perhaps; and whether deliverance or perdition is to be the result depends not on wind or moon, or the mercy of Him who rules them both, but on the caprice of two old birds of prey, two rude gamblers who are reckless of human happiness and affection, are only anxious to win their game, and will stake whatever comes in their way upon their cards.

Those who know the nature of such men may easily imagine how Mary Anne felt. Just now her happiness suited her father, because he could vex Jacob thereby; but let old Jacob come over in submissive mood, and lay all the blame upon his aching back and his agent, peace would be restored she knew, and she sacrificed to the reconciliation of the old sinners. And if her father did go over to Liebiwyl as he had said, he was quite capable, she knew, of leaving them in utter uncertainty as to his plans till he had made a good bargain about the timber, and then coolly bidding them give themselves no trouble about the affair, it did not suit him. Whenever a knock came to the door, she started; if a car passed, she trembled till she had ascertained that old Jacob was not seated in it; nor, when her father went out, had she a moment's peace till she discovered where he had been, and in what mood he had returned.

However, one day succeeded the other without bringing any change of mind either to old Jacob or her father; but now Sunday was come, and whether the farmer would go off driving, or, if he did, whither he would drive, no one knew. There were no family consultations held in this house, as in many others; here it was all unmitigated despotism. The father intended his sons to be rich, and took means accordingly, but he was sole commander, and no one dared to interfere with his rule; and if he ever suspected a son of courage enough to raise his head and betray a will of his own, that head got such a rap that it was glad to duck under again. He taught his sons farming, and buying and selling, but if he fancied they were beginning to find out that they knew nearly as much of both as their father, he was capable of selling a horse they had purchased much under its value, in order to mortify them. This was his mode of government; and if any one ventured to inquire his intentions, he either gave no answer at all, or misled them by a false one. Only occasionally he would let out a thing or two to his wife, provided she kept herself in the background, and were very silent and deferential. If, however, she came forward or showed curiosity, he would soon tell her that no one would ever think of letting such an idiot as she was into anything unless they wanted it to be known in the streets, and bid her go and feed the sow, which was all women were fit for, and the less they poked their nose into anything higher the better.

But, however, there is no man who has not certain hours in which he relaxes, finds it a relief to take off his periwig, to be what he is, and to talk of what he happens to be thinking of, nor are there many like Louis the Fourteenth, who was never revealed in his natural condition, but always bewigged, even to his valet-de-chambre. Accordingly, the farmer would sometimes condescend to expound himself a little to his wife, and then, if she very much applauded and admired him, she had perhaps a few favoured hours in which she might persuade herself that they were on friendly terms. But she had to keep this persuasion to herself, else she got a smart rap over the knuckles to let her know her husband chose her to be his servant, not his friend. What she discovered in these unguarded hours she would often tell Mary Anne, who was discreet, and would not betray her, but her sons never heard a word of it, for they showed a sovereign contempt for their womankind, and gave them plainly to understand, on every occasion, who their future rulers were to be.

It was not often that the farmer went out at all on a Sunday, unless business led him to take a drive either to look after wood, or a cow, or some other secular purpose. Sunday was his day for going over his accounts, and in the afternoon some one generally came over, also on business, to see him, either the butcher, or the tax-gatherer, or a neighbour who wanted shrewd advice or a loan of money.

On this particular Sunday he followed his usual custom, and Mary Anne's only terror was lest old Jacob should drive over; but, at all events, she knew what was going on, and had, so to speak, her father under her eye. But what was her consternation when, as soon as dinner was over, he put on his Sunday clothes, had his hat brushed, and set off without telling whither, only it was in the direction of a public-house that old Jacob was well known to frequent on Sundays, and which lay between his village of Schüliwyl and the nearest village to Dorngrüt.

Mary Anne felt herself irresistibly impelled to follow her father, but before she could get ready he was out of sight; however, she determined to go after him. She felt so miserable, she told her mother she thought she must have a breath of air.

'Very well, go,' said the latter; 'but mind that you are back in time to get things ready for your father. There is no longer any trusting the maids, whatever one may tell them; if they see the point of a young fellow's shoe behind seven hedges, there is no getting them home for any sake.'

Mary Anne took the direction in which her father had gone, but not a trace of him could she find. There were roads diverging in several directions. She did not choose; she only went straight on, and soon saw before her the village in which their parish church stood; and now all of a sudden she was perplexed as to what reason she should give inquirers for being there. If she had said she wanted to take a walk, she would have been stared at like a hornless bull or earless pig; and up to the present time respectable country girls would be ashamed of saying they were taking a walk without a purpose. They are to be met, indeed, but they have some errand to the shoemaker, or they want to see how their flax or their hemp has turned out, or some other practical reason of the kind.

All at once the bells began to ring for the catechising, and the sound came soothingly and comfortingly to her heavy heart, like the oil flowing down Aaron's head, and whispered of peace, and before her a shelter seemed to open wide. Yes, she thought to herself, she would go to the catechising once more. She had never been since she got permission to attend the Lord's Table. It is not the fashion for farmers' daughters to attend the catechising. There is nothing to be done there in the way of match-making; no one to be met; and they would but get laughed at for going. It is only poor girls, and sometimes, too, a thoughtful youth or two, who are found there. Those who are solitary in the world, and to whom the church seems a home, feel a yearning for the teacher who opens out to them a higher sphere of thought; whose words show that he has a heart for their wants and sorrows, that he pities and sympathizes, and would exert all his energies to rescue them from the misery and penalty of sin. Such as these rejoice to hear the old, yet ever new teaching; and when they feel that the ground rocks beneath their feet, and the waves of the world threaten to sweep them away, they turn their eyes to the faithful pastor, and think, if he knew it, what would he say? Such as these need no pretence for attending the catechising.

Mary Anne, too, had always felt drawn to the minister; he seemed to her kinder and better than any one in the world. While she was under the usual course of instruction by him, no power on earth could have prevented her regular attendance; and when it was over it left such a blank, she felt as though she had lost some one by death, and that some one the dearest she had; and often since then she had said to her mother, 'I think I will go to the catechising,' but her mother had replied, 'What can you be dreaming of, you simpleton? I should think you must have had enough of catechising by this time. No creature thinks of going there; the neighbours would all laugh at you.' And the poor girl had allowed herself to be dissuaded. Thus it is that many parents keep back their children not only from God's house, but from God himself. Oh, ye unwise ones, when these children bring your grey hairs with sorrow to the grave, how will you rue your folly, and cry to God? but between you and Him will stand your ruined children, those children whose souls you have helped to destroy.

But now Mary Anne felt she would like to go in

once more, and at the same moment it occurred to her that if asked what took her, she could tell inquirers that a young lad on their farm was there, and she wanted to know how he got on in his catechism, and whether the pastor would give him a confirmation-ticket or not. Having hit upon this justification of her conduct, the young girl moderated her pace, and walked composedly into the village, as beseemed the daughter of so considerable a farmer, trying indeed to reach the church as much unobserved as possible, but when questioned, assigning the good reason above given, which generally led to the remonstrance, 'Dear, what does it signify? just let them settle it between them; whether you go or not, it will only be a matter of chance, or of the humour the pastor happens to be in. Come along with us; one only falls asleep in church, and they are dancing at the public-house.'

When Mary Anne entered the church, the bells were over, the pastor had given out the psalm, the organ was already playing, and the children looked round at her with such wondering eyes that she grew quite red, and half regretted having come.

While the organ was going on, her thoughts followed her father, pictured his meeting with old Jacob, and their reconciliation. Then she looked at the steps before the font, and thought how fearful it would be to kneel there beside one so decrepid in frame and hardened in sin, and to be sold to him, soul and body, as still happens amongst Christians, and oftener in the higher ranks of society than any other. The hateful figure of her aged suitor grew clearer and clearer before her mind's eye, till she actually *saw* him kneeling there, saw him by her side, saw the pastor read on and on, and came nearer and nearer to the place where she would have to say 'Yes,' and her heart grew more oppressed each moment, till at length she felt she must choke, or cry out for all the church to hear, 'No, no; to all eternity, no.' All at once the organ stopped, but she only recovered gradually from her distress. Her bodice, her collar, all that she wore seemed too tight for her; for when any one's heart is thus straitened and oppressed, no dress can be roomy enough; nay, even God's wide world is all too narrow. But, on the other hand, when the pressure is only exercised by outer circumstances, there may still be peace and freedom in the heart, if only that heart be right with God.

And now the pastor began to speak, and say how changeable was everything in this world of ours,— the temper of the sky, as well as the condition of the earth; how rain followed on sunshine, winter on summer, bad years on good, and tribulation on joy. But this alternation was neither accidental nor evil; on the contrary, it came from God's fatherly hand. This, however, was an important truth, and one it behoved us to remember, that whatever the changes without, there should be no such fluctuation in the human soul. Man should raise himself above changes to a permanent immutable being. He should be like, not to the ever-shifting world, but to his Father in heaven, with whom is no variableness neither shadow of turning. But in order to be so, he must know certainly, and bear in mind continually, that he is a child beneath a Father's eye, a Father who numbers each hair on His children's heads, and lets none fall without His pleasure; who gives every good thing, and appoints every chastisement. So only shall man be able to retain a filial spirit, thankful to his Father in prosperous days, patient and resigned in evil, humble and calm as to the future, because sure that all things work together for good to them that love God. But if a human being fail to keep his eyes thus firmly and steadfastly fixed on God, he becomes affected by the instability of the world, and changes colour with every outer change, as the lives of so many evidence too well,—lives in which we may see arrogance alternate with abjectness, pride with meanness, vain display with apathy, frivolity with gloom. We had only to look into our homes to find that where God is forgotten, where in prosperity He is not praised, arrogance and presumption too surely dwell; self is idolized, others are despised. But let the least contrariety occur, and see how these people rage and fret; let real trial come, and see how they despair; how constantly, in short, their peace is disturbed,—in prosperity by haughtiness, in misfortune by pusillanimity, in their youth by vanity, in their age by discontent. They complain ever more and more of the world, and with good cause, for the more power over us we allow to the world, the harder master does it become. We are like fading leaves in the storm, never knowing when the foot will pass that shall tread us down, or the wave that shall sweep us away. If we had overcome the world, and united our lives to God, all these complaints would cease, the world would be once more a paradise. Yes, many a lowly cottage, on which God's eye is felt to rest, becomes a peaceful and precious sanctuary; while many a stately dwelling holds only misery,—regret and gloom are there, for God's love never shines into it, nor do any remember that God's eye keeps guard above them. In care and anxiety, vexation and complaint, strife and wrangling, envy and discontent, they tread their way to the grave. Misery was their portion here below; what will become of them above? And yet God's saving hand was near to them also, but they would not open their eyes; would, if they could, have stoned all those who sought to open them. But you, my children, oh never never forget that it is your Heavenly Father, and not blind chance, that rules over you. Whatever comes, comes from His hand; therefore practise thankfulness and humility, patience and trust in your faithful God and Father who is in heaven.

Thus the pastor tenderly instructed the young ones before him, in alternate question and answer. It was all very familiar to Mary Anne, for she had often and often heard it in substance, if not in these very words,—though indeed even many of the actual words surged up from that wondrous secret chamber of the consciousness, where lies so much we deem forgotten, to revive in some future crisis of our lives. The old days, too, returned, in which, as a merry, thoughtless girl, she had listened to all the pastor said with great reverence, while attaching no particular meaning to it; had held his words, as it were, as pearls and jewels, delightful to contemplate, but to be respectfully laid by, there being no immediate use for them. So, indeed, it generally is. Teaching is like seed, which must lie for a season dormant, buried out of sight, before it springs up by its own inherent energy. What shoots up suddenly, suddenly dies down. It is life that must brood over, and, as it were, vivify God's words within the heart of man. At first Mary Anne felt as though the merry former days had returned, but she did not feel this long. The words had a different sound now; they no longer glided smoothly into her heart. They shook it as they fell into its deeper recesses; they woke solemn echoes there. *Life* gave them a meaning; life bore witness to their truth; life woke up from slumber what had long lain forgotten. Yes, her home was indeed dark and drear, for it lacked God; none blessed Him in prosperity, none inquired His will; selfishness prevailed; and therefore was there such discomfort and disunion. This Mary Anne had long felt, but never so clearly as now; nor had she ever discovered how, in spite of her own sense of its wretchedness, she too was in bondage to the evil influences of her home. God was not her comfort; she did not look for peace in prayer; her faith had little power over her moods; she was not in the habit of discerning the Divine will in outer events; in short, her life was essentially godless, even though she was neither unbelieving nor vicious.

Was not she in her sorrows and distresses a mere leaf in the wind? had she not felt herself dependent on chance and caprice, forgetful that she too was God's child, and safe in His hand, and that a firm purpose undertaken in His name, and with His blessing, was the best weapon against chronic anxiety?

When the last psalm had been sung, and the blessing given, and the sacristan had opened the door, Mary Anne reluctantly went out of the cool peaceful church into the hot and dusty road ; she felt, as it were, the germ of a better life within her, and would fain have spent the holy moments in the holy place. But she had to leave with the rest, and found herself in the village without knowing where she meant to go next. That, however, was soon decided for her. First, the shopwoman called her in, then out came the landlady, and said the fiddlers were already there, and the dancing just going to begin. Thus the world surrounded the young girl at once, and sucked her in. She did not know where else to go, she had no excuse to give, nay, who could say ? the landlady might even know something of importance to her. But she was grave and silent : the world did not penetrate below the surface ; the wine could not drown, the fiddler could not overpower the thoughts within. She did not care to join the dancers ; and as soon as the landlady had had a few words with her, and exhorted her to remain firm—a better husband than Andrew would never be found ; and she knew things of old Jacob which, could they be told, would make a living toad, nay, a dead one, seem a more desirable partner than such an old Moloch,— Mary Anne paid for what she had had, and went her way, the pastor's words prevailing over the fiddling and dancing.

More and more firmly she resolved to resist this marriage with old Jacob, should the project be ever revived. After all, there was no necessity: there could be no actual constraint; she was not to do it to help her parents, but merely to increase the property of brothers who had already enough. If they would not let her have Andrew, so be it; she would even submit to that; and yet she yearned more than ever after a home where there was peace and contentment, of which God was the Sun and Sovereign, where the day began and ended with Him. There she thought she should indeed be happy and safe, should be prayerful and obedient all her days, never give a cross answer, never make a sour face any more; and the loveliest pictures rose before her fancy of how she should behave and manage, how faithful a wife, and how good a daughter she would prove,—loving her husband, beloved by him, and in good repute and favour with all around.

Thus Heaven and Earth seemed both to stand before her, and both were one; and wrapped in thought she walked slowly on, till a loud savage barking woke her out of her dream. It was her great brown dog, who had a trick of flying out after all passers-by. Alas! how many heavens there are from which a cur's bark, or even the mewing of a simple cat, suffices to expel us! Mary Anne stood still, and looked at her house, computed all that was within, and came to the conclusion that being well off does not depend upon corn-stacks or haystacks, manure heaps or money-bags, and that she should not care if they were all burnt up together. And yet that this should be her home was God's will, like the rest; and had she been a beggar's daughter, ragged and dirty, would she ever have seen Andrew? Ought she to murmur, then, and be so thankless? No indeed; she was bound to acknowledge the blessings she had. She would give up Andrew, if need were; but she would not accept Jacob, come what might. She was not born to be a sacrifice to her brothers; that God willed this was nowhere written.

The sun set, and Mary Anne went home tolerably self-possessed, whatever news her father might bring in with him; for it is only so long as we are irresolute that our anguish of terror endures; when once we have taken our resolve, or even only believe ourselves to have taken it, things look quite different.

The great dog came forward to greet her, wagging his stump of a tail as much as he could, for though a savage creature he was not without gratitude. There was perfect stillness round the house, except that the ducks were quacking about the dunghill, and the sheep bleated behind the railings, but the maids were, as her mother had rightly surmised, still absent. The pigs grunted loudly as Mary Anne passed them, for they knew very well who it was, and when she entered the house her mother groaned in the back room, disturbed out of her dream by the grating sound made by the door (everything grated at Dorngrüt).

'Is it you?' she cried, settling her cap straight on her head; 'what o'clock is it? It must be time to set the fire on, go and be sharp about it; the sow's supper has got to be seen to, and ours too, and as for those that are not back in time let them go without.'

Mary Anne, a faithful adjutant, although without a gay uniform, went and fed the pigs in her mother's stead, when, just as she was about to clean their trough, her father came by, opened the door where she was; and how the poor girl's heart beat while he contemplated his swine—not indeed on their account, but on old Jacob's,—is only to be duly conceived by one who is waiting for a sentence of death from the paternal lips!

'They are not doing badly,' he said; 'we shall be able to sell two early in the autumn to the Burgdorf butcher for a good round sum, and if we fatten up the others till Candlemas they will weigh each about seventy or eighty pounds; and if you like to go with me to-morrow up yonder to Liebiwyl, mind that you are ready by five o'clock.'

One often hears people talk of feeling as though they had been shot, but really no expression can adequately convey Mary Anne's sensations. She did not know whether she was standing on her head or her heels, or flying through the air with the pig-trough, and before she could collect herself to reply, her father had gone off to feed the horses, growling over the good-for-nothingness of the young folk, who had not had enough of dancing and drinking, or returned home, though it was six o'clock. He did not consider that they had all calculated upon his returning later, as indeed he had done himself, and were mistaken, as he had been. He had gone off to meet old Jacob, accidentally as it were, and meet him he did, but not in the mood he hoped for. The old fellow took things very coolly, was neither startled nor angry—hardly indeed noticed the farmer when he entered,—merely observed casually as he passed him that he had been prevented coming the week before, he had had a touch of pain in his back; but perhaps next week, if he found time, would do; to which the farmer merely replied, that he could not say how things might go; could make no promise; unforeseen hindrances would often arise; and then he too began to discuss indifferent subjects. As soon as he had finished his wine he set off homewards, refusing all entreaties to remain longer. He had something to look after, he said, and if one's heart were set upon a matter, one had best see to it in time; many a good thing had been lost by waiting, and afterwards regretted to no purpose. These words struck old Jacob, who revolved the speech a good deal, and thought to himself, 'Is that a hint or a rebuff?' At length he decided that it was only said to urge him on, which was mistaken policy; when cats want to catch mice they must know how to watch quietly, and bide their time. But people may be over cunning, and biding our time and letting it go by are pretty nearly akin.

Mary Anne, for very joy, could hardly give her mother an account of what had passed, but she ended by saying : 'Do you, mother, go with father; it is so long since you have been from home, and never up yonder.'

The mother was a good deal annoyed at her husband having made choice of the young girl for his companion, and, as is often the case, her anger extended to her daughter, whose fault it in no way was.

'If he had wanted me,' she said, 'he could have asked me; but well I know that he sets no value upon me, is indeed ashamed of me; and now, if he were to pay me for it, I would not go with him.'

This, however, remained to be proved, for when the farmer had made up his mind he seldom changed it, at all events he did not on this occasion. The poor woman was indeed right; he was ashamed of her,—thought her awkward, nor could she ever speak a word to please him. If she agreed with him, it gave him no satisfaction; if she contradicted him, he was furious. He would far rather have his pretty daughter with him—had the same feeling which makes a man prefer driving a handsome horse to a screw, and looked on her with a certain complacency, as he might have done on a thoroughbred cow, or anything else that reflected credit on himself. He always grinned with a sort of delight when his girl was admired, and felt a malicious pleasure in holding her up, like a tempting piece of bacon, before the young fellows, making their mouths water, and then disappointing them by snatching her away.

As for Mary Anne herself, she was indescribably happy, and her happiness had come upon her unlooked for and complete as an angel's out of heaven. She kept flitting about in the kitchen till her mother had to send her out of it, then went to her little room and turned all her things upside down by way of preparation for the morrow, then discovered she had left out what she did not want, and put what she did back into her drawers. She had no wish to appear decked out, only neat and respectable, and as she ought; and it is a difficult thing for a girl exactly to hit this happy medium, unless she has been in the habit of seeing it from her youth exemplified by her mother.

And indeed it is no such easy matter, especially when it is not habitual, to devise an attire that shall be neither smart nor dowdy, an attire that shall compel every one to admit that it is exactly the right thing, neither more or less. If there be a ribbon too many, or one too few, anything glaring or grimy, anything torn or superfluous, all labour is in vain, and the country maiden may be pronounced a slattern or a conceited minx. It is no uncommon thing indeed to see a gorgeous silk apron and coarse clothing; or a beautiful white straw hat, with feathers and ribbons so dirty you would not care to touch them with the tongs; or smart silk mittens covering hands that have rings on their fingers, and at their finger-ends claws like a hawk's; or gold chains round the neck, and untidy hair; or open work stockings with holes in their heels, and cobbled shoes. It really is difficult for a girl to be right in all particulars, to have a certain harmony in her attire itself, and that attire, moreover, in conformity with season and place; not to go to the communion, for instance, like a peacock; or to wear light-coloured clothes in winter, when her face is purple with cold. But of all difficulties the greatest is to dress properly when you are setting off to be inspected by your lover's family, when, according to the old saw—'Too little and too much the same, may often mar a maiden's game.' An old woman has sharp eyes, can see round many a corner not meant for her; and, moreover, she has often odd fancies of her own, and takes exception at what others might like.

Mary Anne had a natural taste in these matters, and a gift of neatness; everything became her; everything looked well upon her, and yet there was no appearance of any great thought or care bestowed upon her clothes. Still there was one thing that she felt to be much against her: she could not often buy what she liked best, but had things given her either by her father or mother, who had never heard of taste, and liked glaring colours and a cheap showy article. Often indeed the poor girl had shed tears over the presents made to her, and yet she had to wear them, or her parents would have been offended; but to be sure she chose her own time for doing so.

It may therefore be supposed that on this occasion her dress afforded her a subject of much earnest deliberation.

It was late at night before Mary Anne could get to sleep, her room seemed so hot and oppressive, and just as she was dropping off a dread came over her of having heard it rain. Up she jumped, put her face out of the window, and with that sleep was gone. But he quickly returned and pressed down her eyelids till she started up again with a scream, scared by a dream of the great dog having wings and spreading them for flight. However, sleep is a benign power, not easily offended; the greatest friend indeed we have on earth. Night after night he puts his sweet goblet to our lips and strengthens us for fresh daily work, and as a mother who will offer again and again the healing draught her sickly child pushes away, so does he. Only sometimes, when life runs low, and he knows there is great need to think day and night of heaven, because the 'narrow gate' is still too distant, he consents to stand aside and give the aged time for meditation. Alas! that so often his gracious intent should be misunderstood, and the waking hours spent in thinking only of the present world.

For the third time, then, sleep came back to Mary Anne, and brought with him sweet dreams that did not startle, that lulled, and hushed, and wrapped her in delight till smiles played around her like perfume round a flower. The finest of days began to dawn; golden rays fell upon the lovely girl, but did not disturb her, did but gild her dreams, which were at their sweetest when her mother's voice broke in upon them.

'Look you, if you mean to go you had better get up; a pretty thing indeed to be lying in bed in this way till the last moment, and leaving all the trouble to me!'

At that Mary Anne leapt up as if a cannon had been fired off in her ear, and stood in the middle of the little room for some while, not knowing where she was till she saw the bright light shining in, and her clothes ranged round on chairs and table.

'Good gracious, mother, have I then overslept myself, and I so fully meant to be up early? Please don't be angry with me, I will be ready in no time.'

The Dorngrüt farmer was not to be trifled with, and indeed, waiting is the last thing a despot of his stamp will ever consent to. This his daughter very well knew, and therefore dressed herself with inconceivable speed; but when this was done, the drops stood upon her brow, which fortunately was not unbecoming to her. Fortunate, too, was it that she could drink her coffee boiling hot—though the thing in itself is unadvisable,—for her father was already on the move; and taking up his whip left the room, which was as much as to say, 'I am off, if any one wants to come with me, let them look sharp.'

In this particular Mary Anne had been properly drilled by her father, who had neither consideration nor patience for any one, and who, as soon as he was seated, was in the habit of saying 'Gee-up' at once, leaving his companions to jump in or remain behind as they liked. He had at all events taught his daughter punctuality and activity, and therefore she was, as we have seen, ready in a wonderfully short time (what girls can do in that way when needs must, is inconceivable), had neither forgotten her pocket-handkerchief nor her mittens (though these, to be sure, she only put on as she was going from the kitchen to the gig); at all events, when her father seated himself her foot was already on the step, and even he on this occasion was not brute enough to say 'Gee-up' till she was fairly in. Her mother followed to the vehicle, in spite of the mortification of having to stay at home, hoping perhaps for a friendly word or two from her old man.

'See you get on well with the work to-day,' he said, 'and spread the manure on the mossy field, that all may be ready when I come back.—Gee-up, Dobbin,' and after two cuts of the whip Dobbin began to jog sleepily on.

'He is and always will be a brute,' muttered his wife, and went back to her kitchen; but whether she alluded to Dobbin or to her old man she did not more exactly specify.

PART III.

I.

A YOUNG GIRL'S ORDEAL.

IT was a wondrously beautiful morning that on which father and daughter drove off from Dorngrüt to encounter an important day. The sun shone brightly, the air was fresh, the grass was spangled with great dew-drops, that gave back all the colours of the rainbow, and gradually Dobbin got up his spirits and trotted more rapidly along.

There is something quite peculiar in its effect upon the mind, in advancing to meet our fate, under the fresh bracing breeze of early morning, and many a brave standard-bearer and gallant rifleman has experienced this before now on his way to the battle-field or the shooting-ground. But how much more must a poor young girl's heart throb when it is nearing the goal of all its wishes, more especially if it be escaping a hell and seemingly about to enter a heaven; truly her state baffles all expression; and yet the nearer this heaven, the greater the anxiety, the more giddy seems the gulf that yawns between hope and possession, the more fertile the imagination becomes in conjuring up all hindrances that may yet intervene before the promised land be really won. When the young cornet rides into the battle, he has only God and himself to depend upon, and when the rifleman takes his aim, nothing but air lies between him and the target. But how much harder the position of a girl sitting by the side of a despotic father, who is silently revolving plans of his own, while she is driven by him to undergo the inspection of her lover's whole family—father, mother, and sister,—who have also probably private views and opinions of their own, all of which may come between her and her heart's desire.

The farmer said little—he was thinking of his timber bargain; his daughter said even less—the exchange of hearts being a still more absorbing subject of thought. Sometimes old Dobbin's pace appeared to her so slow that she could hardly refrain from urging him on, and then again he seemed to have wings, and she thought she must cry out 'O father, father, do make him go slower.' All at once her father drew up—

'Good gracious! what place is this?' cried Mary Anne suddenly, horrified to find that they were already at their journey's end.

A YOUNG GIRL'S ORDEAL.

'Herrlige,' her father replied, throwing the reins to the stable-boy, and bidding him unharness the horse, who was to be left there till the afternoon. Now then Mary Anne understood that the rest of the way had to be walked, and that Liebiwyl was somewhere near. Her father followed the horse into the stable, and she had to stand between the gig and public-house, not knowing where to go; and when invited in by the waiting-maid said she would rather wait for her father and see what he meant to do. By and by it appeared he meant to go in, and his daughter followed him. Soon they were joined by the landlord, who welcomed them cordially, and asked what it was particularly that brought them into that part of the world. The Dorngrüt farmer upon this waxed confidential, and said he had a purchase of timber to make, and thought he would look in, in hopes the landlord would be able to direct him to where he might get it cheapest and best.

'As to wood,' said the landlord, 'one has no end of trouble with it, it's all carried away, and very soon we shall hardly be able to get our own sawn. The sawyers saw only what they themselves have to sell, and keep us farmers waiting till our timber gets worm-eaten, and whether we storm or entreat they contrive to put us off. Well-seasoned timber is very scarce; here and there some may be got at a farmer's, but not often; however, there may be something to suit you at the saw-mill.'

'Is it far off?' asked the farmer.

'O no, not a quarter of an hour's turn down there to the right.'

'I have been told that the farmer at Liebiwyl has always got a store,' said he of Dorngrüt.

'That is,' replied the landlord, 'that he always keeps some for his own use, but not for sale, though he will oblige people too, now and then. Do you know him?'

'Not I,' said the farmer. 'His son got knocked about at the fire that broke out in the village next to us, and was left for dead; our people happened to find him and bring him in, and he told me if I ever wanted anything I had but to go to him, whatever his father had would be at my service. But I know what that way of obliging means. One is afraid of bargaining, and so one gets finely cheated.'

'Have no fear,' said the landlord; 'if the son has told you that, you'll be sure to find what you want there, and better and cheaper than anywhere else. Even if it were inconvenient to them, they would never go back from his word. They are quite a family apart; if all were like them the world would be a better place. I take nearly all their calves, and they are always satisfied with getting a fair price; and when they buy, pay a fair price down, and never worry one's life out with chaffering. One need have no fear of buying pigs from them by the weight, they'll never be found stuffed out with cherry-stones. With such folks 'tis easy dealing; but in general, farmers have got quite unreasonable, and won't take a landlord's word for anything.'

'No great harm in that,' said the other; 'farmers get keener-witted day by day, and they need to do so if they don't want to be skinned alive, or to fare like the hares, who get scarcer and scarcer the more sportsmen there are. Are these people rich?'

'That they are,' said the landlord; 'they are farmers of the old stamp; they have struck root; they don't merely hang on by the branches, and live from hand-to-mouth, as so many do now-a-days. If you take my advice, you'll go there for your timber; you'll never regret it.'

'At all events, I'll go and have a look at the saw-mill first,' decided the farmer. 'Do they both lie the same way?'

'No,' said the landlord, 'the ways turn off by yonder house with the red roof, and you must return as far as that from the saw-mill to go up to Liebiwyl.'

Accordingly, when the father and daughter had reached the house with the red roof, the former said to Mary Anne—

'Go you up; if they chance not to be at home you can have them called, so that I need not have long to wait, for we must get home to-day, and there's a long way to go.'

So he turned off to the left hand, leaving Mary Anne in the middle of the road. Gladly would she have sunk into the earth had there been a hole for her, but stand there till her father returned she dared not; she must needs go on to the right, cost her what it would.

True, Mary Anne was not what is commonly meant by shy; she knew that she was a person of some consequence in her part of the country, and could give an answer or knock at a door without any blushing or embarrassment. But there is a shyness, an internal shyness so to speak, which is not seen as such, and often is not believed in. It is something indefinable: in part a modest reluctance to disturb or trouble any one, in part a dread of bringing one's own personality into contact with that of a stranger, a dislike to reveal to strange eyes, or to express to strange ears what stirs our inmost heart. Shyness of this kind many a man will take with him to his grave, and it exists, though disguised in many a woman's nature as the best portion of it; but its special home is in the heart of a young girl, though she often strives hard to conceal it, and does this he more, the more important she feels the actual crisis to be. Mary Anne, under the pressure of love and sorrow, had allowed Andrew to look into her soul, had given herself to him without much circumlocution, for she had, as it were, saved his life, and that consciousness unlocked her heart. But now she had to go to a house where she had never before been, she had to knock and explain who she was. What Andrew had said about her she could not tell, nor whether she would be welcome, nor what she herself should say. Perhaps she should go to the wrong house and be laughed at, or she might find no one at home but a cross dog, say one like her own, and then what should she do?

Thus surmising, she walked timidly and anxiously along a narrow lane between two hedges, and ere long heard the sweep of a scythe through the grass behind the hedge on her right, and then a voice say—

'I'll tell you what it is: they won't be here to-day; it's too late.'

To which another voice, that struck her as wonderfully familiar, replied—

'I don't know that, they may come yet; it's a a long way.'

'Depend upon it,' said the first voice, 'they won't come at all; they only wanted to put you off quietly. They have made a fool of you, and I'd wager anything they were called in church yesterday.'

'No such thing,' said the other voice, 'the girl would never have done that; she would have sent me word.'

'Pooh,' said the first speaker, 'never trust to any girl, they are all alike in the end. Whatever fuss they have made before, when the time for going to church is come, they are ready.'

'You should not lump them all together in that way,' said the other voice. 'There are many sorts of girls, just as there are of young men; and depend upon it mine would not have acted so, she would have sent me word.'

'She must then be a rare specimen,' was the reply. 'What is she like now? I have a great curiosity to see her.'

'I can't describe her properly,' said the other voice; 'you must wait till you do see her, and then you are sure to be pleased. She is almost as tall as her mother, but yet not a mere beanstalk; she has a lovely complexion, not deep red, but not like a washed-out stocking either, long plaits, dark eyes, and wonderfully beautiful teeth; when she opens her mouth you fancy you see the gates of paradise, and at times such a kind look in her eyes, you feel yourself, as it were, melting away. Otherwise her face is grave, almost as if she was going to order one to do something.'

'Have you ever seen her angry?' broke in the other.

'I made her angry, I think, that night of the fire, but as soon as I knew her again she was gone.'

'Take care, then, what you are about, and look before you leap. I for my part would not marry any girl if I had not seen her angry, downright angry, as angry as it was in her nature to be, and if this did not come about naturally, I would never rest till I had put her into a passion.'

'And why so, pray? You are always such an odd fellow, Christy.'

'Look here,' said Christy, 'it is well to make sure how they look and what they do when they are in a passion, and what it is that puts them in one. I'll tell you something that no one else knows: I too took it once into my head that I would marry; the girl was as white and smooth as satin, and as sweet as gingerbread; you would have thought butter would hardly melt in her mouth; that her eyes could do nothing but smile, or her voice rise above a whisper. I used to be on pins and needles the whole day till evening came and I could get away to her. On one occasion I went to a house where there was dancing going on; she was not there; I waited, but still she did not come; so just to kill the time I took out another girl, danced two or three times with her, and gave her half a bottle of wine.

While we were at it, in came my sweetheart; whether she had been waiting for me out of doors I don't know, but she made eyes at me that seemed as if they reached my head, and had each of them five talons like a vulture's. She would have nothing to say to me, darted about the room like a wasp against a window, and then off with her, home, like one possessed. I jumped up and followed her, and overtook her not far from her own house; but when I tried to explain and excuse myself, I saw what a girl in a passion can be. She looked ten times sourer than ever, with her nose turned up, her eyes out of her head, and in a thick hoarse voice she abused me in a way I never came in for before. When I heard her go on in such an unseemly fashion, looking like a raging bull, and storming like a half-drunk Frenchman, my love suddenly changed to disgust. Rather a wild-cat than such a one as she, thought I, and off I ran as fast as I could, and never got over my dread of her following me till I found myself safe in bed at home. I felt as if some lumbering waggon had gone over me, and yet, strange to say, instead of being killed I had got up unhurt; and I took an oath never to marry, or at least never to marry unless I had seen the girl in a thorough passion, and knew what she was like then. You see how it is: we only flatter and coax them, and if they look the least cross keep asking what is it, what is it? and bowing and scraping, and billing and cooing about them, so that they can't be much put out if they would; and so it goes on till we get them, and then we think, now they are caught, there is no need to go on catching; and we let things take their course, and the girl does the same, and begins to put out her horns as she had been accustomed to do before, and so nature peeps out on both sides; no more keeping off the storm by coaxing and flattering; howling and gnashing of teeth begins, and each complains that he has been taken in. That, brother, is the way of it; and if I had been married when I saw that face I told you of, I should have lost my senses; but I was single and could run away, thank God! So have a care what you are about. I wonder whether your sweetheart still looks pretty when she is in a pet.'

And so saying Christy pitched a forkful of clover into the cart, and then stood still as if petrified. Through a hole in the hedge he saw a girl's face with a pair of sparkling eyes earnestly fixed upon him.

'What do you think? What sort of a face do I make?' said the girl, when she saw that she was discovered, and a mischievous smile played round her lips, Christy meanwhile standing helpless as butter in the sun; and no one knows how long he might have remained there, had not Andrew dashed forward as soon as he caught the sound of Mary Anne's voice. One easily understands that she could not go on when she heard herself talked of; but she did not want to overhear, only to show herself, though she was too shy to interrupt Christy, and therefore remained standing till she was discovered.

When Andrew joyfully bade her welcome, in God's name, and said what a delight it was to see her, he had almost begun to doubt her,—nothing remained of the grave expression which Christy had seen; she smiled very sweetly, and said—

'Will you never then trust me? What I promise I perform. My father wished me to come with him; he is getting old, and is not fond of driving alone.'

Now then Christy ventured to come forward, shook hands, bade her welcome, and observed that she must not be offended at what he had blurted out; he had a way of saying things half in fun, and must not be heeded. But he proposed that they should go to the house, else people might think they had gone mad and were speaking to the hazel-bushes.

From the clover field the farm-house could be reached without passing by any other dwelling; it stood in a large orchard with an open space around it, but nowhere were there any splinters of wood or scattered straws to be seen—everything was neat as though it was a festival; bright flowers in the windows, and on the broad terrace an old dog sunning himself, who without any barking came wagging up to the new-comers. Christian was hewing away in the wood-house, Annie arranging seeds, and Lizzie cleaning the milk-pails by the fountain. She was the first to see Mary Anne walking with Andrew behind the clover cart, and, dropping her pails, she shot in through the back door, out at the front, called her mother—

'She is coming, she is coming!' and off again as quick as thought, without heeding her mother's admonition—

' Now, Lizzie, there you are with your wild ways, and you know how much I dislike any want of civility. What will she think?' and the handsome matron advanced with all the greater friendliness to meet Mary Anne, bade her welcome in God's name, said how she had longed to see her, and how pleased she should be if she liked Liebiwyl, that she should remain with them always. But now she must come in and tell them how her father was.

When they got to the door Lizzie re-appeared, but with an embroidered collar round her throat, and a clean apron, and almost forgot in the earnestness of her gaze to welcome the stranger. But what indeed is there of such importance to a young girl as the outward semblance and whole attire of another? Till she knows the exact cut and colour of every item the new-comer has on, she has no peace! However friendly the meeting of the two girls may be, however warm their mutual welcome, they always look at each other much in the same way as two wrestlers who shake hands before they begin their trial of strength. It is however fortunate that each of the girls, having taken each other's measure, generally come to the conclusion: 'Well, thank God, if I am not so pretty as she, I don't see much reason to envy her. But I shall never rest till I have a collar or a bodice just like hers, or perhaps even handsomer.' Whether the two now in question inwardly settled the point in this way they never told, but it is highly probable, for their manner increased in friendship after their mental comparison, which shows that the result had been pleasant to each, and if so, both alike would have been right, for all depended upon the ground of preference. Seen from the point of sight of gentility, Mary Anne would have won the day, for she was slenderer and had more regular features; while, judged by the country standard, Lizzie would have been approved as more lively, merry, and fresh-complexioned.

The clean kitchen, the handsome, bright, large room, made a great impression upon Mary Anne; they had nothing of the kind at home; and when she looked out of the kitchen-door into the gay garden, over fields and meadows, in the middle of which the well-built house rose stately and free, she was obliged to own that she had never seen a more beautiful farm, and her breast thrilled with the idea of the dignified and enviable position its mistress would enjoy. And yet she felt oppressed, uncomfortable, ill at ease, just as some people do all day long when there is to be a thunderstorm before night. Everybody was kind; everything was done to please her; in spite of her refusal the best coffee, such as she never drank at home, was set before her, with cheese and white bread; all the family found time to keep her company, and no one seemed annoyed at losing a busy working day for a young girl's sake.

She felt that a far higher degree of good breeding prevailed at Liebiwyl than at Dorngrüt, a kind of propriety and refinement, not to be learned in foreign parts or put on at will; a something compounded of a good-humour and mutual respect which have grown habitual, and affect the behaviour of parents to children and children to parents just as much when there are no strangers by. Very different was it in her home, where self-assertion and contempt for the feelings of others were the order of the day.

The poor girl felt the full distress of the contrast,

and knew that when her father came she should be thoroughly ashamed of him. But our inmost feelings have sometimes a strange way of misrepresenting themselves—humiliation looks like pride, and depression like indifference and ungeniality. The more Mary Anne felt the discomfort arising from a sense of inferiority, the less could she control her own manner, and the darker grew the cloud that shadowed her. Andrew, who saw that cloud passing over her, was on thorns, but he did not know its cause, and went on labouring hard to show her off in a good light, but the more he laboured the gloomier she looked. We all know what it is to be anxious that our loved ones should appear to advantage before others; we would have them outdo themselves, that we may reap the delight of hearing them admired. Alas, how many a mother has had in utter despair to carry out some howling child she had wanted to display, she almost bursting with vexation as her darling with rage!

But her feelings are nothing compared to those of a lover who is introducing the girl of his choice to his parents, and would have her both behave like an angel and be treated like one. He has two anxieties on his mind, the demeanour of his parents and that of his bride—now it seems something is going wrong in this direction, now in that, till he works himself into a kind of fever, is the very one to blunder, and at last feels like an impatient weaver with a tangled skein of wool. Andrew did not indeed commit himself thus, his was too noble a nature, but he went through untold distress. His dear one was so strange, so silent, so almost repellent, that he hardly recognised her, began to fear there had been some omission somewhere, or that Christy's words had rankled. He himself became all the kinder, as Mary Anne was well aware; but it only brought on a choking sensation, and scarcely could she utter a word. Her father's arrival made a diversion, but did not seem to have any exhilarating effect upon her. She felt a positive repugnance to him, and had all the trouble in the world not to express it. Although she did not herself know very well what to do, she longed to instruct him what to say and not to say, and if Andrew sat on thorns, Mary Anne may be said to have sat on live coals. Her father, on the contrary, made himself thoroughly at home; ate and drank twice as much as usual, as it was not at his own expense, bought timber, and as he got it much under its value, bought twice as much as he wanted, and observing their liberal way of dealing, would have gone on to buy half their stock of horses and cattle at half price, if Christian had not been wise enough to declare that as he should want all his teams in harvest, and that so large a family as his required a good deal of milk, he could part with neither horse nor cow; upon which the Dorngrüt farmer cast his eyes upon a handsome calf, and as that could neither draw carts nor give milk, could do nothing, indeed, but eat and look well, the same excuse would not avail, and he got it much below its value, as all were well aware of, though no one made faces over it but old Dorngrüt himself, who laughed heartily in his sleeve, and thought he should carry it all his own way with these people. Mary Anne was not present at this achievement of his, she was with Lizzie looking over the garden. But on their way home she could not refrain from telling her father she felt quite ashamed at his manner of getting so much out of the family, and received this answer—

'Be as much ashamed as you like, it costs nothing. But if you are not an utter fool you may lay this to heart, that the time for shaking pears is when they are ready to fall.'

Thus the morning passed, and now they had all to return to the best room, where such a dinner was prepared as Dorngrüt had never seen, and everything was so neatly arranged and well cooked that Mary Anne was perfectly amazed, and more than ever indignant with her father, who ate again as if he had not had a morsel before. The more, however, he got through the less could she touch, so that the good hosts were quite distressed, and made many apologies for offering them so poor a repast; had they known of their visit beforehand they would have been better prepared, and the next time they would look about for something that would please her,—all which embarrassed Mary Anne more and more; she felt a contraction in her throat, and could only play with the meat on her plate. This was a real grief to Annie, who could not help seizing an opportunity of asking Andrew 'what she could have done wrong, that the girl should be so silent and should eat nothing—was she always so?'

'No,' sighed Andrew, 'she is generally friendly and talkative. I don't think it is anybody's fault; but the drive must have been too much for her, and her head must ache, as is often the case with women.

This was Andrew's attempt at an explanation, but he himself was far from satisfied with it.

During the dinner nothing was said of the main point, but when no one could eat more, and the wine had been put down and praised deservedly (for it was no sour griping stuff from Erlach or Berne), Christian, after Annie giving him many a wink, inquired—

'And now, how do things stand between us? if you agree to this match, we are quite willing. We are getting old, and cannot tell how much longer we shall be here, and therefore it would be a comfort to us to know to whom things were to go. We've often told our son that he ought to marry, but he could never fancy any girl well enough till he saw yours, and he's awfully set upon her. She too, I fancy, does not object to him, and so, if it suits you, I think we may as well bring about a marriage. I don't want to make any particular boast, but I do think if they come together and look after things, they will have more than they want as long as they live.'

Annie wiped her eyes. Christy and Lizzie had left the room as soon as their father began his speech. Andrew and Mary Anne were both silent; while the Dorngrüt farmer impaled a tempting-looking bit of ham, and at length replied that he had not exactly come on that errand, and if he had known they were so much in earnest he should perhaps have let the timber be. Not indeed that he had anything against them; he was quite satisfied as to their respectability, and, as far as he could see, their wealth. But they were a long way off, and he should never know how his child was going on, and that was what should concern a father most. They might half kill her, he should never hear it till it was too late. And he must say on that head he was most particular; he could stand a good deal, but to have one of his children ill-treated was a thing he did not believe he could stand, it would drive him wild. (Here Mary Anne opened very wide eyes indeed, and, though she was silent, those eyes said as plain as they could, ' O father, what a falsehood!') He was well aware, indeed, that there was not much to be done with girls; they were there to be married off, but parents were there to see how they married. Had he chosen to give Mary Anne to the first comer, she might almost have been a grandmother by this time!

And now Annie took up the conversation, and said they had to thank him for having been so careful of his child, and hoped he would think with them that the dear Lord had kept his girl for their Andrew. He need have no fear of her not being happy with him. Let him only inquire what character they all had; as for her, she had often vowed before God and man never to be a bad mother-in-law, and a son's wife, if only she behaved tolerably, would be as well cared for with them as at home. On that head he might make his mind perfectly easy.

To which the farmer replied that he did not mean any offence, but as people brewed so they must bake. The girl was not in his way. To be sure, it might be time for her to marry, but, on the other hand, he had always plenty of food, and plenty of work for her. However, he should like to hear what they thought of doing in the event of his any way coming into it.

'That,' said Christian, 'is a thing of course.

Andrew is the youngest, and will take the farm on reasonable terms, and give the others what is right.'

'That's the very point that should be legally settled,' replied the farmer; 'it often happens that those who get the land fare worst, and have to pay more than they keep, which does not answer, the farmers get ground down and the lawyers and shopkeepers crow over them. The best plan is to have everything settled in one's lifetime; then one has things in one's own hand, and when once the farm is legally made over, the thing is done, and no one can squeeze much more out of it.'

'That is not necessary here,' said Christian, 'and would only cause needless expense. As a matter of course, the farm goes to the youngest; no one has a word to say against that, nor will any one expect him to give too much for it. It is the custom of the country that the property should be kept together, and so it ought to be. If it were to be divided, there would be an end of us farmers, and things would go to rack and ruin. I have heard how this works in other countries. Thank God, it is not so with us. The land goes to one, and so he can keep himself respectably, and bring up a family; and where children are of the right sort there is never any difficulty about sharing, and no one wishes to see the place where they were born disturbed, but, on the contrary, are proud that it should remain a well-to-do farm, as it has for generations been. They know that as long as they live it will still be a kind of home to them, and that they need never apply to the parish. No one wishes things to be otherwise than they are; when the parents die the youngest is still the youngest, the farm is his, and there is an end of it.'

'Yes, yes,' said the other, 'that would be all very well if one could insure it, but we never know how people will turn out, or what they will be after. Therefore it is always wise to be beforehand with them, and it strikes me that you should at once sell the farm to the youngest, so that he may know how he stands. What is it worth?'

Christian replied that he had never had it very exactly valued, his late father had always said that between brothers it was worth about sixty thousand pounds; but since then he had added to it, and land had risen in value; no one could say how much it might bring in now, if it were put up to auction.

'So then you would be willing to give up the farm to him for about half its value, seeing he would have debts beside, and would find it hard enough to get on?' said old Dorngrüt.

To which Christian replied that the debts would be very small, the farm was well stocked, and the wood on it valuable; that, in short, if Andrew took the farm at a valuation of fifty thousand,—and it was well worth more, all would be well satisfied, and Andrew would get a good third more than the others. He would have no difficulty in paying off the charges upon the property, and whatever he got with his wife need never go that way. But as to using his other children ill, he was not going to begin to do that in his old days, nor would he have grandchildren and great-grandchildren coming to him in the other world and reproaching him before God for having made them beggars. There were many places, he was well aware, where only one inherited, and the others got merely a miserable pittance, and he had always shuddered at this, not only on account of the younger children, but because one pound unjustly won was sure to devour ten, as might be seen any day. Many a child ran barefoot because his grandfather had been a rascal to his own flesh and blood. That he would never be; and if he had had more children, or if Christy had seen fit to marry, he should never have wished to keep him at home and make him work throughout his best days on the farm, for the sake of the youngest, but he would have helped him to set up in life for himself. Those were his views. Andrew should have what was right, and none of them grudged it him, but more than that should never be his; they loved all their children, and would not wrong the one for the other. Upon which the Dorngrüt farmer observed that he need not take up the subject in so high a tone; others had surely a right to give their opinion, and each could act as he liked, they had not gone too far as yet. But, once for all, he was not going to give his daughter to a poor fellow weighed down by heavy charges, and that they might consider a settled point.

Here Annie interfered, and begged he would not take amiss what Christian said, he was only speaking generally. But indeed Andrew would in no way be weighed down with debts. As to the charges on the property, the very timber he might cut down would almost defray them, nor would he be ever pressed in any way. Again, no one knew, if only the settlement were just and fair, what might happen; neither of the others were married as yet, though unfair dealings might drive them to it. 'But what do you think of it?' said she, turning suddenly to Mary Anne; 'you are the most nearly concerned, and you have not said a single word as yet?'

This unexpected question made Mary Anne start as though a cannon had gone off behind her. During the conversation her heart had been in her mouth. It was her happiness that was in the market, nor could she feel at all sure how the bargaining would end; and if she took any part in the discussion, she feared she might complicate things still further. Therefore she merely replied timidly, 'She should be satisfied whatever way they settled it. Girls had not much to say in such matters; they had but to take things as they came.'

The poor girl did not know that one straightforward outspoken word is a hundred times better than an evasive answer; but there are many beside a young thing with her heart in her mouth who habitually take refuge in evasion. O how gladly would she have had her father refrain from mixing up himself in the matter, and leave all to God and to this worthy family! How gladly would she have told them that she should be satisfied with anything, if only she could escape from her miserable home, and take refuge here! But then she feared to make her father still more ungracious and grasping out of very opposition; while at the same time she was not unprincipled enough to support him in his policy; and after all, by her indefinite answer, she only offended him and gave pain to the others,—utterly failed to conciliate either party.

'And you, too, what do you say?' asked the farmer, turning to Andrew; 'you are the one most nearly concerned, after all, and I should think you would approve my views, which are all for your advantage.'

With a heavy heart Andrew replied that the state of things with him was as follows :—He loved Mary Anne; he thought she would turn out the same sort of woman as his mother; and never would she have to complain of unkind dealing on his part. He had consequently never even asked what she had, or would bring; and even if she had nothing, it was all one to him. But for this very reason he thought he ought to be a little trusted, and supposed likely to do what was right. He had no wish to wrong his brother and sister in any way, and family ties were sacred things.

'I should have thought a man's skin nearer to him than his clothes,' said the farmer, 'and that when he had set his heart upon a wife, he would not trouble himself about his relations. But it is all the same to me; I did not come on this account. If I could have settled my girl uncommonly well up here, I should have had no objection; else, if she must be married at all, I can find her a dozen husbands nearer home, and then I shall know how things stand, and shall have her under my eye. There is another who has been long set upon her, and she will never find so good a match. The girl herself thinks him too old; but by and by she'll give up such foolish fancies, and agree that the older the better. For his own part, he had no objection to make in that quarter, and before long she would see things with his eyes. But now, if they were to get back to-day, it was high time to set out.'

'Not so,' said Christian; 'we don't mean this; we have no wish to break off the match. What we have said has not been ill-meant, and every one has a right to speak his own mind. The lad is very dear to us, and we shall not stand out for a few pounds more or less. When two people love each other, money should not come between them. His heart is set on the girl, and we have nothing to say against her, though, to be sure, we don't know her, and it might have been as well to know each other a little beforehand. But, as has been said, we live a long way off, and that, too, has its advantages; there is such a thing as being too near. It is the way of the world. Mountains don't meet, but human beings do; and when once they have met and taken to each other, they should not be parted. That's my opinion. How do you think the matter should be settled? All that can be done shall.'

'What do you think, girl?' said the farmer, 'it's your affair; speak out, can't you?'

But Mary Anne was in no condition to speak out. Her heart was torn with agonizing suspense, as might be that of some gambler who had staked all he had on one card, and now with fixed gaze watched the banker's deliberate proceedings. Every thing increased her torture; everything said made her angry with the speaker. She felt as though she would give all her prospects, here and hereafter, to have things settled one way or the other. Her father was hopelessly obstinate, she knew; nothing was to be expected from him. All she had to trust to was the other side; and therefore she was the more distracted at the difficulties they raised, more especially pained that Andrew should admit any. If he only loved her properly, she kept thinking, he would see no obstacles; would come in to everything in order to win her, and afterwards things could have been settled as he saw fit. Therefore her reply was to the effect that she could never have believed it would have been an affair requiring so much deliberation; but she had nothing to say to it. However the parents might settle it, she should be satisfied; but this bargaining was very painful to her, and she must say she would rather not have been present at it.

'And so it is to me,' replied her father, 'and therefore I will state my conditions once for all: the farm must be given up to your son for forty thousand pounds, so that as soon as he is married his wife may take the whole management of the house; and should Andrew die before her, and leave no children, she must inherit the farm out and out. Otherwise, I will never give my consent.'

Andrew grew very pale when he heard this, and his lips trembled as though he were about to speak; but he tried in vain, not one word could he utter. Something venomous rose up within him which was foreign to his nature; a pride was stirred which he had never before known to exist. Were they, then, to come from down yonder, and to suppose that up here there was only stupidity to be encountered, and that people might be treated like fools and idiots? Had the girl, then, no love for him, but merely for his farm? and while he did not even inquire whether she had a penny of dower, was he to be ground down to the uttermost? Was he indeed such a wretched sort of fellow as to require gilding before a girl would take him? He began to feel that in himself alone he was well worth her love, and a greater prize, without any means at all, than many another with a hundred thousand pounds. Our good Andrew, in short, was tempted to overlook the fact that, even if a girl had proper scales for weighing a man's intrinsic merits, which is very seldom the case, those merits went for nothing in the scales her parents were accustomed to employ, unless he could add to them wealth or position. But this he forgot for the while; and then he could not read Mary Anne's heart, but only her face, which had fretted him the whole day. A mighty struggle went on in his breast, and he felt capable of any effort, any sacrifice, to assert his wounded self-respect.

Now, women have an especial faculty for interpreting expressions of countenance, and this faculty is a key to men's hearts which would confer upon them too absolute dominion over the latter, if it were not counterbalanced by a strong spirit of contradiction, which prevents their patiently overcoming the feeling they discern and disapprove, and makes them insist upon expelling it at once by violent measures. Mothers are skilfuller in this respect than wives; their love is generally more unselfish; they see into the heart of their sons (more clearly, curious to say, than into that of their daughters); but they do not put themselves at once into an attitude of antagonism; rather they seek to change, to modify by gentleness, just as you must make butter soft before you mould it, and melt iron before it can be cast.

Accordingly both Mary Anne and Annie read in Andrew's face the invisible characters written on the wondrous table of our hearts by an invisible hand. Mary Anne got hot and cold both as she interpreted them, and she could not for her life have uttered one kind word, and if forced to speak, a bitter torrent would have found its way. But Annie rapidly interposed, and said—

'These were subjects they had not thought of discussing. She, for her part, would gladly give up further trouble and responsibility, and the sooner Andrew brought a daughter-in-law home, the better pleased should she be, and willingly would she give up the management to her; she was not very strong, and wanted rest, and although she had never been used to be ordered about, yet no one need trouble himself about her. But, as to the others, they must be consulted; their interests were concerned, and when things were thoroughly understood and settled beforehand, it prevented all quarrelling later. There was nothing to be feared from Christy; but if Lizzie married no one knew what sort of husband she might get, therefore it would be better to talk the matter over with them before it was finally settled.'

'I think you are quite right,' said Christian. 'Where are they now? they can easily be called.'

A shadow crossed Annie's face, and she was just going to speak, when the old farmer observed—

'There was no such great hurry about it; if they were called in now they might suppose he was set upon its being decided at once, and that he by no means was; on the contrary, he would far rather both parties should remain free; no one knew what

A YOUNG GIRL'S ORDEAL.

might happen,—a few days might alter the whole aspect of things. The family ought to have an opportunity of talking it over together, and if this proposal suited them they could let him know. If no message came, things were but as they were, it was all one to him. Indeed, he had never thoroughly liked the match, and if it were not that he saw his daughter wished it, he would rather hear no more about it. He was willing to please her, but they were not on that account to suppose they could do what they liked with him. Girls could always be consoled; and to play the fool and fret for what could not be had was not the way in his family. If one would not do, there were others, or if there were none, there were her parents. However, there was no time now for talking it over any more, it was already four o'clock, and they had a long way to go.'

And now he began to sigh and groan over his timber. If only he could get it over, he wanted it badly, and did not know how to get it carried; all hands were full just now, and every morning at two o'clock he had to send two teams into the field. As for the calf, he could get that brought over by some chance messenger or other; but the timber required time and horses, and he could not for his life tell how to manage. If he hired, it would add no one knows how much to the price of the timber, and so forth.

'Don't be uneasy about that,' quietly interposed Annie, 'we can always contrive to carry a load of timber, and at the same time we can send our decision, and settle the matter for good and all. If it suits you, we will say Thursday or Friday next.'

'I have not agreed for the carrying,' returned the farmer, 'and if it is to cost a great deal I would rather wait.'

'No agreement is wanted,' said Christian; 'an offer is an offer, and we don't mean to take any money for that.'

'If that's your offer,' was the answer, 'it shall be accepted, with thanks; all days are nearly alike to me, the Friday would even suit me better than the Thursday, and they need not bring fodder with them, I have plenty. To be sure, I have not got many oats, but the hay is excellent, and if anything more is wanted there is some refuse corn. But now there is nothing for it but getting off; it will be night long before we are home.'

At which all declared he must not be in a hurry; at all events, he must eat and drink again before he set out. To this he made no very resolute objection —began tossing off glass after glass, and no one knows how long he might have sat there, had not Mary Anne kept urging him to set off. Her heart was indeed over full, her head throbbed, everything reeled around her, and she would have given the world to lay her head down on the bed in some dark room, there to weep away her chafed and sorrowful love. She was undone to get away, for she felt she was losing her self-control; feelings were overmastering her to which it is not well to yield, since no one can tell where they may lead us. She was in the same condition as a cloud, ready indeed, to pour itself out, but whether in rain or hail depends not on the cloud, but rather on the stratum of air through which its contents have to pass, and the wind that urges them along. And so Mary Anne brought about the departure; but even then she was not gracious. She looked displeased, and she was so with every one; with herself, because she could hardly keep back her tears; with her father, who had gone on so as to discourage the others; with Andrew and his family, for pondering and deliberating as though it were a mere matter of business, while to a young impatient heart whose all was staked upon the event deliberation was intolerable. It was a stroke of diplomacy which induced Annie to postpone the final decision; but she did so with no unfriendly intent. She saw how stormy the mood of both lovers was, and she did not wish the storm to break out. There are moments in private and public life both, when you must wait and let things blow over if you don't want uproar, and these crises require a tact which is not always forthcoming. But poor Mary Anne did not understand this, and to have to go home in uncertainty and suspense, to be driven out from the haven she had so hoped for, into the perilous deep, where sharks and old Jacobs might begin to snap at her again, almost drove her to despair. They all went together as far as the village, but little got said; and at parting, though many a customary phrase was used, there was not one hearty word exchanged; nay, though the tears stood in the eyes of several of them, do what they would no one could hit upon the right thing to say; and, indeed, this right thing is but seldom present to the mind, and even when present, strength to utter it is often wanting. Our moods are like the sky, very rarely indeed entirely free from clouds.

II.

PROS AND CONS.

THE parting over, Mary Anne sat gloomily by her father's side, and he, having more than once asked a question and received no answer, turned round and saw that she was holding her handkerchief to her face.

'Are you crying?' he said.

'No,' she replied; 'but I have got a cold.'

'I don't see why you should cry,' returned her father, 'let things go as they will. If you settle yonder, you are provided for; if they draw back, something else will turn up. They are stupid old-fashioned people, who have ways of their own, and think themselves mighty wise, while they are really up to nothing at all, and I could do what I liked with them in buying and selling. I have not seen such a slow set for a long time. For that reason we must make them follow our lead from the first; if they once had you under their finger and thumb Heaven knows what they would make of you, and so I had to look sharp after your interest, the more so as you did not choose to open your mouth.'

'But, father,' Mary Anne at last replied, 'suppose they don't choose to come into your views? You were very hard upon them.'

'Well, even so, I have got my timber cheap, and a calf that I can make money by. But don't you be uneasy, they'll do it, they won't like to draw back. They'll be ashamed of not going through with it after asking us to come over, in a way to make us think they were sure to agree. It was for us to take time to consider, not for them. They should esteem it an honour that we thought it worth while to go all that way to look at their goat's home in the mountains. But it is the young fellow that I am most vexed with; after all, he was the one chiefly concerned, and should have spoken out then, after being so pressing before, yet not one word did he say. There must be some screw loose there, otherwise he would not have needed to go to such a distance for a wife, or to be so anxious about it. We have done very well to look sharp, and not snatch at him in a hurry; as things stand now, we can afford to wait.'

Mary Anne knew her father, and at any other time this speech of his would have made no impression, but now it increased the dissatisfied mood in which it found her, gave certain vague feelings a definite direction, embittered her temper, overpowered her love; in short, it did what mischief-making insinuations generally succeed in doing,—blew an irritation that would else have died down into a blaze; and who does not know how much such a blaze may consume? Oh, insinuations are devilish, and mischief-making damnable! When the Evil One first tried it with Eve, estranging her thereby from her Maker, and making her question the stringency of His commandment, he knew well the nature of the seed he was sowing in our world, for mischief-making blunts our sense of truth, deprives us of all trust in goodness, is, in short, the handle by which Satan continually lays hold of foolish souls, for he who has once opened his ears to it may be said to sit on an inclined plane having the abyss at its foot, and let but one push be given him, down, down he goes, and all is over.

All those, therefore, who practise mischief-making, are servants of the devil, and just as a butcher's boy and a butcher's dog hunt and drive calves to the slaughter-house, so do they drive souls to destruction. Oh, my brothers, remember this when you have received a slight offence, and some one seeks to dilate and distend it till it fills heart and soul to bursting; see that you free yourselves from such an influence, clothe yourselves with humility, arm yourselves with meekness, take the shield of faith, and, sheltering behind it, cry: 'Get thee behind me, Satan, I will not heed thee.'

No doubt, however, this is difficult; for when a man is out of tune, is offended, or hurt, his efforts are not immediately directed to rectify the discord or remove the cause of pain, but rather some strange perversity impels him to aggravate and exasperate both pain and discord, and often he gives this perverse instinct free scope, not considering who it is instils it. We have a good expression for the right course: to break one's-self; if a man cannot break himself of such or such a habit, he is, we say, but a poor creature after all. Now, such perverse tendencies must be relentlessly broken off; broken plants have no more power of growth, they wither up, and there is an end of them.

But poor Mary Anne could not do this very well, for what her father had begun her mother went on with. She would have rejoiced indeed had the match been settled, for Andrew, she felt sure, would prove a kind son-in-law, who would sometimes make her presents of a pound of coffee or so, and she thought she might have taken refuge with him when her own family were tired of her. But that things should be left in this state of suspense was the greatest offence to her. As for her old man, he was the most audacious and grasping creature, and behaved no doubt like a brute, but there was nothing else to be expected of him, because so he had ever been, and ever so would be. But she did think it too bad of Andrew; she could never forgive him for having come into all this delaying and deliberating. There must be something wrong there, and though he might have eyes full of love, yet he must have told his parents a different tale, and he and they were acting in concert. She hoped Mary Anne would show them that the Dorngrüt people were not to be trifled with, and even if he came with good news, he ought to be kept some time in suspense as to whether she would accept him or not. 'Lord bless us! they must not think that we have not enough to eat here, and don't know what's what. Rich he may be, and well off in many ways he might make you, but don't let him suppose, if you do go to his wild place up yonder, that you do so to be ruled and managed, else you might as well be at home, but rather to be made comfortable, and to have your own way.'

Such talk as this soured Mary Anne; and though it did at times strike her that, after all, the views of the Liebiwyl family were not so unreasonable, yet this idea got no firm grip of her mind. She fancied that every one looked at her as though they knew she had been over to be inspected, and were not sorry that she came back without a decision in her favour. And, moreover, she resolved that on Friday, when Andrew came over, she would be very cool to him, would not show herself for a long time, and even if he brought the best news in the world, would keep him in suspense, that he might learn once for all how he ought to treat her, and what she expected from him.

Meanwhile, it so happened that old Jacob appeared again on the scene, and was more pressing and conformable than ever before. Perhaps he had got wind of their late excursion, perhaps he had other reasons for wishing to get married. At all events, one evening up he hobbled, as it were by accident, sat himself down on the bench before the kitchen, asked for the farmer, and meanwhile entertained the good woman of the house with an account of his wealth and various possessions. And when at length the father appeared, with a very dry and surly air, old Jacob casually remarked that he had had something on his mind of late, but now he had got over it, and therefore here he was again to see how things stood between them. People had said all sorts of things about their daughter that night of the fire, not indeed that he believed them, still it was well to inquire, and when a man lived so far off as he did, it took a long while to get to the rights of things. Therefore, lately he had been in no hurry, but now he felt anxious that matters should come to a point; he knew now that people had told lies, but how long he was to live no one knew, and the end often came sooner than was expected. There was a small innkeeper in the next village to him, who the day before yesterday had gone to bed as well as could be, and the next morning was found dead, and no human creature had heard him or knew how he had died. It had given him a turn; he should not like that kind of end, and when people got into years, they should always have some one with them who could see how things were going on, and could manage to read a prayer or two, if it came to that.

'To be sure,' replied the good woman. 'I too have often thought, when my old man has coughed so badly it seemed his heart must break, that it would be no bad thing if I kept a prayer-book ready at hand, no one knows what may happen, and it does not do to have to look for a thing in a hurry, more particularly when 'tis what you are not much in the habit of using. And then one might be too late, and I should be sorry for that, for something might hang upon it, and one would wish a poor soul to have every chance it could, and to leave its sins behind it.'

'You are a fool,' said her husband, 'and don't know what you are talking of. Go and feed the pigs; don't you hear how hungry they are? That's always the way with women; they meddle with what does not concern them, and forget their proper business; and the devil only knows what would become of things if one were not always at them one way or other.'

'Why, yes, there is a good deal of truth in that,' said Jacob; 'but all the same it is well, too, to take some thought about one's soul, so that, come what will, one may have done the best for one's-self. I often feel so strange; everything turns round me, and I could fancy I was driving my cart far, far, ever so far away, and yet all the while there I am in the very same place. I shall not go on much longer, I fear, I fear! Well, well, do what we will, we have all got to go. But, as I've already said, I should not like to die all alone, with no one to pray for me. I've lived long, and perhaps I've done things that had better not have been done, and that I should be glad to leave behind me, and to get rid of. And so I have determined not to put any more hindrances in the way. Is she at home, your young girl? where is she?'

Thus old Jacob expounded his views, and the farmer was not sorry to hear them, but said things were not to be done in a jiffy like that. They had no lawyer at hand, and then the girl herself would need a deal of fresh talking over. She had got to think nothing would come of it, and had perhaps taken other notions in her head. But at all events, he should like to be told what kind of a settlement Jacob had now resolved upon.

Upon this old Jacob was seized with such a dreadful fit of coughing that it was long before he could get breath enough to answer.

'Ay, ay,' said he at last, 'this won't go on much longer, and it's said, "What you do, do quickly." I must go home now; I can't stand the night air. But come to me one of these first days, and depend upon it things shall be all made right, only don't put off. One never knows what cause one may have to regret it.' And wishing them a good evening, he hobbled away.

'You are a cunning old rascal, that's what you are,' muttered the farmer, looking after him.

But for all that, the near prospect of Jacob's death made an impression upon him, and he came to the conclusion that the matter must be looked to. Mary Anne understood the case perfectly, but the more she hated Jacob, the more angry was she with Andrew, because subjected to new persecutions from which she might have been for ever secured if he had not been so over-cautious, but had come in at once to her father's plans.

Neither, indeed, was the sky quite serene above Liebiwyl. When the family returned from accompanying their visitors, they only exchanged a few broken words on indifferent subjects. No one asked the other, 'What do you think of the match?' or 'How do you like them?' but Annie told Lizzie she must go and gather her more beans. Christian said that he could fancy there was sure to be a storm. Andrew asked whether he should let off the water, and Christy remarked that the second hay crop looked promising. Thus they returned home, and then each set about his own work as if nothing had happened, greatly to the annoyance of Lizzie, who always suffered from having to keep back her thoughts; however, she knew that when her father and mother did not introduce a subject of such importance, it was not her place to do so. But as she was looking out a basket for the beans, Christy passed her, and she could not resist going up to him and asking, 'How have you liked her?'

'Not amiss,' said he, 'but she is either shy or sulky, and I'm not sure which it is.'

'As for me,' said Lizzie, 'I cannot make out what on earth Andrew can see in her, he who is generally so very particular, and could find no one to his taste. To be sure, she is pretty enough; but there are plenty of others nearer home as pretty as she is. But she has no idea of talking. I tried every possible subject, shooting-matches and markets, young men and young girls, but nothing could I get from her but a dry 'Yes' and 'No.' And then, what a proud puss she is! Not a friendly word did she speak to any of the maids, and you should have seen the faces they made at her. And as to her manners, I think nothing of them. I saw her put a bit of meat on her fork with her fingers; and what a pocket-handkerchief she had, so small and thin! I should have been ashamed to carry such a thing about. I daresay she never uses one at home.'

'You are always the same mischievous girl,' said Christy. 'Think, if any one heard you, what would they say? In a strange place, you can be as prim and proper as in church, and see what you are at home. Perhaps it's just the reverse with her, and she is better at home than with strangers.'

'You are a wicked Christy,' said Lizzie, 'but wait a little and I'll have my revenge. Because I talk confidentially to you, as to a friend, see how you turn upon me.'

'Don't be angry,' said her brother, 'I am only repeating what I heard last Sunday. There was a man in the public-house who maintained that there were two kinds of girls; the one good for abroad, the other good for home; some who behaved very prettily out of doors, and others in; some who showed pleasant faces in the village, and very sour faces in the kitchen; and that this makes it very difficult to be sure of them, for, for the most part, one sees them away from home, and has no idea what they look like in the kitchen, or when they are shelling beans, and turning everybody into ridicule.'

'Very well,' said Lizzie, 'wait and see. I'll never speak a confidential word to you again, and when you want the doctor, you may run for him yourself,' and off she went to get her beans.

When all were gone to bed, and Christian and Annie found themselves in their own room, they remained long silent, but Christian kept sighing.

'What ails thee?' asked his wife.

'I don't myself know," replied he; 'but somehow I feel so out of spirits; and what I am to say about this affair puzzles me; it only half pleases me.'

'What is it you object to?' asked Annie.

'The girl,' replied Christian, 'is well enough; I have nothing to say against her, though she would not have been the worse for a little more graciousness; but the old man did provoke me. He is one who thinks no one as shrewd as himself, and that when he gets out of his own village he has to do with half-witted people. He knew well enough where he was, and yet he behaved as if in the market,—seemed to take it for granted we had no sense, and bargained in a way I should have been ashamed of amongst utter strangers. I do believe he would have tried to buy the very clothes off our backs, if I had not said we wanted them.'

'That's a habit,' said Annie. 'One man has one way, another another; and those who frequent markets a good deal come to think they are always there.'

'That may be,' said Christian, 'and besides, it's no matter to me; but the conditions he made are really disgraceful. If he had meant to give a good deal, he might have had a right to require a good deal too; but to give nothing, and to want everything, is really quite out of the way. He went on as though there was not a girl in the world beside his daughter.

'Oh,' said Annie, 'that's their way down yonder. If you give in to them they'll take all you have, if you refuse they will put up with less. He annoyed me too, and above all Andrew; I was sorry for him. But what do you think we had better do?'

'I advise letting the children settle it amongst themselves,' said Christian; 'as to the price of the farm, that's their affair, but as to our giving it up at once, I object to that. And I did not think it pretty behaviour in the girl not to check her father when he proposed it; she ought to have shown more feeling, and refused to turn us out. I must say, that if we are to have a covetous, cross-grained young woman to succeed us in the farm, it will make me turn in my grave.'

'We will hope better things,' said Annie, 'Andrew declares she is not that, but dislikes the goings on at her house. Not, indeed, that we can be very sure; many a one fancies while in their parents' house that they should like to have things different, and yet when they set up housekeeping themselves it's on the very same plan. But we will hope the best; perhaps she did not know what to say; was ashamed of her father, and did not dare show it. There is nothing so painful, or that makes one show to such bad advantage, as being ashamed of any one and yet not daring to speak out for fear of making matters worse. In my young days, I knew what it was to be ready to sink into the earth on my father's account; and it's only they who have gone through it who can tell the effect it takes upon one. Therefore, we must hope the best; very probably this was the case with her. If she could disguise her nature to take in Andrew, why did she not do so to please us? Perhaps hers is a disposition that must show all it feels, and that is not the worst kind. One can get on a hundred times better with a person who lets you see her real feelings, than with one who can put on any manner she likes,—look one way, and think another.'

'You always make the best of everything,' said Christian, 'and you are right; it is far wiser than making the worst. But marrying is always a serious thing; and even when both are in the main worthy and right-minded, they may go on ill unless they thoroughly understand each other, and have patience to give each other a hearing. There must always be one ready to make peace when the world or self-will comes in to divide. But as for that, Andrew knows what he is about, and has his eyes fixed on the right place; and besides, he is not cowardly; and if he sees that the match cannot come off, he won't think himself bound to cling to the cart till it upsets; if there's no help for it, he will make up his mind to do without her.'

'It will be a terrible blow to him too,' said Annie. 'No doubt 'tis a serious matter for us; but, thank God, we are of one mind, and the Lord is our peace. We won't contend any more for anything in the world; who knows how soon it may slip away from under our feet? all we have to do is to give good advice, and to pray the Almighty to lead our children on in the narrow way as well as ourselves. And so He will; I have no anxiety; He is the same Lord who has led us. When we came together we were very different from what we are, yet He has guided us until now, when, God be praised, we can worship Him with upright hearts; and my comfort is that the prayers of pious parents build children's houses. For though, indeed, we are nothing to boast of, yet I know and feel that our Lord looks on us as His; we shall not lack His blessing, and He will give strength to our boy whatever happens. Will you, or shall I?'

'Do you pray,' said Christian.

'Our Father which art in heaven, prayed Annie, 'forgive us our debts, as we forgive our debtors; visit not our sins upon our children, but think upon them for good. Not, Lord, that we would ask Thee to make them rich or important, but to preserve them in Thy ways; to grant them peace in their hearts, and peace in their homes, and happiness for a heaven. Keep up between them brotherly love, that each may be a comfort to the other, a pillow to rest on when the heart is heavy and trouble seems at hand. Let nothing come between them, neither the devil nor man. And whoever shall come into this house, bless, O Father, likewise; receive her into Thy covenant; lead her by Thy Spirit; let her be as an angel who shall show us heaven more clearly. Give to Andrew a right wife, with the right spirit; one who loves peace, and labours for it, and for whatever leads to eternal life. Give meekness and patience to both of them, that they may never lose faith and hope in each other; that the sun may never go down upon their wrath; that they may never fall asleep without joining in prayer, and receiving Thy blessing. O Father, often have I prayed to Thee thus; but when the heart is sincere Thou wilt not weary of hearing prayer, and who knows how much longer I may have power to pray? In all things, then, be it as Thou wilt, Lord, only forget not our children, and have mercy upon our souls.'

'Amen,' said Christian.

On the following day it almost seemed as though there were a death in the house; a silent sadness prevailed, the cause of which all refrained from touching on; everybody went about his business in the quietest way possible, and seemed to court solitude, as though there were some inward as well as outward work to be got through. This habit of silent cogitation is an old-world virtue, inherent in strong reticent natures, and very favourable to a man's best interests. The servants were perfectly aware that something was going on, and a natural instinct inclined them to make themselves as scarce as they could to give scope for private conversation. But for all that not a word was said till Wednesday evening, when the household having gone to rest, Christian, who had been smoking his short pipe on the bench by the door, proposed that they should all go in, the wind was cold, and they had something to talk over.

When all the family were assembled indoors, the father inquired—

'Who is to drive?'

'I think I shall,' said Andrew.

'Which cart will you take?'

'I think the widest.'

'Is it not too heavy?'

'I have six trees to load it with, and therefore it must be a strong cart.'

'Is not that too much?' inquired Christian.

'It can be done; the road is good, the timber is dry and will pack close; and to take it over at once will save me a second journey,' replied Andrew.

'If you can manage it I am quite content,' said his father.

'But what answer are you going to give?' said Christy; 'that too must be talked over.'

'Oh, I have thought it over; a short one,' replied Andrew, shading his face with his hand as though the light hurt his eyes.

'There may be short answers of many kinds,' suggested Christian.

'There is but one answer possible,' said Andrew. 'The old man's conditions are not to be thought of. I will not have all your comfort destroyed for me, and for what end?—for a match that no human being can insure turning out well. At first I thought of letting the servant drive over; but then it occurred to me that what I had myself begun it was proper I should myself end. And then too I thought of the girl; I am sorry for her, she really is not what she seemed to be here; I find I should like just to see her once more, and after that things must take their chance.'

'Why, what do you mean?' said Christy; 'a thing must first be well talked over before one loses heart and throws it to one side.'

'There is no use in talking over it,' replied Andrew; 'the old man has put the case in such a way that there is no making anything of it. The infamous old dog knows very well what he is about; he does not mean the match to take place; he only wants to egg another on by it. I saw what he was about well enough; but before I have done with him I shall let the old rascal know that we are as good as he any day, and better indeed as for that.'

'Nay, nay,' said his mother, 'you must do nothing of the kind; when one loves a girl, one must not run her father down, but esteem him for her sake whatever he may be in himself; but now let us talk the matter over quietly, instead of giving it up in a pet. What do you mean? what is out of the question? what is it that you consider so unfair and wrong?'

'Why,' replied Andrew, 'in the first place he insists upon the farm being sold to me for forty thousand pounds—at about half its value. I don't suppose that you would wish to run me up to the very highest price, but if I got it at his I should be a rogue, and should get as much very nearly as both brother and sister put together.'

'What!' cried Lizzie, 'should I get as much as twenty thousand pounds? Take the farm for anything you like if I'm to have such a fine portion as that. I shall have my pick out of the whole country, and you shall see what airs I shall give myself from this very moment!'

'Come, come,' said Christian, 'this is no matter for joking.'

'I am perfectly serious, father, not joking at all,' said Lizzie.

'If that's the case, brother,' put in Christy, 'that point is settled so far as Lizzie goes, and here I am to witness to what she has said, and to silence her husband if he should ever try to be troublesome. I quite agree with her; so as to this first point you may consider it decided.'

'You are both very good to me,' said Andrew, 'but you know very well there is another point which can never be thought of. Well, one must speak of it; it is about the matter of inheritance. Is not that an unheard-of thing? Suppose the farm was mine, and she to inherit after my death, no one knows what quarrels and miseries might ensue, and yet I would not have you wronged for anything in the world.'

'I don't wish to mix myself up much in that matter,' said Christian, 'but how would it answer to settle it so that in such a case Christy should be entitled to buy it from her at the same price at which you get it? That would not be unjust; she would at all events carry off a good round sum with her, and I must own it would be a pang to me that the property should thus unexpectedly go out of the family, and I know none of the people around would like it either. Not, I hope, that you are at all likely to die, but no one knows what may happen.'

'I too have felt,' said Christy, 'that it would be a very great trial to me to go away from here, but I should not have said so, one does not like to be the only obstacle. If it could be arranged as my father proposes, I should be quite content; and if the wood had not got too much thinned meanwhile, I could afford to give her even more than you pay for the farm. So I really think the girl may venture herself up here; let things go how they will, she will not fare badly, and I doubt her ever doing better.'

'But besides that,' continued Andrew, 'it's a

shame that all the sacrifices should be on one side, and a marriage made on the plan of " Heads I win, tails you lose." I confess that I don't like settling so much upon a wife, and getting, in all probability, nothing with her. It is just as though there were something objectionable about me which it required money to get over, and yet I don't know, when one comes to calculate, that one of us is not as good as the other, after all. There is an arrogance and an insolence in it that makes me tingle all over.'

'Nay,' interposed his mother, 'if you really love the girl, don't give that a thought; when once you are married, the Lord will soon send you a way out of this difficulty, depend upon it. It's no use to tease yourself about a case which a hundred to one will never come to pass, and for two who are fond of each other to split thus, is not to be thought of. Real love is a very rare thing, and a trifle must not be allowed to cross it; people should remember that it is great luck to meet with such love once in one's life, it will scarcely be to be had twice. Therefore, if your brother and sister make no objection, I think you ought to close with their offer. If your sweetheart's nature be the kind I hope, she will remember their kindness all her life.'

'She has a good heart,' said Andrew; 'she really

is much better than she showed herself here. I myself could not understand her behaviour, but she will have to tell me what was wrong with her.'

'Then,' said Christian, 'everything may be considered settled, without any quarrelling or grasping, as so often happens; this rejoices my heart, and so let it remain, it will answer to you all even in this life, and people can do each other many a good turn when there is a kind feeling and perfect understanding between them. Remember that, children.'

'Nay,' said Andrew, 'it is not all settled yet; there is still another point that has nothing to do with money, and that therefore will, I hope, not give us very much trouble. But I must find out whether the girl really loves me or not, and whether for my sake she will give in to others, and control herself a little.'

'Why, what is the matter now?' said Lizzie. 'Have I displeased her in any way, and must I leave the house? If that be so, I'm not afraid; with twenty thousand pounds to back me, I can have my banns called next Sunday, not with one, but two if I like.'

'Do have done with your absurdities,' her mother interposed, 'no one is thinking about you; you must be put up with anyhow, so long as your father and I are here.'

'Yes, mother, and that is what I mean,' said Andrew; 'but did not you hear the old fellow talk of the farm being given up to me! what he meant was that you should resign all interest in it, and I take it up on my own account, profits and responsibilities and all, and then Mary Anne would be mistress here.'

'Well, and if it were so,' said Annie, 'if there's nothing worse than that, no one need grudge me a little rest; at all events, I make no objection to it.'

'Well, mother,' continued Andrew, 'this is what I do object to, and never will hear of. As long as you live you shall rule the house, shall manage and provide as you have always done, else I should have no pleasure in living here.'

'You are a foolish fellow,' returned his mother. 'Why should you not? a young woman may manage better than an old one; let her at all events try it, if she likes. It is often very irksome to young wives to have to conform to the ways of other houses.'

'Irksome or not irksome, mother, whether I bring in a wife here or not, I insist that so long as you are able you retain the rule and management of the household. Please God, you and my father will go on here just as of old, and my wife be as much a daughter to you as Lizzie is. That is what I am resolved upon.'

'Don't be too positive on that point,' said his mother. 'I don't see why you should lay such stress upon it; self-will does not answer.'

'Mother, it is not self-will; I have thought the matter over well. We have customs of our own here of which we need not be ashamed; we have enough, and there is something for others; so it has always been as long as can be remembered, so it shall always be so long as we remain here. It would be pain and grief to us all to have these customs altered. But down there they have very different ways, and I don't want their ways brought in here, they would never suit me. And, moreover, they would give occasion for much ridicule and much gossip, neither of which I should like. My wife comes into my house, and when there she must adopt my ways, and suit herself to my tastes; there is nothing unreasonable, I think, in that. But she must learn these ways, she knows nothing of them as yet. And our mother is one who will teach a daughter-in-law by love; she will not expect everything to come right at once, she will have patience with her as she has ever had with us; a son's wife will be happy with her, and will learn, almost unconsciously, under her teaching, what is reasonable and proper, and what makes for peace. But if my wife were at once to assume the management she would do so in her own way, according to what she has seen at home; she might forget to ask my mother's advice, and if my mother gave her opinion unasked, who knows whether she would be guided by it, whether she might not think of overruling my mother, and then all would go wrong? For if I had to say to her, "Mother used to do so and so;" or "We are accustomed to have things different, ask mother how they should be," who knows whether she would not become jealous, and fancy I loved mother better than her, and plague her heart and mine out by fretting and fuming? And if we did not set her right we should be all uncomfortable, and peace and contentment would be gone.'

'Oh, but surely she will not turn out this kind,' said Christian; 'you must know the one you have so set your heart upon.'

'Father, how can I know her?' replied Andrew. 'I know my mother, and can trust her; she will never plague my wife. But as to how a girl is to turn out, who can say? who can see beforehand what is in them? Some have thought a good deal depended upon sunshine or rain on the wedding-day, and that if it rained then they should have a terrible time of it all through their married life. At all events, something, never mind how small, may come between hearts, and then all is destroyed and spoiled.'

'Indeed yes,' said Annie; 'have we not ourselves experienced this; and not when we were young, but steady-going elderly folks?'

'Therefore,' Andrew went on, 'I prefer playing the safer game. One can easily conform to family customs when one is as a child in the house; but if once one begins to rule, a spirit of independence and self-will comes in. And my mother is wise enough, if by any chance the girl knows how to do a thing better than herself, to let her do it. Mother is not one who thinks it the way to manage to depreciate another's work; she will take everything well, and make the best of everything, and therefore I wish my wife to be under her guidance, and taught by her, and for this reason I will not undertake the farm.'

'I believe you are quite right too,' said his father, 'but if you lay so much stress upon this she will be offended, and will throw you up. You had better give some other reason, at all events.'

'No, father, that will I not; forgive me for saying so; but there is such a thing as being too subservient. They will end by thinking that they can carry all before them, and the girl will get it into her head that she is better than we, and is doing us all a favour, and that never answers. I never could stand it for my part, and even if you did not say much about it, you would feel it in the same way.'

'I would not lay too much stress on that,' said his mother, 'if other things went right. I think it is only a matter of opinion on your part, and perhaps a mistaken one, and to let it come between you would be going too far.'

'Mother,' returned Andrew, 'it is never well that all the giving way should be on one side. As it is, we have given way far more than I like; in the main we are coming in to all the old fellow's suggestions, which he had no right to make, while we hear not a word of what he means to do. What I now insist on is a mere secondary affair, which only concerns the girl herself, and which her father has nothing to do with. If she loves me, she will be too glad to oblige me, if not, very well, I find out in good time what I have to expect; for what a sweetheart will not do to please one, a wife never will, one may be pretty sure.'

'You are wrong there,' cried Annie; 'indeed and indeed you are. When I look back to what I was when I married your father, and compare it with what I am now, I seem to be another person. Fond of him as I was, I was always afraid of giving in to him too much; afraid of spoiling him; and whenever he asked me any favour, I invariably made a great fuss about granting it, whereas I was always enforcing sacrifices upon him, not exactly in earnest, but I wanted to see whether he loved me thoroughly, and if he had refused me anything I should have gone on in a most unreasonable way, as though the greatest misfortune had befallen me. If Christian had been less kind, if he had stood out as positively as you are doing, Heaven knows what would have happened! I do not think we should ever have come together. So it was with me in old days; but now I feel I would consent to anything he liked, and nothing could be too much to do for him. Things are changed. It grieves me to think of your being determined to fight out this point; it seems a sort of tempting Providence; perhaps a word or a look will be all that is needed. And people are not to suppose that when they first marry they are as they ever will be. Love and reason, like a hearth-stone, must be used daily before they are good for much. When my dear mother was alive, that was always her text.'

'Mother, understand me aright,' said Andrew. 'I would on no account fight about an indifferent point just to see who would give in; that should never be done between married people, and insisting on one's own way merely because it is one's way, is wretched work, as you truly say. But in this case it is an affair of right and wrong. Here the question is, first, whether a young woman is to submit to an old, or an old woman to a young, whether one's father and mother are to be set aside like a pair of worn-out shoes, or a mere inexperienced girl guided and taught to respect parents so long as it pleases God to spare them ; and, in the second place, whether a wife is to obey her husband as the Bible enjoins, or the husband to be led by the nose by the wife ? I must say, mother, if I were in your place, I should not wish to give up such a point as this, and I thought you loved me too much not to take some trouble to improve and instruct my wife. But I see how it is : the whole thing displeases you ; you do not like the girl, therefore you would rather have nothing to say to her, and live apart. I see this, and therefore it had better be given up ; better to speak out in time than afterwards to say, " I thought so, I knew how it would turn out, I was sure of it, only I did not like to speak my mind." '

' Come, come,' said Christian, ' don't get angry ; you ought to know that your mother's intentions are kinder than those you assign to her, and that she has never yet grudged any trouble taken for you. But in the main you are right, and I can but approve you ; to take the helm and push parents out of their places is certainly not the proper course, unless they prefer it, or one of them dies. To be sure, if I or your mother were to be removed, that would alter the case ; your undertaking the farm would then be right ; for to manage a house well man and wife must work together. For if the mother dies and the son's wife rule the household, and her husband remains working under his father, she is set over his head, and if the father dies and the mother manages, while the wife is only as it were a maid in the house, that does not answer either. But while father and mother both survive, son and son's wife fare alike; both are helpers, and neither has anything to complain of. In that you are not so far wrong, but I will not interfere with it. Give the matter a fuller consideration, and think how you would feel if the whole thing came to nothing, and what people would say.'

'Oh, as for that,' said Andrew, 'I have no anxiety. People know pretty well what we are, and so on which side the fault must lie.'

'You simple soul,' said his father, 'you think that, do you? I should have fancied you knew people better. Have not you found out that there are many whose delight it is to find a flaw in the best characters; and don't you know that whatever one may be, one is sure to have enemies as well as friends, and that nothing brings them to light so certainly as a broken-off match? It sets them all croaking worse than the frogs in Zealand (I was there once with a cargo of wine, and thought they would have driven me mad). When a wedding fails to come off, the fault is sure to be laid all on one side, according to the disposition of those who discuss it. There will be no end of unkind things said of us, of our means, our position, our characters. No one will ever get at the exact rights of it. Some will have it one way, some the other; but we know what sort of reports the Dorngrüt farmer is likely to spread; and depend upon it, Andrew, so only plenty of mud be thrown, some is sure to stick. Believe me, you will have vexation enough in consequence, and it will be a disadvantage to you all your life long, however innocent you may be; and this I tell you, not that you should come in to whatever they require, but that you should know beforehand all you will have to go through, and not say later, that if you had only known, you would not have acted as you did. And now good-night, and take care of yourself, so that, happen what will, you may be able to bear up. You have it all in your own hands, and you remind me of one at the helm who has to go down the rapids. Take care of yourself, and look sharp about you.'

And now outwardly there remained no more to be done but to get ready, and to set off. Nothing further was said on the subject, but each reverted to silent cogitation; and, as we have before observed, when people are right-minded, a good deal comes out of thinking; more perhaps than out of talking.

III.

AN HONEST WOOER.

ANY one who could have watched the proceedings at Liebiwyl on the following day, would have inevitably concluded Christy to be the bridegroom, and about to make a triumphant progress through the country. Almost all the morning through he was busy with the horses, taking one after the other from the stable to the fountain, and never having done washing and curry-combing them. Lizzie, who observed in passing how often he put their tails into the bucket, and then combed and brushed them out, gave it as her opinion that it was a pity he did not turn lady's maid; many a noble lady would be glad to have him.

'I think,' replied Christy, 'many a farmer's daughter might find me equally useful; but there are some of them I should not so well like to groom as these horses.

'Oh, nonsense with your scruples, indeed, as if I didn't know which makes the most fuss about cleanliness, a young girl or an old bachelor, who at last gets too idle to change his shirt more than twice a year.'

Upon which Christy gave her such a sprinkling with the wet tail of one of the horses that her shrieks were piteous.

'O you wretch! O Heavens! was ever the like? my new petticoat! O my goodness! my petticoat that I had put on for the first time to-day!'

In the afternoon Christy took the harness in hand, and drove them almost wild in the kitchen by the variety of things he wanted. Now it was a soft piece of linen, then of flannel, then a cupful of vinegar, then of oil, etc. For Christy was bent upon showing who they were, and what sort of a team Liebiwyl could send out. Like all old bachelors, he had more of the cat than the dog about him, attached himself even more to places than people. Not but that the best of cats are affectionate to people too, will run before the farmeress as far as the cabbage-garden, and accompany the daughter of the house to the first turning, but after that they find their way home again. So, too, old bachelor uncles. They are fond of people, to be sure, especially of those who keep the coffee-pot hot for them when they are behind their time. They are fond, too, of a child who shows a preference for them, and will go to sleep in their arms but above all, it is the house they cling to, the house they think of, the credit and glory of the house they are anxious to preserve. Hence it was that Christy was so careful about the handsome turn-out. It should be talked of far and wide, so should those to whom it belonged, by the people down yonder, where there were no well-ordered houses to speak of.

The fashionable world lays great stress upon a handsome equipage. Two horses are pretty well, but four are much better; four are aristocratic. The farmer is aristocratic in this; he must at least have four horses,—a pair of discreet mares for wheelers, two frisky young geldings in front. The former draw loyally from the first, the latter dance about to begin with; but when necessity comes, in the person of the driver, or the waggon has to go up hill, then they too work with a will; and it is a real delight to guide such a team through wood and field, when man and horses are so thoroughly used to each other that the whip is scarcely needed, and a word can bend the whole four to his will. Therefore, in Berne the whip is a kind of sceptre, and to know how to drive a point of honour. We often read how fond fashionable young Englishmen are of playing the coachman, and Parisians, who are

2 C

given to aping them, try their hand at it too; but in this they do but emulate our farmers, in whose lives the making over the whip to a son is an important event, that elevates the latter to a coadjutor and representative. The whip is indeed a marshal's baton, which the king only gives to his best soldiers. Accordingly, what a sensation it creates amongst us when a father takes back the whip he has once made over! Parental anger has no more dire threat than this: 'I'll have the whip from thee.' It almost amounts to a disinheritance, and is felt to be a disgrace equal to the degradation of a general to the ranks. And this punishment is not only threatened, but sometimes carried into execution, if a waggon gets upset, or a horse injured, or a young man pays his addresses to a girl of whom his father does not approve, or frequents a public-house that he dislikes, or other grave offences of the kind.

At Liebiwyl it was to Andrew that the whip belonged; Christy had never wished for it, and therefore he turned all his attention to the state of the turn-out, and pleased himself with the thought of the admiration and inquiry the four noble brown horses drawing their heavy load so easily would occasion. When he fastened on the timber and fodder he did not spare strong chains; and on Andrew remarking that so many were not needed, the road being good, Christy maintained it was better to have too many than too few; the chains were there, and he was glad that those people down yonder should see that there were plenty of them to be had at Liebiwyl, instead of the wretched old ropes that they were in the habit of tying their timber with, and even of those they had not enough, but were often obliged to jump down and borrow.

About three on the Friday morning Andrew meant to set out, and to set out alone. His father had offered to accompany him. Let things go as they might, he argued, two were better than one. But Andrew declined; he preferred to settle this most important affair of his life alone, unshackled by any advice, according to his own judgment, as behoved a man.

When such an expedition as this is impending there is not much sleep to be had in a farm-house the night before, though no one seems the worse for it the next day. Things are otherwise in a gentleman's family, where the cook frets for three weeks if she has had to get up on one occasion at five, and seven weeks if at four. The horses have to be well fed, and whoever has this to do seldom goes to bed at all; for farm-horses eat slowly, and eat a great deal, and like plenty of time for eating. And if in the stable all this trouble is taken for the lord of the whip, still less is he forgotten in the house. The mother lies down in her clothes for fear she should oversleep herself, for the driver ought to have a good breakfast as well as his horses, not merely a something warmed up, but a solid bit of beef and an omelette, the remnants of which, if any there be, are given to the faithful attendant who has been watching in the stable. A good mother is generally herself the cook—does not trust to a maid when her son has to make an early start. Indeed, the genuine old-fashioned manager is always the one to kindle and to put out the fire; she is the priestess of the house, the mistress of the hearth; the fire is her servant and must obey her, and there is something wondrously touching and venerable in this rule over fire and hearth which is the especial province of the true housewife.

Thus it was at Liebiwyl on this eventful morning. When Andrew had done his breakfast the team was all harnessed and ready, the servants had got up unbidden to lend a hand. Annie had had a long talk with her boy, and had exhorted him not to be over scrupulous, nor to think about her in the matter of domestic management; so only that the girl were good-tempered and willing, she would be certain to get on well with her whichever way it went. Also, he was to be sure to think over all that his father had said; when things had gone so far it was never well to draw back, and give rise to endless scandal. Christian called out from the bedroom—

'Do you want money? the key is in my breeches pocket, take whatever you like.'

And then he too had another short talk with his son, in which he told him he had only to see that he got the girl since his heart was set upon her; when once he had her he could surely manage her his own way; after all, she was but a girl.

'And for that very reason,' replied Andrew, 'we are not to place ourselves so entirely under her feet as to make her suppose we have nothing to do all our days but dance attendance upon her. If afterwards she found that things were not as she was led to expect, we should perhaps have tears and complaints that she had been taken in. And she would be right, too, if we failed to deal openly with her. That I mean to do. I shall speak out beforehand, father, and bring things to the test once for all.'

'Do as you will,' said Christian, 'I can't say but what you are right; only, whatever happens, don't take it too much to heart; try to think all is for the best.'

'I will do what I can,' said Andrew, shaking hands with his father, wishing him a good morning, and leaving the house.

The whip was fastened to the saddle-horse, who rubbed his head affectionately against his young master when he came to take it, while Christy lighted the all-responsible driver.

'Are the oats put in?' inquired Andrew, who had not forgotten the farmer's sly hint on that score.

'I put in half a measure and more,' replied his brother; 'I thought you might like to give a treat to your father-in-law's horses. Oats must be uncommon scarce down yonder.'

At the last moment out came their mother, with her lantern, and asked—

'Have you left nothing behind? have you your handkerchief and some whipcord in your pocket?'

'Yes, mother, I believe I have everything,' said Andrew.

'Well, then, fare you well,' said she; 'take care of yourself; may all go well with you, and don't be too late coming home. God bless and keep you.'

'Now, then, in God's name,' said Andrew, raising his whip, and steadily set off the horses; and carefully Christy showed a light till they got out of the yard into the road. It was rather a close shave to get through the gate, but that afforded a display of skill, and was the very reason why the gate was never enlarged, but the new posts always put in the old holes. The young master of the whip would have felt it a disgrace not to be able to pass through as small a space as his predecessors, and the whole village would have rung with the rumour: 'The young farmer, Andrew, will never be anything of a driver so long as he lives; only think, they have been obliged to widen the gate for him, though it has been driven through for a hundred years back, and always found wide enough till now.'

As usual, Andrew got through perfectly well, and in spite of his heavy load drove rapidly along the road. Meanwhile, having his four fine horses under his command, it was perhaps natural that his feeling of self-respect should grow stronger and stronger, as well as his persuasion that he was perfectly right in refusing to be dealt with as one who required to bribe a girl to accept him.

Love is a strange contradictory thing altogether, it is proud and it is humble; it bears all things, and explodes like gunpowder at the merest spark; it is sweet as new milk, and, like it, gets sour with a change of wind; it will give up life and refuse a trifle; will spontaneously offer goods and chattels, and withhold a farthing if the farthing be claimed; it will endure the severest ordeal, and at last despise the reward for which that ordeal was endured.

When Kunigunde threw her glove among the lions, Delorges leapt after and recovered it. But when he returned, sword on side and triumph in his breast, his spirit was up ; and he felt his life a thing of too much value to have been staked upon a fleeting caprice ; and that she who could so play with a life had no heart for deeper and worthier feelings. Therefore, when he re-entered her presence, he flung the glove in her face, and refused her thanks contemptuously. And this kind of self-respect must ever accompany all worthy love of a human being (love to God is different, and necessarily linked with humility), else it is no better than a mere animal feeling, that is bent upon its gratification at any cost, or some longing for wealth or rank : covetousness or ambition disguising themselves as love. Not but that the best of men are in some bondage to the flesh, and dependent more or less on external conditions and influences. I hold him to be indeed baptized of the Spirit and of fire who can bear an equal mind in ragged trousers or with royal crown ; at the head of a hundred thousand men, or sweeping a crossing ; hungry and thirsty, or seated at some Lord Mayor's table. He who could remain the same in all these varieties of circumstance, retain the same composure and self-respect, be at once lofty and simple, were a man indeed, a very prince of men, too great for any Valhalla. Which of us has not experienced the difference brought about in himself by different people and different surroundings, how he seems sometimes one person on entering a room and another on leaving it; bold or timid, suspicious or confiding, sentimental or sarcastic, as the case may be? The fact is, like chemical substances, we act and react on each other, so that according to the nature with which I come in contact I am repelled or attracted, modified, metamorphosed,—I am, in short, a different product altogether.

And now I would ask whether it was not to be expected, from that particular compound, a young handsome fellow with strength and skill, whip, saddle, and four fine horses exciting universal admiration,—that he should feel an increase of self-esteem, and a conviction that his personality deserved to be weighed in the balance, and not merely his silver and gold? The first time he had walked over anxious and timid; now there was nothing boastful or arrogant about him, but still he was full of firm resolve ; and, as he drove up to Dorngrüt, not only did his fine brown horses hold up their heads, but so did their master his as well, and gallantly and gleefully as they trotted on, so did he crack his resounding whip. This time he had not long to wait; up came Mary Anne with her sweetest smiles, held out her hand, and said—

'O how I have longed for, and almost thought you would not come! Do you bring good news?'

And with that she looked up lovingly into his eyes; and while he held one hand, she caressed the fiery Dragoon with the other, who neighed and pawed as if just out of the stable.

'I think I do,' replied Andrew. 'My people have been uncommonly kind to me; so much so that I am really ashamed of myself.'

'O heavens! how rejoiced I am you can never believe. Only think, that old wretch Jacob has been over and promised all sorts of things, set my father longing for him again by making believe that he should soon die, so that I have been in deadly terror lest my father should be on with him again. But, however, he has not done that, he has given him a refusal, only I fear, I fear that if the least obstacle arise as to our affair, I shall never escape old Jacob. And I would rather die.'

'Have no fear,' said Andrew.

Then out came Mary Anne's mother, who, as the young man held out his hand, replied—-

'Mine is so dirty I can hardly venture to give it you. I have been greasing my old man's shoes. It's a good thing that you are come; the girl has almost stared her eyes out of her head, though I said you could not be here till the evening. But is there no one about to help you to unload, and show you where to take the horses? It's very hot, and it will be bad for them to stand sweating here. Do look, girl, where those good-for-nothing boobies are.'

But Mary Anne did not even hear her mother; she kept close to Andrew, admiring his horses, and telling him how unhappy she had been, how the three or four days had seemed to her an eternity; she did not think she could have survived another. Such confessions as these young girls will in general only make *tête-à-tête;* before others they do not choose to show how deeply their heart is involved, nay, there are some who even think it unbecoming to let the secret out to their lover. They are curious creatures, young girls, and will never be rightly understood till it is known and admitted that many are actresses by nature, and many more brought up to act, so that the number of those who dare to show what they are is but small, or who are not misled by stupid mothers, stupid governesses, or stupid books, into playing a stupid part badly, instead of letting the fairest thing about them, their pure, earnest love, appear in all its undisguised beauty.

'You are a great fool to run on this way,' observed Mary Anne's mother. 'However fond you may be of a man, you should not let him find it out; you should always keep it half nailed down, otherwise he will soon come to think he may do what he likes with you, as you will find out before you have done. But you are not listening to me, and I must go myself to look after those good-for-nothing lads, who are never to be had when wanted.'

So, walking off to the house, she screamed out, in a shrill voice—

'I say, is no one about?'

Upon this, out came the farmer, and said the others were busy with the manure, and he himself would help to unload. He was not half so friendly as his womankind, came forward slowly, walked round the load of timber before he went up to Andrew; and when at last he did so, instead of bidding him the customary welcome in God's name, asked—

'Have you brought me the trees I chose, or others?'

'As to that,' returned Andrew, 'you can look at them, you will probably know them again; and whether they are the same or not, you'll not have much fault to find with this load; finer timber you will hardly find. But be so good as to tell me where I am to drive to; the waggon must be unloaded, and I should be glad to get the horses out of the sun.'

The farmer showed him the place. There were heaps of earth about, and the road was very narrow for such a load.

'You'll scarcely be able to drive in there,' said the farmer.

'We will see,' said Andrew, raising his whip; and without any shouting or storming, the horses, guided at will by a word or two, made their way safely and swiftly to the place in question.

'You are used to driving, the farmer almost involuntarily admitted. Perhaps he would have been rather pleased than otherwise if Andrew had upset the whole load.

'Only look,' cried his wife, 'how well he can drive, to be sure! I don't believe any one of our lads could have done that; but do go and look for eggs; we must have them. I have not enough for an omelette in the cellar, and when one has never a penny in one's pocket, and an old brute for a husband, what can one do if one wants a bit of white bread, or a wigg every now and then, but give one's eggs to the egg-woman?'

'Mother, I don't know where the hens lay,' replied Mary Anne, and darting off after the horses, helped to unharness them, in spite of her father's injunctions to let them alone.

'You don't know where the nests are indeed,' said her mother, 'as if there was ever a girl who did not find out where hens laid! But she is ready to eat up the young fellow, that's what it is; and if nothing were to come of it, I believe she would go out of her senses. Well, well, I like him too; there is nothing beggarly or pinching about his ways. I wonder if he has brought me a present; it would be pretty behaviour in him, more particularly if I have to use up my eggs for him.'

It was a distress to Andrew to have to squeeze his horses into the dark, close stable, and to remain in uncertainty as to how they would fare there with the other horses, who were running wild about it, and who seemed much disposed to kick at all new comers. But he had to set about unloading with the old man; and perhaps nothing could be more annoying to a quick, energetic young fellow who liked to get things out of his hands rapidly, than to be obliged to share a task of this kind with a person who was so tediously slow and clumsy that Andrew did not know whether it was natural, or done purposely to aggravate. And when, moreover, this quick young fellow had an important piece of business impending—when he waited to know whether he was to have his sweetheart or not,—such an ordeal became doubly distressing. The old man wanted to get as much work out of him as he could, and to detain him as long; added to which Andrew had constantly to run into the stable, where all the horses were kicking and plunging as if they would knock it down. At length he tied his saddle-horse in advance of the others, for he knew he could trust him to clear and keep a place for himself. Having done this, when next a neighing was heard, and the farmer suggested that he should run in and see what was going on, Andrew coolly replied—

'They will all do very well, I hope; they can't eat each other up.'

But the neighing continuing, the farmer ran off to judge for himself, for it struck him that his horses might get the worst of it; and so he brought the whip to bear upon them all, but Andrew's horses came in for the sharpest cuts.

It was pretty far on in the day when they went in to dinner, and in the meanwhile Mary Anne's countenance had considerably clouded over.

'We cannot treat you,' she said, 'as you treated us. You must excuse our fare. All I can say is that it is clean.'

'Don't trouble yourself,' said Andrew, 'I should have been sorry if you had made a stranger of me. It really is too bad that I should be sitting down to dinner here again so soon; but since it is there I must even consent to it in God's name.'

But the inward annoyance Mary Anne felt at her mother having nothing nice to set before him—no handsome china, nor glasses, nor knives and forks, such as she had seen at Liebiwyl,—Andrew could not read. All he saw was the cloud upon her face.

'What can be the matter with her again,' he kept thinking; 'so smiling a little before, and so gloomy now? Is she one of the capricious sort, or has she had a dispute with the old woman?'

Now it is easy to see what sort of expression a face wears, but difficult to know what gives rise to that expression. It is much the same with clouds on the brow as in the sky. We often see them rise before our eyes out of the fog-bank, and know them to be rain-clouds, children of the cold, bitter northeast wind, but often too we cannot trace their origin. They come and go, we know not whence or how all we do know is that they change the brightest sky into gloom; and so it is with the clouds on a maiden's face. Well would it sometimes be for her if it could be more accurately understood whence these spring, for many a cloud which rises from troubled affection looks exactly like the result of illtemper. One kind, loving word might disperse it into a tender smile, distil it into a penitent tear; and yet to all appearance it portends thunder and lightning, or even earthquake.

In this case Andrew did not see the source of the sudden cloud, and hence he thought it a suspicious symptom, and would have given much had it not been there. The coffee tasted bitter to him, and the omelette, in which, to tell the truth, the lack of eggs was supplied by flour, most thoroughly unpalatable. And the less Mary Anne herself approved it, and the less Andrew ate of it, the more out of sorts she grew; nay, at last she was downright angry, yet she would not let it appear in words. She knew that children never get a worse name than for contradiction or depreciation of their parents in the presence of others, and this she never did, not even when her heart was ready to burst. In such cases it was her wont to retire to her own room, throw herself on her bed, and have a hearty cry, perhaps shutting her door with more emphasis than usual. On this occasion she could not make her escape, could do nothing but give the cat a push; but when a young girl's heart is so heavy laden, is there, I would ask, any adequate relief to be got out of a mere push to a cat?

'And now, what sort of an answer do you bring?' asked the farmer, when the wine had been set upon the table. 'I would rather, for my part, that nothing came of it; but since the affair has got wind, I should like to know whether my proposals suit you. But, as I said, I would rather it did not come off, because when a cat smells roast meat, she does not care to run after mice.'

'Yes, and many a cat might have starved to death if she had waited till she got the roast meat she smelt,' replied Andrew.

'Be it as it may with cats,' said the farmer, 'it is

so with me; and if I had not given my word, I should never give it now.'

'And you,' inquired Andrew, turning to Mary Anne, 'are you too inclined to repent?'

'I am exactly the same as I was,' replied Mary Anne.

'Why, then,' said Andrew, 'I hope there will be no hitch in the matter; my family have been so kind to me, and have come in to every point. The farm is to be settled upon me for forty thousand pounds, and if I die without children, Mary Anne may have that sum, and do as she likes with it.'

'May have the farm, you mean?' interposed the farmer.

'No,' said Andrew. 'The farm has been as long as any one can remember in the family, and it would pain us to let it go out of it. Therefore Christy intends, should he survive me, to purchase it back, on account of keeping it in the family.'

'What, what, young man,' replied the farmer, 'are we to have all the bargaining over again? Do you suppose we do not know which is of most value, the farm or the forty thousand pounds? I should not have thought you so barefaced as that. But that's not all that you have in your head, I am sure; so out with it at once, that we may know where we are.'

To which Andrew suggested he did not think

there was anything unfair in what he had said about the eventual disposition of the farm. A hundred to one it would never come to that; and that was the only thing they laid any stress upon. The full possession of the farm he should come into at the death of either father or mother; until then its management would be carried on in their names, which must be pretty much the same thing to the farmer, he supposed.

Upon which the old man rose up—'Indeed, you suppose that, do you? You are cunning enough to try and slip that down my throat, and flatter yourself I do not see what you are at.'

'Nay indeed,' said Andrew; 'I had no underhand purpose, and have nothing that wants to be slipped down.'

'Don't be an idiot,' said the farmer; 'you are not so simple surely as not to see the difference between entering upon the property for forty thousand pounds at the present time or twenty years hence, or still later perhaps, for when one wants to get rid of them, people are never so obliging as to die. If you had the farm at once you might make something by it in the course of the next twenty years, and it is never the custom to pay as much rent to the old people as though they were strangers; so that they are able to get on, nothing more is wanted.'

'The old people are not to be dealt with hardly,

I should think,' observed Andrew. 'You would not surely wish your children to use you worse than any one else?'

'That has nothing to do with the matter, and concerns no one but myself,' retorted the farmer; 'but as we brew so we bake, and people need not suppose that I have not my eyes about me.'

'No one does suppose it,' replied Andrew; 'and I have no doubt my parents will annually give me whatever is fair and right.'

'But why then will you not let the case stand as I put it, since after all it comes much to the same thing?' asked the farmer.

'Well, then,' said Andrew with a heavy heart, 'I must just speak out honestly and plainly. My mother has done much for me, and is a good woman if ever there was one, and I will not have her thrown aside as if her day were done; it would grieve her too much; she never could stand it, even though she raised no objection. And then we have our own ways, and your ways are different, and one gets accustomed to one's own, and if all our ways were to be suddenly changed, it would give people much scope for gossip and ridicule, therefore it seems to me desirable that Mary Anne should come and be the child of the house and learn our habits and how things are managed with us, and when our mother is taken from us she will then be able to carry on in the way that we approve. She will have no hard time of it with us; no one will ever want her to overwork herself; and indeed it will be much easier and better for her than undertaking the whole of the management at once, and if she is only kind to my mother, she will find her the easiest person in the world to deal with.'

'I approve of that,' said the farmer's wife, 'but you must be very unlike other families to go on so about a mother. Here she is never thought of, unless to be flown at and blamed for whatever goes wrong. And if we had a hundred children to marry, I should never appear in the matter, unless linen was wanted, sheets, tablecloths, and the like, and then I should get well abused for not having them by me. And I should like to know how I can when the flax is all sold away from me in the way it is.'

'If once you take to prating,' said her husband, 'we shall never get to the end of our business at all; so shut up, will you?'

Meanwhile Andrew was assuring Mary Anne that his mother would treat her exactly like her own child, and that it was far better for her to be gradually shown how things should be, than at once to have to rule and manage without knowing how. It was easier to help those who were kindly disposed to instruct, than to hold the reins ourselves without any experience. And Mary Anne had thoroughly approved his views, and declared she should much prefer to have it so; it would make her terribly anxious, to have the care of such a household as theirs thrown upon her all at once. She had seen plainly how unlike the ways of one family might be to those of another. Meanwhile the farmer had reduced his wife to silence, and now returned to the charge.

'The match cannot come off,' he said; 'I will pay you for the timber. I see pretty plainly what you want—to have my girl for a servant, and take us in by your cunning. Therefore it is best to break it all off. As I said, when I scent roast meat, I don't need to run after mice; I will go and get the money.'

'But, father,' pleaded Mary Anne, 'I like much better that things should be so. I agree to it thoroughly; what should I do with ordering and managing when I know nothing about it? I have perfect confidence in them all.'

'You don't understand the subject,' said her father, 'and therefore need not interfere.'

'But surely, father,' urged the poor girl, 'it concerns me most after all. I must have a voice in it.'

'If you must,' said he, 'you'll find that it will have no effect. What is said is said;' and off he went to get the money.

'But, good heavens!' said Andrew, 'what an unreasonable man your father is! Are we then not to be allowed to speak out our opinion when we want no more than is fair? We are not such poor mean creatures as to let ourselves be dictated to, and made to give way in everything?'

'He is always so,' said Mary Anne. 'He gets his own way in all parish matters, and thinks he must do the same at home. He is turning old Jacob in his head again; the old wretch has got round him, I see. But do you give in, I beseech you, for God's sake. I can make nothing of my father; I know too well what he is set upon, and he never cared for me. You must rescue me if you love me; you must give in to his wish, and I promise you I will be a child to your parents, whether you have the farm or have not. When once I have made my escape from here, when once we are together, we can settle things as we like, no one will have any right to interfere, and whatever you wish I will come in to,—that I solemnly promise.'

'I believe you fully,' said Andrew; 'I know that you love me; but this is for life and death, and your father is right in saying that as we brew so we must bake. As far as I myself am concerned, there is nothing I would not do; but I cannot go and promise for the rest; and it is not just that they should all have to sacrifice themselves for my sake, and let themselves be trampled upon. I could not ask them to do so.'

'But do not you then love me? and whatever you

wish, the others will agree to; I saw how they all clung to you, and if you do not come in to my father's plans, he will break off and be on with old Jacob again. Think of me.'

'You are dear to me, dearer than myself,' returned Andrew; 'but if your father has a will of his own, are we to have none, and is ours in any way unreasonable? am I to throw father and mother aside?'

'Believe me, only believe me: I will be a child to them; I will be submissive. Am I not used to being so? But let it be as my father likes, else he will bid you go away, and what once he says he never retracts,' said the young girl imploringly, as she went up close to Andrew, and looked lovingly and sorrowfully into his face. Andrew's heart was wrung; he threw his arm around her, and pressed her to him.

'How dear you are to me,' said he, 'you little know. Had I seven lives I would give you them all, for they would be my own. I know you would keep your word, and do right. But I might die the first week of our marriage, and then others would get possession of you, and you could have no will of your own.'

'You will not die,' said Mary Anne; 'we must trust to God.'

'Yes,' said Andrew; 'but our actions are our

own, trusting will not alter their consequences. God has ordered it so, that we may learn to look well what we are about.'

'Listen, listen,' said Mary Anne. 'Now he is counting out the money; he will soon have done. O promise me that you will say "Yes" to everything, and settle it at once.'

'But, my girl,' insisted Andrew, 'just think if I were to die, and had to lie there, and feel that as soon as I was buried my people would have to turn their backs upon their old home; think, my girl, how I should feel, how you would feel, and whether I could have the face to pray for my poor soul, or hope for a happy death.'

'Hush, hush, my father has done. The very first day we can change it all, only promise my father what he insists on; we need not keep our promise more than we like, only contrive so as to take me away.'

'But shall I deceive your father then, and my own family too? Shall we build our happiness upon falsehood and double-dealing? Nay, love, that will never do. We will remain firm and faithful to each other, and never suffer men to part us; then we may indeed trust to God, and we shall be sure to come together, and with a safe conscience.'

'Listen, he is shutting down the chest, he is coming; for the dear Lord's sake say whatever he wants you, or else you do not love me, and I will have nothing more to do with you, and wish I had never seen you. On my knees I beseech you,' cried Mary Anne, in a low tremulous voice, with lips turned pale, and eyes fixed in their sockets.

And before Andrew could reply, in came her father, never asked a word about his decision, but paid down upon the table, on which Mary Anne leant trembling, his debt, in small piles of the worst possible money.

'There you have it,' said he; 'you will be in a hurry to get home, and I will not detain you.'

At this Andrew went up to the table; the money he did not even look at, but a dire conflict was going on in his breast. He was unwilling, he said, to leave in this manner, and surely a reasonable word or two might be allowed him. As to money and property, he would not stand out; what could be done should. He had shown that he had no interested motives, never even having inquired whether the girl was to have any fortune or not. At present they had enough, and for the future they could trust to God; and whether there was or was not anything more to come, with God's help he hoped they should be able to get on. But now he was about to disclose something to them, and they might make what they liked of it. In most families from time to time there would arise some discord or other; often, with God's help, it got worked away, often it did not. There was once something of the sort in theirs, and at that time his father had turned it in his head whether he should not give up the farm to him. But on reflecting, he had determined that his wife did not deserve that at his hands, as she had brought him a considerable property, and was a manager who had thought for everybody, and good sense in everything, and such a one ought not to be set aside while still in possession of her energies, because to lose authority and occupation might prey upon her spirits. It involved a heavy responsibility, merely on account of some temporal advantage to set aside one to whom God had spared all her faculties. That was the view his father took. Otherwise, he would have been quite ready to give up and let his son take his place. 'And shall I,' Andrew went on, 'shall I feel otherwise about my mother, who has been a true mother to me, from the first hour until now, who is always the first and the last in the house when there is anything to be done for any of us, and has never thought of rest for herself, even when she wanted it, or shown us unkindness in any way? I really have not the conscience to do such a thing, and, dear as the girl is to me, I would not take such responsibility before God and man; but my wife will never be worse off, or have less, on that account. And remember this, that you too have children, and never know what may happen to you, or how much reason you may have to rejoice that your children behave well towards you.'

'What do you run on to me so about your mother for?' said the farmer. 'I have nothing to do with her; and as to my children, they will have to do pretty much what I choose. You have heard that what has been said is final; count your money; I will go and tell them to put your horses to, and you can set out.'

Unconsciously the tears were running down Andrew's cheeks, and Mary Anne stood pale, silent, lips quivering, by the table.

'Is it possible?' said Andrew. 'I never heard before, and never could have believed, that a man who himself had children, could have wished to set one against one's parents. But we will remain true to each other, and then no one will be able long to divide us.'

And so saying, he held out his hand to Mary Anne. But she still stood speechless there, her lips trembling, and her dark eyes dilating.

'Give me but one kind word,' implored Andrew; 'I will rest upon it, and trust to God, and if you ever want me just send a message; the landlady will gladly do so much for you.'

And so saying, he would have taken her in his arms, but at that she fired up, and thrust him rudely away.

'Go out of my sight, don't touch me; now I know what your love for me is worth,' she cried in a broken voice. 'Have I not prayed to you, and how have you heard me; promised and vowed, and how have you trusted me? Yes, trust in the same way to God, and He will forsake you as you have forsaken me.'

Andrew tried to speak, but she would not listen to him.

'Go away,' she cried, 'I want neither to see nor hear you more. One word, and you might have saved me, and you would not speak it, and you leave me thus, and now' . . . .

And her words breaking down into convulsive sobs, she rushed into the next room, flung herself on the bed, and wept till it shook under her.

Andrew was struck dumb and terrified; he wanted to soothe, to explain; went up to the bed, begged for one kind word or look, would have taken her hand; but she would not hear him, and if he touched her, shrank away as though his hand had been a snake. As he was standing there, heart-broken to have to part from her in such a state, her mother came in, and said—

'Leave the girl alone, it's of no use now. Why

did you go and spoil the whole thing? It was your doing. No doubt it is right and proper to be kind to a mother, and every now and then to give her a present, but to make such a fuss as this about her is downright stupid, and does no good. One day or other she must leave the farm, and a little sooner or later what does it signify? I know I should be glad enough if some one would take the trouble off my hands, and I could get a little peace and comfort, a drop of coffee, and an eatable morsel every now and then. But now you had better go; not another word will you get from the girl; she is a dreadful one to cry when she once gives way, and if the old man finds you here he will be in a rage.'

'It goes to my heart to leave her,' said Andrew.

'It's your own fault,' replied she; 'take your money and be off, there is no help for it now.'

'You must come at once,' called out a gruff voice through the door; 'no human being can harness your devils of horses.'

'I'll do it,' cried Andrew; and once more went up to Mary Anne and implored her to give him one kind word, and for God's sake not to let him take leave of her thus. But sobs were all her answer, and she buried her head still deeper in the bed-clothes.

'Come, come,' urged her mother, 'I hear the old man. Take your money; nothing would induce her to give you a kind word,' and sweeping the coins into Andrew's hat she put it into his hand.

'Farewell!' she said, 'and don't be vexed; things won't always go as we would have them, and it's well to get early used to this.'

'It's high time you should come,' said the farmer. 'Such a wild set of horses I have never had in my stable before!'

Anger and grief were boiling in Andrew's breast, and the old man's speech afforded them a kind of outlet.

'If they are reasonably treated they will show themselves more reasonable than many a man,' said he.

'I suppose you want to teach me how to manage horses,' said the farmer, 'but you are rather too young for that.'

'Nothing of the kind,' retorted Andrew, 'it would be too long a task.'

'What do you mean?' asked the farmer.

'There are many kinds of people, and many kinds of horses, and some can bear what drives others wild; it all depends upon habit.'

'You must have trained yours very ill then,' said the farmer.

Andrew's answer was lost in the stable. There was a tremendous uproar going on there,—farm-servants standing with sticks and whips, thumping and clashing; his horses kicking and plunging; the others had been driven away. When he saw how things stood, he turned them all out with their whips and sticks, and began to speak to his horses, who, as soon as they heard his familiar voice, appeared to understand that the hour of deliverance from their wretched thraldom was come, neighed loudly, turned their heads round, and though they still danced about, left off biting and kicking. He harnessed and bridled them gently and deliberately, for he was really sorry for the horses; and the consequence was that they became quite docile, and followed him willingly out of the stable; but the moment they saw the farmer and his servants he had sad trouble with them again. One wanted to be off here, the other there; probably the shortest way home they could find. Andrew had to manage them all unaided, for as soon as any of the men approached them, the horses reared and kicked; and to add to his difficulties, he had to deal with an angry mare, upon whom he had, in his agitation, put the wrong gear, and who strongly objected to being a leader; but she had to submit to it, for her master would make no change, though the Dragoon would really have suited him far better as the saddle-horse.

During this hard work (for to harness and put-to four bewildered horses is no slight affair), Andrew had attained to some composure; and in proportion as his horses quieted down so did he. Very calmly he gathered his things together, searched for a chain which had been overlooked, whether intentionally or not he did not inquire, emptied the bag of oats into the farmer's chest, gave two francs to one of the servants, went up to the farmer and said—

'Good-bye, and thank you for your hospitality.'

'You have nothing to thank me for,' returned the latter; 'thank you for carrying for me. I don't inquire what it costs, as it was your own offer.'

Andrew took no notice of this speech, but sprang into his saddle, his refractory mare rearing as high as she could, and all four horses neighing loudly; but he reined them in with a strong hand, and made them proceed at a leisurely pace, in spite of the one he rode dancing under him, and it was only when they had gone about a hundred yards from the house that he permitted them to fall into a trot, which became quicker and quicker and soon carried him out of sight.

'That's a proud young fellow,' said one of the servants, 'who knows how to ride and to manage horses.'

'And knows, too, the proper thing to do,' added the other, who had got the tip.

The farmer stood for a few minutes looking thoughtfully after Andrew, with his hands in his waistcoat pockets; then suddenly turning upon the servants, said they had stared long enough, and it was high time to turn to work again—they had wasted nearly half a day—and then he walked away from the house, followed by the great brown dog.

IV.

SILENT SORROW.

ANDREW'S team trotted along swiftly, but swifter coursed the blood through his veins. The pace seemed intolerably slow to him, his limbs twitched with impatience, and half unconsciously he urged the horses to their fullest speed. Anger and sorrow, love and pain, pride and humiliation, all boiled together within him; and just as wind fans the flames, so this rapid drive did but increase the fierce excitement of his mood.

It is always a very peculiar sensation to have to return home after a refusal, whether it be downright or delicate, administered by parents, or by the girl herself; in every case it is a spark that fires a train within us, and gives rise to strange explosions there. Of course all trains are not alike; there is more powder in some than others, nor are the fireworks all of the same colour, but they have a good deal in common; and a refusal, dress it out as you will, is a most uncomfortable thing.

Andrew's case, however, had some striking peculiarities about it. He had not failed through any want of energy on his part. The girl loved him, he was able to satisfy her parents' monetary requirements, and yet he was rejected, rejected with contempt by the old man; while the girl herself turned angrily away from him, and would not speak one kind word. And yet he had been right, only they were unreasonable, and hence the wreck of all his happiness. Now, there is nothing more incomprehensible and exasperating than the unreason of others, and those who suffer from it generally fall into a mood of antagonism to all the world, and even the world's Maker. So it was with Andrew. Earth seemed to him an abominable place, from whence he would gladly gallop away; nor had he any comfort in looking up to Heaven, which was responsible for having called so much sheer folly into existence. It was well for him that he came across nothing on which to vent his indignation but a dog who ran out to bark at the horses, and who in return got a cut with the whip which sent him howling home, and possibly cured him of his barking habits altogether.

Gradually, however, this fever cooled down, and the vague sensation of rage changed into a definite train of thought. Over and over again he revolved the past, and tried to discover whether he himself had been in any measure to blame. When he thought of the farmer, his arm began to twitch, and woe to the horse who committed the least indiscretion at these moments, for Andrew felt as though it were old Dorngrüt who was receiving the cuts of the whip, and that the harder they were the more good they did him. Then his thoughts glided off to Mary Anne, and there remained, though in a distracted condition. At first he was bitterly angry with her, but gradually something within him seemed to take her part; he began to put himself in her place, and from her point of view look upon the assent required as merely a formal affair, by which he need not have been really bound. He remembered how his mother had warned him not to lay too great stress upon this point, and to question whether he had done well to refuse to trust the young girl, as she so implored, and to leave her in the power of a brutal father, who snapped his fingers at duty and justice. Was it indeed only wilfulness and obstinacy on his part, and not the unreasonableness of others, that had wrecked the happiness of two hearts? And while these doubts prevailed, but that there was a thick hedge bordering the narrow road on both sides, who knows whether he might not have turned round at once, and galloped off to

Dorngrüt, to expiate his fault by an unqualified assent to everything required?

But again, this internal advocate for the other side had been confronted all along by a terrible image, and this image came nearer and nearer, and grew stronger and stronger in all its details,—the image of the quivering, passionate girl in her convulsive excitement, her pallor, the flashing of her eyes, her colourless lips, her rude repulses, her wild gestures, her ungovernable sobs and tears. Never had he seen any human being in such a state, never his mother, or Lizzie, or the servant-maids; all indeed might be angry or cross at times, might answer sharply, sigh deeply, might even have a fit of crying, and for a while prefer not to show their faces; but no one that he knew had ever shown such complete want of self-control, such relentless desperation and rage. What Christy had told him of a girl in a passion now recurred to his mind; Mary Anne had been just as bad. Was he not fortunate to have seen this in time, to have discovered the evil in its full extent before it was too late; for how wretched would it have been to have married such a woman, and what a disgrace to have brought home one who was liable to a something unknown to his own family, a something that looked like madness, and which might perhaps come on often, possibly in public as well as before her husband

and his parents ? Andrew had heard of the falling sickness, but an attack of this kind seemed to him worse. It had distorted the girl's face to such a degree that he hardly knew her, had made her actually a repulsive object, that a man would gladly get as far from as possible. Thus the last recollection rose before his much perturbed mind in ever darker colours, till at length he was almost ashamed of his suit, and rejoiced at its issue.

The last impression, last word, last look, and all associated with them, make so strong an impression upon one who is going away, that a peculiar importance should ever be attached to their character, more particularly by a young girl. No need for her to assume an artificial sweetness; but at least she should be able so to control herself as never to appear out of temper. There is indeed a lofty, sublime indignation which exalts a maiden to a goddess, but this is rare; all other anger distorts, renders ugly, and the roughest clown who knows nothing of the beautiful is yet sensible of the repulsive appearance thus created. True, it is rather hard to demand from a girl the habitual self-control few men practise, and perhaps men are even more to blame for failing to do so; but in them anger is not so unlovely and unlovable as in woman. This is a matter of feeling and taste ; and as it is taste and feeling that render us so susceptible of feminine beauty and charm, the converse is unavoidable.

True also, just as there may be a complication of circumstances which leads a man through rage to murder, and subjects him to a murderer's doom, and yet leaves in our hearts a feeling of compassion for him, and a hope that he may find mercy before God; so sorrow, pain, disappointment may, as it were, almost unavoidably force a girl into a mood that alienates her lover's heart. She could not do otherwise; it was not to be expected from her character; but for all that the effect, the impression is made, is a *fait accompli*. What shall undo it now? What shall blot out the image that ever floats before his mind? Who can avert the consequences of such an image? With all Mary Anne had to offend her,—her earnest wish of belonging to Andrew frustrated, her belief that her hopes of deliverance lay in him, her conviction that he would make any sacrifice to obtain her, disappointed,—who would not have done much the same? who can venture to say they too might not have sobbed and wept? But what the eye has seen remains seen, and many never think at all of what gave rise to it; others do now and then, but such thoughts generally come long after the event, and are soon dispelled.

It was not so, however, with Andrew; these excusing thoughts rose ever before the accusing image; for the good soil in his nature was deep, and flowers sprung up in it rather than weeds, and love warmed it like a sun. The image of the angry girl was the bad fairy who crept into the garden of his soul, and sought to transform the one he loved into an unsightly dragon; a weir-wolf with flaming eyes; a savage hyena, with gnashing teeth and hoary hair bristling with rage. But like a true knight his better mind fought loyally against the bad fairy; and when she sought to exercise her spells over his beloved, interposed its good broadsword between them and defeated the wicked magic. And the more intense the inner conflict became, the more the outward excitement died down. Andrew sat calmly in his saddle, guided his horses quietly along, and whoever greeted the handsome driver received a friendly word or bow in return.

Compassion for Mary Anne ultimately won the day; he pitied her from the ground of his heart; he viewed the rude conduct of the farmer more patiently; a man like that had no moral sense, and did not know better. He was glad he had betrayed no particular vexation, had controlled himself till he got a hundred yards from the house. But one feeling was permanent with him, that all was over, that there was an infinite abyss between him and Dorngrüt, that the past days were irretrievably gone—were like a lost world with which fancy might still play, but which has no connexion with the future. That so it should be grieved him; for who does not sorrow over the grave of a dead love? who would not shudder to know when the sun had set that it could never rise again? And as a true man stands by such a grave as this, well may tear after tear roll down; but for all that he does not throw himself down into it; a strong hand sustains him, the faith that nothing happens by chance, but comes from that Father's hand who orders the courses of the stars, and numbers the hairs of our head. Such a man does not beat his breast, or tear his hair, and accuse himself as a murderer. When a course of action has been well considered, and every proper effort made, 'tis but evidence of confusion of mind or childish impatience to cry out against it because the result has not corresponded with our wishes. Right and wrong are not to be judged by consequences. And so in Andrew's case the more composed he grew, the more he admitted and felt his loss, the less he suffered from any doubt as to the nature of his decision.

He could not have acted otherwise; not only had he pledged himself to a certain line of conduct, but it was the right line; and right is not to be twisted, like a beanstalk, this way or that according to circumstances; it is not a sum of money with which we can speculate at will, nor care to lose a portion.

In this straightforward way of just doing right lies endless comfort, but at the same time it requires no small strength; it involves being faithful to the end, relinquishing the illusory hope of reaching the goal as well by a series of turnings and twistings as by keeping the straight path; of being wiser than God, and the artificers of our own happiness.

Often, indeed, this is grievously difficult to human wisdom and human weakness, because we, in our short-sightedness, are given to fear danger in unflinching persistence, and to see safety and expediency in twistings and turnings. But when we trust to the latter, the result is something very different from our expectations; we find ourselves with a millstone round our neck, insecure in our footing, and the deep sea below us, and what have we to look to then?

One comfort upheld Andrew more and more; he had uprightly and loyally adhered to what he knew to be right, and he could trust God with the rest! But this can never be done by one who has merely shifted and temporized, flattered himself, given way, twisted, haggled, and yet failed after all to accomplish his desire.

It was late before Andrew got home, where all were anxiously awaiting him, and interpreting this lateness of return as a sign things had gone well;

indeed, Lizzie spoke of going to bed, for she felt certain he would not be back at all to-night, and would lay any wager they liked about it.

'I would take it,' said Christy, 'were there any chance of your paying it; but you've no money. Andrew is as certain to come home as hay is certainly not straw. It is possible that the farmer down yonder may sometimes have a man as a guest, though I doubt it. I have been there, and it was but little he offered me; but nothing would induce him to keep four horses for a whole night. He never even asked me to go into the stable and put up ours for an hour or so. I know his sort pretty well.'

Soon afterwards the sound of wheels was heard in the stillness of the night.

'There he is.'

'No,' the others cried, 'that's not he; he would drive faster than that surely.'

But Christy contradicted them; and during the discussion, quietly, and without any cracking of his whip, Andrew drove the waggon in at the gate.

'He has not succeeded,' said his mother.

Silence and sadness now prevailed in Liebiwyl; but the different members of the family were more intimately united than ever in the bonds of an unspoken affection. Which of us does not know how strangely deserted and still the house out of which a loved one has been carried to the grave; how empty and desolate life seems as we return thence; how we miss something, go where we will, while, at the same time, we lovingly press around the one who is the most stricken by the blow, and would fain make up by our increased tenderness for what has been taken from him; how indeed the affection of all hearts burns clearer and purer than ever before, just as the sun never shines so brightly as after a heavy storm! This is the blessing of true love; it is itself the balsam for the wounds it inflicts.

So it was at Liebiwyl. Each voice took a gentler tone in speaking to Andrew, every one tried to do what they could for him, and to show him how dear he was to them all, but little or nothing was said on the subject of the refusal. Of course, he told them how he had fared, and the whole family felt it deeply; the young people being especially indignant with Mary Anne, and Lizzie confiding to Christy that she could never so have used any one for whom she had a spark of love. The parents were most aggrieved by the insolence of the old farmer to a family at least his equals; as to the girl, she was but a child, and behaved like one, but it was to be hoped there were not many such old men. The mother hinted that she had had her fears, and would willingly have yielded for her part;

but no one blamed Andrew, the thing was over, and what is the use, in such a case, of saying, 'I should have done so and so,' or 'You should.' It's easy to be wise after the event, says the proverb, and experience bears this out. Before it, indeed, good advice is scarce; but after, every infant has enough and to spare, and presses it upon you gratis. Nothing is more aggravating than such a display of cheap wisdom when of no manner of use, and this Andrew was spared.

Annie grieved most especially at her hope of a daughter-in-law being over, or at all events indefinitely postponed; she had so wished to see installed the one who was to succeed her in the management of the house. But she never thought of proposing a new love to her son, a premature proposition of the kind only increasing sorrow, and one of the bitterest fruits of affection being the attempt to pour happiness upon a heart that has no desire for it. And she was rewarded for her discretion, for Andrew sought more and more the companionship of his mother, who would talk to him of old times, and acquaint him with past family customs and family antecedents as far back as she knew them.

But for all this Andrew had an inner life of his own, which, dearly as he loved her, he did not reveal to his mother; it was his past life of love, his lost vanished days. Such vanished days as these are like the traditions of a former golden age, with this difference, that national traditions grow ever fainter, while in a lover's heart that past time shines brighter and brighter, just as the evening glow is often deepest the lower the sun sinks. But the fairer the tints of that sunset of love, the deeper his resolve not to attempt to conquer back the vanished magic land from the depths of the sea. And hence he hid it in the depths of his soul, and veiled it in resolute silence, for he knew how apt people are to wish to recover the past, how fain they would restore the lost to one they love, often losing more in the attempt than they could have regained even if successful. He knew his mother's unselfishness and affection for him, and how, could she but discover what was going on within him, she would sacrifice her own life to knit again the severed bond, and win back for him what he still held so dear. But it was his solemn conviction that it was better so, and this conviction stood firm as a rock in the waves, though coloured by the sunset red, and surrounded by the salt foam of loving sorrow. He avoided all allusion to it, and all questionings, feeling how easily one single word might become a magic word strong enough to burst bonds and shiver rocks; a diver to bring up to sight the sunken treasure; an overmastering impulse stronger than his deliberate will. But when he was alone he lived over those days of love, and constantly they put on some new beauty, sweeter seemed the maiden, and sweeter the tie between them. Therefore he liked to be alone, and often got up at night to lean out of his window and lose himself in delicious dreams. When he looked up to the starry wain that ever holds its steadfast course through the sky, his thoughts adverted to the dark house at Dorngrüt over which that constellation would silently pass in its brilliant majesty; he thought of his sweetheart beneath that low roof, and wondered whether he still lived in her heart, and whether she too sometimes called up the sorrowful image of the past. He would have given his life to have that question answered. If indeed it were so, how gladly would his spirit have left the body, left house and home and all, to animate the image that she bore in her heart! Oh, what a sweet life of ideal joy would that be, to watch each morning the unclosing of her eyes, to hear her pray to God for him, to receive the first greeting of her loving thoughts, to accompany her every step throughout the day, in lonely places to hear her call on his name, to feel the kisses that her fancy bestowed! Andrew would have given half his days if he could only have read in those stars above him what was passing in that young girl's heart. Often he thought to himself, 'If we never meet again in this world, and both die, shall we see and know each other in the next? Will there still be something to divide us there, or shall we dwell together in unclouded love?' Thus he dreamed and wondered, and devised many a romantic scheme for going to Dorngrüt and finding out how things stood. He might make his appearance there as a beggar, or a servant wanting a place, or he might pay a quiet visit in his own person to the landlady, and hear something from her, or wander round the house by night. These and many other plans he revolved, and carried none of them into execution, not from indecision, or doubting which of them was best, but because, in spite of his day-dreaming, his conviction that things ought to remain as they were held its ground; and often as he longed to talk out his thoughts to his mother, the certainty that she would throw all her influence into the scale of his yearning wishes, not of his steadfast will, kept him resolutely silent.

This quiet loving uneventful family life began, after a while, to look a little tedious to Lizzie, and she took to longing for something more stirring and varied. Now it is singular how much in common there is between young men and wasps. So long as a pear is hard and sour, wasps may indeed fly round it, but that is all; they never settle; the moment it begins to ripen the greedy creatures scent it from afar, come about it in clusters, and never quit till they have devoured it all between them; that is their way. But young men, though like wasps in finding out a hundred miles off when pears begin to grow soft and sweet, yet differ in this, that each wants the whole pear for himself, and has no idea of partnership in the matter. And if a young girl is not at once snapped up, it is often because there are too many hovering round, and she cannot find out who would appropriate her most pleasantly and tenderly.

So now it was with Lizzie; the young men seemed to have gone wild about her, and many an offer was made, but all in vain. A young farmer whom she had known from childhood, a schoolfellow whom she had teased and laughed at, quarrelled with, scratched, slapped, and in every way tormented from the first year of schooling to the last, and ever since delighted to turn into ridicule, slipped himself in amongst the rest of the wasps who were buzzing about the dainty pear. Lizzie made more fun of him than ever, aimed all the shafts of her wit and malice against him in such a way that her mother often had to check her, and beg her to hold her peace, and remember that there was such a thing as going too far. This would quiet her for a while, but she soon relapsed, and became more intolerably pert than ever.

Now, one Sunday when Christian was alone, taking charge of the house, this very young man came up to Liebiwyl, and asked him to give him his daughter. Naturally Christian was greatly startled, and replied—

'Ulric, you have taken me unawares, I never gave you a thought. As far as I myself am concerned, I should have no objections to make; but I must talk it over with my family, and I don't know what the girl herself might say.'

'As for her,' replied Ulric, 'it is all right.'

'That's strange,' said Christian; 'I think you must be mistaken.'

'One thing is certain,' replied the suitor; 'she has as good as promised me, and she can never have gone so far as to do so in jest.'

'I should hope not indeed,' said Christian; 'such matters are not to be trifled with. But yet I can't help wondering that it should be so; and if any one else had told it me I should not have believed them.'

'It's just the same with me; I should not have believed it either if I had heard it from any one else; not but what she has always taken my fancy, and I could have been fond enough of her long ago. But she always made such fun of me, and quarrelled with me, and went on so that I could not venture to think of it; on the contrary, I used always to say to myself, whoever marries her will be led a pretty kind of life. The other day I chanced to be at the new baths in Herrlige, standing about and looking on, and not knowing whether I would dance or not, or what exactly I wanted, when some one tapped me on the shoulder, and said : " Poor fellow, has he spilt oil, or what is it? But look here, I have something in prospect for you. If you will have three dances with me, and come with me a bit of the way home, I'll give you half a bottle of wine, and perhaps a pennyworth of cheese and a crumb of bread, but nothing more." And there I stood staring with my mouth open, not knowing what this could mean, because it has been your Lizzie's way to make a fool of me whenever she could, and I took it for granted she was at her old pranks then. But when I made no answer, she went on : " Listen, Ulric, you can do me a real kindness ; there are two wild beasts after me— dreadful fellows ; I don't know whether they are gentlemen, or what sort of creatures they are ; the one gives himself out as a lawyer, and the other a doctor, but they are both as rude as they can be, and I don't think our milkman could go on in a more uncouth way, though he does come from the Canton of Lucerne. I am downright afraid of them, and I don't want the disgrace of being seen with them on the road, and dancing with them. I have such confidence in you, I am sure you will never leave me in the lurch." I vow I did not know whether I was standing on my head or my heels, but I was pleased enough to see that she sent the others about their business, and could not help thinking I was not so disagreeable to her as I had always supposed. But I had no end of trouble before I could get her to consent to my coming here to ask for her; and after all, she would insist upon not being present herself, which would have been the proper thing, and what I had meant. "I might go," she said, "if I liked, but no one would see her home till midnight."

'She is always the same,' said Christian; 'but there is no harm in her; quite the contrary. I am very fond of her, and if once she settles down she will make a capital housewife. But just now she is full of frolic, and unless she is at some mischief or other all day long, she does not think life worth having. But that will pass off with her as with others; no need for any other cure than time. If you like to venture upon her, I shall willingly give my consent; but think what you are about, she is a ticklish girl to deal with.'

'Ay, indeed,' Ulric was beginning, 'I have reason to know that—,' when Christian, who sat nearest to the barn, was under the impression that he heard a sound behind the closed door, and thinking it might be one of the maids, who were given to poke their noses everywhere, got up more rapidly than his wont, and opened the door, when it seemed to him as though certain bundles of straw which had been pushed into a corner were shaking in an odd way, and on moving them, who should he find but his own little daughter sitting there, and listening to the negotiations? Christian burst out into a hearty laugh, and Lizzie herself was not in the least disconcerted. She had wanted, she said, to know how a youth of Ulric's stamp would set about making an offer, and suspected that something might get said that she should never hear in any other way, and it had been exactly as she thought.

'You,' said she, turning to her suitor, 'you need not have said anything about my giving you leave to come, for whether I would take you or not was not the question, but what my father would say; and as for that, I have given no actual promise.'

Poor Ulric stood there aghast, till Christian interposed. His daughter had heard what had been said, and such things were not subjects for jesting. But there was no occasion to announce it just yet, at all events. The thanksgiving season (the holy season, as it is called) was coming on; and besides, he would rather it was kept back for a time on Andrew's account, a wedding just now would revive the remembrance of his own failure. But she must tell her mother, and that this very evening; it would be a comfort to her, for when one had such a thoughtless little girl one never knew what trouble she might bring one, whereas, once married, her husband could look after her and take care of her.

At this, Lizzie was almost cross, and said—

'Very well, then, father, if I give you so much trouble, it's high time I should leave; but I thought I conducted myself in a way that need not have much alarmed you.'

'I don't complain of thee, child,' said Christian; 'but how great our own weakness is we are generally the last to know, and if we get through life respectably, we have to thank God for it, rather than ourselves.'

V.

THE HOLY SEASON.

IT was the so-called holy season in harvest, which ends with the day of humiliation and thanksgiving, now close at hand.

The holy season! Are not, then, all seasons and days alike given us for our growth in holiness, and ought not all to be dedicated to God? But we poor men are so prone to make bargains with Heaven, to set aside a portion for God, and dispose of the rest in our own way. For a few days many of us are willing to be thoughtful and serious, and these we call holy days, flattering ourselves the Lord will be satisfied with this compromise, and comfortably returning to our old way of life, almost like a glutton who intentionally fasts for a few hours in order to guzzle by and by with greater zest. For the perverted mind perverts the best things, and can even change the means of grace into a snare.

But for all that, there is something very beautiful about our four holy periods, our four spiritual seasons of the year, each having its special influence over the human mind, and all, by their constant recurrence, tending to ward off spiritual slumber. When one harvest is already garnered, and the young seed beginning to sprout for another, when the leaves are growing yellow on the trees, and the ripe fruit shows bright between them, then should man remember that he too is a tree from which fruit will be required, that the human race is the great world-field, to be judged by what it brings forth. We ought, with our spiritual eye, to behold our Lord daily visiting His trees, seeking fruit thereon, and ourselves to search anxiously for what our Lord looks for. This will give rise within us to humility and godly sorrow; for how little fruit does man, the crown of creation, bear, compared to the abundance that the trees display (and even that little is flecked and worm-eaten)! how sparse and sickly the growth of the wheat on the great field of the world; how ripe and luxuriant that of the tares the enemy has sown among it! With thoughts such as these will come the stream of repentant tears, the inward yearning after Him who came to seek the lost, and to open heaven. Such a day of penitence and thanksgiving admonishes us that we are still wanderers in the wilderness, but that God has sent us a deliverer and a guide, and encourages us to be happy and thankful in the wilderness, for beyond it lies the land of promise, which all shall reach who follow that guide.

In country places this anniversary is very solemnly kept. Even the evening before is quietly spent, and on the day itself a wondrous stillness prevails throughout the district. There are few farmers who, during its course, think of taking a horse out of the stable; no one is to be met on the road but church-goers, or sermon-hunters, whom curiosity drives to some other than the parish church, to hear how their neighbours are lectured for their faults. Meanwhile the pastor has been earnestly and devoutly meditating upon his discourse, contemplating the seed-field, seeking to discover whence comes the blight that most threatens the harvest, and laying before his people the conclusion to which he has arrived,—not imperiously as a lord over God's heritage, but humbly and sorrowfully, conscious that he is himself a member of the flock, and only different, it may be, from the rest, in a quicker eye to discern, and readier tongue to point out, the spiritual sicknesses common to him and them.

At Liebiwyl the day had always been religiously observed and spent in quiet retirement, nor, except in times of sickness, would any member of the household fail to attend church at least once, and the pastor's discourses would long afford matter for grave conversation.

On this particular festival people do not walk slowly and leisurely to church; on the contrary, the dense stream pours rapidly along; no one likes to be late, all are bent upon finding places. The older people are, the earlier they set out, and the church, at least in fine weather, is full before the preacher enters, more solemnly and earnestly even than usual, knowing that what stirs in his breast is stirring too in that of the great majority of his hearers; and in full hope that the Lord will enable him to find the right words in which to clothe the thoughts that all are sharing.

Christian and Annie had both been reflecting how eventful a year this last had been to them, how, in its course, the Lord had both chastened and blessed them more signally than ever before. The evening before, they had had a long conversation on this subject, and on that of their dear Andrew's fate, and had fallen asleep at a much later hour than usual. The consequence was that they somewhat overslept themselves in the morning, to Annie's dismay, for on days such as these she disliked any hurry or bustle, knowing how difficult it was, amidst the press of domestic matters, to obtain the quietude of spirit so essential to the right receiving of God's word. But to her great amazement she found that the chief part of the morning's work was done, and everything laid ready, so that she would have her whole time to herself. These preparations were quite unusual; young people generally leaving early rising to old; and therefore it was in a tone of surprise that she asked Lizzie, who was busy at the hearth, who had called her.

'Oh, good morning, mother,' said Lizzie, turning round with a blushing face, 'so you too are awake?'

'God give thee a good day,' replied Annie; 'but do tell me why thou art up so soon, and who woke thee?'

'No one, mother; but I have been thinking over things, and taking myself to task a little; and it has struck me that it would be better in future if I were to get up first and you remain in bed; you want rest more than I, and then by the time I am obliged to get up I shall be used to it.'

'Well,' said her mother, 'it will do you no harm, I daresay; but tell me how such sensible thoughts ever found their way into your giddy little pate?'

'Ah, mother,' said Lizzie, 'indeed it is not but what I often have serious thoughts, only I can't show them as others do. It is true I have many faults, but I deny that I am not bent in earnest upon improving, and if ever I want to be, not equal to you, mother dear, but anything like you, and that I do want, I know I have a great deal to do, and a long way before me. I was thinking of this yesterday, and it made me serious enough, I can tell you, and I determined to set out this very morning on the better way, and to try to walk in your steps, for I cannot tell how long a time the Lord will give me. It is so soon over with us poor creatures; one never knows when or how, and many take no thought of it.'

'You are right,' said her mother, 'and young wives especially should bethink them of this, and if they want to be really happy, let them follow the Lord. Therefore, child, I rejoice that you have such thoughts, and I own I should not have given you credit for them. Go on like this, and I shall be able to die happy, for you are the one about whom I have had the most anxiety. But none of the three have given me heartier delight than you are doing now, and indeed I cannot remember a morning that ever began for me more happily than this; for what is it makes the happiness of parents but their children? and the greatest happiness of all is to see them good and pious, that so we may all meet together in heaven. If I could only know how it would fare with Andrew, and whether he would yet be happy, I should be ready and willing to die.'

'Don't talk of such a thing, dear mother; die indeed, when we want you more and more every day we live! Don't you always tell us, if we ever speak in this way, to hold our peace, and to take care we say nothing sinful?'

'That is a different thing, quite, child,' returned the mother. 'When the trees are grown we take their props away; to leave them longer would only do harm. And so our dear Lord does; He knows when the proper time is come. But as we are too early for breakfast, I will go and dress for church; I don't like to set out in a hurry, and to get there out of breath.'

It was a beautiful autumn day; the air was mild and clear, and already full of the sound of bells; when they died down in one direction they swelled louder in another. They resembled loving parents addressing their children; as soon as the father's earnest voice was hushed, the mother's, more gently, but with equal fervour, took up the strain.

On most occasions, light-footed youth is in advance of all others, but on this day, old grannies take the lead, setting out very early, with slow pace and many a halt, grey-headed men walking along with them, talking of past days, and of the kind of sermons preached when they were young. What indeed is the human race but one great company marching onward to the grave, and seeking to pass through its dark portals to a radiant heaven; and is it not fit that the aged should lead the van and prepare the way for the young, who part so much less readily with Earth's sunshine? Yet 'tis touching too to see these old folk heading the funeral procession, going so believingly and piously to meet their Lord, walking so trustfully amid graves, quite resigned to the thought of lying down in one of those narrow beds.

Annie was among the first; and many a poor old granny was proud and pleased, and held herself up more erect than she had done for ten years before, to walk with the good Liebiwyl farmeress, who had kind questions and friendly words for all. Oh, it is marvellous how much good a genial nature can do; it comforts and cheers like the light of the sun! When the old dames got to the church, every one wanted to know where the pastor would best be heard, and looked out for a seat with a back, or near a wall, where they could sit at ease, for sometimes they remarked the minister would spin it out, and they got fearfully weary of sitting straight up. Gradually the church filled, the bells rang, the schoolmaster read—and read with spirit, for he was determined to make himself heard above the bells, —when all at once there was a great stillness, the pastor appeared in the lofty pulpit, pale, and evidently a good deal moved, and, having finished his private prayer, gave the psalm out in a low voice.

Loud and solemn rose the song of praise, devoutly impressing the hearts of all, and humbly they invoked a blessing on the word of life. Eagerly did they wait to know what text the pastor would make choice of, and these were the words that met their ear: 'If it seem evil unto you to serve the Lord, choose you this day whom ye will serve, whether the gods which your fathers served on the other side of the flood, or the gods of the Amorites in whose land ye dwell: but as for me and my house, we will serve the Lord.'

It was a striking text certainly, but to many it appeared strange that the pastor should speak now-a-days of choosing whom they would serve; that was surely a settled thing long ago; they were all Christians, they opined.

The minister's sermon began with a remark to which he desired, he said, to call particular attention, namely, how all fallen nations would be found to have, during their decline, more and more neglected what the Old Testament laid especial stress upon, and the corner-stone of which was the Fifth Commandment: 'Honour thy father and thy mother, that thy days may be long in the land which the Lord thy God giveth thee'—he desired, he repeated, to call their serious attention to the family, and its importance. The family had been the earliest temple, the father the first priest.

Family piety was ever rewarded by the Lord, and family irreligion punished. 'Read,' he said, 'the history of Isaac, and the discord between his children; of Jacob, and the disorders of his house; of Eli, and his sons; of David, and his darling Absalom, who brought the greatest misery upon him, and you will find that the sorrows of the parent spring from the bad bringing up of the children. When the family grew into a people, they built a common house of prayer in remembrance of the fact that they were all still essentially only one family, each separate home continued to be the temple of its inmates, the home-life a daily service, the father's rule a priestly office. Accordingly, the Jews had only one common temple, that at Jerusalem, which enclosed the whole people as one family, while, in the intervals of the great festivals, each house was a holy place, where the head of the family worshipped God with those whom God had given him; every other sort of temple, or altar set up in groves or on high places being a token of apostasy and idol-worship, a sign that they had forgotten to sanctify the domestic temple, that they and their house would no longer serve the Lord. Nor was this condition in any way done away with by the New Covenant,—merely exalted and sanctified. Each Christian was to be a priest, his house a temple, his family an altar, from which a sweet savour of righteousness should rise to heaven; our church is nothing more than the one common house of prayer destined to remind us that although necessarily compelled to live in different dwellings, we are all still one great family, and that, though the circumstances of those dwellings may indeed be greatly varied, some of them being palaces and some hovels, this neither makes us better nor worse in the eyes of God, the essential is the state of our hearts and our families, and the account we are prepared to give Him of these.

'Dear hearers,' the pastor went on, 'this is our day of humiliation. We are here to feel conscious of our miserable estate, and to bemoan it. If each one of you were bid to speak aloud his causes of complaint, they would, I doubt not, be found many and deep. But how seldom do people seek for the ground, the root of their wretchedness, where it really lies! It is men's way to complain of everything but their own perversity, their own departure from God. My dear hearers, I will now tell over to you a few of the chief complaints we are sure to hear, in the course even of a brief conversation with our neighbours, and, if you call to your remembrance others that I omit, you will find them all referable to the same source.

'It is not of him or her self that each complains; no, the husband sighs over the wife, the wife over the husband; the wife is pronounced no longer the mother, the visible providence, the nurse of the household, careful for the bodily and spiritual subsistence of all its members; the wife laments over her husband's extravagance or idleness, and neglect of family ties. The parents complain of their children's lack of duty and obedience, and of their contempt for all but their own new-fangled ways. You complain of servants as covetous, negligent, and dishonest, caring for nothing but their wages, and earning them by mere eye-service. You complain of the poor in general, that they claim as a right what is given to them in charity, that they are envious, thriftless, discontented. You complain of teachers and schools, and of how your children seem to grow more useless the more they learn there, and have nothing to show for it after their schooling is over. You complain of government and governors, of their actions and blunders, of their inaction and neglect; in short, your causes of complaint are so many, that you know very well it is impossible to produce them all. Is this the case, or is it not? But on whom do these complaints recoil? On you, parents; on you, masters and mistresses. Is your house a holy temple; is there an altar there on which you offer to the God who has so gloriously revealed Himself in both covenants, what He claims at your hands, yourselves, your nearest and dearest above all? Or

have you not rather forsaken this temple, sought out
each for himself high places to suit his taste, delighted to frequent these, raised altars there, and
sacrificed to your self-chosen deities, body and soul,
health and happiness, sons and daughters, men-
servants and maid-servants, private property and
love of country, everything, in short, that falls into
your idolatrous grasp?'

Such was the drift of the pastor's discourse, closed
by much loving admonition, and in deep humility.
His hearers knew, he said, that from this language of
condemnation he in no way excepted himself, for,
whenever a particular spiritual malady prevailed, it
was but seldom that any entirely escaped, and all of
them were liable to the spirit of the age, which
either brought disease or was disease;—just as when
any epidemic was in the air, as for instance dysentery
now was among themselves, even those who escaped
fatal attacks generally came in for a slight sense of
illness and discomfort, and he held that none of
them, certainly not he himself, were justified in
thanking God that they were not as others. But he
earnestly and tenderly besought them, by the
mercies of God, to return to the reasonable service
of which Paul spoke, the presenting their bodies a
living sacrifice, the confessing openly before all men
that they and their house would serve the Lord, and
the standing to this confession in daily life. Should

numbers of misled and unhappy souls stand up so boldly for their dead idols, and should not they for the living God?

During the whole of the pastor's discourse there was a deep and devout silence in the church; few were there who did not inwardly confess that he was right, and many an eye was wet as his hearers thought over the state of their own homes, and began to understand the secret of their misery. Others, again, recalled their family history, and clearly traced what had disturbed and what restored their domestic peace, and how it prospered or declined according as the sacred fire on the home altar burned dim or bright. And many a poor woman silently wiped away a tear as she thought into whose service her husband had entered, and resolved thenceforth to be herself all the more on that account a faithful priestess of the Lord. Many a husband rejoiced that to his wife home was everything, while others sighed over a contrary conviction. And many a child too seemed to understand a parent's claim more clearly than when the sermon began, and to resolve upon more cheerful obedience.

Our good Annie was deeply moved; a kind of heavenly life seemed to stir within her, she felt such a tender melancholy, and yet such an inexpressible peace. Her family rose before her mind's

eye good and loving, she could rejoice in them
before God and man; she thought with delight of
her home, her perfect union with Christian in
thought and feeling, and how they both alike desired to serve the Lord; and her children, too, were
so dutiful, so attached, so free from all germ of discord between themselves, that she did not doubt
their maintaining the family in this happy state,
not only before men, but God. She realized how
blessed a thing it is when parents can confidently
say, 'Lord, now lettest thou thy servant depart in
peace;' and this they only can when they know
that their children are rooted in faith, and their
names written in the book of life. Annie felt no
pride, did not pray thus with herself, 'God, I thank
thee that my house is not as other houses;' but she
rejoiced with all her heart to believe that when God
should call her hence, she need not fear to have
lived in vain, she had not buried the pound
intrusted to her, but returned it to her Lord with
usury; she had founded a family in the fear of God,
brought up three children for Him, strong to master
the world, not mastered by it; and can a mother
come before God with any more precious offering
than a pious household and pious children? True,
one shadow fell athwart her joy; it was her gravelooking Andrew, who never complained, but seldom
laughed, got through a great deal of work, but pre-

ferred to do it alone, and then gave way to an evident dejection, which had not escaped the mother's eye. It was her terror lest he should remain alone in the world, the silent wish to see the one who on some future day was to take her place, stand by his side before the holy domestic altar; this shadow it was that clouded the loving mother's eyes; but they soon shone again with cheerful trust: the Lord, who had helped them hitherto, who had done all things well, would He not help them still, and ought she not to say, with full resignation, 'Thy will, not mine, be done'? And accordingly she composed herself, and went home cheerful and strengthened; she felt as though she was being carried thither, she had not for years walked so lightly and well.

The sermon had made an impression upon the congregation at large, and met with far more than average commendation. The pastor is right, they said; the home is the root of all, and if anything goes wrong there, there may be as much corn or hay as you like, it's all to no purpose.

'Yes,' said a pert tailor, 'and what pleased me most was our minister's admitting that the school was of very little use, and that children learnt next to nothing there. If I did not teach mine at home, they would make nothing of their schooling. And since the minister himself says so, why, so it must be. But I should not have thought he would have had the sense to see it, still less to allow it, and consequently I must respect him, and believe that he says the truth, but more than half of them do nothing of the kind.'

What a joyful thing is the return home from church, when the peace of God dwells there, when there is no disturbing influence awaiting us; when some have been quietly engaged in necessary domestic duties, and others finding fresh strength, fresh light and comfort in God's house, and all assemble around the family table in quiet contentment, these pleased to listen, and those to tell, what the sermon taught! Such a scene helps us to understand what St. Paul meant by eating and drinking to the glory of God, and on such eating and drinking God's blessing rests.

VI.

DEATH THE RECONCILER.

'I SHALL stay at home alone this afternoon,' said Annie. 'I don't wish any one else to do so; on such a day as this no one should put off going to church, and if the pastor gives as good a sermon as in the morning, all may get some good from it, and it were a thousand pities you should not all hear it. And I want you to bring me some rice back with you, about half a dozen pounds or so. I heard a sad account of the ravages dysentery is making; at Stephen Glause's there are four children down with it, and the mother as well; not one can help the other, and they are very poor. That is a fearful condition, and I am more sorry for them than I can say. When you are all back again I will step over and see what is to be done to help them: one can't let things go on so; think if it were our own case—so many sick at once, and no one able to take care of the other, and nothing in the house, and perhaps no creature to go for the doctor.'

'Mother,' said Christy, 'send over; one of the maids will go for you, or, if not, wait till morning. It's a good step to those people, and you have already had the walk to church.'

'I can't send any of the maids,' replied his mother; 'they would not see what was wanting, and the poor souls might not be able, or might not like to tell them; you know yourself, Christy, how troublesome it is, when one is very ill, to be questioned right and left. What is wanted is a person who can see with half an eye how things stand. The maids might have all the good-will in the world, but they have no experience; one must be used to nursing before one can be of any comfort to the sick.'

'Then wait till the morning,' returned he.

'But, Christy, what would you say if you were ailing, and I was told of it at midday, and replied, " Well, well, he must wait, and if it is convenient I will see to him in the morning"?'

'Yes, mother,' argued Christy, 'but this is not the same case: I am your child.'

'True, indeed, it is not the same case; here there are four children, not one, down in this dreadful disorder, and not one can do anything for the other, but help to wail and weep. And to spend a night so, only think how fearful!'

'But you cannot do them any good,' persisted Christy.

'You don't know that; I believe I can. It will do them some good to see that they are cared for, and not utterly forsaken by all. Just think, one of them might die in the night, and no one be there to take it away from among the living.'

'But, mother, surely you will never stay there through the night?' replied Christy.

'I am not sure of that,' said Annie; 'it must depend upon how I find them, but if I am not home in good time, don't be uneasy about me, and make sure that I am there. Even if I find some one with them, I shall very probably have to send her off to fetch whatever may be wanted.'

'But, mother, don't go at all yourself; they say dysentery is catching; send one of the maids,' pleaded Christy, coming out at last with his real meaning.

'O Christy, Christy, what are you thinking of? Oh, for shame! To want to seem to be kind and charitable, and to send over a poor maid, who has nothing but her health, when we dare not venture ourselves, and to make her run all the danger while we have all the credit, and no one thanks her! No, Christy, that has never been our custom hitherto, and I trust never will be.'

In the cottages of the poor there is no disease, cholera and small-pox excepted, more distressing and disgusting than dysentery. Where there is perhaps only one bed, and that a bad one, and the rest of the family have to make up a sort of lair with a few ragged blankets, either on the stove or in an empty bedstead, or perhaps on the table, where no one has more than two shirts, the one on, the other hung on the hedge to dry, no store of provisions of any kind laid in, even the wood for daily use having to be daily collected, it may easily be imagined what wretchedness must attend a disease where cleanliness, ventilation, good food, and warmth are the great essentials.

When the household returned from the afternoon service, Annie set off, no one opposing her further, but all offering to go with her, and, when she positively declined their company, imploring her to remember her age, and to return soon.

Although Annie had often seen poverty and misery before, she had never pictured to herself such utter destitution as she now found. She had brought several things with her, rice, and some clean shirts for the children, as well as bread, and even cream, which she had heard had a soothing effect. But she found no wood, no butter, and a fearful deficiency of linen and all means of cleanliness, so that she was almost sickened on entering. As it was Sunday, there were a few neighbours there, and some had brought with them bread, salt and smoked meat, etc., others laid down a few pence, and exclaimed—

'Good gracious! how dreadful, I could not breathe here for one single hour; it is too shocking.'

Others had rendered a little manual help, but, that done, they said they must go home, or there would be no dinner cooked there to-day; as to who was to replace them here, they took no thought. Others went up and down, asking questions, answering them, and deciding that probably all would die except the mother, and it was doubtful whether she would get over it, but no one had fairly grappled with the exigencies of the case till Annie came.

Annie at once assumed the management. To so intelligent a housewife disorder is intolerable; she has an instinctive faculty of putting everything and everybody into their proper places, and organizing different activities into a whole, so that they may not nullify, but aid each other. And this a woman of her sense and experience does, not in whirlwind fashion, but gently and persuasively, so that each one feels to have fallen in the right position unconsciously, and flatters herself she is of particular service, and that had she not been present everything would have gone wrong. One neighbour was sent off to the doctor, and on her way told to call at

Liebiwyl for various articles; another directed to bring in wood, another butter; rice and milk was set upon the fire, the room was cleaned and ventilated, and the more that got done the less was said, so that the poor suffering woman declared she really thought she was better already.

'If people only knew what to do, they were always willing enough,' she observed; 'but the knowledge was the great thing, and few possessed it.'

In the evening, Lizzie came over heavily laden, bringing a message that her mother was to go home, and she would remain in her stead. But say what she would she could not stir her mother. When once so energetic a woman has taken a matter in hand, there is no persuading her to give it up; she becomes feverishly active in the cause, and convinced that no one can replace her. And besides, there was another reason. Any one who has ever seen the children of the poor struggling between life and death, knows that there is something infinitely touching about them. Generally speaking, they get, even in their earliest years, an impression that they are a burden, and that it is on their account their parents have such a hard fight with life. If this is not positively told them, they can see it all the same. When they are quite infants the mother caresses them, and the father will take them up in his arms, but as soon as they begin to walk alone a gradual process of alienation sets in, unless, indeed, in the case of some particularly pretty and taking child that gets a special hold of the parents' hearts. But this is quite an exception, and generally made in favour of the youngest. The others have to take care of themselves, and to grow accustomed to hardship, no one fondles or attends to them, there is no time for it. A hard school this for tender hearts, and one in which many get their life crushed out; and yet there is a sort of mercy too in it. It is an effectual schooling for a hard life, just as poles have to be hardened in the fire (alas! they often get scarred there) in order that they may not rot in water, snow, and earth. Such a system results in a kind of submissiveness, a habit of suffering and bearing without complaint, and this we often observe in the sick children of the poor. They do not scream, they do not cry; in the worst shivering fit of fever they lie quiet on some wretchedly uncomfortable bed; their lips are parched and brown, a broken cup with something to drink in it stands on the stove, but no one has time to reach it them; they suffer and are silent, their eyes are indeed fixed upon the cup, but they wait till their mother, in passing by, remarks the look, and says, 'Will you have a drop to drink?' When we contrast with these the children of the rich, in their exacting ways, their incapability of bearing pain quietly, their screams, which all the attendance around them often fails to check, one's heart is perplexed and saddened, one begins to doubt which is best qualified for life, the rich child or the poor, and to wonder more and more why it should be so difficult to hit the happy medium, to harden the heart into endurance, yet keep it tender to the touch of love.

The sick children of whom we are now speaking had passed through the school of hardship; they lay quiet, resigned, silent; any one seeing them there dull and listless in dirt and discomfort, might have doubted whether they felt or thought at all, or had any idea of the meaning of death and recovery, of which people spoke so much in their hearing. They made no sign, at all events. But when the handsome kind elderly woman took them up one by one, washed them, put clean clothes on them, caressed them, laid them comfortably down, and gave them something sweet and warm to drink, it seemed as though their dormant consciousness awoke, as though they might venture to be heard, and the youngest, a pale but lovely little girl with curling light hair all round her head, asked—

'Are you my godmother, then?'

'Yes, child,' said Annie, 'I will be thy godmother?'

'Then you will not go away from us? You will

stay here till we are dead, and mammy is well again?'

'Yes, thou sweet child, I won't leave thee,' Annie had replied, and now she was positively unable to tear herself away.

The children, particularly this little pale fair thing, had wound themselves about her heart; she felt as if she were their grandmother, as if, were she to forsake them, God would require them at her hands. Not however that this was the reason she assigned to Lizzie; nay, it very generally happens that in explaining our motives we may seem explicit, and yet omit the very one which is the most influential of all. For how indeed should we reveal that of which we are not yet conscious? and how often our resolve starts up like a ghost out of the mist, and it is only when it does thus stand out before us that we begin to find reasons to justify its existence!

No one else, she told Lizzie, knew how to make proper rice-broth for a case like this; generally the rice was not half boiled, and when you came to pour it out there was nothing but water at the top and hard grains at the bottom, and the great point in rice-broth was to have it of one consistency throughout, as the doctor had told her, and she was just going to prepare it herself. Then, again, the children had to take their medicine; their mother said no one would be able to get it down their throats, but taken it must be; and she thought if they would do so for any one they would for her, they seemed to have got used to her; at all events, she must try. And it was far easier for her to remain than to walk home again. In the morning they might send the horse and gig for her, and if any one replaced her then she would return; for when once things were set agoing, nearer neighbours would be sure to come forward. But they must not forget to bring more chaff to stuff the beds, and one of the counterpanes that were hanging up in the granary. Do what she would, poor Lizzie had to go home alone, and Annie remained to nurse and attend to the sufferers in spite of all the sick woman's arguments. She could not, she dared not, accept such goodness, the poor creature said, she should never know how to repay it. If it had been a case of childbirth, it would be different, would be customary, then one woman did want another, and she should have been most thankful, but with such a complaint as this it was quite out of the question. If Annie would be so good as to put the drink on the stove, they would manage very well. And when Annie persisted in her intention, she fell to crying, and said she never could have believed there was such a good woman in the world, and then a woman of her consequence too, who wanted for nothing on earth, and need not do a thing of the kind for the sake of getting to heaven, for she was sure of going there anyhow, as she knew quite well. But what good it did her herself to keep warm, instead of being up every moment, no words could say.

At length the messenger to the doctor returned with physic, and the tidings that he would be there early in the morning, and that they were to take the medicine every hour, and to drink the broth as thick as they could. Perhaps he should begin some other treatment in the morning.

'Nay, surely not,' said the poor woman; 'he won't be so hard upon us as to want to doctor us any more, when we have to get up to our work.'

'Don't be anxious about that,' said Annie; 'just take it now, and then try to fall asleep. I know something about doctors; and very often what we think the oddest thing to do turns out the wisest.'

And upon that she addressed herself to the children, who hitherto had stoutly resisted all physic, and in her kind caressing way began with the youngest, promising her some good broth after it, and the child swallowed it, and declared it was quite nice,—she could never have believed doctors' stuff tasted like that.

'Have you never had any before?' asked Annie.

'No; but I have often been told if I did not go to bed at once I should be sick, and then I should have to take doctors' stuff, and that it was something that stank and tasted most horribly.'

'You see that was a mistake,' said Annie.

And then she persuaded the other children, and they gulped it down too, partly because the youngest had done so, and partly because they were afraid to refuse the good kind stranger.

Night had set in, the mother fell asleep. Annie, who was constantly occupied either with the children or with cooking, wanted a light, and soon found the lamp, but as to any oil, in vain she looked for it in all possible places where oil could be kept, and then, in a whisper, asked one of the children where it was.

'We have had none since yesterday,' replied the child.

Fortunately it was moonlight, and a very bright one, though for all that it was inconvenient enough. Whenever Annie got a quiet quarter of an hour to sit down, she kept thinking over and over again, 'No oil, and four sick children! What a thing! We farmers have no idea how these people live; we are really too well off. What would become of me if any one thing were wanting in my household, and I had to lie sleepless only one night long without coffee, or flour, though I knew quite well I might get any quantity I liked on the morrow? And here there is nothing; no bread, no money, and all are sick. Neither to have, nor know how to get, that I could not stand. And yet I must if our Lord God had willed it so, but I don't know how I should have borne it, but borne it I needs must had it been His will. Oh, when one has the power to give, how little one can tell the feelings of others who have to receive! If I had had to see my children lying in such wretched rags, so thin and pale, with nothing but skin on their poor little bones. Oh, Lord, if I had had to see that, surely surely I never could have gone through it! And if God had given me the choice between wealth and children, either to see them in that miserable condition or not have them at all, which should I have chosen? But how gracious God above is in not putting such questions, not leading us into temptation, but ordering things as He sees best! But I can't help thinking that if I had to part with all, and had nothing for my children, and they lying sick, and I unable even to beg for them, it would surely rend my heart, and yet I would not part with them; what good would it do me to be rich, and to have no longer any children? I should weep myself to death, and have only one thought: O that I had them still, had them still! What a lovely child that is,' Annie went on thinking, as she moved to take up the youngest little girl, on whose small face and golden curls the moonlight fell.

'Oh, poor child, what is to become of thee; what a hard life will be thine, and how rich many a lady would feel if she had thee! Then thou wouldst be in a very different bed, and no one knows how many would be attending on thee. But God has ordered it thus, and He must know why. Only we blind mortals cannot understand it. Oh, how much there is that we never can understand! Why should not this poor soul have had more given her; we could have got on with less, and should still have been far from her condition, and from not having money to buy oil. But 'tis the Lord's doing, and it is right, and must be right; the one thing needful is that, whether rich or poor, we should not fall into sin; that the rich should not sin against the poor, or the poor against the rich. No, indeed, I will not sin against the poor so long as I live. If Christian could but see this room! Not but what Christian is kind, particularly of late, but if he could look at these children, and this misery, he would still better understand how I feel when any one begs from me. I must give, in God's name; how can I tell how the people are faring at home? Why, look at this! Christian has a good heart, and does not so much need to see for himself, but there are others who are downright cruel, and delight in oppressing the poor, would suck their life's-blood if they could,—brutal wretches that they are; God forgive me for saying so. But, indeed, every man and every woman ought to know how their fellow-creatures may suffer, and what misery really is. There are so many complainers who are never contented, and, though not knowing what trouble means, do not think themselves well off, and sin fearfully through envy and murmuring. Oh, when one can slip into a warm bed, sound and well, and know that one's children are all covered up comfortably, and have all they want, how thankful one ought to be, and how one should praise and bless God!'

Such were Annie's thoughts during this night, nor would she for any money have been without this experience.

When one day passes much like another, and people go seldom from home, they can know but little of life in general; and thought becomes so limited to self, and things connected with self, that it is difficult to realize that elsewhere circumstances and feelings are quite unlike our own, and that ours too may soon be radically changed. For misfortune may easily overtake us; a stride or two and it is within our very doors; and Annie asked herself how she should resist it if it unexpectedly came upon her; and determined that the reason so many people remained hard and apathetic was their ignorance of what was going on elsewhere; and that their rebellious despair in the hour of trouble arose from their having forgotten the ups and downs of life, and how the Lord may send trial before nightfall, not only into a poor hovel, but into the handsomest of farm-houses as well.

The night flew rapidly by; it was blest to Annie and the invalids both; and when the dawn broke, it lighted up peaceful sleep and happy faces. With morning came several people, and among them Christian himself, with a gloomy countenance, but with all that was required. Annie knew that gloomy expression well, and insisted upon Christian tying the horse up and coming into the little room, to see for himself how destitute they were, and how pitiful the children looked. But this did not brighten Christian's face; he thought that for all that his wife need not have spent the night there; let things be as bad as they would, he could not reconcile himself to that.

'Come away now, at all events,' said he.

'Must you go?' said the little girl; 'no, godmother, stay with me, you promised me you would,' and she clung round Annie's neck, and was hardly to be composed by promises of all kinds; while the other children, though they said less, showed plainly by their grave looks how sorry they were to part with the kind friend who had done so much for them. As for the poor sick woman, she kept crying, and could say little, but that she hoped their

Father in Heaven would repay it to her; such another woman there was not in the whole world; and neither in this life nor the next should she ever forget the past night; it was just as though an angel had been there watching over them. When Christian heard this the clouds cleared away from his countenance, he began to comprehend what Annie had done, his heart grew tender and full of compassion, his manner changed to friendliness. They should not be forgotten, he said, for all he took his wife away; but she was growing old, and could not stand more fatigue. But they were not to be uneasy, they were better already, and when they were well again they had only to come up yonder and he would see what could be done. This was a great deal from Christian, who generally left all such speeches to his wife, and what she told him on their way home touched him still more.

It was a cool autumnal morning, a sharp north wind blew in their faces, and before they got to Liebiwyl Annie was thoroughly chilled. She had been heated in the close cottage, and had not put on any additional clothing when she got into the gig; no one thought of it for so short a way. Then she had eaten little or nothing for many hours; she had not liked to take the broth from the children, and there was nothing else. To an elderly woman, a chill upon an empty stomach was a serious matter; however, Lizzie, she said, would be sure to have thought of making some coffee, and she owned she had never wanted it so much in all her life before.

She was quite right, the coffee was all ready, and Annie thoroughly enjoyed it; but at every mouthful she stopped to say, 'O children, we don't know how well off we are, and how the poor suffer; here we have good food, a warm bed, and if I want anything I can have it got out of the cellar or the barn; oh, we don't know what a comfort that is, and how much we have to be thankful for!'

Her children were all at her to go and lie down at once, that she might recover herself after her fatigue, and with great difficulty they got her to do so; but she was so full of what she had seen, that she would rather have kept talking it over with them the whole morning.

'Do go to sleep, mother,' Lizzie said half-a-dozen times before Annie would let her away.

It was 'Just hear this, just think of this,' all the time, and it was long before sleep came at all, and then it was broken and uneasy. Lizzie had only put the door to, not shut it, that she might hear if her mother called. She heard her speaking,—went in, and found her asleep.

'Come here,' she called to Andrew, 'come and

listen how mother is talking in her sleep; had I better waken her?'

'I should let her sleep,' said Andrew; 'she has such a tender heart, and these poor people have so terribly distressed her, she can't throw it off at once. I trust it's nothing more, but don't go away, and watch her well.'

Annie awoke with a headache, but said nothing about it; was thoroughly unwell, but would not allow it, however anxiously questioned. She was afraid of their all saying: 'Now, mother, why will you go and do such things; did not we tell you it was far too much for you?' This kind of fear is very common, and much to be deprecated; it leads to many concealments that have serious results. Often it arises from some secret consciousness of imprudence; often from too great consideration for the feelings of others; sometimes, too, from a dread of being lectured and tutored,—certain persons having a terrible love of tutoring, which could never get gratified as regards grown-up people, unless they were to fall sick now and then. Woe betide one who betrays that there is something wrong with him in presence of this lecturing race, it affords them a first-rate opportunity for that familiar exordium: 'Have I not told you this or that over and over again? Now you see that I was right; you would not believe me, but you are convinced now, I hope; at all events you cannot lay your illness to any want of proper warning on my part,' etc. etc.

Annie's family were not of this stamp, but for all that they might not have fully appreciated the wisdom of letting bygones be bygones; they would probably have said: 'Mother, why will you go and fancy you are still twenty years old? Mother, why will you not believe us, and let us take more care of you?' And so Annie concealed the fact that to the headache were added internal pains, and the premonitory symptoms of the prevailing complaint. She made herself some tea as privately as she could, and as she only drank it when she could do so unobserved, she did not take much. At length, however, Lizzie and Christian found her out.

'Mother, you are not well, what is it? oh tell us, mother; you are not as usual.'

'It's nothing of any consequence,' said Annie. 'It's only a little indigestion; it will soon pass off. I have been taking some camomile-tea for it.'

'The doctor must be sent for instantly,' said Christian, 'this can't be allowed to go on; who knows where it might stop?'

'That would be a pretty joke indeed,' said Annie, 'to send for the doctor because of a slight bowel-complaint; why, he would only laugh at us. We can have some rice-soup made, and if it does not pass off we can see to it then.'

'Ay,' said Christian, 'many a one has slipped away because of not seeing to it at once; the doctor must be had.'

'At all events,' pleaded Annie, 'do let us wait till morning, and if I am not better then we can send. And, besides, some one must go to the village for oil, and see that our lamp is properly trimmed; we have hardly any oil left, and I can't rest till a fresh supply is brought in; I know now what it is to have no oil in the house.'

The following day Annie was no better, but rather worse, the complaint went on, and she was very weak. The doctor was sent for the first thing in the morning, with strict injunctions to come directly. The messenger returned with the announcement that the mother must take the greatest care of herself, her symptoms were not to be trifled with; dysentery was sadly about, and a very bad kind too. He, the doctor, would be over in the afternoon, and meanwhile he sent medicine to be taken at once. When this message came it seemed as though the house had been struck by lightning; there was not a face but grew pale, not a hand but trembled; no one had thought of this, the very idea of their mother getting the dreaded complaint had occurred to none of them, not even to Christy. In spite of his warning as to its contagious nature, all he had meant was that his mother ought not to trouble herself, and run risks to serve poor miserable creatures picked up from the streets as though they were her own family. 'Lord Jesus! the mother has got dysentery,' was the wail of every one, down to the parish lad working on the farm, who was found crying bitterly behind the house, and saying that if she was taken from him he had no creature left to him on earth; and that she had promised him, if he behaved well, a new coat at Christmas, and would surely have given it him. As for Christian he was utterly prostrated, was almost beside himself; if he wanted to leave the house he was a long while before he could find the way to the door. No one knew exactly why they were all so terrified; there seemed no danger as yet; the doctor had only cautioned them. But their mother had never been ill—never kept her room; they all looked to her as to the visible providence of the household, from whom all their comfort proceeded; and the idea of having her laid up, nay, of her perhaps dying, came over them for the first time as a possibility, and struck them down as by a thunderbolt. When Lizzie gave her mother the medicine, the tears coursed down her cheeks, and her hand trembled so violently that she could neither hold the spoon nor pour out the drops, she was obliged to get Andrew to help her. Meanwhile Annie herself remained quite calm, and did all she could to comfort them: they must not, she said, go on in this way about an illness that had not yet fairly set in; and if it did, it was not certain that she should die of it; and if she did, the time must have come some day; and whether it was a little sooner or a little later, they had great cause to thank God for sparing them so long to each other. Twenty years ago, indeed, she would have been a serious loss to them, but now they were all able to get on very well without her.

When the doctor came in the afternoon, dysentery had begun. What an agony to the whole household! The doctor at first looked very grave, and said, 'Exactly so; this is what I feared.' But when he saw the sorrowful faces about him, he took a more cheerful tone, and bade them keep up their spirits, or they would distress the patient. All that he could do for her he would, and he hoped it might not be God's will to take such a good woman away. She would be a terrible loss to the poor, and indeed to every one. They all went with him out of the house to ask further questions,—to beg him to devote himself to the case, to do all that man could, and to tell them what there was that they could do, —the more the better; and when they returned, one dropped down here, and the other there, their faces hid in their hands, then crept quietly in to see how mother was going on. Everybody wanted to watch, to have a share in the nursing, to do a something to promote her recovery; and in the morning even the milkman was up much earlier than usual; he could not get his sleep owing to his anxiety to know what kind of a night she had had. For he said if ever there was anything the matter with a servant, the mother was always there to comfort him; many a night she had lost her sleep on his account, and he had found her at his bedside with a cup in her hand; and though very probably at the time he had made wry faces at the dose, yet the kindness did him good, and the sense of being cared for, though he was only a servant.

The attack was a severe one for an elderly woman, and the doctor went on looking very grave, enjoined the greatest care, and was himself most assiduous in his attendance. The first thing in the morning he was there, and generally returned in the evening; and as to the family, none of them took off their clothes. If they were not to be all in the room at once, still not one would hear of going to bed; and if they dropped off to sleep for a little time, anxiety soon waked them, and there they were, listening at the mother's door.

The doctor had expressly forbidden the admittance of strangers into the sick-room, because it would only disturb and harass the patient, more especially in a case like this. But it was no easy matter to enforce his orders. As soon as it was noised abroad that the Liebiwyl farmeress was ill, people came from far and wide, intent upon paying her a visit. Her room would never have been empty could they have had their way. One would have exclaimed, 'Gracious goodness, how ill she looks; she'll never hold out till morning!' Another would have said, 'Ay, but still she may come round; many a person has been far worse, and for all that has come round in the end.' Some would have shuddered, and all would have wept. Poor women would have raised a loud wail, and on taking leave have said, 'Well, well, I shall never see you again; but I will pray God to have mercy upon your sins;' or else, 'I must go home, so farewell; and if we are never to meet again here below, I hope we shall yet come together above.' All which the family had the greatest difficulty in preventing, for the Bernese peasantry believe that they have a right to enter a sick-room, and there are many who look upon it as a positive sin to forbid access to the sufferer, and explain it by surmising that he or she must be in terrible spiritual distress, and disclosing things that had better not be heard.

On this occasion the visitors were received with all kindness, and plenty to eat and drink set before them; but the doctor's orders were pleaded as im-

perative. Nevertheless, few believed in them. Some
thought the good woman was already dead, and
looked so ghastly that her family did not like her
to be seen; others set it down as pride; others
again whispered that perhaps she had some wishes
to express which her relations did not mean to carry
out,—wanted to give away this or that to some one
or other (she had always been a kind-hearted soul),
and her children grudged it. Thus people went on
in their usual uncharitable and unreasoning way,
hardly conscious indeed of the character of their
remarks, and let us hope better, for the most part,
than their words.

Meanwhile, Annie said nothing about dying, and
that made her family very hopeful. She must herself know how she was, they thought, better than
any one else could; and surely if she believed herself in danger, she would tell them so; therefore
they took heart again, and trusted all would be well.
And one morning, when the dysentery seemed to
have ceased, great was the joy of all. As to her
being still very weak, why, nothing else could be
expected. She herself positively insisted on their
all going out to the field. Andrew, she said, would
remain with her. He had sat up all night, and
might perhaps get a little sleep. If she were to be
less well, they would be at hand, and could be
called in at once. It was very fine and bright out

of doors, and there was a good deal of work to be done. But in spite of that, each felt reluctant to leave, nor was there one who did not pretend to have left something behind, in order to have an excuse for looking in again to see whether there was nothing that could be done for mother.

'Are they all gone?' Annie at length inquired.

'I believe so,' said Andrew; 'I hear no one about.'

'Then come and sit close beside me. I have something to say to you, and cannot raise my voice. Hear me, child. I shall not be here long, and I want to open my heart to you.'

'Oh, mother, don't say that; you will be better by and by. Will you not try to get a little sleep?'

'There is no time for sleeping now,' said Annie; 'my day is done, and a long sleep will soon set in. Hush! don't speak; give me your hand. It is God's will that some should go and others come. But my great grief, indeed my only grief, is that no one has come to replace me here,—no one to whom, when my day's work is done, I can intrust my husband and my children. This does grieve me. Hitherto I have not liked to ask you how you felt about it. I saw you had a good deal to get over, and could do it best alone. But now I want to know something. Do you still love that girl, or have you another in your mind? for a wife you must have. Lizzie will soon go to her husband, I to my Father in Heaven; you must have some one here.'

'No, truly, mother, I have never given any other girl a thought; how could I?'

'Then you love that same one still?'

'Mother, I ought not, but I cannot get her out of my mind; and when I try to think of something else, there she is still, always before my eyes.'

'Listen, child, this delights me! then you will marry her when I am gone?'

'What are you thinking of, mother? that would look as if I had been waiting for your death, and had got you out of my way. No, mother, no one shall think that. And, besides, I can't forget the eyes she made,—so angry, mother; they flashed fire; and not a kind word would she speak, though I besought her for God's sake, as I had never besought any human being before; yet not one little word, not one; I could not have behaved so to my greatest enemy. And shall I go now and kneel to her, and, as it were, say, Thank God, my mother is dead! and to a girl like that, who would not even speak to me! Mother, if, as my wife, she had gone on in that raging way, I should have been the most miserable fool in all the world, must have blushed for myself and her in the presence of every one, even the maids and farm-servants.'

'Child, you must not take it in that light. All

those who know anything about us know you have not been looking out for my death, and as to others what matters it? And you must not carry it with such a high hand towards the girl either. It's not right to cast her away because of an angry moment, and she loving you—only think if our Lord God were to deal with us so.'

'Nay, mother, if she had loved me she could not have used me so; and besides, she had already shown temper here; I did not know what to make of it then, it grieved me to my heart.'

'I was a good deal struck with that too, child, and at first I fancied that she did not like us, or thought we had not made enough of her, and it gave me a distrust of her. But all at once it seemed to me that I could read into her heart as plainly as though she had had a window in her breast; but the fact was, I saw it reflected in my own, and it was my experience that taught me to understand her. Oh, child! believe me, when one looks back to what one was one's-self, and how one thought and acted, it is just as though one could read an invisible writing, of which people in general don't know the letters, let alone understanding the meaning. So it was with me. I have never spoken much of my father, though I have prayed for him a good deal. He was very hard to live with, and fond of drink; and I often felt as if I could have sunk into the earth when people were by. I said little, but I used to look sad and glum, exactly like that young girl. I could not, at such a time, have spoken a pleasant word to a creature to save my life; if I had tried, I should have burst out crying. And yet I was much fonder of my father than she of hers; and he never was half so bad as to bargaining and grasping. It was that that depressed the poor girl: she did like us, and observed that our ways were unlike theirs. I saw how she took notice of different things; and then she was so anxious to get away from home, particularly as they wanted to marry her to an old man; so that when her father made such unfair proposals, she was almost beside herself with the suspense. She would gladly have opposed him if she could, but she dared not trust herself; feared to burst out crying, or to make bad worse. I was truly sorry for her. And so it must have been. I fancy I see it all—at her own home, when you and the old man stood out against each other, her poor heart was too full, and at last all its pent-up grief broke out, and many, you may take my word for it, would have gone on still worse.'

'Mother, I do believe you,' said Andrew, 'that this led to its so happening, but it should not have happened, and I have no heart for a woman who, under any circumstances, can make such eyes and refuse to speak a single word. One person has a dread of this, another of that, and I have a horror of all the neighbours talking of my wife's temper, and how at times she is not herself.'

'Hear me, child,' pleaded his mother; 'you are unforgiving; will you cast away the poor girl for one angry fit that arose from her being so fond of you? Believe me, those who are bent upon a wife without a fault are generally punished; the over-careful are oftenest deceived, because true-hearted girls don't think of dissembling, but the cunning ones see what their game is, and play it. Believe me, you will never get a faultless wife, and it's much better for you to know her faults beforehand. Believe me, when we are young we can all fly into a passion. Choose as carefully as you will, unless you practise love and patience, unless you are gentle and forbearing, a husband that a wife must esteem,—unless God helps you to be this, all your choosing will do little for you. You are so fond of me, and want to make me out a pattern for your wife; but can you expect from a young creature what you do from an old one who has had so much to teach her? Andrew, is this fair? Believe me, if you had known me when I was young, you would never have taken me, I should have been far too wild and high-tempered for you. But what are we in the world for but to grow better? You cast away the poor child, and never think what it must have been to have one's whole happiness depending upon one single word, and yet for that word not to get spoken, and all one's happiness to vanish out of one's grasp. Only think of that! And the girl had to look on, and dared not interfere; and could you expect her to continue calm? Why, Andrew, only think of it! A more cunning one would have thrown her arms about you, and tried what coaxing and flattery would do; this girl honestly showed what was in her, and this, Andrew, you turn against her! No, no, you will not, must not; promise me that you will forgive and seek her out. Promise it me; think that you too have sins, and need of mercy. This is my only wish as to this world; if it were fulfilled, I could die in peace. Believe me, I have considered the matter well; I know how much there is in home influence; in another house than this I should have been quite different. There are houses in which it seems as if a good spirit dwelt; one can't help getting better and better there; who knows, perhaps I shall see one here yet?'

'Mother, you are talking too much; shall I get you anything?' asked Andrew.

'Will you promise me to look after this girl again?'

'Mother, how can I? Shall I expose myself to being driven away like a dog? I would do so if I were to receive a kind word from her; but as it is, I must believe that she does not love me; she has made no sign since we parted.'

At that moment he saw a strange light pass over his mother's face; she folded her hands, to his sudden terror.

'Mother, mother, what ails you?' he asked.

His mother's eyes were fixed upon the outer room; she pointed thither; he turned round, and there, on the threshold, her head leaning on the door-post, stood Mary Anne, pale, thin, and weeping bitterly! Andrew stood petrified, not a sound could he utter, not a step could he take. The poor girl stretched out her hands imploringly to him.

'Bring her here,' whispered Annie, in a low voice

Mechanically, as it were, her son obeyed her, and she clasped the hands of both in hers, and said—

'Now I see that the Lord loves me. I had one last wish, and He has granted it me. Remain together, be faithful, be open to one another; whatever is in the heart of either let the other know it, that there may be no misunderstandings between you. Misunderstandings are fearful things, they grow up so fast, and divide hearts so sadly. Remember that, remember our case, and love each other always; think that I am looking on you. Andrew, go, run, call them, it won't be long now, I feel, I am getting so cold, and I should like to see them all once more. Run, run.'

When he was gone she turned to Mary Anne—

'You do love him; you will do all you can to make him happy?'

At that the young girl fell on her knees by the bedside, and sobbed out, 'O mother, mother, you are not a mortal, you are an angel; O that I could but be like you!'

'No; no angel,—a poor weak creature,' said Annie; 'but perhaps God will make me one soon. If you only wish it, and keep close to our Saviour, you may be one too; you will be better than I, you have had a harder school than I had. Only love him always, and be open with him. I am awfully fond of him myself—almost too fond of him,—but he is so good, a better boy there is not on the face of the earth. You will love him, will you not, and come into his ways? Take my word for it, you will be happy; you don't yet know how good he is, and what a heart he has. I am sorry to part with him. I love him, I cannot say how much; but our Lord will forgive me for it, for it was He that gave him. Raise me a little; I want to sit up, I am getting to feel so strange, so cold, and yet such a brightness before my eyes. Can the other world be opening upon me? If they would but come! I should like to see them all together, and you with them. If he was to be sick, you would take care of him, and see that he did not overwork? Do you hear them;

are they coming? If only they would come! Cover me up better; I feel as though I were freezing about the heart. If ever you are angry, don't show it; just steal away and pray "Our Father." O God, O God, what is this? I thought I saw my mother.'

The whole family came hurrying in weeping. Mary Anne started, and tried to make way for them at the bedside; she felt they had a better right to be there; she was but a stranger, yet she too sorrowed deeply. But Annie held her hand fast, and whispered—

'Our child! Love her—She is the new mother—Don't be vexed with me for anything, and think of me, all of you. And you go on loving me,' she said to Christian; 'I will try to keep a place beside me in heaven for you.'

Then she folded her hands, her pale lips trembled, her eyes gave one bright upward look. Gently they closed, gently the head dropped to one side. Earth was poorer for the loss of a good wife and a good mother.